WAY OF ESCAPE

WAY OF ESCAPE

by

Ann Fillmore

BOSON BOOKS
Raleigh

Published by
Boson Books, a division of C&M Online Media Inc.
3905 Meadow Field Lane
Raleigh, NC 27606-4470
cm@cmonline.com

ISBN (paper): 978-0-917990-98-4
ISBN (ebook): 0-917990-41-2

http://www.bosonbooks.com

Cover art by Joel Barr

Table of Contents

Dedication

To my father, Daniel Hughes Fillmore, 1905—1986
an unsung hero who saved countless lives
US Public Health Service, 1940—1965

and with gratitude
To all the people in all the organizations who have selflessly striven to bring equality to women all over the world. It is said that women need merely a minimum of an eighth grade education to realize they can be more powerful than anything on earth. Let us pray that such education will be made available to all girls in this generation.

Without strong mothers, there can be no future for humanity's children.

CHAPTER 1: VIA DOLOROSA

Snow was falling gently on Golgotha as Carl-Joran hurried down the hushed and somber shadowed steps of the Via Dolorosa, the Street of Sorrows.

The wet, overhanging, heavy canvas awnings, garish store signs, and banners had lost any color they might have possessed. Here and there a dry snowflake made its way and landed with a *spittt* on the broad stone steps, worn by thousands of years of footfalls, including those of Christ who had labored up and up, carrying his cross on his bloodied shoulders.

Palestinian shopkeepers dragged barred shutters across storefronts and locked doors and windows tight against the impending darkness and the onset of curfew. They hustled to finish before the Israeli soldiers, sauntering along the lower streets with their rifles slung loosely, would come up the stairwells.

Carl-Joran wanted to be out of the Palestinian quarter before dark. It wasn't healthy for him with the number of enemies he'd made among the ultra-conservative Muslims to be in Jerusalem alone. Besides, he was dead. For two weeks now, he was officially deceased and supposed to remain so.

Halima would be furious that he had left Haifa. Her long black face, so like a thoroughbred horse in its intensity, would storm and those sable brown eyes, seething fire, would confront him. It had taken the tall Swede months to become accustomed to a woman boss who could snort him down nose to nose. Her shoulders weren't as wide as his, but her height and energy were on a par.

At the gate stood the familiar cream-white Mercedes, its door being held open by the small Palestinian chauffeur. Carl-Joran slid into the back seat with a long sigh of relief.

"To the Nof," he told Taqi.

"Yes, Baron," replied the tiny man putting the car into gear. They rolled carefully down the tight streets and headed for the highway leading northwest to Haifa. On such a cold, dark Sunday evening, there would be few travelers and they should make good time. Perhaps three hours? A late supper and a hot shower would reward Carl-Joran's return to his living quarters on the top floor of the Nof Hotel.

Traffic, although light as expected, was its usual deadly game. In a country where buses and trucks were driven by former tank corps personnel and jet pilots, taxis by Palestinian day laborers and personal cars a rare commodity, the highways and byways tended to be high-speed killing fields. In addition, lights in the countryside were almost nonexistent and traffic signs and signals meaningless. Wandering donkeys and sheep had right-of-way, unless they got whapped by a passing truck, which turned them into semipermanent speed bumps. Traveling was always chancy at best and dangerous at worst and that didn't take into account the occasional bombings and terrorist attacks.

Having a driver as skilled as Taqi Nabil-Nasiri d'Din was of tremendous benefit to the clinic. About sixty years old, the former Lebanese Christian Palestinian engineer who looked like a gray-haired dwarf, would have given over his life, in fact, in a way, had done just that, to help the Emigrant Women cause.

Carl-Joran did not know much of Taqi's private history, except that, through the EW's influence, he had acquired a very rare Israeli residency permit and was working as a chauffeur and sometimes tourist guide.

Taqi had never confided in Carl-Joran, and Halima had done no more than hint that Taqi's devotion had to do with a daughter who at the time of her death ten years ago had been working as a nanny in a royal Kuwaiti family. No one had been able to help Taqi rescue her when she'd struck out with a broken vase in defense of herself against being raped by a visiting houseguest. No one dared even step in to testify on her behalf at her trial. Taqi called her death by garroting a murder, and over the years of EW's existence the clinic's staff had come quickly to believe in such statements.

Palestinian and Swede made no small talk as the darkness settled around the speeding car. Carl-Joran dozed fitfully. Sound sleep was impossible due to the jolting turns and kidney-shocking bumps in the road. One of the EW's larger expenses was keeping the old Mercedes-Benz in operable condition. In moments of awareness, Carl-Joran pondered the news he'd managed to acquire on Golgotha from their American representative Barbara Monday. It was not good.

Just outside of Haifa, the smoother going on the improved highway let the big Swede fall into a troubled sleep where he was once more flying through the air on the blast's shockwave, crashing into the garbage heap and dying—again. The pain...the pain...the screams...

A hand shook him. Shook him again. And again.

"Baron, Baron Hermelin," Taqi was repeating over and over with great respect. "We have arrived at the Nof."

Carl-Joran opened his stinging, tired eyes. "Ah, thank you, Taqi."

"Please for me to say, you must let Dr. Legesse help you some more. You did dream of Cairo, you were crying," the small man said softly.

"Yes, yes, I promise to tell Halima," Carl-Joran fibbed and nodding at Taqi, crawled from the car and stretched. There was a warmish breeze coming off the Mediterranean. It crept up the cliff side and softly caressed his face. The contrast between Jerusalem and Haifa was almost hard for a body to take. Ohhh, thought Carl-Joran, that bed is going to feel so comfortable! He bent his long frame and waved at Taqi, "Good night."

Taqi smiled wanly and drove off, leaving Carl-Joran to stuff his huge hands in his pockets and amble into the lighted hotel entry.

Built narrow and stark upright off the cliff edge that soared above the Baha'i gardens and, further below, the harbor area of Haifa, the Nof Hotel was not the finest in the city, but it was certainly the most pleasant, in Carl-Joran's opinion. Besides the incredible view, it had an excellent Chinese restaurant in the lower floor, and where in Israel could a hungry person order Chinese take-away delivered to the room at midnight on Sunday?

The doorman acknowledged the arrival of the familiar giant Swede; the desk clerk saluted tiredly and pulled the day's messages from the slot, holding them out for Carl-Joran to snatch as he moved across the dark blue carpet to the elevator.

His room, or rather, small suite, was on the top floor. Facing him, upon entry, were the wide French doors whose curtains he never closed. They opened onto a balcony from which could be seen the vast expanse of black night and sparkling city lights that filled his rooms with their glow. Beyond the city was the ever-busy harbor. There were constant booms, bumps, whistles, and tugboat toots as the ships docked, were unloaded and loaded. From the hillside immediately below the hotel, the soft spotlights of the Baha'i Gardens and the gold-roofed Temple to the Bab scattered tinted shadows on his ceiling.

He dropped the messages, unread, on a coffee table to let them mate with others of their kind. He was certain that's what happened, as the stack seemed to be increasing exponentially like coat hangers in a closed closet. Next, he dropped his lanky hindquarters into a chair, pulled off his boots and smelly socks. His hand went to the phone; he dialed the Chinese restaurant by memory and ordered several large dishes. Because he was their favorite customer, they would also include his usual pints of imported Swedish beer without asking. Probably the owner himself would deliver the meal. Carl-Joran hauled himself to his big feet. A trail of soiled clothes marked his path to the shower.

The excellent meal awaited him when he came out in his purple bathrobe. He vigorously toweled his shaggy mop of hair, which, he noticed in the bureau mirror, was beginning to resemble the winter coats of the little dun-colored horses that dotted the hillsides around his castle in Norrkoping. He needed a haircut, badly, and they'd have to trim his bushy eyebrows. Luckily, he could at least go out in public enough to take care of such things here in Haifa, as he was relatively safe this far into Israel from prying Arab or Iranian security forces' eyes. The towel was cast off to be with the soiled clothes. The maid would take care of them. He sat to eat and at the same time typed into his laptop some rough notes on the day's events.

He'd met up with the tour group Barbara Monday had traveled with near the Russian Orthodox shrine inside the immense Christian Church of the Holy Sepulchre on top of Golgotha. The church is filled with shrines devoted to the death of Jesus. This particular shrine was very small, maybe six feet long by three feet wide by five-and-a-half feet high at most. It housed the supposed tomb, made of huge stone slabs, where Christ had been laid after crucifixion.

Since there was no way Carl-Joran could have comfortably, perhaps even uncomfortably, fit into the shrine with any other body, he'd waited for Barbara to do her touristy stuff and exit. They had casually walked side by side to the dark, untended section of the maze of shrines and conversed as if discussing the state of disorder of Christian churchdom, a not uncommon topic for tourists when viewing the chaos of disrepair of this mausoleum.

Barbara was her usual gorgeous, alert, and headstrong self. She'd recently had her rich brown hair sharply cut to above her ears and of course she wore exceptionally stylish New York clothes: a dark, wool suit with a heavy silk blouse and leather boots. She was young for the work she had chosen to do—perhaps thirty now and adamantly single.

Right out of her Master's degree studies, she became attached as a consultant to UNESCO. That was still her official job. Unofficially, she was coming to spend most of her hours as the American representative of the Society for Emigrant Women, known as EW, with the blessings of the UN; at least, those in the UN who knew of EW's operations.

Barbara gave him the message as casually as possible. The last thing they wanted to do was attract attention. Last week, sources in the underground run by a coalition of American battered women's shelters had approached her regarding a woman who needed to be rescued. This was a woman the shelters could not begin to assist long-term, as it would have been highly dangerous for their own personnel, as well as for her. Any day now, Polly Marie—the last name was left out of the conversation—would be severely terminated in an arranged accident by her famous husband's hired killers if the EW did not act. Because the situation was too dangerous to even discuss on the phone or over the Internet, Monday had flown to Tel Aviv and taken a tour bus to quietly meet with Carl-Joran in the bitter cold on Golgotha.

Arrangements would have to be made as they had been made many times before.

Whatever would work to extricate Polly Marie would be considered, whether it would involve Dr. Halima Legesse faking some medical excuse for a trip to Sweden or even declaring the woman dead or disguising her as a man. Whatever worked.

The food in Carl-Joran's stomach, plus the two beers, went right to his head. His eyes closed and he caught himself only at the last second, falling forward into the remains of the kung pau chicken. As he stumbled across the room, he managed to strip off his robe before tumbling onto the bed. He kicked the extra blanket over his poor feet, which hung over the bottom of the bed, as always. His eyes shut.

A metallic rattle startled him. Hot food smells, the warm reek of camel and donkey dung, unwashed people milling back and forth as the big official black car with little Swedish embassy flags fluttering on the front pushed its way through the afternoon bazaar. He was relieved the meeting was finished. As Swedish consulate to Israel, he was always stuck with receptions and parties and official dos of one sort or another and this do had been at the Swedish embassy in Cairo. He was glad to be done with it and he wanted to be done with Cairo, which was not one of his favorite cities.

Who was this driver? Not someone he knew. Usually he wasn't so careless. The heat was oppressing him. Sweat trickled through the dun-blond hair on his chest and diverted into rivulets along his ribs and he considered leaning forward to ask the driver why the air conditioning wasn't on.

The bazaar scattered into tight alleyways that fronted garages and mews converted into flats. Tighter and tighter. The limo stopped. There was no reason to stop. Carl-Joran let a window down slightly. This was not any one of the many avenues leading to his hotel. Then the driver bailed out.

At that moment, Carl-Joran knew the chill of fear that made the heat vanish, the sweltering sun darken. He got the wide back door open, his head and shoulders out before the pressure vacuum of the exploding shell extruded the rest of him at high velocity from the rising, disintegrating vehicle. He was blown along the roadway like a seed popped from a squeezed grape tha-upppp! to land with astonishing force in a pile of trash.

Gas fumes raging in searing green light whirled along the tarmac and pieces of flaming car tumbled out of the sky like tiny comets, cascading around him. He burrowed into the pile of old boxes, broken glass and plastic bags. Blood seeped over the dusty pavement. He slipped in it. The flames, the smell of burning, the screams of bystanders, themselves burning and cut to shreds by the flying hot metal, and glass shards. Smoke and gas fumes roiled through the alley, filled the nostrils. He crawled and crawled through endless mounds of garbage and camel shit. His stinging knees left trails of blood along the mess in the street's drain. He crawled for he knew not how far or how long.

Muted light, noises—a hospital ward. He was naked. A kind nurse explained in broken English that his clothes had been seared off him, along with his ID, but by the grace of a beneficent Allah, his only wounds were thousands of shard cuts and a skin burn about equal to a day of lying unprotected on a beach. Several people had been killed, she related before being pushed aside by Dr. Halima Legesse in doctor's greens. "You may leave us," Halima said to the nurse and the little Egyptian nurse vanished.

Halima whispered urgently, "Don't say your name, Baron. Don't speak. You are dead. Carl-Joran Hermelin is dead."

She forced him to his feet and into strange clothes plus an Arab headscarf to wrap around his entire face. Her voice repeating, "This is good. This is an opportunity. Sadiq-Fath will believe you are dead. Our enemy will think you are gone and he will get careless."

Carl-Joran tried to say something and she pressed a firm hand into his back, ordering, "Be quiet, do as I say and you'll be safe. We're leaving. Come now. Taqi's waiting downstairs. We're going back to Haifa."

Sneaking along the corridors, ducking out the employees' exit, quietly, unobserved, unnoticed. Taqi held the Mercedes's door open.

Halima was screaming at him…

"Hermelin! Hermelin! Wake up from the dream!"

Carl-Joran brushed at the air around him.

"You'll not be hitting me!" she warned.

He forced open one eye. This was his hotel room. He was at the No?. He could see the swirl of gold and brown of Dr. Halima Legesse's full-length Ethiopian dress. That accursed bellboy had fallen to her wiles again and let her in. He moaned, "Go away. I was just asleep."

Legesse had no mercy. Arms akimbo, large knobby hands splayed onto her hips, she bellowed, "It is noon."

"No," he insisted, putting a pillow over his head.

She grabbed it and smacked him with it. "Get up. We all are to meet in one hour. Get up."

"At least let me put on my clothes!" he begged.

"You are awake? You are not going to go back to sleep?"

"Yes," he half sat up, pulling the sheet around his nakedness. Halima may be a doctor and she may have seen and doctored most of his body at one time or another, but he did want to retain some modesty. He jerked back his pillow and laid it on the sheet in his lap.

"Yes, you will go back to sleep?" she queried snidely.

"No, no," he shook his head emphatically and squinted up at her. The bright sunlight coming in the windows blinded him. "I'm getting up. I promise. Okay?"

"Okay. You be there." She grabbed up the laptop from the table. "Are your notes in here? A little something we can make sense of?"

"Yes," he ran a hand through his unruly hair, "yes, yes, take it with you. Then you can't accuse me of forgetting it later."

She closed the small computer, put it under one arm, and slung around on her sandaled heels, her long skirt swishing noisily as she walked out of the room, and Carl-Joran heard the hall door close behind her.

"But I will eat breakfast first!" he shouted rebelliously at the door.

CHAPTER 2: FIFTY

M rs. Bonnie Ixey looked in her bathroom mirror with studied and somewhat anxious appraisal to see if any great change had taken place at the arrival of a half-century of life.

To her delighted surprise, she discovered that the person she'd regarded in this mirror for years she'd not really appreciated. This face, which had never quite been pretty, had kept its cheery smile and thereby produced charming smile wrinkles. The thick and wavy mousy brown hair, so like in quality her father's shock of pale gold hair, had slowly become a pile of shining silver tresses, her pink skin glowed with health from her good diet, hours spent working in the garden, and her long hikes. Besides, she still had every one of her sparkling white teeth. The ugly duckling had transformed into a rather elegant though diminutive swan. What a nice birthday present!

Bonnie Mari (Seastrand) Ixey was one of those interesting people who had looked old from birth. Fully grown she was a frail hair's breadth under five feet, four inches tall. Her baby pictures showed a wrinkled elfin face with an expression of incalculable wisdom.

Her dear mother had said the premature baby Bonnie rarely cried, that the little pixie observed everything with great intensity and eerily, as if remembering lives lived before or not yet lived. Bonnie in her younger years considered herself to be her mom's descendent more than her father's and thought with utmost rationality that the mystic baby expression could well have been severe nearsightedness.

Fifty years ago today, Dell Drachet had given birth only moments after a dory from a Liberian merchant cargo ship put her and her new husband, Bo Pers Seastrand, ashore in a no-name fishing village on the eastern coast of Mexico. The black seaman in charge of smuggling them had been relieved to see the last of the strange couple and had motored the dory back to the big cargo ship as fast as it could go.

Bonnie, just after her tenth birthday, had found in an old sea chest in the attic, the yellowed, neatly folded transport papers for her parents slid into oversized Swiss passports. She had excitedly unfolded the papers. She could not read much of what was in them. She was able to recognize that they were official documents of some sort from what the English language portion said and this portion was repeated in Arabic and

French and spoke of emigrant passage for two "Swiss undesirables" from Marrakesh. She had not asked her parents about the papers, knowing full well the emotions such memories could incite and the anger her father would most likely display. So, she had discreetly refolded the papers and put them away where she'd found them. They became a treasure for her, a bit of evidence of the reality of her parents as human beings with a history neither of them ever would admit.

When Bonnie was twelve, she and a girlfriend went to see *Casablanca*. Yes, of course, it all made sense! *Her* parents must have been just like Victor Lazlow and Ilse Lund from Rick's Cafe. Perhaps her father had been a famous resistance fighter and her mother madly in love with Rick Blaine...that would have certainly been preferable to her father!

It was shortly after this private determination that she had asked her mom quietly one evening about the papers and had received no more reply than a placid, "They were necessary because of the Cold War, dearest." A couple months later, she bucked up the courage to broach the subject to her father, the tall and icy blue-eyed Bo Pers Sjostrand. The anger had not come. He had merely shaken his head and said, "Taking a freighter from Algiers was the only way your mother and I could escape and hide."

Once her parents had been plunked down on that Mexican beach, Dell Bonnie Drachet Sjostrand began having labor pains. An old *bruja*, medicine witch, in the village had midwived Dell. With ancient skills she had saved the six-week preemie by wrapping the tiny Bonnie in a tattered, soft wool blanket and placing her in a warm potting kiln where she remained for three weeks, except to be taken out for cuddling and feeding.

Bonnie's birth wasn't officially registered until the Swedish-Scottish couple with Swiss passports arrived in San Luis Obispo, California, a month later as Mr. and Mrs. Bo Pers Seastrand. Bonnie was never sure how that had been accomplished, how they'd come across the Mexican-US border, how the Swedish name had been translated into English. No one ever spoke of that lost month or of how her father came so quickly after arrival to teach in the engineering college and her mother to work as a nurse in the local hospital.

Such opposites! Her mother, Dell Bonnie, was as dark and emotional as only a Drachet Celt from the Scottish Highlands could be. Her father epitomized the stoic and somber Swede from the heart of a cold country. A lot of history hung about them, little of which Bonnie grasped since both had remained secretive to the end.

Perhaps that's why in college Bonnie Seastrand chose to become a research librarian. Perhaps it was the need to find out things beyond the mysterious half-truths with which her parents had raised her. She, in contrast to both of them, had led a peaceful life for the most part. A long marriage, two grown daughters: Mari Dell, who had gotten married last year and was now a Williams, and the elder Trisha Svea still single, who would be coming to the house later.

Her daughters were beautiful. That had worried Bonnie during their childhood because her husband Ike had been downright ugly. But he was a sweet soul with whom she'd shared twenty-five good years. Ike had lived with flowers, farmed flowers, adored his way of life and his family. He was considerably older than Bonnie, and he'd died last year. Life went on. She sighed.

The clunk, clatter of the mail dropping into the box brought her out of the bathroom and out of her deep reverie. More birthday cards probably, what fun!

She was right. There was a handful. There was also a letter from a foreign country. Who did she know who was traveling in icy Sweden in the dead of winter?

No, this was not a wayward friend traveling. This envelope portended some bureaucratic function for it was a long, very official-looking brown thing with one of those suspicious transparent windows. The stamp read: *Sverige*. Yes, that was Sweden. The postmark was Norrkoping. The return address meant nothing to her. Swedish she did not understand. French she could manage, and Spanish and Italian and a teensy bit of German. No, she didn't understand any of the return address.

She forced herself to fix a strong cup of coffee, to sit at the kitchen nook and stir the honey and cream into her coffee, to take a bite of the breakfast smorgas sandwich she'd made. Then she searched around briefly for her reading glasses, finding them on the bedstead. She really must, she promised herself again, buy a couple more pairs of reading glasses so she didn't have to constantly search for the damned things As she sat back down at the breakfast nook and took another bite of the sandwich, she laughed gently.

Bonnie had early in childhood learned to laugh at herself in a very healthy way. Take the whole business of being so nearsighted. In the fifth grade, a school nurse appeared one day to check for vision problems among the students. When put with her toes behind the taped line,

Bonnie was asked, as had been the others, to read the chart. Bonnie had responded, "What chart?"

The nurse, a no-nonsense sort, had rather gruffly inquired, "How about the big E?"

To this day, Bonnie remembered answering, "What big E?"

Because she'd always been seated in the front row by the teachers, little smarty-pants, teacher's pet, the girl who couldn't see over the big boys, a very bright Bonnie had never had to read the chalk board beyond ten feet away.

Her elfish appearance was not improved by the coke-bottle-thick spectacles prescribed by the optometrist. As soon as she could overcome her parents' objections she got contact lenses, which, at the time, were heavy, made of glass, and extremely uncomfortable. The wonderful sense of freedom from spectacles though made up for any discomfort. Only lately, after her arms grew too short to read well any more, did she use glasses, but only to read.

Of course, at sixteen, she had had to put up with her mom's constant nagging about how those new-fangled lenses would cut her eyeballs or that she was sure to lose a lens up inside her brain or some other horrific disaster. After all, her mom had been a nurse. Her mother's concern was better than her dad's nonreaction, which consisted of a cold, hurtful, "Well, those expensive lenses haven't improved your looks enough to attract a boyfriend."

Going off to college was the best thing that ever happened to Bonnie, and at Stanford were the biggest libraries she'd ever seen. It was there, in her senior year, she met Ike Ixey attending college on the Vet's Bill. He was studying horticulture and after their marriage, she put him through his PhD at California State College at Davis. Within months after his graduation, his father helped him invest in a piece of farm property just north of San Luis Obispo on the California coast which became their home, and Ike's flower farm.

But Bonnie could not stay content with her husband's flowers. She continued her schooling past her PhD, worked for the University of California library system and her world grew beyond books and old-fashioned research to the reference sources of an entirely new era of communication. She had become enamored with computers. Now, she was working out of her own home as a specialist in literary references for professors and students and anyone else who had to write papers or find obscure quotes or whatever.

Bonnie sipped her coffee and finished the sandwich. Today was Saturday. She would not work. She would relax and enjoy.

At that moment, the suspense could be held back no longer. She ripped open the mystery envelope and took out the flimsy airmail papers—two pages, precisely typed and stapled together. It was obviously a notice of some kind beginning with a heading that read something-something Norrkoping Pastorkirche, plus a form to fill out to return. A big official government emblem was impressed upon the whole thing. Near the middle of the first page was a crest of some sort next to the name: Hermelin. The spidery signature at the end was printed underneath: *Birgitta Algbak.*

Why in heaven's name would a very official looking document be coming from Sweden? And why was it addressed to: Bonnie Mari Ixey (Sjostrand) Hermelin? She had never known anyone named Hermelin, much less been close enough to any male soul to have acquired the name, although whoever sent this form had done considerable and thorough homework. Not only had this Birgitta Algbak gotten Bonnie's middle name right, they'd spelled her maiden name of Seastrand in the old Swedish—Sjostrand.

For the millionth time she regretted deeply that her father had never taught her Swedish, had made a point in fact to never even speak it in her presence. She remembered how, if he were on the phone to a friend he would switch to English when she came near, as if he wanted her to be clean of the language.

She tried to fathom some more of the words on the form. She got what was to be put in the lines headed by *mormor, morfar* and *farmor, farfar,* although she had no idea whose mother's mother, mother's father and father's mother, father's father they pertained to. She also recognized *barnen,* but whose children?

To be given such an intriguing puzzle was the best birthday present she could ever have received. Although unknown fates had delivered it, she was ready to believe it meant good things. Her book-loving mind was already into images of Strindberg and Ibsen, *Dream Play* and *Wild Strawberries,* and sleigh bells and little red wooden horses…no, it wouldn't be anything bad on her birthday. It couldn't be.

The front door swung open and Bonnie heard Trisha come bouncing in. Tall like her father and sturdy like Bonnie's father, Trisha had just graduated from college to a job as basketball coach at Morro Bay High School. The big feet made clumping noises all down the hall.

"Hi, Mom, you home? Dell and Lou will be arriving at two this afternoon. Mom?"

"In the kitchen, dearest." Bonnie smiled at her red-haired Trisha, clattering across the linoleum to enthusiastically hug her with such strength it almost crushed her head. When she could catch her breath, after Trisha had poured her own coffee and sat down, Bonnie asked, "Who do we know that still reads fluent Swedish?"

"Huh?" Trisha reached for the letter which Bonnie gingerly let her have. Trisha, slightly dyslexic, struggled with the small print then said, "Looks like an official document of some sort."

"I think it is." Bonnie took it back, afraid that her ham-handed daughter would inadvertently rip it.

"Wouldn't be anything concerning farmor's family, would it?" she scowled. "If it is, it won't be anything good."

"Trish. Shame. Just because we know so little about your Grandpa Seastrand's past doesn't mean there was shadiness going on."

"I don't know, Mom," Trisha continued, doubtful, "official documents always seem to demand payment of some sort at the bottom line."

Bonnie tried to keep her cheeriness past the pessimistic assault. "Let's see it as a door to adventure, okay? It is my birthday after all."

"Yeah, Mom," Trisha leaned over and gave her another brutal head-hug. "Happy birthday, old lady."

"I do love you," Bonnie laughed from her daughter's armpit. "Do release me, dear."

Trisha let go and leaned back to scowl again at the letter. "I don't know, Mom. I don't know. Aren't you a bit old for adventure?"

A shivery shimmer of…anticipation perhaps, went down Bonnie's spine. She had had only one instance in her life that could have qualified as an adventure. One itsy-bitsy adventure out of all her fifty years—and the memory of it would come forward unbidden every so often, vividly, like the brightest of lights in a foggy night, like an acrylic-colored painting that hung on a wall long enough its presence was taken for granted. Well, no, upon closer examination, more like a painting that had aged and needed cleaning. The colors of the time seemed to have faded like the tie-dyed T-shirts they'd worn.

Oh, my, she thought as she tried to recall the faces of the people involved and the places during the summer of all summers. The magical places, the music of the Beatles and Joan Baez, folk songs around a campfire on a beach…dreamlike images. They had lost any sense of reality. That's too bad. That's really too bad. How sad. How very sad. Tears welled up in her eyes and she turned from Trisha with the excuse of putting the letter safely into a drawer in the kitchen telephone desk. Odd to react this way, Bonnie thought and shut the drawer firmly.

"What time did you say Dell was arriving?" Bonnie covered her emotions.

"Two. She called from Sea-Tac. The snow in Seattle has let up and they'll get out on time. They'll fly into Paso Robles and rent a car. I offered to drive up 46 and get them but..." Trisha paused, "You okay?"

"Oh, of course," Bonnie stood, heading for the coffee pot.

"Damned menopause. Damned hot flashes." She waved her other hand at her face like a fan. "Never know when they're gonna hit."

"Maybe you should go on estrogen."

"Nah." Bonnie poured coffee for them both. "I'll take care of it. Nothing more soy in my diet and a few pieces of licorice won't cure. Not to worry." And then she remembered discussing all this menopause stuff with Lena last week over coffee. Bonnie had been updating the reference system at the Morro Bay Library and had met Lena, who told stories to the kids who sat absolutely still listening to her lyrical Skona Swedish accent make the old fairy tales come real. Lena could translate the letter.

It was all Bonnie could do to pay attention to her daughter at this moment. Besides, Bonnie consoled herself, it's Monday. There was no way to find Lena's phone number as she didn't know her last name and the library was closed on Mondays and...and...Bonnie calmed herself. And maybe, as her pessimistic daughter had said, there would be a bottom line to the form. Perhaps she should be cautious. Perhaps.

"—got permission from old Toppenish to order those new hoops installed," Trisha was chattering and Bonnie struggled to be a good mom and listen. "It's such a pain to get around that old fart—"

Bonnie's hand was slowly moving toward the desk and the phone. Maybe the chief librarian would know Lena's phone number. What was that librarian's name? Blast this forgetfulness!

"Mom? That hot flash getting worse?" Trisha asked, puzzled and concerned.

"Uh, no. No." Bonnie smiled and put her attention back onto her daughter and the incredibly boring story of basketball hoops and the boring principal of Trisha's school...until, unbidden, the image of a white flower with a yellow center popped into her head and the chief librarian's name followed quickly after. Crannell. Under C. Daisy

Crannell. In the address book. In the drawer under the phone. Near where she'd stuck the letter.

"Mom?"

CHAPTER 3: STEALING WOMEN AWAY

We know Baron Hermelin is dead because our Egyptian operatives sent us a copy of his death certificate," said the lieutenant, dropping the faxes onto his commander's desk, "so why did Barbara Monday travel to Jerusalem yesterday? Who from EW did she contact now that Hermelin is gone?"

The sun would be setting soon over the golden dunes outside his office window. Commander Gurgin Ali Yusef, chief of the Saudi Security Forces, reluctantly moved his gaze from the beautiful desert world outside to his lieutenant standing in front of his desk. The craggy faced chief tapped his manicured fingernails on his big, expensive oak desk before stirring the faxes around and regarding his underling with intensity. "When did you find out she was in Israel?"

The lieutenant put his hands behind his back. "We didn't, actually. An operative who happened to be at the Boston airport spotted her in the El Al security enclosure. The only El Al plane leaving that afternoon was to Tel Aviv. He called our operative in Bethlehem who bribed a tour bus operator who found out Monday went to Jerusalem with a tour group specifically to the Christian church on Golgotha."

"But why?" Commander Yusef pounded a meaty fist on the desk. "Is she arranging to take more women from our country?" His black eyes seethed with possessive anger. "Our women!"

"There was no way to follow her in Jerusalem, sir, it was late evening just before curfew and the Israeli soldiers were patrolling the area heavily," the troubled lieutenant answered. "All we had was the Boston operative's assurance that she arrived back in Boston yesterday and immediately caught the train to New York. Our staff at the UN says she is in her office this morning."

"Why can't we get someone into Haifa to watch EW?" muttered Commander Yusef. "Damn! It would make things much easier for us!"

Unable to respond, the lieutenant grimaced.

"You may go," Yusef barked, "and bring me any update on Monday's movements."

"Yes, sir." The lieutenant slid out of the office, relieved to be gone from the hard old man's presence.

The reddish gold light of the late afternoon shadowed Commander Yusef's sun-dried face making the wrinkles and creases look like saber cuts. He knew his men regarded him as a brutal old warrior. So be it. Discipline was more important than any other quality in his command. The rule of order, the rule of the Koran, the rule of male authority, *his* authority had to be maintained. Coming to a decision he was reluctant to make, he picked up the telephone. "Faruq," he growled at his personal aide on the other end, "get me Tidewater."

"Yessir," the meek man in the outer office responded and immediately punched the code for Virginia, USA and obtaining a satellite connect, put in Agent Marion Tidewater's private number.

The secretaries were busily fussing with coffeepots and plates of doughnuts as the unlikely looking Tidewater came along the hallway. Unlikely because, with his closely trimmed black beard and moustache, balding head, chunky nose and stout body, he would have appeared more likely to be wearing a yarmulke and heading into a synagogue for a *bet midrash*. His ancestry, though, was not member of the tribe; his ancestry was linked to one of the multitude of the original Youngs of Utah. That is, his guiding light was Moroni, not Moses. There was a strong likelihood that this had helped him acquire one of the top positions in the Agency, one that specially dealt with Arab intelligence as the requirements for clean living plus the attitude toward women were quite similar and acknowledged by the powers-that-be higher up.

Standing with one foot out of Tidewater's office, phone to ear, his newly assigned personal assistant and computer geek, Russ Snow, waved frantically at him to hurry. Tidewater picked up his pace, smiled only briefly at his secretary as she put a cup of coffee in his hand. The dancing Snow, covering the mouthpiece, held out the phone as his boss entered the office.

"Yusef," whispered the young man, pointing at the phone.

"Ahhh," said Tidewater, seating himself. Then with a cold smile, he said into the phone, "Commander, good morning, or rather afternoon to you." He listened for several minutes and, pursing his thin, grayish-pale pink lips, responded, "No, I don't think they're after Saudi women this time. Monday deals mostly with our women, with American women. Remember how she and the baron got the senator's wife out, got her into Costa Rica as a butterfly collector before we could even send an agent to the Miami airport? Monday's sneaky as a coyote."

He listened for a moment before saying, "Uh, coyotes are varmints, sorta like wild dogs. We got 'em all over the West. They kill sheep. Really sneaky critters." He listened again. "Right. I thank you very much for letting me know. And I especially thank you for that update on the Hermelin's death. He was a real pain in the butt." With deliberateness almost of intention, Tidewater said sympathetically into the phone, "Too bad we can't get rid of the whole Emigrant Women outfit."

He paused, listened. "Right. I'll see what my sources come up with. Yeah, I'd like to know more about the hit, like who did it. I'll send him a thank you card." Tidewater laughed. "Okay, Commander Yusef, talk at ya later."

Snow, who had been making himself unobtrusive next to the filing cabinet, turned around. "What's Emigrant Women? And who's this baron person?"

Marion Tidewater twiddled his pencil and regarded the tall, dark-haired young man with envy. Tidewater was short and he had never had much hair and he certainly was losing his youth. Time did that to a man. To women too, the thought of his wife and twenty-five years of marriage flashed through his mind. And Snow? Although deeply tanned, Russell Snow was most probably one of the Arizona Snows, once looked at askance by the Mormon Church as renegades because of their avowed determination to maintain polygamous marriages. About ten years ago, negotiations about the situation, and the polygamous men's agreement to at least be quiet about the marriages, allowed the church to take them back in good standing. Still it wasn't wise to give away too much information to an underling…just tell him what he could already read in the reports.

"Baron Carl-Joran Hermelin." Tidewater pronounced each name as close to how he imagined a Swede would say it, thus making them sound like something off the Muppet show. "He's one of those do-gooders who wrecks everybody else's way of life. Close as we can tell, about five years ago he lost his wife to cancer. Instead of just getting married again, he set out to help…to help women," Tidewater related in an almost puzzled tone. "Guess he thought of himself as some sort of Schweitzer or Wallenberg or something. Anyway, he has, or had, a vast fortune, even a castle in Sweden. Maybe it was Legesse who talked him into helping. Dr. Halima Legesse is the brains of Emigrant Women. She's a black doctor, a gyn-ob who was exiled from Ethiopia 'cause of her stand against the government's war over there. She settled in Haifa, Israel, and started giving aid to women on the run. Emigrant Women or EW. It's a society, an organization for taking women out of a country's borders illegally. At first it was sorta like a battered women's shelter. Now it's a damned international underground railroad. They pull families apart, take a woman right away from her husband. Just like that." Tidewater snapped his fingers and shook his head in disbelief. "What gall to take a wife right out of the family!"

"Maybe if the woman's really in danger...?" Snow offered tentatively.

"She should get the hell out and call the police, let them handle it," said Tidewater with certainty.

"I've heard sometimes it can be pretty bad," the young man said, thinking of what his sister's friend on the reservation had gone through. "Some men go nutso."

"Guess there are a few crazy fellows out there," Tidewater looked over his desk for his phone list, "but overall if a woman's a good wife, a man's gonna be happy." He picked up a couple files. No list.

Snow decided not to pursue his side of the question. Obviously his new boss wasn't hearing what Snow wanted to get across and Snow had learned well from his elders. Listen well. Listen until the man wants to talk no more. So Russ Snow asked in a helpful manner, "What are you searching for? It may be something I put in a drawer."

"My phone list."

"Top drawer on the right."

Marion Tidewater pulled open the drawer, "Ahhh." He flipped to S and found Sadiq-Fath, Quddus Sadiq-Fath, the *darughih* of the Iranian secret police. Sadiq-Fath had once translated darughih as high constable, which was a leftover from the British rule of years ago. Of course, the weasely, vicious man was also a graduate of the Agency's best training schools and by providential circumstance, in the same graduating class as Tidewater. Perhaps Quddus was a friend, if that relationship could be said to exist among these ruthless men. Such is the way of international security forces. Tidewater waved the open book at Snow. "Get me this guy. It's past work hours in Iran but he can be found. He'll talk to me."

Snow took the proffered address book and nodded. "Will do, sir." As he stepped from the room, the briefest of speculations went through his head about why his boss was hotly against an organization that helped women emigrate, how such an organization could be considered subversive. It was merely an intellectual kind of questioning though. Russ would know when he had a need to know or when he decided he needed to know he'd set some forces moving through his Internet connections.

He punched up a satellite link to Tehran, Iran, and didn't even look in his boss's book. Russ had been hired because of his expertise with computers and as far as he was concerned, any idiot could find any of the phone numbers or e-mail addresses to contact the darughih of Iran without the use of paper.

With long, loping strides, Carl-Joran jogged downhill, cutting across the tightly curved road back and forth, past the little markets busy on this Monday afternoon. He stopped, puffing lightly, at his favorite hole-in-the-wall cafe and was quickly served Turkish coffee and a huge plate of bagels with assorted fillings. This coffee was the real stuff, as an American might say. The cup was not more than two inches across and it truly would keep one of the small sugar spoons upright if stuck into the grounds at the bottom. The rich taste was due to the raw honey-sugar that had been brewed into the blend. Carl-Joran stood against the high table with all the other customers getting their after-lunch caffeine fix, and sipped slowly, savoring the tiny helping. He felt the *crinch* across his forehead as the caffeine went to his brain.

A horn, deep and sonorous, *booppped* outside, and turning, Carl-Joran saw the familiar cream-white Mercedes-Benz. Taqi had found him. He grabbed up the last bagel, stuffed it with vinegar soaked cucumbers, wrapped a paper towel napkin around it, and dashed to the car. Pulling open the back door, he bent way down to crawl in, one long leg at a time.

"Good day, Baron," a richly masculine voice said from within.

Carl-Joran, his bagel dripping vinegar, squeezed onto the seat. "How are you, Haji Mansur?"

The solid, powerfully centered man taking up the rest of back seat was the baron's age, though his full beard and curly hair already had gray streaks. His long abba, a soft black wool full-length robe, was pulled around him for warmth and on his head was a low, hat-like dark red turban, with checked scarf about his neck. This was the proper, conservative clothing for a haji; that is, a Muslim holy man of the Sunni tradition who had made the pilgrimage to Mecca.

Carl-Joran breathed in the smell of the man, much like a horse lover or a farmer relishes the enveloping odors of a familiar environment. Habib Mansur always filled his space with the gentle aroma of sandalwood. The sable brown eyes held the quality of an old wolf, wise, unyielding, and fearless. Such a man would have looked not the least out of place riding beside the Prophet, sword in hand, galloping across the plains of Arabia centuries ago.

"I am in fine health this day," he exclaimed, slapping his knee. "We will have a good meeting."

"Yes, undoubtedly," agreed Carl-Joran and how could he not agree? Habib had been personally responsible for the rescue of a half-dozen women from the harems of the Saudi and Kuwaiti sheikhs. His being along today meant they were ready to go into one of those countries again. And why would a conservative Sunni rescue women from the very practices his religion embraced?

Carl-Joran knew of the sister Habib had lost to a violent husband years ago. Despite his influence, Habib had been unable to break the codes which kept the girl of sixteen in the clutches of the older man until she died in childbirth of...officially the diagnosis had been miscarriage. But Halima had told Carl-Joran it was massive internal bleeding from being beaten so badly. And the reason for that final beating?

Halima had looked away when she related to Carl-Joran that the doctor, after an ultrasound ordered by the husband to determine the sex of the child at six months, had told the husband, not the girl, that she was carrying a girl child. In a rage, the husband had decided to force her to abort. How ironic that the modern technical device should give the husband the power to kill for such an ancient reason, Halima had murmured.

As the big Mercedes whirred down the steep hill, Carl-Joran leaned forward. "Taqi, you okay this morning?"

"Very good, Baron," responded the little Palestinian. He didn't turn around as they were approaching the thoroughfare at the bottom of the hill where they would turn to go to the harbor. Traffic was heavy along here and Taqi concentrated on changing lanes so they could scoot in behind a lorry that was also heading toward the docks. It took only moments to reach the big brick building that housed the EW's headquarters. On the outside, this building looked exactly like other warehouses along the water. No sign announced it.

As Taqi opened the car door for the haji, a thin Indian man with a neatly trimmed pitch-black beard and a glowing blue silk turban pedaled madly up on a bicycle. He shoved the conveyance into a parking slot, attached a lock, stood, and looked around as Haji Mansur and the tall Swede came toward him.

"It is so good to see you both," the Sikh beamed nervously as he bowed.

Mansur bowed in response, "And to have you here, Mr. Prakash."

"Siddhu, what's happening, my man?" Carl-Joran clapped the frailer man on the shoulder.

Siddhu Singh Prakash stumbled forward and grinned mightily, "The meeting happens, Baron."

They filed in. It was not a warehouse inside. An office-like room took up the front space. Across the office wall was a large, beautifully painted sign that read in big green letters: SOCIETY FOR EMIGRANT WOMEN and under the English in other colors: SOCIETÉ POUR LES EMIGRES FEMININE, ASOCIACION PARA LOS MUJERES EMIGRANTE, SOCIETET PA KVINNOR UTVANDRARE and so on in numerous languages including Hebrew.

Devi Hamberg, the EW's secretary, her curly black hair disheveled and her eyes sparkling, clothed in the Israeli teens' common outfit—khaki pants and white blouse—greeted them as she retrieved a sheaf of papers from the humming printer.

She motioned with her head toward the wide double doors leading to a long hallway and said, "Dr. Legesse is pacing the floor. You better not keep her waiting much longer!"

Siddhu paused at Devi's desk long enough to pick up a large notebook and the printout. He scurried to catch up to the other men as they hurried along the hallway.

They passed rooms, designed like hotel suites, for women needing shelter, walked past the actual medical clinic, and near the far end, rounded the hallway, glancing into the big windows of the childcare room from which the noises of little people playing filtered through.

The men pushed open another double door and entered a vast room, warm with purple-red Persian carpeting and soft yellow-tan walls. There were a TV and VCR in one corner, an overhead projector and screen at the front, and a large map across the back wall. The entire center of the room was taken by a stunning black-and-white, long curved table made of metal and plastic with matching chairs padded with tan-gold pillows. At the top of the table's curve stood the majestic Dr. Halima Legesse.

"It is time," she said gruffly. In front of her was Carl-Joran's laptop computer.

Siddhu hustled up to her and bowed, "We are so sorry to be late, Doctor." He put down the notebook and paper and sat across from a very handsome, delicately boned, older woman with dark brown hair tied back in a bun. She had on a tailored, white-cotton pants suit. Carl-Joran smiled, almost flirting, as, recognizing Dr. Rachel Bar-Fischer, he held out his hand to her.

"How do you do?" she asked.

"I'm fine, Dr. Fischer. And how is the drug business?"

She laughed. "Our anti-drug unit is coming along."

Haji Mansur shook hands with her next, saying, "It is a shame such a thing has become needed in Israel."

"We can only be thankful we have so few cases and most of them immigrants," she replied, and then added, "Your chief invited me to observe your meeting today."

"Ah-hem!" Dr. Legesse pointed. "If you men will be seated, we do business."

The men promptly sat.

"You go first, Siddhu, so we can know the present state of our finances," Dr. Legesse also sat and nodded at the Sikh.

For the next fifteen minutes, Siddhu Singh Prakash expostulated on accounts and transfer of funds and the amounts needed for the projects on hand. When he stopped to take a breath, Dr. Legesse said, "Let's you and me finish the accounts after we discuss cases. We have to find out what more will be needed." She turned to Haji Mansur, "Habib, tell us about the princess."

The black abba-cape made a shhh-shhh as he leaned forward and pulled a small notebook from an inside pocket. Opening the back of it, he translated from his beautiful Arabic script into English. "Princess Zhara i-Shibl is eighteen and unmarried," began Habib Mansur, "which is two or three years past the age when most girls are married in conservative Arab families. She is the daughter of Sheikh Rassid i-Shibl's first wife and thus her marriage is considered to be very important for political reasons. Her father had years ago arranged a match for her with the powerful ruler of a neighboring tribe, Sheikh Sultan Mustafa Bayigani. It probably won't be a tremendous surprise to you all that Bayigani is sixty-five years old and has nine wives already. Zhara objects and has objected since she was twelve. She has been brave enough to say out loud that she doesn't want to go through with this marriage. The only way she has avoided the marriage to date was staying at a private school in Paris for the last five years. We know she even has a French boyfriend. Her father has found out. Last week, he had her brought back to Saudi under court order. If Zhara again refuses the arranged marriage, he will have no choice but to let the court execute her as an adulterer."

Carl-Joran nodded. It was not an uncommon story. Several years ago, just such a princess, sixteen-years-old, was snatched right from her school dormitory in England by Saudi operatives, brought home, and stoned to death for disobeying the judgment of the Saudi court that she be married to the family's choice. Her boyfriend, another Arab boy she'd met in London, was later caught and kidnapped out of England, brought back to Saudi Arabia and executed by public beheading in the village square on charges of adultery.

Carl-Joran turned to Habib and asked, "How did we hear about Princess Zhara?"

He answered, "Through the girl's headmistress in the Paris school who called the Torture Treatment Centre. Zhara tried to hide in the woman's house, almost got the poor woman killed."

Dr. Legesse spoke up, "I've set up refuge for her in Switzerland at the Bergenstock School, you remember, Professor Freda Englich? The woman who took our escapee from Guatemala? She is ready to receive our princess as soon as we can get her out and she can protect her in that mountain retreat."

"Where in Saudi is she?" asked Carl-Joran, a gleam in his eye.

"Up in the north, at her father's compound," Habib Mansur replied. "It is not far from the Kuwaiti border."

Dr. Legesse pointed a long, bony finger at Carl-Joran, "Don't even think about going in there, Baron. Habib will be meeting Tahireh Ibrahim and they have a plan well laid out."

Carl-Joran squirmed. "Tahireh worked on the last rescue in Kuwait only a couple months ago. She's cutting it awful close, you know. She's a Baha'i, they'll be watching her because of that anyway."

"Tahireh will remain all covered in black, with even her face mask on while we are in Lebanon," Habib said lightly, "and you know the Arab men can't tell one woman from another. They simply don't look at women in black robes."

"Haji..." Carl-Joran began to protest.

Halima Legesse insisted, "It is done, Baron. Do not try to involve yourself. They will be taking the princess to the American air base in Kuwait and she'll be flying out as an airman's wife. Tahireh has much experience doing this."

Haji Habib patted his tall friend on the arm and added, "Zhara will be meeting Professor Englich right at the airplane in Geneva and going directly to the school."

"If our sworn enemy Quddus Sadiq-Fath finds out," Carl-Joran warned, "Tahireh won't live long. Nor you either, my dear Haji."

"We will be careful," Habib, in a very kind way, needled his friend. "After all, we have done this before, my dear baron. Besides, we are not in Iran, we will be in Saudi Arabia and Kuwait."

The Indian accountant spoke up, "Baron. We must have transfer of funds to the Saudi bank where Habib can have access tomorrow. He will need several thousand dollars for bribes. Getting a princess out will cost a lot."

"No problem. The living estate grant should have taken effect by now," said Carl-Joran, "and all the monies in that one Swiss account will have been turned over to the EW's account."

"Good," Siddhu said, relaxing a bit, "because our own accounts, as I have been very careful to enumerate, are quite low."

"Speaking of Kuwait," Halima Legesse said, "Lori Dubbayaway in Thailand sent us e-mail yesterday."

"Another servant girl in horrible circumstances, I bet you," interjected Habib, shaking his head.

"Yes," Dr. Legesse nodded. "Mr. Sanjay Pandharpurkar, the father of a fifteen-year-old girl named Milind, is terrified for her safety. Same story almost exactly as what happened to our own Taqi's daughter. Milind came with a shipload of teenagers from Thailand and Indonesia to work for the rich Arabs. She ended up as a kitchen helper in the Syrian embassy in Kuwait. At a big party, the son of a Saudi diplomat tried to rape her and she stabbed him with a butcher knife. Cut him pretty badly. She's due to be executed next week. The father is begging Lori for help. Lori says Carin Smoland in Sweden has a place for her if we can get her to Stockholm, and I've gotten confirmation by e-mail from Carin that all's ready there."

Carl-Joran shook his head and said harshly, "Are you going to have Tahireh rescue little Milind too?"

"No," Dr. Legesse shot back at him, "she couldn't do it anyway. The girl's in prison."

"So how...?" Carl-Joran began.

Habib Mansur broke in, "I have a contact in Kuwait. A good man who can do the job with enough bribery money. Shamsi has already been to the girl's holding cell and used some of his own money to pay off some guards."

"That's great," said Carl-Joran and stretched out his long legs, "we can get him more money. That's the least of our problems."

"Then," said Dr. Legesse, "I will have Devi send all concerned word to that effect. If your Mr. Shamsi..."

"Mr. Shamsi Granfa," interjected Habib.

"Right, if Granfa can carry this out without our personnel being needed, so much the better." Halima looked around at Carl-Joran, raised her black eyebrows.

"Ready for my tale now?" he inquired, reaching for his laptop.

"Yes." Halima glowered at him, "Although I am very angry at you for going out of Haifa."

"I know, I know," Carl-Joran motioned her to calm down. "I was absolutely safe." He turned on his little screen and peered at it intently, struggling to decipher what, last night, had been perfectly intelligible to him. "Now, here we go, I think. I met Barbara Monday at the Church of the Holy Sepulchre. She has a woman in the US ready to come out, a Polly..."

"Valentine," Dr. Legesse blurted, "that is the code name."

"Valentine it is, then," said Carl-Joran. "Anyway, the woman is already in the Los Angeles shelter system and will be moved discreetly to the airport holding area and will be arriving in Miami in a couple days. She'll have to be disguised and shipped out of the US from there. She's the wife of a famous basketball hero and if we don't move fast, she'll become the accidentally-dead-in-a-car-or-boat-wreck wife."

Dr. Bar-Fischer shook her head, "And I thought my drug unit was full of pain and suffering."

"It goes on and on," said Dr. Legesse. "Is Monday ready for her?"

Hermelin nodded. "She's all prepared on her end. You have to contact Judge Moabi in Uganda."

"No problem," Halima Legesse agreed. "Give me the particulars on paper and I'll have Devi e-mail her. In return, Kandella has..." Halima picked up a computer printout and read, "'from Judge Kandella Moabi—I have a woman and two daughters living in Somalia. Fumilayo Makwaia, daughters Jo and Esie, who are asking for refuge so the daughters will not have to be circumcised. Can we put them at EW for a while?'" Halima looked at Siddhu, "Do we have space?"

Siddhu thought a moment, "If they can arrive here next weekend we can keep them for a week. After that they will have to be moved."

"Okay," said Halima, satisfied, "I'll tell Kandella." She sighed and held up a telephone message note. "Oh, my, I do wish he would get a computer and get online. This phone call is from our dear friend and helper Lama Kazi Padma in northern India."

"Another sati?" asked Siddhu Singh Prakash, referring to the Hindu custom of wives being expected to sit on the pyre of their deceased husband and burn with him.

Halima Legesse shook her head, her ringlets quivered. "No, Lama Padma has been asked by a woman's group to stop a murder. It is common knowledge in the village where they work that a young wife Shai Nanek will be killed by the old man's sons from the first marriage the moment that he dies. They want the inheritance."

"How much is the inheritance?" Carl-Joran interrupted. "Four pigs and a flock of chickens?"

"No, a bit more than that," Halima gave her heckler a crooked smile. "The old man owns a fairly substantial restaurant business near the lakes."

"Ahhh, then she is in danger," Habib spoke up. "In India that is a fortune."

Halima nodded. "The Lama has also sent the same message on to his brother-in-law, Vaughn Eames in London, who has worked with us many times. We're hoping he can do something. And that's it for today, my people! Except you, Siddhu—you and I have to confer."

He nodded in agreement.

Dr. Bar-Fischer sighed. "Well, you know I will help if I am able. We can always put someone in our drug unit at the hospital. Perhaps those women from Africa? It would be a good place to hide a mother and daughters."

"Thank you, Rachel," said Halima. "We'll keep you in mind. Okay, Baron Hermelin, when Siddhu and I are finished, you and he must arrange the money we need and then all will be underway. Habib can go to Saudi Arabia and Barbara Monday can get the Valentine case out and the women can be flown in from Africa and so on." She sighed with a relieved note of finality.

"Right away, Halima, boss-lady!" Carl-Joran said in his inimitable American-Swedish accent, and jokingly to Siddhu, "Aren't you glad you don't have a name like Monday."

"It is better than Friday," Siddhu commented with his Indian accent, "because everyone would say, Thank goodness it is Friday!"

The group laughed as if humor would help ease the load each had just taken on, the burden of life and death, the seriousness of their missions.

"Who chose the name Valentine," asked Habib Mansur, standing, "for Monday's lady?"

"Probably Monday chose it," said Carl-Joran, getting to his feet.

"So it is Monday's Valentine!" Siddhu giggled. "We must go out this Monday and send money to Monday for her Valentine."

Everyone laughed and the Swede responded, "We'll do that, Siddhu. I'll meet you at the Swiss bank after I have a haircut." Carl-Joran waved at the two women, "See you soon."

"You stay out of trouble, Baron!" Halima insisted loudly.

"Of course!" he responded lightly.

"Goodbye," said Habib and bowed formally to the women.

"Good luck," said both women simultaneously and they watched the two men exit and listened to their footsteps go down the hall. "I wish," said Rachel Bar-Fischer, "I could have found a man like the baron when I was younger."

"Wouldn't any woman!" whispered Halima Legesse rising to her full height.

Siddhu Singh Prakash spread out his printouts and prepared to brief Halima on the further intricacies of their present funding status.

Darughih Quddus Sadiq-Fath slid one hairy leg off the plush sleeping mat and was about to push the satin cover aside when a timid knock came at the big door. That should be dinner arriving. He leaned back and patted the slender leg of the boy on the bed next to him. "Put on a robe and set our table."

"Yes, master," said the beautiful lad, hopping from the other side of the bed and wrapped a kaftan, as flowing and white as the sand outside, around himself.

A more confident knock came, the door opened a crack and a gravely old voice announced, "Sadiq-Fath, sir, you have a phone call."

That would be his second in command, Ali Fur Muhit. The boy, poised near the knee-high, expensively carved serving table, glanced inquiringly at the man. With a firm signal, Sadiq-Fath waved the boy out of the room. The boy hurried into the bath area and closed the door behind him. Sadiq-Fath pulled a silk shirt over his head and a half robe around his waist.

He said to the door, "Come in."

Two people entered, the servant girl with dinner and Muhit, the crusty warrior who'd been Sadiq-Fath's assistant for so many years he was a virtual institution. Ali's eyes were clouded. Cataracts. Years of being out on the desert, one war after another, fighting his commander's battles. There would come a day when he'd have to go in for surgery and Sadiq-Fath knew the man would have to be ordered to go.

Muhit had a cell phone in his hand. "Call coming in from Tidewater in Virginia. He's got news about EW."

Sadiq-Fath's whole face screwed up. "I'll take it." He reached out his hand.

Ali Muhit said in rough English into the phone, "Mr. Snow, you have Mr. Tidewater on the phone, yes?" He then handed it to his commander. "One minute, sir."

The servant girl, a pretty one from the Philippines, was standing patiently by the serving table, tray in hand. Sadiq-Fath motioned her to put it down and leave. She did. Ali Muhit bent over and lifted the lids of the plates letting the wonderful aromas of cumin, nutmeg, and saffron escape.

"Help yourself," said Sadiq-Fath, sitting again on the edge of the bed as he put the phone to his ear. Ali immediately dug into the big bowls of steaming food. The phone clicked on the other end and there was the familiar voice.

"Hello? Is this Quddus?"

"Yes, Marion. And how is Mr. Tidewater tonight?" Sadiq-Fath's English was not only American, but with a Los Angeles accent that demonstrated his years spent at California State University in San Jose as a student of criminology.

"Hey there old buddy! It's darned near lunch time here," came Marion Tidewater's voice enthusiastically. "How ya doing?"

"I'm fine, Marion. How's it going with you?" Sadiq-Fath had a smile drawn tightly across his teeth. He had let this man consider him a friend since their Agency training together. He was useful. It cost Quddus a lot in tolerance. He would much rather have dispensed with the overbearing, crass, ugly little American.

"I'm just fine, but I wanted to share some hot news with you. Get your input."

"My assistant says it is about Emigrant Women. You know I am always interested in that organization." Quddus moved to the table, unable to resist the food that Ali was consuming.

"Well, first," came Tidewater's words, "we gotta discuss Barbara Monday."

"Monday!" Quddus growled, and then winked at Ali as he lowered himself to a cross-legged sitting position across from him, "That American whore. I will have her in jail one fine day, my private jail..."

"She went to Jerusalem."

"Hmmm." The Persian commander made his tone more neutral, and the food, which had halted halfway to his mouth, continued.

Tidewater said, "She met with someone from EW, what else? But since our good ol' buddy Hermelin's taken care of, who would she have contacted?"

Quddus swallowed the excellent dahl and hummus along with a piece of pita and pursed his lips, "Maybe their accountant, that Sikh Prakash."

"Nah, the Indian wouldn't leave Haifa, I was considering Halima Legesse herself."

"Dr. Legesse does not do errands." This was said with a touch of respect, and then Quddus Sadiq-Fath sighed dramatically, "I had hoped once the baron was...eliminated, we would not have to worry so much about these people."

"Yes, and by the way," Tidewater slyly inquired, "you got any, uh, information on how the baron met his end?"

"Ahhh," laughed Sadic-Fath, his powerful jaw muscles loosening from their continual clenching for a brief second, "he had a little accident in his limousine in Cairo a couple weeks ago. Something about a grenade launcher that blew up a large part of the street. Lots of casualties, I am told."

"Well, well," Tidewater responded, "those things happen, don't they?"

"They certainly do. One of those radical Muslim sects which cause so much trouble in Egypt claimed responsibility," Sadiq-Fath added.

"Yeah, I bet." Tidewater said.

"So," the Persian commander folded his legs under the table and leaned an elbow onto it, "let's talk about Barbara Monday."

"Yes, she's up to something."

"Hmmm, didn't expect her to go to Israel like that," said Sadiq-Fath tantalizingly. "We knew Smoland in Stockholm was working with Dubbayaway in Thailand on a case relating to Arab interests. We think it has to do with a Sanjay Pandharpurkar whose daughter is being held in Kuwait for knifing a young Saudi fellow."

"Didn't know about Smoland 'cause we don't have much interest in Sweden," said Tidewater.

"In consequence you would not know," gloated Sadiq-Fath, "about what has happened with Baron Hermelin's estate?"

"No, should I?" Tidewater responded, curious.

"It has been given, in its entirety, to a woman, a widow named Mrs. Bonnie Ixey. It is a big surprise to everyone." Sadiq-Fath paused, relishing both the shocked grunt on the other end of the phone and the excellent food. He ate a few bites of the saffron rice dish. "We have an agent on this Mrs. Ixey already. She's in California, has a couple of grown daughters."

"How did that happen? Awarding the estate to her, that is." Tidewater's incredulous voice came over the line a bit staticky. The satellite was moving along in its orbit and the transmission hadn't yet shifted to another uplink.

"One of our agents in Sweden got a copy of the government's records. Bonnie and the baron were married back when she was in college. Ever so briefly, before Hermelin disappeared again and the couple never bothered to divorce. She is and has been for all these years, his official wife."

"Well, I'll be damned." Marion Tidewater's chair could be heard squeaking.

"She will have to go to Sweden to the castle to do business and deal with the baron's son, Sture."

"Bet the boy is madder 'an hell."

"I imagine he is furious. No one knew, maybe even they had considered it invalid, the baron and this Ixey woman. But," the Persian commander laughed cruelly, "How will EW operate without the estate's money? Sooner or later, the organization must contact Mrs. Ixey and persuade her to join its efforts or go broke. I thought," Sadiq-Fath said with intense cunning, "if the old woman can be eliminated, the estate will be in total chaos and this nuisance, this EW, will disappear!"

"Sounds like a plan," Tidewater said with only the briefest of hesitation, quickly realizing he'd just agreed to some poor woman's assassination. "We'll put an operative on at this end and keep their movements posted here."

"No need," said Quddus Sadiq-Fath, knowing full well Tidewater would assign an operative anyway as soon as they'd hung up, "as I said, we have it covered. Oh, and you might like to know, our Los Angeles agent has heard a rumor through the police there, that your Barbara Monday is helping an American woman escape. I assume they'll be using the EW's pipeline. We don't know who this person is except she is the wife of someone famous, perhaps a movie star. That is probably why Monday flew to Tel Aviv, to avoid the paparazzi."

"One of *our* women! In that damned underground railway EW runs!" Tidewater exclaimed, "No way, not again."

"You know, Monday may be a whore of the Satanists, but she's damned good at her work," Sadiq-Fath nodded to himself. He couldn't resist taunting the hated American, "I believe she could sneak anyone she wanted out of your country."

"We'll see about this," snarled Tidewater. "Okay, Quddus, thanks for everything. Be sure to tell me if I can help you in any way. Talk at ya later, buddy!"

"You too, Marion." Quddus cut the connection, handed the phone to Ali Muhit who had to wipe the grease off his hands first before laying it on the floor nearby. "Time for you to leave," said Sadiq-Fath to his assistant, "and take the phone with you." Sadiq-Fath glanced back at the bath area. "I want privacy, for the entire rest of the night. Understood!"

"Yessir," Ali Muhit grabbed up the phone and saluting, left.

As soon as the big door had closed tightly, Sadiq-Fath ordered loudly, "Come out, young one," and the boy emerged, "have some dinner with me."

The boy bowed, knelt close. "Thank you, sir."

Russ Snow regarded his boss with perturbation. Tidewater's chin was crunched onto his chest in what seemed to be immensely serious deliberation. "You okay, Mr. Tidewater?"

The beady brown eyes shot up and focused on the young man.

"Sure, son. Couldn't be better." Tidewater stretched and grinned broadly, dissembling. "Got more information out of that old bastard Quddus than I could ever have hoped. You pay attention, Snow. All you have to do with these Arab guys is start them bragging on themselves and bingo! they blab their heads off." As he stood, he pushed his shirttail back into his pants. "I'm going to lunch. You," he pointed at the young man, "find out where a Mrs. Bonnie Ixey lives. She's in California somewhere. I want all the particulars on that woman by the time I get back. Family, kids, hobbies, everything. And look up who the operative closest to her is. I want to talk to him. Okay? See if we can have her under observation by dinner time."

Marion Tidewater went to the office door and opening it, regarded his secretary with appreciation. Maybe she'd like lunch at the Top Hat, he thought. Bet she never gets to eat such a fancy lunch. To Russ, he said, "Be back in a couple hours."

"Yessir," said Russ Snow, deliberately not watching his boss walk over to the secretary's desk.

The barber brushed the trimmings of white-blond hair from Carl-Joran's shoulders and onto the floor. Even with the chair at the lowest rung, the barber still had to stand on a stool for this tall fellow. With the kind of gratuity the baron gave though, the barber would have brought in a stepladder if he'd had to. He swung the Swedish man around and handed him a mirror.

"Thanks," said Carl-Joran, noting only that more of the blond had turned white.

The barber took off the plastic cloak and pulled the tissue away from the big man's neck. "I'm glad you're satisfied so easily."

"You always do a good job," the big man stood, pulled some bills from his wallet, and paid. "See you in a month or so." As Carl-Joran stepped through the door, onto the busy street, Siddhu hurried up on his bicycle.

"Ah, you look much handsomer now," said Siddhu, "so are we ready then?"

"Yes, let's walk." They went briskly together along the pavement with Siddhu pushing his bicycle. The breeze from the Mediterranean was warming the late winter's afternoon, and as they arrived at the Bank of Switzerland, Carl-Joran said, "Wouldn't it be nice to take a holiday for a couple weeks somewhere warm, like Southern California or Hawaii?"

"It surely would," responded Siddhu, parking his bike and following Hermelin into the entry and first security room of the quiet bank, "but you know Doctor Legesse would be very upset with you if you tried to leave."

"I know," grumbled Carl-Joran, as they passed along the corridor and through the guard station before being allowed to go up to a counter, "that's one part of this being dead business that I find extremely irritating. She hasn't told me yet how long I have to be deceased."

The teller, a penguin-dressed Israeli man who knew the big Swede, hustled over. "What can I do for you today, Baron Hermelin?"

"I need to move some money," he explained.

"Then we will do that," said the teller smiling. After making out the correct forms, the teller bowed and walked back into the rear security area.

What usually took only moments began to stretch into a considerable amount of time. Carl-Joran looked down at Siddhu and shrugged. He leaned his tall body around the corner and peered through the thick glass windows. Just barely, he could see the teller's black-suited form rather animatedly talking to someone not visible to Carl-Joran, and the teller's back was uncomfortably stiff and his arms intermittently jerked in some sort of pleading motion.

"I don't like this," said Carl-Joran to Siddhu, "this is not good."

"What? What is happening?" Siddhu tried to lean around like his large counterpart, but was unsuccessful.

Three more minutes and the teller and an expensively dressed young man came out of the security area. The young man, younger than the teller, introduced himself as the bank manager. He had probably been sent directly to Haifa from the main bank in Zurich.

"'Ello, yes," said the manager, whose accent immediately confirmed Carl-Joran's suspicions, "there is a very strange problem on your account, Baron." He laid some computer printouts on the desk. "If you see it says from the main bank that you…that you are *tot*. I mean, obviously, you are not dead. You are standing right here alive. But, *mein* baron, we cannot get into your accounts. None of them. You see on the forms, they all say your accounts are all to be put in your inheritor's name and until that has officially happened, they are frozen. I am very sorry, Baron. I am so sorry." The young man was beside himself and the teller hovered like a distraught groom.

Carl-Joran's face had the appearance of a boxer who's been hit one too many times and is about to go down for the count.

Siddhu Singh Prakash, not much better, stared at the young manager, then at his friend and gently tugged at Carl-Joran's sweatshirt sleeve. "Baron, is he saying you cannot put money in the EW account here in Israel? Is he?"

"I guess that's the upshot," said Carl-Joran.

"What will we do?" Siddhu almost screeched, "Nothing can happen."

"I'll call my son," Carl-Joran said. "Don't worry. We'll get this straightened out." He smiled at the worried bank manager and the dancing penguin and nodded, "It'll be dealt with. And, you don't say anything about having seen me alive, here, correct?"

The bank manager bowed again, "Naturally not, no. Of course, Baron, because we are here to help, Herr Hermelin."

They hurried out of the bank and along the street until Carl-Joran could whistle a taxi, which sped them, along with Siddhu's bicycle, to the top of the steep hill and to the door of the Nof Hotel. Carl-Joran paid the driver and they were quickly up the elevator and into the big Swede's room.

The little red light on the phone was blinking madly. Messages—Carl-Joran called the desk. All of them were from Sture, the very person he was about to call, his son and the number was the castle's. Sture was at home. Carl-Joran got hold of the international operator and was rung through to Sweden and to his castle.

"*Far!*" Sture almost shouted into the phone when he heard his father's voice. "Dad! What the hell is going on? I can't get any money from our bank. I must go to Stockholm, I should have gone today, to the Karolinska Institute and see my professor...and, and..."

"But, *min son*, the accounts should all have come directly to you, except for the one that goes to Emigrant Women. They weren't to go into probate, they were in trust accounts." Carl-Joran dropped heavily onto the bed. Siddhu sat quietly in a chair at the table and waited patiently while the man spoke in Swedish, which he didn't understand. Carl-Joran went on, "There was to be no probate, none at all. I assure you. Everything was in trust funds and assigned accounts. It was all taken care of."

"Well, it's not!" exclaimed Sture Nojd Hermelin. "All I got is what's in the housekeeping account and in my own savings account. Everything is closed up!"

"Damnation! The lawyer must have gotten confused," said Carl-Joran. "Can you call Inge Person? Can you see what's happened and call me right back?"

"I already got a call in to whoever's in the office," said Sture. "As soon as they answer, I'll ring you."

"Okay, I'll be waiting right here in my hotel room." He hung up and Siddhu jumped to his feet and waved his hands. He was about to speak when Carl-Joran said firmly, "It'll be taken care of. Just...wait. Wait. Sture is getting hold of our attorney."

"But...but...but...," Siddhu sputtered.

"Don't!" insisted Carl-Joran. "Here, I'll order up some tea." He grabbed the phone and did just that. Siddhu's eyes were wide with anxiety and he began to pace, back and forth, back and forth.

Fifteen very long minutes later, after the strong tea had been delivered and was about to be drunk, the phone in the hotel room rang and Carl-Joran grabbed it up.

"It's me, Far," said Sture on the other end, "and the news is bad. It's a terrible shock."

"What? Tell me," Carl-Joran sat down again on the edge of the bed.

"The Pastorkirche has found someone they say is your real wife, a woman you did not divorce. She is the person who has been given your accounts." Sture, a youngster as tall and strong as his father, could be heard near tears. "Everything, except for my small private account has gone to her. Far, she even owns the castle!"

"It can't be. Your mother, *min alskling* Heda, was my wife. What do they mean my first wife?" Carl-Joran could see the lights coming on in the harbor and around the shiny dome of the Bab's temple down in the Baha'i Gardens immediately below the hotel. He was completely unprepared for such a shock as this. "What name was it? Did they give you a name for this woman who is supposed to be a wife of mine?"

"Mrs. Bonnie Ixey," said Sture. "Now really, Dad, be honest, did you ever know her?"

"Bonnie?" Carl-Joran's lightly tanned face began to blush pink, "Bonnie...I knew a Bonnie once, long ago, but her name was Seastrand, not Ixey."

"Okay, then they're the same," Sture said with horrible resignation. "Here is what the Pastorkirche papers say, 'Bonnie Mari Sjostrand Ixey of Morro Bay, California.'"

"*Aha...min...gud!*" swore the big Swede, "I cannot believe such a thing. That was years and years ago. It is ancient history. Long before you were born, before I came home to Sweden and met your mother, so long ago! The marriage was not even real. It was...it was for...for protection!" and he stopped speaking for a moment. How could he explain all of this to a son who knew nothing of the Contras, of Nicaragua, of guns and drugs in Latin America, of rebellions and refugees, of the exigencies of war and soldiers and terrorists and intrigue? Finally, Carl-Joran took a ragged breath and asked, "You didn't tell the lawyer I was alive, did you?"

"No, that's still a secret, *Pappa*." Sture sighed on the other end with all the implications of not understanding his father at all or his father's crazy friends and crazier business, but putting up with it.

"Okay, then we're safe." The father shifted on the bed and noticed the very anxious Siddhu now pacing at warp speed back and forth, back and forth. "I'll deal with it from here, Sture, I'll take care of things as fast as I can."

"I hope so, Dad. Call me soon, I'll want to be at the Karolinska by noon tomorrow. I'll tell the professors something." Sture rang off.

Carl-Joran hung up the phone. Agonized, he turned to the Indian accountant and switched to English. "We're in a whole bunch of trouble." He said, "We don't have any money."

Siddhu screeched, "Do not say such a thing!"

CHAPTER 4: WEALTH IN AN INSTANT

It was like waiting for a medium to look in her crystal ball, except that Mrs. Lena Falquist Reynolds bore no resemblance to a gypsy palm reader or spirit medium. She was in her late twenties, dressed in an old sweatshirt and jeans, her boyish-cut blonde hair pushed under a scarf, and her face had a minimum of makeup, leaving her gray eyes the most outstanding feature in her lightly tanned face. She peered at the letter though as if it were just such a magical instrument to divine the future.

Bonnie, in the big armchair with the floral patterned cover, tried to be still. The large, comfortable house had that morning quiet only housewives or househusbands know, those moments when everything is suddenly peaceful. The cat, black with a white chin, having finished its morning's wash job, purred in the sun on the windowsill, his little pink tongue absentmindedly left poking out from between sharp fangs. Lena's daughter was in preschool class, her husband, an aeronautics engineer, had gone to work. The world seemed empty of strife. The chubby cat half closed its eyes, settled into encircling paws and with little pink tongue vibrating, began to snore gently.

"I am very sorry," said Lena abruptly, making Bonnie jump a bit, "to have you to sit and to wait a long time." She poked a straying lock of hair back under the scarf. She was slender, with that willowyness found in the southern Swedes from Skona. With a nod, she went on, "You were right, it is a government form and it is complicated. It says this and it says that and then it repeats it and then you have to fill out this form on the back. *Forbaskad byrakratism!*" She shook her head, trying to translate with, "Darn it bureaucracisms!"

"But generally, what does it say?" Bonnie begged.

"Okay, we begin with the *brev*, the letter that is on top," her accent was heavy and she was struggling with the words. "One moment, I get dictionary." She jumped to her feet and hurried to the bookcase in the hall, pulled out two huge orange books, brought them back to the coffee table, and laid them there between her and Bonnie. "*Nu*, we work."

Bonnie was somewhat appalled at the seriousness with which Lena was suddenly taking all this. Perhaps appalled was not the word, perhaps it was fearful. When Bonnie had appeared that morning, Lena had been bright and cheery and had happily served up a tray of rich coffee and supremely delicious, and probably highly caloric, Swedish cookies. All was amiable until Bonnie handed her the envelope with the ominous window and the two sheets of airmail paper. Lena's face had immediately clouded with tension and as she read through the papers, her whole demeanor underwent a transformation.

"You do not know anything of what they write here?" Lena had asked. Bonnie had shaken her head no. It was then Lena had begun the divination of sorts.

The big orange dictionaries looked as formidable as the expression on Lena's face. "Do you see they have your name spelled correctly? That they have translated the name Seastrand to the Swedish Sjostrand?"

"My father's real name was Sjostrand," explained Bonnie, "which makes this all the more mysterious that they should have gotten it right. That's all I could figure out though, except for the blanks where they want the grandmother's name, grandfather's name, and children."

"Ah, yes, here on the back. That is for you to give the Pastorkirche official enough information to register you in the correct book."

"Why? What is a Pastorkirche? What book?"

Lena sighed, struggled for more words. "The Pastorkirche is a very, very old institution. Each area in Sweden has one." She thumbed through the big orange dictionaries. "Ah, you say parish, each parish has one, or county, yes, it can be county. It is like the chief church office of each county. In that office, for centuries, all the people are marked down in a giant book. Of course today everyone is put into a computer list in Stockholm central government as well. All the *fodelsen*, all the *dodsfallen*—that is, the births, the deaths, and you say, the marriage, the divorce, everything that happens to the people in that county."

"But..." Bonnie shook her head again, "why me? Why does this Pastorkirche office want me to fill out a form?" " Ah," Lena leaned back into the couch, "because the Swedes are fanatical people about making records. When you fill out the form, this person can put you in the correct book in the correct Pastorkirche. Do you know where your father was born?"

"A place called Mora. I saw it once on some old papers." Bonnie remembered the yellowed immigration forms hidden away in the trunk, which was now in her own attic, untouched, left as her parents had left it all those years.

"Ah, you are officially going to be registered in Dalarna County. It is a wonderful place, Dalarna. It is where the red horses of wood come from and elfs...is that right? Elfs?"

"Elves. Little fairy people?" Bonnie tried to help.

"Yes, maybe, in Sweden these elfs are very big and not good." Lena looked back at the letter and the form. "Your registration is the second thing. The first thing is this letter. You are being told that you *arvade*," she leaned forward and flipped through the dictionary again. "Ah, you inherit a *aga*, a…a *egendom*. You inherit a…estate."

"An estate!" Bonnie exclaimed. "What estate? Whose estate? Where?"

"Wait, slower, I try to explain," Lena held up one hand. "Someone who is called Carl-Joran Hermelin died two weeks past and the Pastorkirche says you are his *laglighet hustru*. It means you are his legal wife."

Bonnie's mouth dropped open. She could no longer speak.

Lena, putting a finger on the names, held the letter so Bonnie could read them. "Do you know a person who is called Carl-Joran Hermelin?"

Bonnie shook her head.

"It say you are his wife! You must remember him if you did that," said Lena, grinning. "And also, he was a baron."

"Baron?" Bonnie's voice returned with a sharp squeak, "You mean, like a lord, he was royalty?"

Lena nodded. "Yes, you inherit his *slott*—his castle and his land." Lena laughed at the look on Bonnie's face. "You never know this Baron Hermelin? Never?"

Bonnie, completely perplexed, shrugged a big shrug and raised both her hands. "No, never."

Pursing her lips, Lena perused the letter again. "It is very unusual for the Swedish byrakratism to make a mistake on these matters. They have wonderful genealogy records. They are very thorough." The pretty face scowled. "Very thorough, especially when taxes must be paid."

Whirring back over the years, Bonnie tried and tried to remember anyone she'd known who might conceivably have been called anything like Hermelin. Surely, as Lena pointed out, she'd have remembered being married to royalty! Nothing, absolutely nothing came to mind. She shook her head again.

"Well," said Lena, "you are now wealthy. You must fill out this form and send it back so you are registered as Swedish. Then you must travel to Norrkoping and take possession of the castle. Let's see," she returned to the letter, "there is a younger son who lives at the castle. His name is Sture Nojd Hermelin."

"Why didn't he inherit his father's estate?" asked Bonnie.

"Ah, it says you are legitimate, he is not. It says you did not divorce this Carl-Joran Hermelin, so when he married a woman named Heda Bergshem it was not legitimate. This makes Sture Nojd not legitimate."

A thought struck Bonnie. She said the name slowly, "Carl-Joran was his first name?"

"Yes."

"I..." the small, gray-haired woman sat back in the big chair. " Once, I knew a Swedish man named Carl. Many years ago. In college."

"Many Swedish men are named Carl. Many are named Carl-Joran. It is common," said Lena. "What was his last name?"

"I..." and Bonnie thought, this is where things get sticky. She breathed once, twice, and blurted out, "I never actually knew his last name. I mean, his real last name. It was...I was doing a friend a favor. You see..."

"So what was the last name he used?" asked Lena again.

"Mink. He called himself Carl J. Mink." Bonnie felt the blood rush to her face.

"Mink, what means mink?" Lena grabbed up the dictionary and hurried to the word mink.

Bonnie explained, "It's a little white animal whose fur gets made into extremely expensive coats."

"Ah, of course," she said with glee, "I find it. Mink or ermine in Swedish is *hermelin*. I thought so because of the crest." She held up the letter, which had near the middle part with the name Baron Carl-Joran Hermelin: *avliden*, a small imprint of a shield. On each side of the shield were two creatures, one black, one white, which, if the imagination stretched, could be considered to be a mink and an ermine.

"Oh...my...God." Bonnie put a hand to her face as it turned scarlet. Trisha was right. There is a bottom line.

Bonnie had had the one moment in her life that could be considered an adventure. None of it had seemed real. A summer, three months that had gone blindingly fast like a movie speeded up. And once over, she had not looked back. How lucky Ike had died last year, she suddenly thought and the import of the statement hit her hard. What an awful thing to believe! She had had many good years with Eisen Ixey. He had been very good to her. What would he have done though, if he had known? She could feel tears start down her cheeks.

Lena saw them, reached across the coffee table, and took her by the shoulder. "It is sad? What can I do?"

"I don't know," Bonnie shook her head. "I never thought, how could I, that I was bringing you this!"

With a swift movement, the willowy Swedish lady came to sit on the arm of the big, overstuffed chair. "This paper does not say bad things, Bonnie. It says you are rich. It says you are a baroness."

"How could this Pastorkirche have found out about me? About that man? He didn't use his right name. I, myself, never knew his real name. I never knew who he was. I only knew he was in trouble, that he needed help, he needed to hide, and I...I helped." Bonnie wiped the tears from her cheeks.

"You helped him?" Lena bent to look in her face, "You helped him by marriage. Yes? To give him have a green card."

Bonnie nodded. "Yes. And...and more, he could have a new identity for a while."

"Do you know why he needed the identity, a new one?" Lena put an arm around Bonnie's shoulders.

"No. I didn't ask questions. We knew we shouldn't, or couldn't. The only reason I did what I did was because I trusted Toby, Toby Hughes, our leader. We were all in an antiwar group, helping refugees from Latin America, you know, go to someplace safer. One day Toby came to me and asked me, because my father was Swedish, which would make this seem logical to the immigration authorities, he seemed to think, to take care of this man, well, a boy really, who called himself Carl Mink. And I did."

A cloud of doubt came over Lena's face. "Did you get a divorce from this boy, Carl Mink? If you divorced him, you cannot be rich now."

Bonnie shook her head. "I knew Carl Mink was a made-up name. I didn't think the marriage was real. How could it be legal if Mink wasn't Carl's name? And we did everything in secret. My parents didn't know, no one at school knew. We got married in Las Vegas, we honeymooned...I mean, we called it that...and I didn't..." Bonnie choked, "I couldn't tell the man I met the Christmas after Carl went away...I couldn't tell Ike before we married, and I could never, ever have told him later."

"A marriage is a marriage and Mink is the same as Hermelin. It is the same man." Lena nodded. "You have always been Baroness Bonnie Mari Hermelin."

"What will I tell my daughters?" Bonnie asked, not Lena, but herself, and no answer immediately came.

Lena went back to her seat on the couch and poured more of the excellent coffee into Bonnie's cup, stuck a rich butter cookie on the saucer, and forced Bonnie to take saucer and cup in hand. "Do you think Dell and Trisha will object to being rich? Oh, I don't believe they will."

"Probably not," laughed Bonnie, trying to cover her dismay. "Tell me what else the letter says. You said I have to go to Sweden? That I'll be registered as Swedish?"

After pouring her own coffee, stirring sugar into it, and sipping, Lena scanned the letter again. "Umm—yes, because your father was a Swedish citizen, you are a Swedish citizen. So, first you must go to the Norrkoping Pastorkirche office and report to them. You will be given the proper papers and so you will take possession of the Hermelin Slott, the Hermelin Castle. You must decide what will happen to the poor boy, Sture, if he gets any money or property or something. And you must decide what you want to do with the castle and your bank accounts."

"Accounts!" Bonnie almost spit out her coffee. "How many accounts? How much money is there?"

"It only says accounts, it does not say how many," said Lena reading, "but it does say that the total amount of property value and money is, hmmm, let's figure, from the krora to the dollar...around $280 million dollars."

Bonnie forced herself to gently put the cup on the coffee table. Her hands were shaking uncontrollably.

"You know," Lena went on happily, blithely, "a friend of mine won a lottery *pris* in Sweden five years ago; she won eight million kronor. She had lots and lots of trouble. She of a sudden had so many relatives! And so many friends! Before, she never knew these people! She almost lost the money but then she hired an attorney who protect her. I think you must hire an attorney."

"And I better hire one in Sweden!" Bonnie agreed. "Can you ask your friend who hers is?"

"I can ask. I think you must do that," said Lena, secure in her advice.

Bonnie fell back into the big chair and looked at the ceiling. "I think I'm in shock."

"Come, come," Lena waved at her, "we must fill out this form. We must send it special delivery right away. The Pastorkirche official, she is named Birgitta Algbak—what a *komisk*...a comical name!—she must register you immediately in your parish."

"Okay, okay," Bonnie took in a deep breath and sat up. "You read to me and I'll answer."

"First, you must put in the name of your children." Lena had a pen poised.

"Children?" A chill went through Bonnie Ixey. That damned bottom line. Again the thought raced through her mind—what would she tell the girls? But especially, how would she, could she, explain all this to Trisha?

When Bonnie arrived home, to the welcoming big yellow house on Ixey Posie Farm, she sat down hard in a kitchen nook chair and gasped four times. This was not about her sudden wealth. This was about the hideous close call.

She had gotten into her car outside of Lena's, still in a daze. In the corner of her eye, she had noticed what she had thought was a student, a young man, dark, foreign probably, probably up from California Polytechnic State University. There were lots of Middle Eastern students attending Cal Poly down in San Luis Obispo. He was in a droptop, oversized jeep and he started his engine the same moment she did. He drove at a fair distance along behind her.

Then just above the seafood market on that sharp blind curve that Morro Avenue makes, he gunned his engine and slammed the jeep into low gear and roared past her forcing an oncoming delivery truck to swerve and almost crash into her. Front bumpers touching, the truck and her car sat on the curve until she and the truck driver could catch their breaths and step out. They agreed that there was little they could do. No one had been hurt. There were many, many students driving such jeeps at Cal Poly and at the local junior college, Questa. She and the driver had congratulated each other on escaping with their lives and vehicles intact, gotten back in, and driven off.

Slowly, Bonnie turned around in the chair and regarded the bright, warm winter sun reflecting off the patio. Past the patio and the backyard were the rows and rows of winter garden flowers, bulbs, trees, shrubs, and plastic-covered nurseries that were all now tended by a Japanese woman to whom she had given over management after Ike had died last year. The woman had done exceptionally well at converting portions of the land to Oriental spice production. They were going to make an excellent profit from the ginseng alone.

Calmed by the thought of her husband's, her real husband that is, beloved farm being well cared for, her mind went to present matters. Her heart rate went back to normal and her breathing eased. She decided she really needed to talk to the one person who might clear up the whole business about the Carl J. Mink she had been arm-twisted into helping all those years ago. Bonnie swung the chair back and dug through the telephone desk drawer. There at the bottom was an address book she had not looked in since…well, since the college reunion seven years ago.

Beside the name and address and phone number for Toby Hughes was scribbled with a different colored ink the updated phone numbers and addresses for him. There was a home number and a business number. He had been working for Batelen, Inc., a high security think tank for engineering geniuses in Bethesda, Maryland. It would be midafternoon there. Should she call his home, which might mean having to talk to his wife? No, not wise. She'd leave a message at his work.

The number rang and after a series of buzzes, hums, and beeps put her onto his answering machine. "This is the desk of…" said a tinny recording of a female voice, followed by Toby's voice, "Toby Hughes;" then the female voice saying, "Please leave a message."

After the beep, she said slowly and distinctly, "Toby, remember me? Bonnie Ixey? From college? I must talk to you about someone we knew a long time ago, someone you told me was Carl J. Mink. Can you call me right away? This is very important. Thanks. My number, in case you've lost it, is 805-555-3024."

CHAPTER 5: ALGBAK

We have an operative free in San Luis Obispo," said Russ Snow to his boss, "I'm getting him on the phone right now."

Tidewater paused, two files in hand, nodded, put the files into his briefcase, and closed it, setting it upright on the desk so he wouldn't forget to take it home with him. Sitting, Marion Tidewater took the phone from his assistant, covered the mouthpiece, and asked Russ, "What's the name?"

"Claybourne, Curt Claybourne out of the LA station." Russ half whispered.

Into the phone, Marion Tidewater announced himself and proceeded with, "Claybourne, are you assigned anything you can't get out of for a few days?" Tidewater listened and nodded, "Okay, I want you to tail a lady named Bonnie Seastrand Ixey." There was a pause and Tidewater smiled, "Yes, I guess she could be the same as the Ixey of the Ixey Posie Farm. I certainly wouldn't know. Well, as surprising as it is to you, I want you on her...yep, twenty-four hours, so get a sub for when you need it. And do a complete background check."

Tidewater paused again, then answered, "Don't be so sure. The Ixeys may have been stanchions of the community and Mrs. Ixey just a librarian but, trust me, that may be all surface stuff. Don't expect it to be as tame as you believe right now. Especially, keep your eyes peeled for Iranian Security operatives."

Tidewater grinned at whatever was being said on the other end and added, "You betcha, ISF guys. Don't think the Saudis are on it yet. Can't be sure so be careful. Your little librarian's hot property." Another pause and Tidewater said, "You do that. Report daily or if anything major breaks. Yeah, thanks, Agent Claybourne." He handed the phone back to Russ Snow who traded him for the folder in his left hand.

"This," Russ put the phone back as he indicated the manila folder, "is all the material I could collect this afternoon on your Mrs. Bonnie Ixey."

"Thanks, Snow, you're fast," Tidewater heaved his stocky body out of his chair, added the folder to the ones already in his briefcase and headed for the door.

"Ummm, might I ask a question," began Russ, "about this case?"

"Case?" The bulgy black eyes regarded the taller, handsome young man with ill-concealed envy.

"Well, this Ixey thing," Russ plunged ahead. "Just, I'm really new to putting tails on people and doing operative stuff, you know, since I did my first two years here in the documents section."

"Yeah, right," Tidewater paused at the door. "You're obviously good at tracking book-style information down and that's valuable to me, guy. What's more valuable on this side of the building is the real world stuff. So you gotta learn how we do that, right?"

Russ Snow nodded with the proper humility and went on with a very low voice, "For example, why do we care what a battered women's shelter does or what happens to a fifty-year-old widow in Morro Bay, California?"

Tidewater had a hand on the doorknob. He considered for a moment before deciding how much to tell this new man. "It ain't the women really, 'cause they don't have any value to us, it's this international smuggling of persons. We simply don't know how EW does it."

"How'd we even know they were doing it?" Russ got braver.

"That old weasel Sadiq-Fath asked me to look into it on this end about three years ago," laughed Tidewater, grimly. "Seems an EW operative, a haji, an Islamic holy man, no less, got a condemned Baha'i woman smack out of the high security prison in Tabriz. That's in central Iran, for God's sake. Got her to India, we still don't know how, where a Tibetan monk sent her along as a stewardess on a BOAC jet to Australia where she disappeared into the outback. Damned ingenious. Pissed the hell out of Sadiq-Fath."

Tidewater moved into the common room where the secretaries were hustling toward the double security doors and said over his shoulders as an afterthought, "Sadiq-Fath put a fatwa out on the haji and threw in anybody from EW he could identify for good measure."

"A fatwa?" Russ queried.

Tidewater nodded, a grim expression on his face. "That's a death sentence given by the holy guys of Islam. You don't want one of those in your worst nightmare. It's what that writer, Rushdie had put on him. Any righteous Muslim is supposed to kill a person with a fatwa laid on him, on sight. Tried, convicted, and executed in one fell swoop!"

"Shit!" exclaimed Russ. "So what we want to know is how EW manages these rescues?" Snow persisted, staying close.

The senior officer, now moving toward the door and home at a faster pace, glanced back. "Our agency wants the inside scoop on any subversive activity like this."

"Subversive?" Russ Snow raised his thick black eyebrows.

Tidewater stopped in his tracks and gave the new man a penetrating glare, "Damned right, Snow. Somehow these women and often children along with them get expert false passports made, new identities, hustled from one country to another with impunity. Their husbands are completely stymied. Sometimes even parents of the woman are kept in the dark. It's the process, Snow, the system. We wanna know their system." The ugly man glowered. "What EW is doing is illegal. Don't forget that in any ill-advised moments of kind-hearted, liberal, weak-kneed leanings, Snow. It obviates everything HS has in place and our agency don't like it much neither. Hell! It borders on kidnapping."

Snow got the message. Be very careful how he asked questions. Don't give away his own feelings, ever. He smiled and bowed slightly toward his boss. "Well, such an ingenious system will offer me a real challenge. I look forward to solving your puzzle."

The older man seemed mollified. "Yeah, you got a useful curiosity, guy. Keep it bridled, that's all, saddled and reined in. Okay?"

"Sure thing," said Snow.

Tidewater strode after the last of the secretaries toward the big security doors. As he was punching out, he called back to Snow, "Have me beeped if Ixey buys it. ' Cause if she does, we gotta make a move on the baron's money. Okay?"

"Yessir," Snow replied from across the room. He watched his boss go out, watched the big doors latch shut behind the last secretary and he felt a chill cascade down his spine. He went into his cubby and sat down at the computer. The material he'd gathered on Mrs. Bonnie Ixey still glowed on the screen. He was glad he had not succumbed to telling Tidewater that today had been Bonnie Ixey's fiftieth birthday. It would have made Russell Snow seem just that much more a hated liberal. A softhearted wimp. A pussy of the first order.

The tall young man sighed. This was not turning into the job he'd imagined when he'd applied to get out of documents. True, the information-gathering department had taught him a life's worth of computer search skills, but it was deadly dull. Most of it had been straight-out clerical work and of course, he'd been completely desk bound. He'd gone days in mid-December when he hadn't seen daylight at all. He'd come to work at seven a.m. in the pitch dark and gotten loose around six-thirty p.m. when the darkness had settled in again. Certainly this was not a happy situation for a boy from the wilds of northern Minnesota.

When word had come down that he'd gotten the assistantship to Tidewater, everyone, including his former supervisor, had raved. Tidewater had an excellent reputation, or so the portrait had been painted. Adventure lay in wait for Russell Snow. But here, on his first day, he had already become genuinely discomfited. He knew it was due to the fact that his first real assignment, Mrs. Ixey, had, as of today, achieved the age at which a woman became an elder in his tribe and he, Russell Snow, might well have to stand by and report her assassination.

It was a truth that he was not the dedicated tribal warrior his Menomonee father would have desired, although Russ had gone to Harvard, as his Mohican mother had wanted. Russell Snow-from-Night-Sky was, in the eyes of the greater Iroquois nation, a shining example to the coming generations, which was the most important thing the greater Iroquois nation considered in judging people.

That he had chosen to work at the Agency didn't go down well. His father had written it off as Russ's wanting to sow wild oats. Russ had told his dad that the experience in the most complex information gathering organization in the world would assure him a job for the rest of his life. That part, at least, was true.

Russ noted that Mrs. Ixey had an e-mail address. Old lady's up-to-date, he smiled. It was all he could do to keep his fingers from typing out a simple little message and sending it through some nondescript and anonymous source. As he pushed save and filed the information in the bowels of cyberspace, he wondered what he could have said? You're in danger, watch your back, the ISF is after you? He reflected sadly that the chances of her believing such a message were very minimal. A woman her age, with her well-documented staid background, would hardly be able to come to terms with suddenly being the center of international intrigue.

Russ morosely decided to brave the nasty traffic and the miserable snowy weather and go home to his little house near the river. Whatever information might come into the office would be routed over his computer and sent to the one he had at home. He'd rigged that up last year so he'd never be out of touch with the Agency. For safe keeping though, he had established a security code to keep his own stuff private.

Of course, for tonight, this was all dependent on if the snow didn't worsen and knock out power again. He sauntered to the big double doors, slipped his card through the punch-out clock, put in his code, and the latch on the doors clicked open. The cavernous long hallway was chilly compared to the offices. He bundled his down-filled, thigh-length coat around him and threw the hood over his head. He was glad he had kept the trusty old Land Cruiser.

Sture woke up feeling like he had a hangover, which was not true, not this morning. He was too stressed last night to have gone with his buddies into the small village of Norrköping for beer and pizza. He would have been very poor company. And it was lucky he hadn't. His father had called at eleven to tell him nothing could be done about the financial mess in Israel.

Just what the kid needed, Sture thought bitterly. Now he'd have to put off going into Stockholm until this afternoon, perhaps even until tomorrow. His autopsy lab results were all hanging on, waiting for him to arrive. His professor had to be notified that he wouldn't make it to the lecture on child abuse trauma this afternoon and what the accounts department would say...! Damn! Why him?

The bedroom was chilly. They never kept much heat on in the castle and although the living quarters in this wing were tolerable, it still meant a brisk awakening. The six-foot six-inch tall, skinny lad stretched, looked out the window into the darkness through the beautiful lace curtains. Only this year had the centuries-old ones been replaced by some of more modern, washable material, but in exact imitation of the old ones which had been folded away safely in the vast attic with original furniture, paintings—God knows what all was stored up there. Even some weapons and armor, Sture recalled.

Icicles hung from the upper outside window frame and sparkled from the reflected light of his room and the lamps around the faraway stables. Snow, brittle and dry, blew in huge mounds across the balcony. Beyond, in the shadowy early morning darkness, below on what in summer was the broad lawn, deer and a couple of *alg*—the cow-size Swedish moose—picked their way along a deeply trodden, snow-lined path from the frozen river toward the barns. Winter-feed had always been available to the wildlife. Birds in great numbers came, as did the birdwatchers from all over Scandinavia. The predators came too: foxes, wild dogs and cats, stoats, weasels and naturally, what the estate was famous for, mink. Last week, Sven, the head groundskeeper and stable man had sworn he'd seen a wolf. There had been rumors in Sweden for the last five years that some wolves had returned, probably running over the Finnish ice pack straight from Siberia. Maybe. Maybe.

Sture could hear the brittle snow rustle like dried leaves along the balcony. He guessed it was near minus thirty-five degrees Fahrenheit out there with a wind chill factor of about sixty below. Normal for central Sweden in late January.

He buzzed for Gustav before slipping into warm underwear and sweats. He'd change into his polypros before he set off for Norrkoping. He dreaded the whole prospect of going into town, of going to the Pastorkirche. No different than any warm-blooded Swede, he despised the whole business of dealing with bureaucratic officials. Sture, like most Swedish fellows of twenty-two was still very much a kid, comfortable, well cared for, raised in a totally undemanding environment. He would only after college have to face the frantic workaholism of the grown-up Scandinavian existence, and university studies for someone of his status, an incipient Baron with lots of money, could go on for as long as he desired being a student.

Or so it had seemed three days ago. His father's predicament, now Sture's also, was quite rudely interrupting his pleasant lifestyle. He was putting on fuzzy slippers over heavy socks when Gustav knocked discreetly and stuck his grizzled head in.

"*God morgan, ers nad. Vad will er?*"

"*Kom in,*" Sture ordered. "Some breakfast first and then call around my car, I have to go into town this morning."

"*Jawohl, min herrevalde,*" the ancient servant responded. Gustav had been more of an attending parent than his father, but then he'd helped raise his dad too. The ancient one handed the young man a woolen overshirt and reached to help button it and was brushed off by Sture. Gustav backed away politely and asked, "Do you wish to drive yourself or have Krister drive?"

"I'll drive..." said Sture, by habit, and stopped in mid-sentence. " No, have Krister drive. We'll take the big Saab. It'll be sure to make a better impression on those damned bureaucratic toads when I pull up in that."

"*Jawohl, min herrevalde.*" The old man turned to go, thought a moment and said, "*Urskulda mig,* but were you not supposed to be back at the *Karolinska Universitat* today?"

"Yeah, I was supposed to go." Sture grimaced, "More paperwork for Far's estate must be done."

"Aha, it must be important work for your father to interrupt your studies," said Gustav with great deference. He bowed as he went out the door, "I will tell Astrid you wish breakfast? *Ja?*"

"Right, tell her I want a big breakfast. I'll need the energy." Sture went into the bathroom. All the plumbing had been added years after the castle had been built, meaning it was quite aged in and of itself. He and his father had the only two master bedrooms with attached baths, fully updated. The other rooms in this wing had to share a bath and toilet at the end of the long hall. The other wings of the castle had ridiculously small toilets and baths and Sture had once commented that hell would freeze over before the estate invested the huge sums needed to update all of that space. His father, on his way to somewhere else in the world, as usual, had absentmindedly agreed.

The recently installed, under the sink, little hot water cooker was functioning well this morning, giving him plenty of steaming water to wash with. He regarded in the cloudy mirror the attempt he was making to grow a beard like his dad had had at his age. He'd seen photos of the baron as a young man and he loved the swashbuckling appearance the bristled, thick gray-blond beard had given the senior Baron Hermelin. Oh well, Sture mused looking into his own icy blue eyes, it has only been a week. He tried not to be too disappointed. Perhaps it was because his hair was so red. He trimmed the edges and rinsed his face well, scrubbing his pink skin dry with a thick, cream-colored towel.

When he entered the hallway, he could smell from far below in the great kitchen, the wondrous odors of pancakes, ham, coffee, and his most favorite *blabar* syrup. Astrid had picked those blueberries herself last summer from the garden behind the castle.

As his foot hit the first step, he suddenly thought a most distressing thought. Pay...how were they going to pay the servants? Gustav, Astrid, the maids, Krister the chauffeur, Sven, and the stable hands...the only person he could think of who came for free was the postal worker, and in second thought, he or she wasn't free either, really. Taxes, incredibly heavy taxes, paid the salaries and benefits of government workers. Surely there must be housekeeping money available?

Sture sighed deeply and slumped down the wide balustrade stairs. Generations of Hermelins had used those stairs, lords and ladies all. Portraits of them regarded the tall, skinny young Sture as he decided on the second landing, that the attorney's office, Person, Person and Alexanderslund, should come first, then the Pastorkirche. Maybe he could even browbeat Ms. Person into coming with him.

***

The vizier of the i-Shibl family compound was most polite, though Commander Yusef knew full well his soft words were an imperative invitation. The i-Shibl sultanate was of Shi-ite belief and thus, conservative to the point of being only one step removed from the believers who paraded their sacrificial urges.

Commander Gurgin Yusef hung up the phone and wondered with a headshake how Sheikh Sultan i-Shibl's eldest daughter ever had been sent to France for schooling anyway. None of this bother would have taken place if the girl had been kept at home. The commander buzzed his assistant and called for a car to be brought around. If the sheikh sultan wanted him to check out the compound's security, so be it. Gurgin Yusef suspected the real reason for the summons was the sultan's desire to have this tough-looking uniformed commander lecture his daughter on decorous behavior. Which, thought Gurgin, picking up his belt with holster and gun and strapping it on, was like trying to corral the last camel after the others had been scared off by jackals.

His assistant, Faruq, knocked on the door before poking a head in to tell him the Hummer was waiting. Commander Yusef settled his hat on his head and proceeded on his mission. Faruq drove and made good time across the interminable sand and scrubland, arriving at the modernized outer security gate of the i-Shibl's compound in under an hour.

The vizier, that is, the sheikh sultan's number one man and major-domo, waited inside the outer gate. A huge man whom Yusef suspected of having some African forebears, the vizier bowed to the commander and walked alongside the camouflage-colored Hummer as they proceeded through the iron-barred inner gate. The numerous guards were well armed with Uzis. No problems with security here, Yusef harrumphed to himself. Yes, he was being summoned to lecture the girl. He knew it.

At the door of the palace, an obviously Asian servant jumped forward to open the Hummer door for the commander. As he stepped out, the vizier elbowed his way forward.

"Welcome to our home," said the vizier, whose width equaled his height. This was a man of substance. His clothes were of finely woven cotton and silk, his pink-and-blue turban was of silk, he cut a fine figure. "If you will follow me?" His hand, every finger of which had a ring on it, waved forward and they went through the brilliant blue front door.

Commander Yusef was led from room to room, one cool hallway leading into another until he was quite turned around. His general sense was that they were proceeding north, that is, toward the back of the immense structure. The fittings of the rooms, the halls, made it very evident that this sheikh sultan had a substantial oil field on his property.

They crossed a lovely patio with a tinkling fountain and passed into a sizable room with a set of low Roman couches and chairs at the far wall surrounded by large pink-and-blue pillows. On one of the couches was Sheikh Sultan Rassid i-Shibl. He was much younger than Yusef had thought he would be, perhaps thirty-eight, but not more than forty. Slender, small, the sheikh sultan pulled his bright pink, embroidered topcoat vest down with a jerk to cover the top of his whitish-gold cotton trousers as he stood. This was a tense and unhappy man, the commander noted.

"How do you like my modest domicile so far, Commander?" asked the sheikh sultan.

"It is of inestimable beauty, your majesty," he replied and cut to the chase. "Your security lacks of nothing that I can detect."

The small man nodded. He was being told what he intimately knew already. "I would have you look at the back wall and installations before you leave. Vizier Rida will take you that way as you leave. Now, may we share coffee? Some breakfast?"

"If your majesty pleases," the stocky commander bowed. He also realized the vizier had vanished. A silent, cunning one that fellow...

i-Shibl sent a servant scurrying and he himself sat in one of the low chairs next to a table, inviting the commander to do the same. Yusef pulled up a pillow and sat in front of the man, decorously making himself shorter than the sultan. He had not achieved the rank of commander without learning all the necessary manners around royalty.

The ritual of coffee and food was precisely accomplished. The servants were well trained. The preparation didn't take long and the conversation remained on security, despite that moment's acknowledgement of it's being topflight already. Yusef noted as they conversed that i-Shibl had probably been educated in England, or at least in an English-speaking school. The man mentioned in passing his hobby of desert biology, in particular, the study of the small lichens that grew on the lee side of dunes where moisture would collect in minuscule quantities at night. That seemed to be the cue for a woman to appear.

The vizier brought her in. Despite her full covering in colorful dress and scarf, the commander could tell this was a woman in her mid-thirties and, he suspected, a very good-looking one. From the two strands of hair that peeked from her scarf, she could be seen to have dark auburn hair.

"My first wife," said i-Shibl.

Neither man stood. The commander simply gazed past her, the polite thing to do. She lowered herself onto an uncomfortable chair on the other side of the large room.

"Jani," said the sultan, "come closer."

She got to her feet and approached to within a couple yards.

"This," i-Shibl said, "is the reason for our daughter Zhara's unruly behavior. When I was a very young man, attending the Birmingham University in England, I met Jani Felice McCreesh. Her father is an engineer from Ireland, her mother a Saudi citizen. I believed Jani had been happy to marry me. We had a good life until I came back here to take the rule after my father died. I thought Jani was fitting in well here. Then five years ago, as is the custom if the first wife can give no sons, I took a second wife. Jani insisted shortly afterward to send our eldest daughter, Zhara, to school and this woman chose a girls' school in Paris." The man sighed.

Commander Yusef, quiet and attentive the whole time, saw the slightest nod from Jani at the mention of the daughter. Ah, yes, i-Shibl was right, here was the cause of the dissension. Secretly, perhaps even unconsciously, although Yusef suspected not, Jani Felice McCreesh i-Shibl had converted her daughter to wanting more Western ways. This was becoming so common! Despicable, he snorted.

"You must tell your wife not to disobey the teachings of the Koran, my sheikh," said the commander with as much concern as possible, "for if she has the wishes of the Western world in her heart, even if they are unspoken, even if she tries to keep them hidden, she will transmit them like a disease to her children."

"So I have said many times," the sheikh sultan responded with a meaningful look at his first wife. "I sincerely do not think she does it intentionally. Yet," he put his hands into the air almost in supplication, perhaps of Allah, "I am partly to blame. I had a big-screen television put in the common room last year and it is hooked up to a satellite dish." A note of bragging slipped into his voice, "We can pick up hundreds of stations, all of European satellite transmissions, all of ours and some of India's. It is quite extraordinary."

"Television alone did not make your daughter unwilling to be a bride," was the commander's rejoinder.

"Ah, you are right, of course," sighed i-Shibl, motioning the servant to pour more coffee for himself and the old warrior.

Yusef accepted it willingly. This was a superior French espresso blend not usually obtainable by the likes of himself.

"I'm certain," continued i-Shibl, "that being around boys, especially boys of European countries, and being unchaperoned and being in Paris, of all places…" this time he positively glowered at Jani i-Shibl who responded by looking away, far, far away.

The sheikh sultan, holding a tiny coffee cup in hand, stood and walked back to the chair he used as a dais. "Did you know, Commander, that Zhara has had the effrontery to say she wants to marry one of those boys? She will not tell us his name, but I happen to know he is French." i-Shibl laughed cruelly, "Why, he is a commoner to boot. The son of a wealthy Parisian merchant. I am surprised," he growled harshly, "she didn't pick a Jew! There were a number of them at that school!"

Jani seemed imperturbable. Perhaps, no, definitely, she had heard this argument many times already. What must it be like, wondered the hatchet-faced old warrior, to be ripped from your Western world where women drove cars, voted, carried on as if they were men—why, often wore men's clothing—to be brought to the safety and security of a compound where everything was done for you, where you were cared for with all your best interests at heart? The commander smiled past the woman and said to her husband, "Do you wish me to have a word with your daughter?"

The objective of the visit being reached, Sheikh Sultan i-Shibl motioned to the vizier. "I am so delighted you would do that, Commander Yusef! Rida, fetch Zhara."

Vizier Rida quietly nodded and slipped away.

"How is your wife, Commander Yusef, and your son?" i-Shibl asked in an off-handed remark.

"My wife is as well as can be expected," he said, "she will go to Florida next week for her third cancer operation. My son will go with her."

"Oh, I am so sorry to hear she is that ill. Please, give her my regards," said i-Shibl, "and those of my wives."

Zhara must not have been more than a couple rooms away because the big vizier reappeared with her in tow at this point. She was taller than her mother and most probably very distressing to her father being taller than her father. She was dressed in a long skirt made of stunning gold sari material and a white blouse with a scarf that matched the skirt. The scarf was not well wrapped, her eyes and nose and some of her reddish hair could be plainly seen. Yusef felt deeply embarrassed by her forwardness. Rida indicated for her to stand about ten feet away from the old warrior.

Commander Yusef stood and was inwardly dismayed to find the girl was only an inch shorter than he was. "Your father wanted me to have a talk with you. He wants me to remind you of the seriousness of your stubborn behavior."

Her eyes flicked past him and gallantly remained staring at some distant carpet design on the opposite wall.

"I imagine," Commander Yusef went on, trying to be kind in his very gruff way, "that you are aware of the penalty for adultery, and that includes the intention of an adulterous act?"

Her eyes flicked across his face, rudely, and instantly returned to their target on the wall. Yusef resisted the urge to slap her hard, although he bet her father had done it several times, or had had the vizier do it for him.

"I can only plead with you to consider your actions," he continued. "Your marriage to Sheikh Sultan Mustafa Bayigani will assure you of a home, of a future, especially if you give him sons. He is one of the wealthiest landowners in Kuwait. He has the ear of many American governors. I'm sure you may get to travel with his entourage. I see no downside to your situation."

Princess Zhara i-Shibl felt the bile rise in her throat. The image of the aged Sultan Bayigani was enough to make her gag, the mere thought of that man sticking his withered old penis into her made her want to throw up. She suppressed an inner painful, wrenching laugh. At eighteen, most girls in her circumstances, would have been long married, and if not, would not only still be virgins, they wouldn't have the slightest notion of a penis, of sex, of how babies were made. In fact, Arab girls from these conservative families still bought the whole business of the woman determining the sex of the child. Ignorant fools, she swore under her breath.

Her father spoke up, loudly, "She was caught using the telephone last night, Commander. I want you to trace that call. I want to know with whom she spoke."

Ah, the truth comes out, thought Yusef, the real reason he had been summoned here. "Of course, your highness," he smirked. "I can do that with a mere call to the telephone company."

The sheikh sultan waved a royal hand over the heads of the people in the room, stopping at his daughter. "You see, Zhara, nothing you do is secret! You watch out. I will catch your friends and I will have Commander Yusef bring them to trial just as you will go to trial if you do not behave yourself!"

Zhara nodded, solemnly.

"Hear me," Yusef reproached her sternly, "your life is on the line. You can be executed. Do you understand that?"

She cast her eyes down and pretended shame. The rage she had felt as she had been dragged from her teacher's flat in Paris, the all-consuming fire of desire for Emil, she struggled to keep invisible. She knew the passion of *Juliet* and she would have it no other way. Death was so much more preferable than being a slave. How could these men not understand?

The shaming went on for some time, until they got tired. She covertly watched the vizier lead the brutal old commander away toward the back of the house and, inwardly sighed relief at his parting company with them. When she and her mother were dismissed from her father's presence, she grabbed her mother's arm and the two of them scuttled down the hallway to the women's quarters.

"Momma," whispered Zhara, "don't stay! Please don't stay! Come with me when I go."

"My dear, my dear," her mother said softly, patting her beloved daughter's hand, "how can I? It would make the hunt for you all the more intense. I want you safe. That is my only, only wish in life."

As they took off their scarves and Jani her outer robe, Zhara said emphatically, "You know full well, Momma, that after I escape your life won't be worth pennies. It will be just what second wife wants. She has the two sons, she has Father's fancy, you are a fool if you stay. I can tell Haji..."

"Shhh!" Jani put a hand to her daughter's mouth, "Never say that name in here. There are ears in the walls." Jani hugged her daughter tightly. "I do wish you'd been able to hide away with that teacher in Paris. Oh, how I wish you were already safe."

"Momma, I beg you, come with me," Zhara felt the tears starting down her cheeks.

Her mother brushed them with her fingers and whispered, "Let me consider it, Zhara, let me think. I...only if they can assure both our safety."

"That's all I ask," Zhara hugged her back, "think about it."

Into her daughter's ear, the mother whispered in the barest minimum of sound, "Who did you call? Not the haji?"

"Oh, blessed Allah! No!" Zhara laughed out loud. "I ordered pizza for me and my half brothers to eat while we watched *The Empire Strikes Back*."

Her mom threw her head back and laughed with her, the laughter grew into peals of hilarity and like the cap off a bottle of shaken champagne, they giggled until they cried.

Zhara thought with a smile that she could never have been so foolish as to contact the underground through so traceable an instrument as the phone or over the computer. Her news would come by donkey boy, as if she were being held in the encampment of a desert king two thousand years ago. Sad, so sad, how little it's changed. Saudi Arabia of today is little different from the testosterone-driven existence on the dunes of history.

As her and her momma's laughter subsided, she reflected on how wonderful it would be to be shed of all these clothes, of this slavery, and to be in the arms of her beloved Emil.

Commander Yusef got his view of the back battlements and was happy to take his leave shortly thereafter. His thoughts went to the reports he was scheduled to give to two local men regarding catching the daughter of one and the wife of the other—two sisters—driving to town yesterday. Regardless that they were hurrying a sick child, a daughter, to the hospital, they should have had a man to do it. He wasn't sure which had been driving. The hospital personnel who'd reported it hadn't seen them get out of the car. So Yusef would be kind to the women, he would have them fully restricted to quarters, he would give their fathers and husbands heavy fines and make sure the child was well.

Yusef motioned to Faruq to get going. Sitting back, he pulled off his scarf and wiped the sweat from his head. After all, he thought, he could see the women doing such a chancy thing if the youngster had been a son.

Sound carries great distances in clear bitter cold and the brisk wind helped. Sture heard sleigh bells. He paused as he was about to get into the Saab and Krister, holding the door open, looked around also.

"Probably the Johannsons, my lord, exercising their Belgians."

Sture nodded. "Bloody big beasts to keep in shape this time of year. Can you imagine the feed alone..." he ducked into the warm front passenger seat "...not to mention the combing and brushing and hoof trimming and stable cleaning,"

Krister nodded, taking the driver's seat, "and it's every day of every month. Where are we going, *min herre?*"

"To Norrkoping, to Person's office."

"Right, my lord."

The Saab slid forward into the murky darkness and the special snow tires caught on the gritty drive. They were on their way. It was a little over six miles to the gathering of shops and schools called Ostby. They passed skiers, shoooshing along the lane and eventually, passed the four-in-hand huge brown Belgian horses pulling a large sleigh with the bright crystal lamps lit. Old Mr. Johannson was driving and Sture lowered his window to wave. The Belgians were dancing with energy, their breath sending clouds of steam along their backs. Their stable mate, a giant wolfhound romped alongside, seeming to enjoy the sub-zero chill.

Near the Ostby ICA food store, the only place for miles and miles where the local residents could buy supplies, Sture lowered his window again and Krister slowed the car.

"*Hej da!*" he shouted.

The very pretty Katrina, all bundled up in polypro and wool, paused in her long ski strides and her eyes, the only visible part of her body, smiled at him. Her Great Pyrenees dog, massive and white, bumped his muzzle into her. Sture could hear the old dog grumble as the sled he was pulling hit his hind legs. She patted the massive head and said something kind to him that was indistinguishable to Sture. She looked up at the Saab. "Come skiing with me this afternoon!"

"I must return to Stockholm!" Sture shouted back.

Her gloved hand waved a hopeless gesture at him. "You study too much, Sture Nojd!"

"Next week, Katrina, I will ski with you next week!" Sture assured her and let the window slide back up. The Saab moved along the lane, careful to avoid other skiers and dogs with sleds on their way to the ICA store.

"You should be more attentive to that young lady," Krister admonished him gently, "or she'll surely find another young man, my lord."

Sture laughed. "You are quite right, but when will I ever get five spare minutes' time?"

The lane ended at the intersection with the slightly larger road which led to Norrkoping and from there to the big highway which went east, skirting the shore of Lake Malaran, to Stockholm and west, up into the rolling hills, to Dalarna parish. From this point on, they could travel faster and the ten kilometers to Norrkoping would go quickly.

Traffic was fairly heavy once they reached the suburbs of Norrkoping and within a mile of the city boundary, the snow on the road vanished. The entire small city, all the buildings, under the streets, throughout the plazas, was heated by the steam exhaust from the big central electric facility on the tip of Lake Malaran about two miles south of the city. This warmth and lack of snow seemed a wonderful idea at the outset and certainly in the long run it was a lot cheaper than snowplows and individual heating units, but it brought a nuisance none of the planners had counted on—the drunks.

From all over central Sweden, the alcoholics who didn't want to be shut up in care facilities, to which they were entitled, would arrive in Norrkoping along with the freezing weather and first snows. The police would get after them, though without much success because the vagrants would simply move from plaza to park to alleyway gratings.

Sture noted four men and a woman sitting, huddled, just barely visible in the pale lights of the steaming fountain in front of the attorney's office. How, he wondered to himself, was it fairly easy to tell the difference between a male and a female although completely bundled up? The big Saab was parked near the café and after Krister had opened the door for him, then locked up the car, he hustled off to his favorite table for coffee and sandwiches. The bums held out their hands rather dispiritedly as he passed and he gave them nothing. Sture went around the other side of the fountain and avoided them.

Mr. Ingmar Person, the brother, was out, Mr. Alexanderslund was meeting with a client, and Ms. Inge Person, the clerk told Sture, would be with him shortly. Please sit.

He sat.

Inge Person, mid-forties, tall, blond, and regal in her sharply cut yellow suit appeared about five minutes later. She extended her hand to him as he stood. "I am so sorry about your father," she said.

For a second, Sture didn't know what she meant, then remembered that to all these people, Dad was dead. What a farce! he thought and answered, "Yes, yes. Thank you."

"Come into the office," she led him back and indicated a chair in front of her desk. "Isn't there going to be a funeral? Or at least a memorial service?"

"Ummm," Sture's mind was racing, "well, I guess so, as soon as we can get the body out of Egypt. There's still an investigation going on. You know how those countries operate."

"What a shame!" The woman smiled consolingly at him. "What can I do for you this morning, Baron Hermelin?"

"I have to find a way to make sure there is money coming into the housekeeping accounts and into mine. I must pay the servants. I must pay my tuition at college." He scooted forward in his chair and put his hands, clasped into fists, on her desk.

She nodded. "As soon as I found out about the Pastorkirche's decision last week, I began gathering all the paperwork. So far, as I told you over the phone, I've not seen any way to undermine what has happened." Glancing at his huge hands, she said, "I can understand your frustration."

"I don't think so," the young man said firmly, "you don't have an entire castle to run without the slightest idea where the money to operate it will come from. The National Swedish Historical Trust won't cover expenses for our private wing, that's for sure!"

"Did you get a copy of the letter the Pastorkirche sent to your father's first wife?" She opened the rather thick folder containing all of the Hermelin affairs, probably back into the last century, perhaps earlier. Her father's father had passed it on to her father who'd given the trust to her and her brother. Somehow, she had taken over most of the work for the Hermelins and Sture often suspected she had the hots for his Dad. Too bad, he thought through gritted teeth.

"Yes, I got it," he replied almost in a snarl, "and I spoke over the telephone with the person in charge of doing all these investigations, someone named Miss Birgitta Algbak."

"Funny name, isn't it?" Inge Person allowed herself a chuckle.

"Hysterical." Sture sat back in his chair and crossed his arms.

"I'm working as fast as I can, Mr. Hermelin," said the attorney, "I've submitted all sorts of objections, I've asked for a probate court to give an opinion. I've sent an overnight letter to this Bonnie Ixey requesting confirmation on her end, I've sent for the original marriage certificate from the State of Nevada and all residence records from the state of California. I don't know what more I can do!" She raised her hands in semisupplication.

"Why California?" asked Sture.

"That's where they met, or so I understand, and where they lived together for several months until your father, under the name Carl J. Mink, got his green card. It was easier then, for an outlander to do that in the US." She handed the reluctant Sture a photocopy of the form that documented Carl-Joran's US green card.

Sture held it in his hand. "I'll bet Dad didn't even read this or any of the forms before he signed them."

She shrugged. "Regardless, it's still legal and so is the marriage certificate." She dug out another form, glanced at it. "They were married in Las Vegas."

"Is that a state?"

"Ha! Almost," she laughed. "No, it's a gambling city in Nevada, which is next to California, where people can go to get married in a hurry."

"Sounds about right," he muttered, "getting married in a hurry is a gamble."

"So I'm not sure why you're here," she coaxed him, "or what you want from me."

"Money."

Her head went up, then down, her chin falling onto the fluffy cravat tied onto the top of her blouse. She said, "There is an open account for housekeeping, I told you that on the phone. There is your private account which was in trust and which came to you automatically. That's to cover your college tuition. How are your studies coming, by the way?"

"Fine, fine. I graduated from Uppsala last summer and I'm studying medicine in the Karolinska Institute now." He brushed the accomplishment aside and said, "What, exactly, does this first wife inherit? And how will it affect me?"

There was a long silence while Inge Person shuffled through the folder. She produced a sheaf of papers held together with a bright yellow plastic paperclip. "Mrs. Bonnie Ixey," she read, "inherits all the estate, except accounts held in trust for the castle upkeep, your college expenses, and the organization your Dad was helping, Emigrant Women, which has a small Swiss account."

"I had a call from…someone in EW," began Sture—which was the truth, he had, "and they've not been able to access their money."

"Ahhh," she said, "that's because the Swiss banks have a hold on the accounts until the Swedish authorities get a response from Mrs. Ixey confirming her acceptance of the inheritance. You see, the trust accounts are not of one certain amount. They get money from the accounts, which keep monies from the businesses' and investments' profits. So you and the castle can keep on running since they're from Swedish accounts, but EW's account is frozen until the Swiss banks get papers from the Pastorkirche that everything has been transferred."

"Damn it!" swore Sture. "I know Dad wants, er, wanted EW to go on operating without any hiccough. It's probably life and death for them."

"You're probably right. But there's nothing I can do, absolutely nothing. The Swiss banks are a world unto themselves. Not even a Swiss lawyer could do anything for you or EW."

Sture hesitated a moment before springing the real reason he came to her. Taking in a breath, he asked, "Would you come with me to the Pastorkirche to talk to this Birgitta Algbak?"

"Why do you want to talk to her face to face? And why have me come with you?" *Her* had been said with complete distaste.

"Because I don't want to face *her* by myself," explained the giant of a young man rather shamefacedly. "It's devilishly important to find out what's been done, how all this came about and if Algbak has any word from Mrs. Ixey yet. Come on, you're supposed to be my advocate."

Inge Person wrinkled up her handsome face. "I'll charge you for the time, oh yes, I will."

"Thank you, Ms. Person," Sture Hermelin replied in mock ruefulness. "Let's go."

"I'll get my coat." Her sigh of resignation was heart rending.

As they exited the office, she gathered up a handful of kronor for the drunks and, although Sture tried to lead her around the other side of the fountain, as he had come, she went directly past them and slipped the coins into their outstretched hands.

When they had reached the Saab, Sture commented, "That's illegal."

"My own philosophy," she said back, "I feel they have the right to remain free. Why should they be locked up in the winter if they don't want to?"

"'Cause they're sick and they need to dry out," Sture responded with the appropriate explanation. He knocked on the café window where Krister sat, drinking coffee, and reading the *Dagbladet* newspaper. He dropped the paper and jumped to his feet.

"We could walk," Ms. Person said.

"No, we're going to drive up in the Saab," the young man insisted and when Krister opened the back door, he motioned the attorney in, before sliding in himself. "To the church offices," he told Krister.

They drove around the block and down the boulevard that led over the twelfth century bridge into the part of Norrkoping that was much as it had been for centuries. Some of the wooden buildings, painted the traditional dark red, were in the exact spot they had been since the church, always the center of feudal towns, had been established in the ninth century. Archaeologists were finding that some of the huge oak logs, corner pieces of the houses sitting right on the river's edge, had come directly from the hills around Mora far to the east in Dalarna, probably at the same time the church was being constructed. Only recently had the church, a beautiful example of an early Gothic abbey, been renovated, with the help of archaeologists, who managed to save authentic historic features, such as the ancient woodwork, the graffiti on the back walls drawn by bored parishioners in the back pews, and the uneven floor trod by so many feet.

The Saab drove past the freshly whitewashed, small abbey and pulled up at the office next door, which was fairly modern, built in 1920. They parked in a spot quite visible to the rows of lighted windows on the left. Sture and Ms. Person got out and trailed by Krister, who would wait in the lobby, they went into the small area where supplicants to the bureaucratic system could call for various officials. Sture filled out a little piece of paper requesting an interview with Birgitta Algbak. The secretary hurried away.

Minutes passed. White-haired women in business attire came and went from the front desk, collecting other attendees of the system. Finally, a chunky woman, most likely in her mid-fifties with pitch-black hair, so obviously dyed as to hurt one's sensibilities, came to the desk. Half-lens reading glasses hung by a cord around her neck. In her hand was their little paper.

"Sture Hermelin and Ms. Inge Person?" her matronly voice croaked. The absence of a title before Sture's name was emphasized.

Inge pushed ahead in her role as advocate for the Hermelin estate and Sture followed her through the desk gate, which Miss Algbak held open for them. They wandered along through hallways until they reached a tiny office where, as Miss Algbak sat, she motioned them into plastic chairs that had surely been designed for robotic imitations of humans, certainly not for a real human, in front of her desk.

"Why did you come here?" Her directness was accented by sliding her reading glasses onto her nose and peering over them as if examining a couple of bugs that had had the audacity to crawl into her office.

Inge sat on the edge of her uncomfortable chair and began, "We are requesting any update on the status of Baron Hermelin's estate. We understand the Swiss accounts, which feed money into the trusts accounts, are locked up until word comes from the..." She almost said *supposed* and thought better of it, "first Mrs. Hermelin."

A smile of majestic proportions filled the lower part of Miss Algbak's face. The red lipstick she was wearing made it all the more grotesque "Why yes, I imagine young Mr. Hermelin here would like to know when he'll have money available to him."

"It would be useful," Sture glowered.

"Oh, your estate monies can be used at any time. Except for the household budget, most of that trust fund has gone into holdings by the Swedish National Historical Trust."

Inge said, "That happened a long time ago. The entire west wing of the castle is a bed and breakfast for travelers and hikers and scientists visiting the Ostby area. What's of much more urgent concern is the trust fund for the organization Baron Hermelin was working with..."

"You mean that group in Israel?" Miss Algbak's smile became a half sneer. "The one helping battered women? Yes, that is too bad their funds are on hold, but there is nothing I can do until the first," which was said with a severe tone and a told-you-so glance at Sture, "Mrs. Hermelin sends her forms back to us filled out and complete. Even then, legally, we are required to do a thorough check on her to make sure she is the correct person. This will be done after she's come to Sweden and presented herself in person to this office."

There was no doubt in Sture's mind at that moment that Miss Algbak meant to drag this whole process out as long as was possible. "That organization is a very worthy one. You as a woman should be trying your damnedest to help."

"I imagine you feel you are right, *pys*," she responded insultingly by calling him a young twerp, "it is all a matter of opinion, and my opinion has always been that the family together is a much healthier way to live."

Inge's bottom was only barely on the edge of her chair. She was so frustrated she plunged ahead, "Regardless of your opinion, legally you must move forward with the paperwork as soon as the forms are returned by Mrs. Ixey of California, whether she is here in person or not. The

Swiss banks will proceed with monies for Emigrant Women as soon as
you acknowledge Mrs. Ixey's assignment of the estate."

"As an attorney of such good standing," that also came out as an
insult, "you realize we cannot be too careful in these matters, especially
when this has all been such an unusual case." Miss Algbak peered again
over her spectacles, this time giving the attorney a piercing stare that
would have fried lesser mortals than Inge Person who, being one of the
only lawyers in the entire parish, had actually done a number of criminal
trials.

"I'll warrant your finding of Mrs. Ixey and her legitimacy of being
the first wife, I'll even grant your holding up of the accounts as proper
until receipt of Mrs. Ixey's credentials, but," Inge fought back, "I don't
see why you have such antipathy toward an organization such as
Emigrant Women."

An enigmatic frown crossed Birgitta Algbak's face, her body slumped
back into her chair, not in relenting, rather in ownership. One bony, pale
white hand slowly moved to point straight up in the air. "The baron has
his lordship thanks to Swedish royal decree in 1546. The Hermelin
money has come through the good graces of the Swedish people; it would
seem only right," the bureaucrat's righteousness oozed, "that it be
reinvested in Swedish interests. In this instance, he chose to invest in an
Israeli organization. So we shall see…"

"It's a bloody international organization which is headquartered in
Israel for safety!" exclaimed Sture, furious.

"Sweden is a perfectly safe country for women. I've never heard any
complaints." Algbak's pointing finger lowered and pressed upon the
papers in front of her. "He should have founded it here."

"Miss Algbak," the attorney stated in her deepest voice, "Baron
Hermelin was not the founder, nor does…did he have any administrative
capacity with EW. It actually works through the auspices of the United
Nations."

"Not my concern," said Birgitta Algbak and quickly changed the
subject. "My particular goal is to help the Swedish government gain a
way to reestablish tax rights on the Hermelin profits which heretofore
have gone into Swiss banks."

"*Fy fan!*" cursed Sture Hermelin jumping to his feet. "So that's what's
up."

Inge put a hand to his arm and tried to calm him. In a voice fit for
telling a jury the truth, and nothing but, she said to Miss Algbak, "Almost
every penny of the Hermelin wealth was made through investments in

humanitarian enterprises in both Sweden and foreign countries. The baron was amazingly astute at picking starter companies, cottage industries, small ecologically oriented firms, and kicking them into full gear. Reindeer ranching in north Sweden, fish farms in Vietnam, medicinal pharmacology in the African jungle, a factory using hemp for building materials in Mexico, and every bit of that money is accounted for and taxed by the Swedish government." Inge stood also, "No more, Miss Algbak, no more. I'll fight you on this."

Birgitta Algbak smiled sweetly up. "There is only one person who can make any changes in the way things are disposed at this present time."

"That damned Mrs. Ixey," grumbled Sture.

Inge Person's pert blond eyebrows scrunched together, "Bonnie Ixey is an American."

"No...wait!" exclaimed Sture. "Her father was Swedish. I remember seeing it on the copy of the papers Miss Algbak sent her."

Birgitta Algbak nodded. "As soon as Mrs. Ixey officially registers in her Pastorkirche in Dalarna, she becomes a Swedish citizen."

Inge's whole body went rigid. "And her newly acquired holdings become taxable through death duties."

Birgitta Algbak had a thoroughly smug expression on her ugly face.

"Let's leave. It does no good to stay," insisted Sture, pulling on his attorney's arm.

"This does not end here," Inge said grimly as Sture forced her out the door.

"Goodbye, my dears," a self-satisfied Algbak responded.

The two collected Krister in the lobby and, each bundling up against the bitter cold, headed for the big car. It was a relief to be in the warm Saab.

"Back to your office, Ms. Person?" asked Krister.

"Yes," she replied, then turned to her young charge, "what time is it in America, specifically in California?"

"You mean now?" he asked and shrugged, "I'm not sure."

"Pardon me," interrupted Krister, "it's about nine hours earlier than us. My wife's sister lives in Seattle. That's the same time as California."

"Drat. One a.m. That won't do," she reflected. "Sture, what say we give the first Mrs. Hermelin a call around four o'clock this afternoon? Catch her at breakfast."

The Saab pulled up in front of the little café again. The drunks noticed and their expressions looked hopeful.

"Sure, why not?" Sture said. "What do we ask her?"

"When she's coming over? What her decision will be on the funding of EW?" Inge continued more to herself than to the young man, "I'd like to find out if she understands all the implications of this. She may not have any idea at all!"

Sture Hermelin said, "You could well be right. I'm sure old moose's behind didn't tell her everything."

Both Krister and Inge Person laughed at the translation of the bureaucrat's name. Inge went on, "Perhaps that's why the moose's-behind biddy has it in for anyone with money and why she instantly hated me!"

"Why?" Sture inquired, puzzled.

"Her name!" Krister managed between guffaws. "Who could stand having the name *algbak*, moose's back, without going crazy. Every kid in school must have called her *algbakdel*, moose's butt."

"*Bakslug*, that's what she is! Underhanded, conniving...an algbakdel by any other name..." muttered Sture, remaining grim. "Okay, we ring Mrs. Ixey at four today."

"I'll set up a conference call from my office. You be near a phone in the castle. We have a date." She hopped out of the big car, walked back past the drunks, and handed them some more coins.

It was as the big car was heading out along the highway at a higher speed that it happened.

"Dad?" came Sture's voice over the phone, shaky and unsure.

"Yes, *min son*, what news do you have?" It was lunchtime in Haifa. Carl-Joran sat perched on the edge of the bed, phone to ear, Siddhu sat at the table cum desk. He had brought sandwiches from the Jewish deli and was unwrapping them. Halima Legesse stood near the balcony windows looking out toward the harbor.

"Dad, I know you want to hear about money," Sture almost stuttered, "But...Dad, I know you're in danger, but...am I? Now that you're supposedly dead?"

Carl-Joran tensed. "What...?"

"The engine in the Saab blew up."

"Blew up!" the exclamation, although in Swedish, made Halima and Siddhu look around at the tall Swede. "How? Are you hurt?"

"No," said Sture, "only by the grace of God. Krister's face and hands got burnt, not badly. He's home now. The Saab's ruined, Dad. The whole engine blew to pieces and caught fire."

"When did this happen?" asked Carl-Joran.

"Two hours ago. The police came. They're investigating. One of the officers told me he thought someone put sugar in the petrol tank."

"Sture," Carl-Joran was insistent, "you ask the police for the results of their investigation, and then tell me what they found. Okay?"

"Yes, I...I'll do that." The young man sighed deeply, "Dad, tell me the truth, am I in danger from some enemy of yours?"

"I don't see why you should be," responded Carl-Joran sincerely, "There's no reason you should be. That's why I became deceased. So, calm down. Thank God no one was badly hurt. Now, call our insurance company, they should give us a replacement car right away." The frustration of everything as it was made Carl-Joran grit his teeth between words. "Did you talk to the Pastorkirche when you were in Norrkoping?"

"Yes. Ms. Person came with me. We spoke to an absolutely disgusting individual named Algbak." Sture managed to laugh a little, it was harsh and bitter. "Old algbakdel wants to screw over our entire estate and make the government tax all our accounts for death duties. She's managed to do a good job so far. EW is really stuck. Their account is held up until this Mrs. Ixey decides on the disposition of the accounts." He went on to describe everything Miss Algbak had said and finished with, "Ms. Person wants to talk to Mrs. Ixey today, this afternoon, on a conference call."

Carl-Joran agreed and added, "Perhaps Dr. Legesse also?" He looked around at the tall black woman who raised her eyebrows, puzzled at hearing her name in the Swedish conversation, "When are you going to make this phone call?"

"Four this afternoon..." Sture, his voice trembly, interrupted his own words. "Dad, are you sure someone isn't after me like they're after you?"

"I..." the father thought a moment, "I'll have Habib check It wouldn't make sense to put a fatwa on you. There's no reason. That's why I became deceased—to stop such behavior."

"What's a fatwa, Dad?" Sture inquired.

"Umm, it's one of those death sentences fanatic Muslims put on an enemy. Like they did to Rushdie."

"Oh, swell!" Sture tried to joke and then went deadly calm. "Can you find out for certain I'm safe? Was the engine exploding merely an accident? Far, you go have your adventures, but I don't want to get assassinated."

"I'll try to find out. Habib should have some sources he can ask. Okay?" Carl-Joran said firmly, working very hard to keep the fear out of his voice.

Sture sighed again. He was growing old before he had any desire to do so. "Well, Ms. Person will contact us as soon as she makes connection with Mrs. Ixey. Where should she call to get hold of Dr. Legesse?"

"Uh, at EW, that would be safest." Carl-Joran felt terrible. He had not wanted this for his son. It must have been a bad coincidence, someone in Norrkoping who hated the royalty, such people did still exist in Sweden. No way did he want his only son to experience the constant anxiety, the looking over the shoulder, the nightmares that would surely come if it were a fatwa.

This was not what Baron Hermelin had planned five years ago when he offered to help battered women. Somehow he had neglected to consider that in helping the victim he must eventually face the perpetrators, which included the authorities that both condoned abuse and more often than not participated in the societal system that perpetuated the victimization of women. He had believed that he could have his adventures and Sture could peacefully pursue his medical studies. After forcing himself to relax, Carl-Joran said over the phone, "You be careful. You are my only son. I love you very much. I will try to fly home soon and deal with everything."

"You mean you'll be alive again?" Sture asked hopefully, "I sure hope so, this is a mess."

"Let me discuss it here," his father replied. "Goodbye, *kille*."

"Adjo, Far."

The big man clicked off the phone and pensively laid it on the nightstand. He glanced first at Halima Legesse and then at Siddhu Singh Prakash. In English, their common language, he said, "My attorney, Miss Person, will be calling Mrs. Ixey at four this afternoon. That's five o'clock here. She'll make it a conference call and that way, Halima, you'll have a chance to tell Mrs. Ixey about Emigrant Women."

Halima moved closer to the baron. "Did I hear the word fatwa in that conversation?"

Siddhu handed around sandwiches and between bites, the Swede translated for them what Sture had related.

"Your poor car," said Halima. "It is, as you told him, only a bad coincidence. Surely."

"Do you want me to call a meeting?" asked Siddhu.

Halima nodded. "Yes, at five. We can all listen to what Mrs. Ixey has to say."

"I hope she's home when we call." The baron carefully chose one of his dirty sweatshirts from the floor and used it to wipe his mouth.

Cringing, Siddhu handed him a clean napkin. "When will you ever do your laundry?"

Completely unfeigned, the baron replied with the great disappointment an employer might have at an errant servant, "The maid should do it and she hasn't."

Siddhu, sandwich in one hand, used his other hand to gather up some of the soiled clothes. "You have to put these in a laundry bag, my friend, and set it in the hall."

"When did they start that policy?" Carl-Joran asked. "I've been here a year and..."

The elegant Dr. Legesse put a hand to her forehead and pretending great exasperation, exclaimed, "Maybe you have a new maid! Do you know? Have you paid this new one extra?"

"I always leave tips for whoever the maid is," said Carl-Joran perplexed at the suggestion he should be aware of which maid was which. He looked imploringly at Siddhu who had found a stack of laundry bags in the bathroom and had brought them out to show his big friend.

Registering the entreaty, he dropped the bags and raised his hands as if supplicating one of his Hindu gods for assistance, "I am so sorry that I do sometimes question why I must live this life."

"I'm going back to the office," muttered Dr. Legesse, "while you two men solve the really important problems of the world." Shaking her head, she quickly departed.

"This is how you put laundry into the bags," Siddhu instructed the baron and with his quick, efficient movements, he scooped one mound of clothes after the other from the floor and stuffed them into the long white bags.

As the massive Carl-Joran watched his friend bring order to the chaos of the hotel suite, a memory of another thin, bearded man who had been concerned for him many years ago crept, at first slowly, into consciousness. A man who had extracted the young Swede from a very scary situation in Nicaragua and dropped him on the coast of California. A caring man who protected him from the American immigration authorities and finally, in order to hide him from the overly zealous FBI, had gotten him a new identity by arranging a marriage to a plain little lady in the local resistance group. A delightfully cheery, sunny kid, half Scots, half Swede, named Bonnie Seastrand.

That brought a flood of images rising unrelentingly through the morass of his present-day thoughts: the taste of saltwater and the smell of low tide along beaches stretching from Morro Bay to San Simeon; the narrow roads winding through golden dry hills and skirting sheer drop-offs above the surf; the pelicans flying in strict formation on the wave crests; the dark and twisted pines on looming higher cliffs; the log cabin hotel in Big Sur in pounding rain with driftwood blazing in the fireplace, and the woman who had been his first love.

In fact, the emotion he felt surging up from his groin was more than the mere word love could describe.

Where had he hidden this feeling? Where had it secretly resided all these years? How could a person just lose so powerful an emotion and not miss it? Lust, affection, caring, and a kind of respect that bordered on adoration. The pain—oh, such pain! How that separation had ached when he had gone away and his question to himself was answered. He had kept it suppressed so deeply...so long...and the answer was spoken in a small, subconscious voice: because there had been an utter ripping of his soul when he was made to disappear that second time.

Carl-Joran, pushing this revelation to a safer internal place, regarded his Indian friend lugging one laundry bag after another to the door, five in all. Toby Hughes had been very much like Siddhu in height and weight. Toby's beard was much shaggier and lighter colored. Where was that nerdy, bespectacled Toby now, Carl-Joran wondered, and what did he finally do with his life?

CHAPTER 6: OLD FAMILY BUSINESS

There was a wonderful birthday cake in the middle of the table. Dell and Trisha had spent the afternoon making it and tonight would be the official celebration of Bonnie's completion of a half century.

Yesterday had been so stressful. There had been freezing rain in Seattle and the jet that was to carry Dell and Lou to San Francisco was hours late taking off. Once in San Francisco another foul-up meant they were late getting into Paso Robles and the rental cars had all been driven away, even the one they'd supposedly reserved, and Trisha had picked them up after all. They were now comfortably ensconced in the big guest room downstairs.

Bonnie had pushed both girls out of the kitchen after the cake-making exercise, encouraging Trisha to take Lou and Dell on a walk to see the new greenhouses and the exotic herb gardens. Despite many efforts to teach her girls to cook, both had been disappointingly inept. The most they had managed were cakes and cookies and a fairly decent tuna salad if they had been hungry enough. The intricacies of putting together a large meal and getting it onto the table still warm remained beyond them. So Bonnie took charge of her own kitchen and prepared dinner while the rest of the family explored rows of ginseng, echinacea, dong quai, and the koi pond.

Later, the family sat down to a heaping platter of fried fish, parsley boiled potatoes, a lovely green salad with fresh avocados and homemade rolls. Lou wasn't waiting for anyone. The good-looking young man was scooping potatoes onto his plate before Trish had picked up the fish to pass.

He and Dell had finally married a year ago. They'd been living together since Dell's first year in college. He'd been her instructor in Biology 101, of all things. They'd gone scuba diving, a passion of Dell's. He'd taken her onto the research vessel where he spent all of his graduate study hours. And by the end of summer, that had been that. Three years later, Dell was finishing her bachelor's degree in biochemistry and had already been admitted to graduate studies in marine sciences and Lou was within a term of completing his PhD in oceanography. Bonnie liked Lou Williams with his outdoorsy frankness, his lithe strength, and especially, those gorgeous blue eyes.

"Thank you, Mom Ixey!" he exclaimed between the mouthful of potatoes and a bite of fish. "Who says you can't love your mother-in-law."

Dell grinned and helped herself to the salad. "Don't start," she nudged him.

"Hey, it's okay you're a lousy cook," he swallowed, "as long as we can come here to eat once in a while!"

Dell smacked him playfully on the shoulder and they smiled at each other. She had the short stick of the draw as far as Mendelian genetics went. She had inherited all the short genes Bonnie could give her and whatever few short genes might have existed on Ike's side. She'd topped out at only five feet, two inches tall, which was incredibly tiny for the Ixey family in which the merely average person was six feet tall with the shortest Ixey aunt being five feet ten.

Trisha's big hands balanced the salad bowl long enough to serve herself more and then she passed it on to her sister. How unalike these two appeared, thought Bonnie, and grimaced. At that exact moment, the phone rang.

"A salesman," Lou insisted, "they always call during dinner."

"Yeah, Mom," Dell joined in, "leave it be."

But having a bad feeling about doing that, she started to get up and the answering machine came on announcing this as being the Ixey residence. She was reaching for the phone when the beep sounded and a voice from eons past came on.

"Bonnie? This is Toby..."

She grabbed the phone off the hook. "I'm here, uh...let me go in the other room." She held out the phone to Trish to hang up and trotted quickly to the living room.

"I'm sorry," he started, "did I get you at dinner?"

"That's all right," Bonnie responded, "I know you must be a busy man."

"Yes, you could say that. You know that I'm doing engineering analyses for a very high tech firm," he seemed to be speaking to her as if she were a moron or a child. "There are lots of security issues here and I have to be very, very careful who I talk to and what I talk about."

"Well," said Bonnie, "I assumed that was true."

"If you assumed that," Toby's voice was changing, becoming harsher, "then why did you leave a message about Mink on my machine at work?"

"You're the only person I could think of to ask about him," Bonnie went on bravely. "Did you know he died a couple weeks ago?"

"I didn't know. I'm sorry to hear about it. He was always getting in harm's way. It's a wonder he lived to the age he did!" Toby Hughes, cleared his throat, "Now, listen, Bonnie, we won't talk about him any more, will we? Let's just you and me have a nice chat about our own lives."

"Toby, there are some things I must find out, things you might remember," Bonnie insisted. He started to object and she ploughed on, "For example, did you know he was a baron. Were you aware I was marrying Swedish royalty?"

"A what? Royalty!" Toby, incredulous, half laughed, half snarled, "Couldn't have been. The man could hardly read and he could get lost in a parking lot. Giant Carl was by far the clumsiest individual I've ever come across. Him, a baron? Be serious."

"Yes, seriously. He was a wealthy baron, with a castle and an estate and Swiss bank accounts and after we...after he left, he went back to Sweden and got married and he has...had a son," the whole sentence blurted from her mouth and she could feel tears brimming.

"Wait, Bonnie, hold on, I didn't know any of that," Toby's voice pleaded, "I really, honestly didn't. He was a dork I rescued when I was doing that Latin American underground refugee thing. But, and I am really, really dead serious here, we have to quit talking about him. I wasn't going to return your call for fear of this. I can't say any more about him, please!"

"Why?" Bonnie demanded, "Why not? You got me into it. You persuaded me to..."

"We were different back in those days, we believed in different things, we thought we could save people, save the world from its own destructive urges." The words sounded hollow and cavernous, like echoes of old TV shows heard from the apartment next door.

The tears flooded over onto Bonnie's cheeks and trickled down and they registered in her voice. "Carl and I never divorced, Toby. I thought it was a sham marriage, that Mink wasn't his real name."

"It wasn't. He made it up for his passport into the US. I was standing there when he did it. That's all, Ixey, I'm hanging up!" he growled.

"No, not yet!" she screeched, "Mink was his real name, it was a translation from his Swedish name, Hermelin, and we were really married and we've always been married and now he's dead and I've inherited his estate!"

"Christ almighty! You've been in contact with Mink? That's why you called me. No! Don't call me! Don't write! And never, never e-mail me! Don't mention this conversation to anyone. My security clearance is probably down the toilet already! God, if anyone heard…I'll never work again, ever!" The connection on Toby's end cut off.

Bonnie held out the phone receiver and sniffling at it, put it gently into the cradle. People change, she thought, they really do. She stood and turned and there were her two daughters and son-in-law watching. Dell threw her arms around her.

"Mom, what's wrong?" she asked.

Bonnie laid her arms over the small shoulders of her younger daughter. "Ghosts, my dear."

"That's what the letter from Sweden was all about," said Trisha, confirming her own worst prediction. "Told you, there's always a bottom line."

Managing a smile amidst the tears, Bonnie guided her family back to the table. "Sit, children, let's have cake. Come, Dell, you light the candles. Trish, you serve up ice cream, and I will tell you a grand story."

She did not tell them everything. In fact, she kept it simple, extracting all the passion, the anger, the fear. How could she convey the danger to children of this time? They took what she did say well. She sensed they perhaps saw her in a more realistic light, certainly as more human and with a history they had never guessed before.

They wanted to know more and she blushed and refused. Some things were hers alone. Besides, there was this ache beginning in her lower stomach. There was an odd burning sensation in her chest and her breasts tingled. This was no hot flash. This was lust. As she put her story to a close, she inwardly laughed at herself. A fifty-year-old woman with incipient wet dreams—how droll.

"So I'm married into a potentially wealthy family?" was Lou's first comment.

"Yes, you are." Bonnie smiled.

"Right on!" he grinned. "So when do we pack off for Sweden?"

She shook her head. "I'll be going, not the whole herd of us. And I have to make sure Carl's son Sture is okay."

"Mom," Trisha snorted, "the boy's been raised in a castle. What else could he need?"

"We can't know," said Bonnie softly, remembering the big, oafish Carl. "Wealth doesn't provide for everything."

"It won't change me!" Dell insisted rather disdainfully. "I have my love and I know who I am." She hugged her husband and he kissed her on the top of her head.

"I am glad you're grown up before this happened," Bonnie said truthfully. "Becoming wealthy suddenly can be very hard on a family."

"Not us," chuckled Trisha, "we're the Ixeys. I mean, we've done okay. We're not poor ourselves. Dad and you were good providers, Mom."

Bonnie swallowed hard. She didn't want to broach the whole subject of how very much they had inherited, that the baron's wealth was beyond what the flower farm could ever dream of producing. "Um-hum. Ike was a good man. We always had enough to eat and a nice place to live. We've been safe and you've been protected."

At that, Trisha leaned over the table and asked, "What's this about you almost being run off the road this morning?"

"Just some Arab student who didn't know how to drive," she responded and Dell's eyes lit up.

"Arab?" She turned to her sister, "The man we saw by the end of the road, he was black-haired and swarthy. He looked Arab."

"Yeah, Mom, when we went walking earlier there was a guy hanging out near the mailboxes," said Trish, "I sicced Gryphon on him."

Worried, Bonnie asked, "What happened?"

"The guy ran," laughed Dell

"Anyone would run if an eighty-pound Australian Shepherd was after them," Trisha said, "I mean, they wouldn't stop long enough to see he was old and nearly toothless."

Lou shoved his chair back, stood and leaned close to Bonnie, "You don't have some sort of threat against you because of suddenly being rich, do you?"

"Why would I?" she replied.

"Maybe the tabloids are hot on your trail," Lou hugged her, "my mom-in-law, a wild child now fabulously rich, being trailed by secret agents. Who'd-a thought!"

"Oh, my," she fussed, "what an awful thing it would be to have those vultures after you!"

Lou let her go and taking his pipe out of his pocket, made for the front door. "Time for a smoke and since you women are all against my filthy habit, I'll go stand on the veranda."

"I'll come out in a minute," said Dell, "after we do dishes."

"It's not me evicting you," Bonnie contended before he went out the door, "I like the smell of pipe smoke. Reminds me of my father."

"Ugh," muttered Trisha, starting to collect dishes, "Let's not mention Grandpa Seastrand."

Lou waved and shut the door behind him. Ten minutes later, he dashed in and hurried to the kitchen, pipe in hand. It was out. He was flushed from the brisk night air and excitement. Over the clatter of dishes going into the dishwasher, he almost shouted, "There's a different man lurking on the drive."

The women paused in their work and looked at him.

He went on, "Not Arab this time. He's a black guy and he's for real in a trench coat. Kid you not. And he had those night binocular things and when I lit up my pipe, he quit watching and got into a car that was standard government issue. Swear to God! Drove off down the road, but I bet you he didn't go far 'cause I didn't hear that car engine past the bend."

Trisha turned to her mom, a severity creeping into her voice. "What the hell's going on? Do you know? Do you? You aren't keeping something else from us?"

Shaking her head, Bonnie shrugged her shoulders in a strong negative movement. "No, I am not."

"Should we call the police?" Dell looked up at her husband.

"What do you think?" he asked Bonnie directly.

"I don't know…" she began.

Trisha butted in with, "What if this new guy is a cop of some kind?"

"But why?" Bonnie beseeched them. "It doesn't make any sense." She instantly recalled Toby Hughes's consternation. He was terrified that someone would find out about what he'd done with the Latin American refugee rescue group despite its being so far in the past. There was undeniable panic in his voice at the mention of Carl Mink in the present tense. Could it be? Was there danger here? The sudden flavor of fear made her remember that summer when she and Carl were midnight riders hiding from the authorities. A thrill went through her. She stifled it and said, "This is all silly. Who'd want to put surveillance on a flower farm?"

"Never know, Mom," Trisha offered, "maybe they'll invade us while we sleep and steal everything or surround us like Waco and accuse us of raising pot."

"Come on, Trish," her sister giggled uncomfortably, "next you'll be telling ghost stories like when we were kids and you'd scare the bejeezus out of me at bedtime."

"So that's why you two never got to sleep!" exclaimed Bonnie and everyone laughed. "I always wondered and worried about you two being awake most of the night, even on school nights." The subject of strange observers had been astutely set aside. Bonnie was relieved.

They stayed up for a while, playing Clue, and enjoying each other's company. It wasn't until Bonnie was pulling the bedcovers over her that that other sensation she'd had earlier, that almost foreign one...that burning desire for touch crept back, shyly, as if it weren't certain of what its reception would be. Bonnie's only conscious reaction was to consider how long it had been since she'd laid with a man...Ike had been sick for three years before he died. There had been little they could do and she could never see herself being unfaithful. Most of her waking hours had been spent caring for him.

This last year she had stayed alone and avoided male companionship, as she certainly didn't want to end up nursing another old man. She had neglected her sexual self. Perhaps she had even convinced herself she was finished with it. Yet, there was no denying the surge of feeling coming along with the memory of Carl.

She smiled and nestled into the warm covers. Of course, spending an entire summer as they had, why even an old woman could recover her lust with those memories. Suddenly it hit her. The man she had fallen so fiercely in love with those many years ago was dead. He had died two weeks ago. She would not be able to recover him, repair the past, finish the unfinished business. Grief drowned her like a sneaker wave, powerful and cold and with it the guilt of being in grief over a man she'd known for an eternity of mere moments when there had been only immense relief when Ike had passed away after a blink-of-an-eye twenty-six year marriage. Why was that? How sad. How tragic. The tears returned and with them, deep, heavy, dream-filled sleep.

The phone was ringing. She was stretched out on a towel on a beach in the hot sun and a large, golden-haired arm was over her back, a warmly comfortable large body next to her and the waves rumbled in a steady rhythm, hypnotic "Carl..." she spoke to the giant man lying beside her. The phone kept ringing. Answer the damned phone, she swore at the conscious universe.

"Mom!" Trisha shouted from downstairs. "Long distance call coming in for you. Mom!"

She opened her eyes. She was not on a warm beach, she was in her bed and the window was a damp blank gray with early morning fog and Carl was gone forever. A wave of depression matching the gray fog sucked up her soul.

"Mom! Get the phone!"

She struggled into full consciousness, prayed for a cup of coffee, and leaned over to the nightstand, grabbed the cordless phone and sat up. "Okay, Trish, I have it." She clicked it on and put it to her ear. "Yes, hello?"

"Mrs. Ixey?" The voice was female, not old and it had a very strong Swedish accent. "I am Inge Person. I am the *advokat*, you say attorney? For the Hermelin estate."

The woman had pronounced her name as *Pershoon* and Bonnie tried to imitate it as closely as possible. "Yes, I am very glad you called. I wanted to contact a Swedish attorney to find out what all this was about."

"*Jo?* You want an attorney? That is good. You see, I am the *officiell* attorney for the family so I'll be your attorney also." She paused, "You must have an introduction to Baron Hermelin's son. He is on the telephone also, but he is at the castle. *Sture, ar ni dar?*"

"Yes, I am here," said a husky male voice with the same thick Swedish accent and young and so familiar in its cadence it made Bonnie gulp.

"Hello, Sture," she said. "I guess we are related in a way."

"*Ja so,*" he responded. "We are a big surprise to us, *jo?*" There was a note of anxiety, a trying very hard not to offend.

"So," Inge butted in, "we'll soon have another on our telephone. She is the head of an organization you have not met yet. It is the reason we call. You are the owner of money now, Mrs. Ixey, and we must talk to you about this."

"Yes, I want to talk to you also," Bonnie repeated emphatically.

"Good. Because if you do not come to Sweden immediately and take control of the money accounts, this organization will not be able to work."

Bonnie began, "Which organization..." and was interrupted by a loud crackle, buzz, and a dim voice asking if she were on yet. Some more crackle and the voice developed a presence.

"Hello, hello, are you there, Ms. Person?" came the entirely different accent, one that had strong British overtones, and something else Bonnie could not place.

"Yes," said the attorney, "I am here, and Sture and Mrs. Ixey are here. Mrs. Ixey, say hello to Dr. Halima Legesse in Israel."

"Israel?" This was all going rather fast for Bonnie.

"I am Dr. Legesse," the woman spoke, and the power of her personality vibrated along the airwaves, "I am chief of EW, the Society for Emigrant Women. It is for women who are in danger of being killed."

She took a breath and Bonnie interrupted with, "A kind of battered woman's shelter?"

"In a way," Dr. Legesse continued, "although our women must do more than escape from a husband, they must be taken out of their country."

"And you want me to do something?" Bonnie decided to get right to the point.

"You must do something," Inge spoke up.

Sture, his male voice the meekest of the four, said, "You must come to Sweden immediately. You must give the account to me and the other account to Emigrant Women. You must do this today!"

Bonnie felt really overwhelmed. She told herself this is what happened when lots of money came your way. It's what Lena had warned her of. "What do I legally have to do?"

"Legally," replied Inge, "you fly to Sweden and come to Norrkoping and you go to the Pastorkirche, but only with me, and we sign papers for you to take ownership of the accounts. You must also go to the parish of Dalarna, to their Pastorkirche and sign papers. Dalarna is the home of your father's family. That will make you a Swedish citizen. Then you and I must fight the government because when you become a Swedish citizen, they will want to tax your new money for death taxes. Do you understand?"

"Sort of, not very well, I mean, it's a lot to comprehend all at once," admitted Bonnie. "I don't understand why Sture and Emigrant Women can't have money right away. Weren't they using money from accounts before Carl...before the baron's death?"

Sture spoke quickly, his words tumbling over each other, "My case is important because I am now boss of the castle and I also go to my medical studies and the account for doing this is very small. But, the organization of EW is more so important..."

Dr. Legesse broke in, "Yes, EW to date has been funded by transferal of interest money from one of Baron Hermelin's Swiss accounts. That account is now frozen until the bank recognizes you as the legal inheritor.

It means a number of our projects, which involve rescuing women in danger, are on hold."

"That isn't good," said Bonnie, trying to do the best she could in this uncomfortable and confusing situation.

"It is bloody awful," Dr. Legesse went on, "these projects must be carried out immediately, if the women are to survive, and we must have money to move forward."

"Oh, my," said Bonnie. "Okay, I will book passage and fly to Sweden as soon as I can."

"Tomorrow!" Sture blurted.

"Sture, *lugnar er!*" Inge Person ordered the fellow to be still and then explained to Bonnie, "Mrs. Ixey, there is an account you may access right away. Use that one to pay for your tickets, or better, may I reserve the tickets for you on SAS? The Hermelin family has credit with that air service."

"Okay," Bonnie gulped and bravely added, "I'd like to bring my older daughter with me. Is that possible?"

The attorney could be heard smiling. "It is your money. You may do what you want."

"Oh, right. Okay," Bonnie said.

"I will transfer you money and your reservations."

Dr. Legesse interrupted, "Ms. Person, is there a way she could release some money for us to use immediately?"

"I will check on that, and if there is I'll arrange it on her speaking permission."

"Thank you," Dr. Legesse was somewhat relieved.

"That is okay with you?" Inge asked Bonnie.

"Yes, yes. Certainly."

"If we have a new car by the time you arrive," Sture spoke, "I'll send it to the Stockholm airport for you."

"What happened to your car?" asked Bonnie.

"Not my car. It is my father's car, the engine blew up," he explained, nervously.

"That's terrible," said Bonnie.

"Yes. I believe someone blows it up," he went on.

"Did he look like an Arab?" asked Bonnie with a sudden flash of possibility.

"I did not see who do it," Sture said.

Inge interrupted, "Sture, it was an accident."

"No," he insisted, "it was *socker* in the petrol. I bet you."

"Sture, there was a lock on the petrol tank." She sounded put out.

"No," Sture kept on, "the engine is all gone. When the *polis* report comes and it reads sugar, I show you."

Bonnie said, "The reason I ask is because there is an Arab man watching my house as well as another man, a black American man in a trench coat."

"*Verkligen!*" Inge exclaimed, "Why does that happen?"

"Arab," Dr. Legesse's intense concern did not sound pleasant and she stressed, "or Iranian?"

"I can't tell the difference," admitted Bonnie. "But do you think it means something? Because the other day a Middle Eastern-looking man tried to wreck my car."

"You must be very careful," said Dr. Legesse emphatically, "I think it's very wise for you to travel with your daughter. Yes, Ms. Person, you arrange those tickets and we will talk when Mrs. Ixey gets to Sweden. Wait a moment," there was a sudden pause and Bonnie could hear the earnest, quiet murmur of Dr. Legesse and two men discussing the problem, and abruptly Dr. Legesse said into the phone, "Goodbye for now," and she hung up.

"I will send you bank access and tickets immediately," Inge Person assured Bonnie.

"Just fax everything" Bonnie offered, "That's easiest."

"Oh, yes, how good. Thank you." The attorney ended with, "Take care of your self. Goodbye!"

"*Farval!*" said Sture and the phone line clicked several times and Bonnie sat with the hum of an open line.

The fog still snuggled against the window, and faintly it carried the noise of seals barking on the beach. She clicked off the receiver and suddenly her mind became very busy with new chores such as, I'll have to buy a winter coat and some woollies. Except for a couple ski outfits, I have absolutely nothing to wear in very cold weather and Sweden will be cold. And I'll tell Misimoto to watch the house and feed Gryphon...

Halima pushed the speakerphone aside and looked at her team seated around her at the big black-and-white table.

Carl-Joran had an expression of utter dismay on his face. He brushed his five o'clock beard stubble nervously. "She sounds like she did when I knew her." He rubbed his eyes as if they were irritated. He half whispered, "She thinks I'm dead."

"Well, your assignment," Halima pointed her bony finger at him, "is to go to California and make sure she arrives in Sweden safely."

Carl-Joran nodded. He had expected this. Yet...he turned to Haji Habib Mansur, "When do you go for the princess?"

Mansur let his eyes rise to Halima's. "Tomorrow?"

Halima regarded Siddhu, who leaned over his account sheets and his eyes went to the haji. "I have figured that we have enough money for you to do this project. However," the Sikh warned, "if you run into unexpected circumstances or an extra expense, it will be difficult to send you cash because some of what we have left must go to Barbara Monday." He raised a suppliant hand, "If Mrs. Ixey will do the paperwork quickly, we will have no problem. Whatever I have figured for you is with our present financial status."

The majestic Dr. Legesse nodded slowly, "It is up to you, Habib, to go or to wait."

"I would like to go tomorrow," he said with determination. "Princess Zhara grows more restless and the pressure for her to relent and marry is continual. My messenger has told me that her father had the Chief of Saudi Security Forces come to lecture her, so this person of authority is now watching and aware of her case. We must do this quickly and with utmost caution."

"Everything and everyone else is ready?" Halima asked.

Habib nodded. "Tahireh is waiting for me to arrive. All is ready there."

Halima sighed. "I send you on your way then. Salaam!"

"I hope so," Habib Mansur laughed gently.

"Carl-Joran," Halima Legesse regarded the perturbed giant sitting next to her. "I know in your heart of hearts what you wish to do. But you cannot go with him. First, we do not have the money, secondly, it will be too dangerous for you to be in an Arab country, third, your job is to straighten out the money problems. California is your destination."

"Who says it'll be any safer in California?" the big man blurted, "and how could it be less expensive to go there than to go with Habib?"

"You will use your own money to go to California," said Halima with complete surety, "and Sadiq-Fath's agents will be less likely to strike when you are in the United States or in Sweden."

He looked doubtful. "America is a fine place to do violence. It happens all the time."

"Carl-Joran!" she put her hands on her hips and stamped her foot. "You go to California."

"I would really like to know why I can't just come alive again," he sat forward, challenging her.

"No," she said firmly. "We can deal with all this confusion, we could not deal with your real death. Sadiq-Fath must be brought to some kind of justice and we cannot get him into the open if you are around. I am certain he will show himself soon. I am sure!"

The Swede pounded his fist on the table making the room vibrate, "I don't like being dead. It's too damned much trouble."

"I think," the kindly Haji Habib leaned toward Carl-Joran, "you do not want to face this woman you once loved."

Carl-Joran went silent for a full minute. All that could be heard in the room were the voices of the children playing down the hall, the hum of the air vent fans, the tick of the wall clock. With great discomfort, he finally said, "She and I will meet. We will talk. I don't think it is so bad."

Habib laid a sun-tanned hand on Carl-Joran's paler one and smiling, said, "And you both will remember."

Dropping his chin onto his chest, the big Swede shrugged. "I guess so."

"Therefore, you must go to California." Habib nodded, squeezed the big hand briefly, and stood.

"My friend," Carl-Joran stopped him, "may I ask you a favor? Please, if it does not compromise your work?"

"Of course," responded Habib.

"Could you, through your sources, see if Quddus Sadiq-Fath has put a fatwa on my son. And," the big Swede added, "on Bonnie Ixey."

"I will try. I tell you what you already know, that I must ask such questions very, very cautiously. Such information costs a lot of money to get and much more money to be kept from bouncing back to the source."

Carl-Joran nodded. "I understand. Don't do it if it is too expensive and dangerous for you. I suspect the Iranians are already onto both of them." He sighed and frowned. The brown abba swooshed near him as Habib moved away from the table and the smell of sandalwood filled his nostrils.

Habib Mansur half bowed to the doctor. "Halima, my love, I will be on my way. Siddhu, if you will get those funds to me tonight?"

"Yes, certainly," said Siddhu.

Halima stepped around the table and gave Habib a strong hug. "Allah be with you."

"So far he has remained on our side," smiled Habib and hugged her back.

Carl-Joran stood, clapped the man on the shoulder. "My thoughts will be constantly with you," Carl-Joran said.

"And mine with you," said Habib, "for you are quite correct about the United States being violent. It is perhaps more violent than Saudi Arabia."

"Yeah," said Carl-Joran, "I'll be in more danger from guns than anyone in this room."

Habib nodded. "So it is said." He went to the door, "Goodbye, my friends."

As soon as the brown abba had swept from the room and the door sssshhhhhed shut, Carl-Joran swung around to Siddhu, "Where is the money coming from for my trip to California? You know I can't take any out of my accounts, not as me anyway."

"I have no idea," replied Siddhu, "but I will have it by tonight. We must also get you a new passport and identification. You cannot go into the United States as Baron Hermelin."

"Oh!" Carl-Joran straightened, a sudden inspiration striking him. "I remember something important. I have an old United States passport in another name. I've even got citizenship papers somewhere. They're in the name of Carl J. Mink, of course. They were expertly done. Toby Hughes had very good sources."

"Where would those papers be?" asked Siddhu, standing. "If we can get them it will save us a lot of time, and money. Updating a passport is far, far easier than having an entirely new one made."

"In my office in the castle," he replied. "I'll have Sture find them and send them express to you Siddhu, here at EW."

"Good," Halima came up to him and put her knobby finger on his chest, "because I want you to be on a plane to Los Angeles tomorrow evening."

"Yes, ma'am," Carl-Joran agreed, half terrorized, half relieved.

Tidewater, coming back after lunch, poked his head into Russ's cubbyhole. "Snow, what we got on the Ixey woman? Is she still alive?"

"Yessir," responded Russ Snow immediately, "Claybourne turned in a report first thing this morning." The tall Native American handed his boss a one-page e-mail form. "Ixey's older daughter drove to Paso Robles, picked up the younger daughter and husband at the airport, and brought them to the farm. They were having some sort of party. Later in the evening, Claybourne spotted a well-known ISF operative, somebody he knows out of Los Angeles, keeping a watch on the home." Russ chuckled, "The ISF guy got chased by the farm dog, and, 'cause of that dog, Claybourne wasn't able to get a phone tap in until midnight. Just before he went off he recorded a conference call that originated from Sweden. Something about arranging for Mrs. Ixey to fly to Sweden."

"Do say?" Tidewater glanced at the sheet and pursed his lips. "Neither Claybourne nor the dog scared the Iranian away, did they?" There was a slight note of potential disappointment in the question.

"I don't think so," said Russ.

"Who's on now, watching her day activities?"

Russ shrugged, "I'm not sure, sir, someone Claybourne pulled out of the LA office this morning."

"Okay, as long as Ixey's covered." Tidewater went toward his office, saying over his shoulder, "Thanks, Snow, and tell Claybourne that I want him or his sub to call me direct if anything happens to Ixey."

"Yessir," said Russ.

Sitting behind his desk, Marion Tidewater considered calling Sadiq-Fath and immediately put aside the thought. Anything going on in Ixey's life would be reported to that weasel the moment it happened. God knows how many phone taps were in place already and it wouldn't surprise Marion if the ISF man had a video camera link hooked up to her bedroom wall. The woman wouldn't have a private moment from here on out. The only place she'd be relatively safe from harm in the days to come would be on the airliner going to Sweden.

Russ Snow peeked in, "Sir? The fourth party on that conference call was identified. It was Dr. Halima Legesse of Emigrant Women in Haifa."

"Right. Smart move," said Tidewater. "They're going to the source of money as fast as they can."

"Need me for anything else today?" asked Russ.

"I've got three cases here which should be coordinated with their counterparts in Germany." Tidewater pulled three folders from a stack on the desk.

"Are they imperative?" Russ slipped the folders under one arm. "It's just, I'm supposed to go to the pistol range this afternoon and see if I can qualify or if I need more training."

"You should do that," said Tidewater, nodding an affirmative. "Never know when you'll have to take someone out. Those files can wait until tomorrow morning. Go ahead."

"Later then," said Russ and left.

Russ Snow didn't like the firing range. He didn't like the noise, and guns, especially pistols, were low on his list of good things in the world. After all, the only thing a handgun was meant to do was to kill another human. Russ could understand a powerful rifle if there were a meal to put on the table, but even there, he believed as his father had taught him, that the animal life he took should be appeased and shown gratitude. It was a relief when the firearms instructor passed him with high marks. Russ quickly took leave of the firing range and hopped into the old jeep to get on the road. As he clicked his seat belt, he also patted his sharp throwing knife, kept hidden always in a sheath in his belt. Now that was a weapon of choice—deadly, silent, accurate, virtually untraceable.

Arriving home, he laid the knife on the table, poured himself a glass of wine, called the local shop for a pizza to be delivered immediately, and then clicked into the Ixey file. Last night he had rigged a forwarding order into her machine so that unknown to her, whatever was mailed her, or that she shipped out, would also come to him.

"Busy lady," said Russ to himself. She had a stack of e-mail waiting. "Wonder if she always has this much?" he mused. Almost all of it dealt with research projects she was working on for any number of people all over the world. Several libraries had correspondence with her, asking for information and updates. Obviously the woman was extremely computer literate and, in addition, was highly educated and respected. What was it he'd read in her background check? A reference librarian—well, that didn't say it all. For an older woman, she certainly knew how to make use of cyberspace to do business.

A half-dozen personal messages were also there, and one notice from...ah-ha! SAS confirming two tickets, first class, booked from San Francisco to Stockholm, Sunday evening to be picked up at the boarding window. She and her daughter, Trisha would soon be on their way.

Russ imagined her finding this message on her machine sometime this evening or tomorrow morning. How would she react? What would she say? Had she started packing? He wondered what the older daughter was like? It was very, very tempting to peck out a few words, say hello, say he was worried about her, and just press that send button. In a flash, she would know...

The doorbell buzzed. His pizza had arrived.

Princess Zhara i-Shibl felt the breeze off the dunes and smelled the donkeys' approach before any other of her senses caught up. Her heart leapt into her throat. She had paced this wall of the compound each night at this time for a month, waiting, waiting for their nightly arrival, and waiting for something to bob up, but nothing had.

This particular spot on this particular wall was the only chink in her father's fabulous security system. An archway of stone rose about a foot above the huge pipe conduit that brought the water from the deep well half a mile away. Two years ago, their own well in the compound had failed and the new one had been dug, the pipe laid, and the arch in the wall constructed. Outside the wall, a shut-off valve allowed the camel herders and donkey boys to fill a basin for their animals. That way, the raggedy scum, as her father had described the working class and poor nomads, could be kept outside as much as possible.

Since there was, just inside the arch, a beautiful big fountain and pond, it was amazingly easy for the secret messages, enclosed in a bottle or plastic cover, to be reached through the arch and dropped into the pond or vice versa. Tonight, as on other nights, Zhara sat on the bench that edged the pond and dangled her fingers in the water, doing her best to look completely innocent as she teased the colorful koi. She would miss her pet koi. The black and orange one nibbled at her fingertips and even let her pet it. Tonight though, as she sat, playing with the fish and listening intently to the hubbub of noises outside the arch, donkeys braying, herders shouting at their animals, camel drivers gossiping, a plastic panty-hose egg shape suddenly bobbed to the surface.

She knew, as if by some extra sense, that this was it. Her heart did not race any more. A strange calmness enveloped her as she pulled apart the blue egg. The note inside, in the haji's perfect Arabic script, read: "We are on our way. Be ready to go. Do not bring anything with you. Dress everyday in your black robes and wear the mask. You will know when it is time."

Immediately upon reading, she tossed the empty plastic shell back through the archway hole, which signified she'd received the message and thrust the paper into the pond and held it there until the koi had nibbled it to shreds. No one could find it now, it was gone into the tummy of her beloved fish. She let the black and orange koi nibble her fingers again and wished very much she could somehow take him with her. On the other hand, once she had returned to Europe, she could be with Emil and Emil had her dog, her beloved Charlotte. It had been an entire year. Waiting.

She sighed. Now would come the hard job of convincing her mother. She simply could not go away and leave her mother here. It would not do. It would not be safe for her mother. How though...?

The footsteps of the night watchman made her rise hastily. Taking a breath to calm herself, she pulled her hood and robes around her and walked gracefully back to the women's rooms.

The hallways of the Nof Hotel in the early morning were always busy: business people hustling off to meetings and tourists being called for their buses. One of the people bustling around was Siddhu Singh Prakash who at first knocked on the door of the big Swede's rooms, then pounded. Carl-Joran could sleep through an earthquake, thought the thin Indian. The Nof had allowed the EW to secure a room and to install a retinal reader for access. Siddhu had his eyeball scanned, entered the room, and closed the door behind him. Amazingly, Carl-Joran was in the shower, awake and moving around.

Siddhu stuck his head in the bathroom. "Hello, Baron, good morning!"

"*Fy fan!*" came the curse from the steam. "Isn't privacy at all known in other countries?"

"I have good news!" said the Sikh, disregarding Carl-Joran's displeasure. "We have found money for you."

"Get out of my bathroom!"

"Do you want me to order coffee and breakfast?" asked Siddhu.

"It's already ordered. Get some for yourself if you want."

Siddhu went to the phone and ordered tea. Moments later, room service delivered Carl-Joran's breakfast and acknowledged that Siddhu's was on its way. The big Swede appeared by this time, wrapped in a large towel and drying his hair with another one.

"What's the news?" he asked, sitting in front of the breakfast tray and pouring steaming coffee into a cup. "Coffee?"

"No thank you," said Siddhu, "they will bring me tea in a minute. Here," he handed an express packet of papers across the table.

Carl-Joran, coffee in one hand, shook out the packet with the other. An ancient and familiar United States passport, a sheaf of folded papers, and a little brown bank deposit book dropped onto the table. He sipped his coffee and opened the deposit book first. It was a savings account established in Calexico, California at a small local bank. Nine thousand four hundred three dollars and twenty cents was the final amount listed.

He flipped through the pages, there was no stamp to say it had been closed or transferred. Was this money still there? Did the bank exist? He looked up at Siddhu.

"Have you called to see…?"

Siddhu nodded. "This bank was bought out by a larger bank about five years ago. The account was transferred and has accrued interest. They said they have been sending account balance notices to the address listed at the front. I cannot imagine the post office has never told them you do not live there any more." He shrugged. "But the US post office is much different than ours."

"All these years!" Carl-Joran shook his head, put the bank books aside, and opened his old passport. It had long ago expired. The papers: Social security number, work permits, all the accoutrements of having acquired US citizenship. Of course, none of it was legitimate, except for the faded certificate of marriage with the stamp of the Justice of the Peace in Nevada. Astounding. Suddenly the one event he believed had been sham had been legal. Toby Hughes had arranged all of this through the Latin American refugee program. For a second, he flashed back to the Nicaraguan jungles, the machine-gun fire, bombs falling, the desperate rush for cover, the people helping him to escape…and Carl-Joran Hermelin had become Carl Joseph Mink before he'd crossed the Mexican border into Calexico. The last stamp in the passport was Japan, March 26th. As luck would have it, the once Carl Mink would be going back to the United States.

He asked Siddhu, "Have you been to our paper maker yet?"

"No. I wanted to show you the bankbook. I thought you would be pleased." Siddhu smiled, looked around at the tap on the door announcing arrival of his breakfast. As the bellboy with the tray entered, the smell of smoky tea permeated the air. "Ahhhh," said Siddhu, tipping the fellow. "Blessed chai."

"How long until all this is brought up to date?" asked Carl-Joran, taking the cover off his cereal and toast.

"By late this afternoon if we are lucky." Siddhu sugared his tea, putting five teaspoons in and stirring. "I have made reservations on El Al airlines to Los Angeles for Carl Mink, but the earliest I could get was tomorrow morning. Halima will not be happy."

"Could I fly SAS?"

"I will try them when I leave here, and also United and KLM." Siddhu sipped. "You will also need a car once you are in California."

"Please make sure they give me a full-sized one," moaned Carl-Joran. "Last time I ended up with a subcompact. Couldn't even fit in the door."

"That was when you went to London last year," Siddhu regarded the bagel and cheese. "I believe I asked for toast."

"Do we know when Bonnie is scheduled to leave?" The name sounded strange on his tongue. Something from a script long ago memorized and discarded.

"You will have to drive fast. She is to depart on SAS on Sunday. Today is Thursday." Siddhu peeled the cheese from the bagel and ate it plain, between bites of the fruit salad. "I hope all goes according to schedule!"

"So do I," said Carl-Joran, putting milk on his cereal. "I wouldn't want to miss her." How odd to put it that way, he thought to himself, eating the oatmeal, for he had missed her, deep down, somewhere inside, there had been that unspoken emptiness he never quite understood. If he should miss her again? No, he must get her to safety. They, the Iranian Security Force, would be after her because she was, had been...no, was his wife.

He looked up at Siddhu, "Did Habib say anything to you?"

Siddhu shook his head, "No, he had to leave very early this morning. There was a note under my door which begged your forgiveness." Siddhu reached in a coat pocket and handed his friend a flimsy sheet of paper, neatly folded and smelling of sandalwood.

Carl-Joran opened it and read, "Please forgive me but I could acquire no information, which does in itself make me suspicious. My sources will not say anything without an enormous sum of money. Can we assume that your son and Bonnie Ixey are in danger? I believe so. Allah keep them safe and may He bless you. Habib."

Carl-Joran whispered, "Allah go with you, Haji."

Bonnie looked up from her computer screen and blinked. The morning fog that had crept in overnight from the ocean was giving way to sunshine. "My goodness," she said softly. Slowly she picked up the telephone and dialed Trisha's school's number. The office secretary rang through to the room where Trisha Ixey was teaching health class.

After several long rings, a breathless Trisha said, "Hi!", and then shouting behind her, "Quiet down!" The chattering of the kids muted.

"Hi, yourself. This is your mom."

"Must be important to call me here," said Trisha. "What's up? Have the HS or FBI stormed the house yet?"

"Very funny," Bonnie didn't laugh. She had seen an Arab man at the mailboxes again this morning and a woman in a government issue car parked near the bend in the road, binoculars in hand. Bonnie said, "Better get a substitute for a while, kiddo, and go home and pack. We leave Sunday for Sweden."

"Cool."

"And, honey?"

"Yeah, Mom, I know, we need to buy jackets and some fuzzy warm underwear."

"Listen. Guess what?" Bonnie paused for effect, "We're flying first class."

There was a moment of silence before Trisha responded with, "Right on! Way to go!"

"We have to pick up our tickets by six p.m. Sunday at the SAS desk at the San Francisco airport so we better be in San Francisco no later than noon."

"Want to drive up Saturday night and have dinner at the Embarcadero?" asked Trish. hopefully.

"Sounds like a good plan," said her mother.

CHAPTER 7: MISSED OPPORTUNITIES

To keep the wind from whipping it away, the haji pulled his cloak around him as he stepped from the taxi. The air was viciously bitter cold. Dry brittle snow lay in drifting heaps along the cement pathways. It gathered in higher mounds along the eroded niches in the shrub-covered hillsides.

He paid the taxi driver and carefully averting his eyes from the heavily armed Israeli soldiers, walked along the starkly lighted corridor marked with bright orange stripes that designated the sidewalk for the Palestinian day workers coming and going through the Good Gate. So far he had not been challenged and he did not expect to be. His mind was perfectly calm and his body reflected his peaceful demeanor.

Habib had taken a bus from Haifa to Kiriat Shimona, the northernmost kibbutz of Israel, and there caught the taxi that had climbed up the steep road along the ravines. It had deposited him at the open-fronted film and snack stands that catered to the few tourists who visited and the many soldiers who paused long enough in their patrols to buy bagels or potato crisps or steaming coffee.

As Habib stepped onto the sidewalk lined with eight-foot high cross-wire fencing, a slight tremor of fear shivered through him. This portion of the long walk over the Israeli border always made him, and every other Arab who traversed it, feel trapped and helpless. It was designed to do just that. The Israeli Defense Force guards were always on alert, always had their rifles resting ready in their cradled arms along every step of the path.

Habib mixed in with the homebound housemaids, gardeners, mechanics, and other assorted workers up the switchback and into the slightly wider section of the corridor which lay before the actual Gate. It was slow today. The guards at the Gate were patting down persons such as himself in heavy cloaks.

When his turn came, he identified himself and the guard at least acknowledged his title, saying, "I'm sorry, sir, but we do have to search all full-bearded men in abbas, holy men or no."

It went quickly. With the briefest respite of relief, he stepped through the Good Gate and into Lebanon. Although expected through familiarity, Habib Mansur felt an especial ache at the sight of the devastated countryside around him. The snow was deeper here, the wind more biting, the mountains so barren they hurt. There were no trees, no twigs, no bushes, no grass, no birds, no rabbits, nothing. The once plentiful vegetation and famous cedar trees had long ago been used for cooking fires by the encamped refugees. Any creature that had walked or flown had been put in someone's pot for sustenance. Or simply shot and killed for the sport of it by rampaging soldiers of one faction or another.

As peace was settling shakily onto the countryside, moss and lichens were the first to appear in the more inaccessible rifts and, as Habib walked to the taxi queue, he could hear ever so faintly, the jingle of goat bells from behind the far hills to the south. There must be some islands of dried grass over there. Even such minute signs of returning life made him happy.

An aged, battered blue Mercedes was hunkered at the curb. It was the sole taxi available and the driver had only one hand, the absent one undoubtedly a casualty of the war. Habib nodded at him and got into the back seat. It smelled of unwashed humans and perhaps chickens. Yes, in one jagged rip near the center of the seat were some feathers from the last customers' traveling companions.

"To Beirut," Habib ordered the driver and they set off across the desolate land.

Lieutenant Ali Muhit peered through his cloudy eyes at the message being handed him by the computer man sitting in the massive security central command room.

"It's about Habib Mansur and we have an order for urgent notification whenever his name appears," said the young man and Ali Muhit nodded.

Moments later, the battered old warrior was walking into the beautifully appointed office of his boss. At the door to the inner sanctum belonging to Quddus Sadiq-Fath stood two guards from the darughih's Special Operatives. Nearby was the large desk area of Walid, the personal secretary.

Walid blinked like a cat dropped into bright sunlight after being asleep in the shade, "Good day, Muhit, did you want to see the darughih?"

"I've a note to be delivered," responded Ali Muhit.

"Uh, just a minute," Walid said and leaned toward the intercom. "Darughih? Your lieutenant is here." Some mumbles came through the speaker and he nodded. "Yessir."

He waved at Muhit, "Go right in, sir."

Quddus Sadiq-Fath resembled an animation-movie line drawing of a bad guy even to the squared facial features and perfectly trimmed mustache. His khaki uniform was as starched and precise as it could possibly be, giving the cruelly handsome man an almost inhuman look. He was signing directives and reports. The cold, black eyes looked up.

"What have we got?"

"A message from the operative at the Good Gate, sir," the lieutenant lowered his creaky body into the chair closest to the far corner of the antique ebony wood desk. "Haji Mansur has entered Lebanon and is on his way to Beirut."

"Ahhh," Quddus sat back and peaked his fingers together in a church steeple. "I wonder why. Obviously Emigrant Women has sent him on a mission. Is there any indication of where he's headed next?"

"No, sir. None. The taxi dropped him off at the Hilton Hotel." Ali Muhit handed the note to his boss who took it and scanned it.

"Not much here," muttered Sadiq-Fath. "What about our Beirut operatives? Haven't they set up surveillance yet?"

"There was nothing from them today so far. Shall I push them?" The lieutenant sat forward, ready to go.

"Yes, yes," Sadiq-Fath nodded, "and nothing's come in from the operative in California?"

With a frustrated grimace, Muhit shook his head. "Not that you want to hear, Darughih."

"Please tell me what it is that I do not want to hear," the cold eyes sparkled with something approximating humor as the hands dropped to the desk.

"The night operative watching the widow's farm was chased and bitten by the large dog that guards the property. I understand," Ali Muhit could not restrain a crackly chuckle, "the part of the anatomy caught by the dog will render our operative unable to sit down for a while."

"Ha!" the darughih laughed once and went directly on, "So where does that leave us with information about Mrs. Ixey's activities?"

"It meant there was no tap put on her telephone," Muhit confessed, "it means we do not know what her schedule is or when she is due to go to Sweden. We do know she must travel to Norrkoping to register as a

Swedish citizen in order to take over inheritance of the baron's estate, that much we got from our Swedish informant. But, we are handicapped—so to say—in California."

"And Tidewater's operatives? Have they acquired more information than our dog meat?" growled Sadiq-Fath.

"I am afraid they have." Ali Muhit shifted uncomfortably in his chair, "A black agent named Claybourne got a tap on their telephone line last night while Faqir was fending off the dog."

"May Allah preserve us from stupid operatives," the darughih shook his head. "It appears I must call Tidewater to find out what Mrs. Ixey is up to. Do tell me, Lieutenant, do we have a more competent agent on duty now?"

"Yessir," the old man smiled, "this agent brought American hamburgers with him and has managed to convince the mutt he means no harm. So it says in his report at noon today."

"I am pleased," Quddus Sadiq-Fath's voice did not indicate pleasure, "we have established diplomatic relations with the Ixey's dog. What a commendable step! Is there a reason the dog simply wasn't killed?"

Muhit shook his head again, "Not a good idea in the United States, sir. Dogs and cats are considered part of the family. A dead dog would have instantly brought suspicion onto the watchers, and then the local police would have investigated."

"Shame," said Sadiq-Fath, spreading his fingers on the desk, stretching them. "Truly, the Americans are strange people. You are correct though. I remember in university how some of my dorm mates would go to tremendous lengths to have pets in their rooms despite the regulations against them. And spend fantastic sums of money keeping their pets happy and healthy!"

"Yessir," Muhit agreed, shaking his head in mutual mock amazement.

The darughih looked down at his hands and resignedly put his chin on his chest. "I will call Tidewater and find out what is going on. Do we have any tidbits to feed back to him?"

"Only the news of the haji crossing the border into Lebanon."

"Perhaps that will be enough," said Quddus Sadiq-Fath and punching the intercom for Walid, ordered, "Get me a linkup to Marion Tidewater's office immediately."

"Yes, Commander," came the computer guy's voice.

***

Tidewater's secretary was just handing Russ Snow a first cup of coffee as he sat down at the computer in his cubbyhole when the phone rang. She answered it, listened, and handed it to Russ.

"A call coming in from Iran, Mr. Snow, and Mr. Tidewater hasn't arrived yet. You better take it."

"Thank you." Russ accepted the receiver. "I'll deal with it." He waved her out of the tiny room and closed the door after her. "Yes, good morning," he said into the phone.

When the conversation was finished he felt slimy. True, he'd had a good laugh at the image of the Iranian operative running down the street with the farm dog munching on his hinder parts and ripping his pants, but that didn't ease the unpleasant guilt responses about telling Sadiq-Fath of the Ixey's travel schedule. There had, though, been a good trace-off, which would make Tidewater happy. The news about Haji Mansur was undoubtedly valuable.

This was proven accurate a few moments later when Marion Tidewater arrived and Russ handed him the recording of the conversation between himself and the darughih. As he listened, Tidewater's eyebrows went up and he grinned broadly.

"Time to let our buddy Yusef in on this. What a plum!" exclaimed Tidewater reaching for the phone. "Whenever Habib Mansur goes to the Beirut Hilton, you can bet your britches that's the first part of his pilgrimage into Saudi Arabia to rescue some woman and my best guess is he'll be accompanied by Tahireh Ibrahim. Have you read about her in the reports, Snow?"

The Native American shook his head.

Tidewater lifted his phone and said to his secretary, "Lily, honey, get me a satellite link to Saudi Arabia and Commander Yusef's office, will you?" Tidewater glanced up at his personal assistant while waiting for the link-up. "Ibrahim is a Baha'i. She's been on Sadiq-Fath's hit list since she led a woman's revolt back when she was a teenager, which wasn't too many years ago. A bunch of those women were summarily executed, but Ibrahim escaped. I understand she's very beautiful. Too bad she's determined to die young. That happens to anyone going against the Iranian strong men as she has."

Tidewater's attention reverted to the telephone for a moment.

Fascinated, Russ Snow asked, "How does she get her money, I mean, other than what the EW gives in funding operations?"

"I believe she's a model. I know she works at various modeling agencies in France, mostly in Paris. That's where she spends a lot of time volunteering at the Torture Treatment Centre." Dismissively, Tidewater said, "Which is all good stuff. Really too bad she goes and helps someone like Mansur and the EW kidnap women out of Saudi and Iran."

Wanting to keep this flow of information going, Russ prompted with, "What's a Baha'i?"

Tidewater, falling into the pleasure of showing off his eruditeness, continued, "They're some sort of heretical offshoot of the Muslim faith that came out of Iran back about 1860. They've got two prophets, someone called Baha'u'llah and someone called the Bab, who was martyred by the Iranians along with a bunch of his followers. The Baha'u'llah character was kept in prison in Acre for half his life. Not much has changed; the Iranians especially and most any of the Arabs take great delight in torturing and killing Baha'is whenever they can come up with whatever excuse is plausible. It gives the conservative Muslims the shaking willies that Baha'is actually have written into their religious codes that there has to be equality of men and women! There's stuff in there that all religions are one, that there's supposed to be formed some sort of World Justice Court or some such, and so on. Baha'ism has spread all over the world. There are some reports on it in our library..."

The phone buzzed and Tidewater leaned forward, then spoke into the phone, "Hello, Gurgin. Do I have something for you! Yessir, your holy man, ol' Habib Mansur, has checked in at the Beirut Hilton. I suspect you better watch your women!"

Russ Snow didn't want to hear what his boss was relating to Commander Yusef but what choice did he have? His job mandated that he listen and participate. Russ Snow suddenly realized he was more than uncomfortable, he was actually unhappy.

Habib was prepared for the skittering when he turned the bathroom light on, but the sheer number of cockroaches triggered a gut reaction anyway. His stomach tightened and his skin shivered and twitched like a horse trying to shake off flies. In the glare of the unshielded overhead light, most of the big, brown insects ducked down the drains and hustled under warped wainscoting and linoleum cracks. He sighed. It was one of those rare moments when he wished his vow to protect all life wasn't so firm. He would have dearly loved to take off his shoe and use the heel to send some of these hideous creatures to meet their maker.

Once the majority of the insects were in hiding, Habib dealt with his bathroom needs. He was settling back onto one of the two uncomfortable beds when the tap-tap, tap-tap-tap, tap-tap on the door, announced Tahireh's arrival. Before he could stand, she had let herself in.

There was a forceful grace about the woman that demanded attention, and it was neither her expensive Parisian perfume nor the exquisitely cut, full-length woolen dress and tailored chamois-golden greatcoat she had traveled in. Without the high-heeled boots, she stood five feet, six inches tall and her figure was slight. Yet, her energy filled the room. Her dark brown eyes sparkled.

She deposited her overnight bag on the floor, flung off the greatcoat and wool scarf, dropping them onto the other bed and smiled at her dearest friend. Her long tress of dark chestnut brown hair fell in waves down her back all the way to her waist and her skin, the color of coffee with rich cream, glowed in the evening lamp light.

Habib threw his arms open and they embraced, not as lovers, but as compatriots who've shared many terribly dangerous enterprises. Perhaps such a bond is more intense than any romantic connection between humans might ever engender.

"Have you eaten?" Habib asked in an innocent tone, pointing surreptitiously at the ceiling where the multiple smoke alarms and odd wiring running down the wall so obviously indicated eavesdropping apparatus.

"I'm fine," she replied, nodding understanding. "The bellboy should be up in a moment with my suitcase. It was, of course, well searched at the airport. It is always interesting to see how much of my small wardrobe remains after coming through the Beirut airport." She laughed gaily. "So when does this tour you've booked us on depart, dear Habib?"

"As soon as you've rested," he smiled in response, "and put on your proper attire."

"Ah, yes, I must constrain myself again. Oh, how I hate doing that!" She bowed slightly to Habib and indicated the bathroom. "Have you disposed of the inhabitants?"

"Ha! Most of them," he said. "There are a couple though that defy the light, which you will notice I left burning. One truly ugly fellow was sitting on the edge of the sink, watching me as I did my ablutions. A truly insolent little creature."

"You did not kill him?"

"Of course not," he exclaimed in mock disgust, "how could I have determined if it were a he or a she? And I would have felt quite ungentlemanly smacking a female. Besides it would not speak to me."

Tahireh peeked into the loo and groaned. "Your insolent one is still on the sink. Well, I for one have not the compunction you do." She rolled up a tourist pamphlet that extolled the beauties of the now peaceful Lebanon and stepped into the bathroom. A loud kasmaack! resounded from the sink.

"Mon dieu! Le petit va vit!—Goodness, that sucker is fast!" came in French. "But at least he has put himself down the drain hole!" and she stuck her head out of the bathroom long enough to continue in that language, "Tip the bellboy when he comes, oui? Merci."

"Yes, my dear," Habib said in Farsi to the closing bathroom door and as if by cue, there was a knock on the door.

The bellboy, a thin Palestinian lad whose eyes had seen too much for such a young age, slipped the hardcover suitcase inside the room, and no further, and Habib paid him in euros. The boy regarded the holy man with hostile curiosity, aware as he was that the Parisian fancy lady with the Arab name, who'd arrived all by herself, would be staying in the same room as this haji. He turned away after snarling "Merci."

Habib moved the suitcase to the baggage stand. There were corners of blouses sticking from one side and a strap hung from the front. Whoever had done the search had made no pretense of it.

"They really rifled through it, didn't they?" commented Tahireh, coming out of the bathroom. "Let's see if my robe is still wearable." She clicked the snaps. It wouldn't open.

"I'll lean on it," offered Habib, and put his entire weight onto the case. The latches finally gave. There could have been no predicting the mess inside. Tahireh sighed.

"Perhaps you should have met me at the airport after all," she said and dispiritedly fingered through the wreckage of her belongings. Perfume had been spilled, makeup scattered over the clothing, and a bottle of shampoo leaked from the upper compartment. She found her silky robe, which had originally been laid across the top of the clothing, now at the bottom—where, at least, it was relatively unharmed, and jerked it out. Picking up the almost empty shampoo bottle and toiletry case, she stomped back into the bathroom. Another vicious kasmaack! echoed from behind the closed door along with a throaty growl in crudest French, "Take that you insolent beast!"

The shower water started and Habib, smiling, thought how lucky he was to have such a compatriot-in-arms. He turned his attention to a sheaf of papers he had been carrying in his cloak. They were the plans for tomorrow's sortie into the desert. The tricky part would be driving the Land Cruiser through the broad expanse of enemy territory without being noticed. He had managed to round up some fairly inventive disguises, but still and all, the Arab police, as prejudiced and stonehearted as they are, were no fools.

Once he and Tahireh had met up with and joined the nomads and changed over to camel transport, they would be fairly safe. When the shower water stopped, he inquired through the door, "Can we leave tonight?"

"Yes! I want to be gone!" Tahireh's voice came back, "Give me a couple hours to sleep, and then we will go."

"Fine," said Habib, "I will call and tell the rental agency to have keys ready for us." He reached for the phone.

Bonnie walked with a brisk, bouncy step to the barn. The day had turned out to be very pleasant after the fog had burnt off. A bright and sunny winter's day with the smell of low tide and the cry of ravens and gulls, and Bonnie could pick out the raucous chatter of a small flock of wild parakeets in the eucalyptus trees at the bottom of the property.

The massively shaggy Australian Shepherd came bounding from the lower pasture where he'd been diligently counting the ground squirrel population and greeted her as she approached the barn. He was grinning, his tongue lolling in doggy pleasure.

"What have you been up to, Gryph?" she asked, patting him on the broad forehead and noticing the dirt on his front paws and muzzle, laughed and inquired, "Did you get any of those squirrels or just extend the tunnel to China?"

He shook in seeming negation and galloped into the barn ahead of her and promptly set about digging for a mouse in the hay. The old orange barn cat, which'd probably spent hours waiting patiently on the wooden beam above that haystack for that mouse to venture out, regarded the big dog with vile contempt. The cat rose, stretched long, bony legs and knobby back, yawned sharp teeth, and ambled off along the beam toward the ladder to the loft, flicking his tail in a last sign of displeasure.

As Lou and Dell looked around at the sound of Bonnie's footsteps, Gryphon produced some ragged bits of material that looked suspiciously like pockets from the backside of a pair of rayon suit trousers. He gamboled up to the three people, flinging the material like a prize trophy at their feet, then sat, grinning again, waiting for the praise he was expecting.

"Uh-oh," said Dell, reaching for the scrap. She examined it, and then held it up to her mother.

"I'd say Gryph's been protecting us from an intruder."

Bonnie gingerly took the scrap between forefinger and thumb, eyed it warily, and gave it back to Gryphon. "Whoever he attacked hasn't complained to us, at any rate. Here's hoping the poor man doesn't go to the sheriff."

"I don't think that'll happen, Mom Ixey," said Lou, leaning on his pitchfork. "I bet it was one of our spies down at the end of the drive. Maybe that Arab one. And since there's been no complaints, well, those guys don't want to be found out. That's the answer."

"I hate to admit it," said Bonnie, "but you may well have something there." She patted the grinning dog on the head, but Gryph looked disappointed. He'd expected more praise for such a job well done.

"Sure I do," said Lou and, picking up the pitchfork and digging into the manure heap.

Bonnie laughed. "I guess wealth produces these sort of problems." She put an arm around her daughter, "Dell, how long are you and Lou planning to stay? You told me, I'm sure, and not that I would ever dream of pushing you out! It would be nice though if you could stay on a little longer while Trish and I fly to Sweden."

Dell nodded. "We can stay until Lou's teaching term starts late next week. Right, honey?"

He smiled. "We would much rather hang around here and play with horses than be rained on in Seattle."

"And after that, well, I could stay on for a while longer," Dell said, a note of unwillingness in her voice, "I mean, if you think it's necessary."

Bonnie hugged her. "You know I'd never do anything to keep you from that gorgeous man of yours." She kissed her daughter on the cheek, "It's just, I don't understand what's going on here, what with these people spying on us, the whole business of the baron's estate, just...everything."

"And Dad's farm is really important to you," responded Dell, hugging her mom in return. "It's pretty important to us, too. One of us will stay on and take care of it. Although, you know, Misimoto is as dedicated to the farm as we are."

"I know, I know," agreed Bonnie, "and I'll speak to her. Perhaps what I need from you two is simply assurance that you are here, that you will be where I can talk to you." Bonnie turned away and patted a nearby horse on the neck. "I may be your mom, but I'm not above asking for your moral support."

"You'll certainly have it," said Dell and Louis looked around.

"Mom Ixey," he said with conviction, "you can count on us."

"Thanks, children." She turned. "I've got to meet Trish in San Luis. We're going to see if we can find any winter clothes."

Lou said, "Try the ski shops."

"And the outdoors equipment stores," offered Dell.

Bonnie nodded, "And if worse comes to worse, we can shop when we get to Stockholm."

"That might be even more fun, Mom," said Dell, her face lightening up with the thought, "although probably much more expensive." A funny look flitted over her face. "Oh, I guess that doesn't matter any more. Oh, my. What a strange concept."

"Are you flying to San Francisco or driving?" asked Lou, grinning as his wife struggled with the new sensation of being rich.

"You know how Trish is paralyzed with fear in those small planes. We'll drive up tomorrow evening. See Ghirardelli Square, walk down to the Embarcadero, and have a good fish dinner. Spend Sunday at the Exploratorium or the museums," Bonnie felt butterflies start fluttering in her own stomach, "and then we go to the airport. We leave at four on the first leg to New York."

Dell smiled at her mom. "This could be the adventure of a lifetime, Mom."

"Sure could," Lou chimed in. "Lucky lady!"

"I wish I didn't have such bad feelings about those spies who are watching us," Bonnie said, "I wish I knew whether they meant us harm or not."

"They're just observing," insisted Louis. "You'll be okay. You and Trish will be fine."

The silver-haired lady with the lovely skin and blue eyes pursed her lips and tried her best to be cheery. "I'm sure you're right, my dear. I've always wanted to see where your grandfather and the Seastrand family came from. And we'll be staying in a real castle. What could be scary about that?" Bonnie gave them both another hug and walked out of the rich-smelling barn. Gryphon followed her a ways back toward the house until, spotting a taunting ground squirrel far out in the pasture, he scrambled away in a flurry of yelps and barks to vanquish the tiny intruder, who merely popped down his hole to reappear yards away, chattering. It was a long-standing game.

Carl-Joran regarded his reflection in the window of the jet. They had taken off from Tel Aviv airport in bright sunlight and after a brief layover at Boston and six hours more in the sky, they were now on the long, long descent to Los Angeles. The sun was setting ahead of them. Lights, vast numbers of lights were coming on, rows and rows, hillside after hillside, freeway upon freeway became rivers of lights shivering in faint smog that hung year round in the LA basin. He could see enough of himself reflected in the window to be surprised.

The darkening solution he'd used on his hair had changed the complete texture of it and his skin seemed more tan, more lined. When had he aged that much? He didn't remember having crows-feet around his eyes and smile lines near his mouth. The beard he had not shaved yesterday was already past the five o'clock shadow stage and well into prickly and rough. He sighed. With that and the grotesque California beach shirt, white jeans and baseball cap, he looked so much like one of those dreaded American tourists coming home it scared him.

Bump-bump-bump and they landed. "The weather in the Los Angeles basin tonight is clear and dry," announced the pilot, "and you got some ocean winds and it's sixty-five pleasant degrees."

Very similar to what he'd left behind in Haifa, thought Carl-Joran, unlocking his seat belt as the plane pulled into its parking spot. He hated flying in the cattle-car section. It had been years since he'd done it. His little American bank account wouldn't have supported more though. He pulled his briefcase from under the seat, keeping it securely next to him. It contained his precious laptop computer. Hair almost touching the ceiling, he stood and was able to reach above the other passengers as he grabbed his duffel from the overhead compartment and stooping to avoid knocking himself out on the bulkheads, he made his way along the aisle and, gratefully, stretched upright on the ramp. He should, he told himself, immediately go to the rental car desk and pick up the car and get onto Highway 101 up the coast.

The ramp, as all incoming foreign flight ramps do in all airports all over the world, led to an enclosed corridor down which all the passengers trod. After so many hours in flight, everyone was tired and wobbly-kneed. By the time they reached Customs and Immigration, most were beyond grumpy and had become obnoxious.

Into a huge room they went, channeled now into one long line that wound like a snake through the room. Unobtrusively—which wasn't the way in other countries, specifically third world airports where they stood right along the line—guards with guns stood here and there against the wall or behind door edges.

Carl-Joran had a moment's spasm of fear, quelled it and firmly told himself that the passport nestled in his briefcase was not illegal...except for the changed date, more recent photo and immigration entrance and exit stamp pages photocopied from his real Swedish passport. Which did make it a little illegal...though its number did belong to Carl Joseph Mink. The fear tried to come back. He squelched it again. Thank God for his years of martial arts training, even if he had taken it for other reasons. He had never intended to actually *use* it! He had trained in order to overcome his inordinate clumsiness and he had done so. He lowered his heart rate and relaxed. He couldn't wait to write this whole experience down in his little computer file.

His turn came. The immigration officer he ended up with was an older Chicano man who appeared tired and ready to finish his shift. He glanced at Carl-Joran, asked the usual questions: how long had he been in Israel, did he get to visit Jerusalem? Wasn't he scared about the terrorist attacks?

Carl-Joran's American accent now was at home. The answers were no problem. The immigration officer stamped a page and handed the passport back to him. Carl-Joran slipped it back into the briefcase and walked like any other tired, returning tourist past the guards and out of the huge room, down another long corridor and through the giant glass doorway arch that led into the general hustle of LAX.

Immediately in front of the arch, half hidden behind a pillar stood Barbara Monday, sleek and trim in an olive-green cotton suit with a yellow silk blouse that spoke total native Los Angeleno, although Carl-Joran knew she had been born and raised in upstate New York. The woman fitted into her surroundings like a chameleon.

He had to laugh. So much like Tahireh Ibrahim in Paris, and Carin Smoland in Sweden and the older Lori Dubbayaway in Thailand. He had once read a book about the women spies of World War I and II and how extremely deadly they were because of their ability to blend, to make the men around them think they belonged in that place, at the time, with those people. Certainly, the women who moved about doing the rescue assignments for the EW fit very well into their predecessors' roles.

She did not look at him as he stepped through the glass arch. She did not approach him as he walked by her. His eyes couldn't help glancing at her, as any other man's in the crowd did. She looked so attractive. He wrenched his gaze back to the unknown people in the crowd in front of him and went along toward the main exit. She fell in behind him, casually walking as if going to meet someone else.

When she had come abreast close enough for him to hear her above the white noise of the bustling terminal, she said, "I need your help."

Without seeming to talk to her, he said, "I've got to get to Morro Bay tonight."

"It'll only take a couple hours." She sped up enough to get ahead of him as they stepped onto the escalator leading down to the parking garages. "The private investigator hired by Valentine's husband has found where we're keeping her. She has to be moved tonight. She has to be brought to the safe house near here, near LAX, so she can be put on the eight thirty-five a.m. flight to Miami."

"And there's no way you can do it by yourself?" Carl-Joran's face had a gravely perplexed expression.

"If the private investigator has told the husband already, we could have violence," she whispered.

Carl-Joran snorted, replying sarcastically, "I think I win my bet. Okay, lead on, Ms. Monday."

They stepped off the escalator together in the fore-lobby of the garages and both noticed the Arabic-looking individual near the tall potted plant beside an exit, watching Barbara from behind a magazine. Carl-Joran strode away from Barbara, separating from her. The Arab slid away from his potted palm and, sticking the magazine into a nearby chair, followed her through one of the exits leading to the parking garage.

Carl-Joran circled back and went after the Arab, who, once into the garage, paused to see where Barbara was headed. The man was completely absorbed in the fine legs and beautiful rump motion as she swung briskly along toward her rental car. Carl-Joran set his duffel and briefcase against a pillar and quietly came up behind the short, stocky man. As soon as no one was looking their way, he neatly—in a swift, small movement—pinched the side of the man's neck, dropping him like a stone. He caught him, one arm under the shoulders and as if carrying a drunk, took him to an elevator and gently placed him inside, pushing the top-most button. The doors slid shut.

Barbara, in her big rented Oldsmobile, pulled up as Carl-Joran retrieved his duffel and briefcase. He put them in the back seat and climbed into the passenger seat.

"Neatly done, old man," she laughed.

"It is good to practice," he responded. "Where are we going? And I assume you'll drop me off back here at my own car after we're finished?"

"We're on our way to Malibu and yes, you'll be brought right back here." It was dark outside. The roads were black ribbons with huge lights. Barbara finessed her way out of the massive traffic circles around the airport buildings and was quickly onto the San Diego freeway headed north.

A few minutes later, Carl-Joran asked rather plaintively, "Do I really look older with my hair dark?"

"Well," she began, trying to think up an inoffensive way to say what she felt she should say, that is, the truth, and continued with, "I think the dye made your skin seem darker and your beard emphasizes those little lines."

"Oh," he said, disheartened.

"Hey, you're still really handsome for an..." she said and then decided any more might be putting her foot in her mouth.

"*Ja-so*," he muttered.

"I mean, look at Sean Connery and...and Edward Woodward and Clark Gable."

"Mr. Gable is dead." The big Swede loosened his seat belt.

Barbara switched to the fast lane and accelerated. "You're missing my point. Any woman would love to date Sean Connery or Tom Selleck or Clint Eastwood."

"Uh." Carl-Joran replied.

Soon, they left the freeway to turn onto Sunset Drive to wind through the big houses toward the ocean and Pacific Coast Highway.

It was something of a surprise when, after whizzing through Malibu, Barbara turned into the Pepperdine University entrance, but she seemed to know right where to go. Up past the last university building she swung onto a narrow drive that led to a small, dormitory-like structure. She pushed at Carl-Joran. "Get down."

As she parked, she motioned her head toward a black sedan, lights out, windows shaded, half-hidden behind the hedge. Its occupant, a

white man with a buzz haircut, was lighting a cigarette while lowering his
night glasses.

"The PI," she whispered.

Carl-Joran gave one quick nod. He signed to Barbara to put her
hand over the interior car light. She responded immediately by taking a
scarf and pressing it over the light. Smoothly, like a long snake, he
pushed the passenger side door open, slid from the car and amazingly,
for a man so tall, disappeared instantly into the mottled shadows of the
other vehicles, the trees, the fence.

Barbara lowered the scarf. Waited several heartbeats and opened her
door with the light unguarded. The PI's night glasses jerked back up to
his eyes. Deliberately she put her long, beautiful legs out of the car and
walked along the sidewalk where he could observe her. The man's neck
craned around as she passed about fifty feet away bathed in the soft light
from the porch lamp. As she went up the porch steps and under the
shadow of the large portico cover at the front entrance of the building,
the private investigator stubbed out his cigarette, lowered his glasses, and
opened his car door.

At that moment, from below the car window height, Carl-Joran in
one swift motion jerked the car door fully open and hauled the fellow out.
As silently and swiftly as the Arab had been dispatched, the PI was
unconscious. Carl-Joran gently laid the man back into the car seat and
closed the door. Standing upright, he turned and headed for the portico.
Barbara had already gone inside.

He was stopped at the door by a large woman who shook her head at
him. Apologetically, she said, "We know you're a good man, but just wait
here. It's our policy not to let men in. You'll have to wait."

Not more than three minutes passed before Barbara and another
largish woman, whom Carl-Joran guessed was the other half of a lesbian
pair, stepped from the shelter carrying a thick suitcase and a smaller
cosmetic bag. The woman handed both to Carl-Joran.

"Thank you so much, Baron," she smiled, and promptly retreated
back into the building.

Barbara motioned come along to someone behind her, someone who
must not have wanted to leave because Barbara again motioned, and
once more very firmly. A tall, stunningly beautiful black woman,
nervously looking around, staring for a second at the car with the
slumped over private investigator, finally, cautiously, stepped from the
darkness of the doorway like a scared deer.

"Valentine," said Barbara Monday, "this is Baron Carl-Joran Hermelin, your benefactor."

"My God," she breathed softly, her eyes moving up and down, "he's 'bout as big as my husband."

"We'd better go," Carl-Joran urged them, "our sleeping watcher won't be unconscious much longer." He led the way to the Oldsmobile, put the suitcase and bag into the trunk, and held a back door open for Valentine who, herself, had to duck low to get in. Passing that close, Carl-Joran was able to see on her dark skin, with only the interior car light, ugly bruises, half-healed, along the woman's jaw, neck, and lower arms below the short sleeves of her dress. He cringed.

Barbara opened her own door and had the engine started before Carl-Joran had clicked his seat belt. Off they went, back along Pacific Coast Highway, and this time, they stayed on the ocean-side highway until they were past Santa Monica. Barbara wound her way through the busy streets, busy even at this time of the night, and only after some round-about driving through one city street after another to be completely certain she had no one tailing her, did she slip back onto the freeway heading for the airport. The next stop was a ticky-tacky little house stuck between storage units behind an airfreight hanger. The vibrations of the incoming planes shook the car. They were directly under the near-end of the flight path.

"Sorry for the noise," Barbara shouted over her shoulder, then got out and helped Valentine out while Carl-Joran went to the door of the house. He tapped lightly and someone peeked between torn curtains. The curtains fell back in place. The front door creaked opened and Barbara hustled Valentine in. Carl-Joran took her suitcase and bag from the trunk and handed it in the door, which promptly closed with him still on the outside and this time no apologies at all. Over the years, he'd come to accept that this is how it had to be. He had long ago refrained from questioning the women who ran these places about why he, the man who helped support them, was always refused entry. It was not important to him any longer. The job was getting done, so be it.

Not too long and Barbara hurried back. "She's a brave lady," said Barbara. "Holding up a lot better than I would under the circumstances."

"I saw the bruises. I am always amazed at the strength of these women," commented Carl-Joran and, slipping into the passenger seat, put on his seat belt. "What is your schedule now?" he asked Barbara.

"I'm staying at the Airport Hilton tonight, then flying back to New York tomorrow morning. Sometime this week I'll go to Miami and help the crew get Valentine ready for her new life in Africa." Barbara held up her cell phone. "Do you have my number in case you need me to help with the Ixeys?"

He nodded, patted his upper pocket. "Your number is close to my heart."

"Such a romantic!" her New York City accent betraying her origins and she laughed out loud. "You nervous?"

He shrugged. "A little. Of course. Well, a lot. She…Bonnie and I will not meet until we are in the castle. I intend to make sure she will not know I am accompanying her."

"What a shock that meeting will be!" Barbara pulled up to the rental car area. "I envy you, finding your lost love."

"I do not envy me," he snorted, smiled morosely at her, and got out, slamming the door shut behind him. Barbara shook her head and drove away.

It took only moments to retrieve the Saturn. He cringed at its small size, but within another ten minutes he, with only his duffel bag and briefcase to accompany him, was speeding north along the San Diego freeway. Once past Ventura and onto Highway 101, traffic at this midnight hour was minimal and he made better time.

Despite the wider highway, despite all the shopping malls and housing developments that had filled in every empty field between Los Angeles and Santa Barbara, it all was hauntingly familiar. The eucalyptus trees smelled the same, the ocean was the same, the rocky cliffs still brooded over the ocean, and his feelings were flashing back, sharp and clear, as he was physically returning to where they had been.

Trish insisted they take her van. "It's an all-wheel drive, Mom, and it'll be easier to deal with the bags."

"You don't mind leaving it in long term parking?" asked Bonnie and the tall, gawky daughter shrugged.

"It's been in worse places," she muttered, "what with the teams of kids I've had to cart around all over the state."

Gryphon insisted on jumping in and out of the vehicle and Lou had to forcibly shove him out finally, before Trish could take her place at the wheel. The noon sun was warm, though the breeze off the ocean was brisk and chilly. As if sensing what was coming, Bonnie let her face bask in the sun for a moment before getting in.

"Got our tickets?" Trish asked.

Bonnie patted her small fanny pack. "Yep."

Little Misimoto bid them good journey, smiling and bowing. Lou and Dell waved goodbye and Gryphon barked all the way down the drive, until he spotted the stranger standing near the mailbox. Dirt flying, he scrambled across the field only to meet with disappointment as the guy jumped into his car and drove down the road a way. As Trish pulled out of the drive onto the road, another car, the plain white United States government issue car hiding behind the second large oak tree, came to life. The black man in the trench coat was on duty this morning.

"Either we will be exceptionally well taken care of," said Bonnie with some sarcasm, "or this will be a veritable television shoot-'em-up drama all along the coast."

"I hope not the latter, Mom," said Trisha and headed for Highway 1.

Since she wasn't driving, Bonnie could take more notice of the passing scenery. Funny how it is that hills and coastline you've driven by hundreds, if not thousands of times suddenly develop spots you've never seen, consciously that is, when you were driving. A house there, an unusual tree. Or you notice how the winter storms have eaten away at the beach around the lighthouse, or how few tourists are waiting in San Simeon today to tour Hearst Castle. A squadron of pelicans, in as precisely straight formation as a marching band, dipped and skimmed the waves. Bonnie truly loved this part of California.

"Mom, you were right," said Trish, glancing in the mirror, "we've got *both* secret agents on our tail."

Bonnie turned around. There they were. "The Arab fellow doesn't know the road very well," she commented.

Trish nodded. "But the black guy drives like he's got it memorized. Like us." Trisha sighed, "Oh, well. I'm not going to try outrunning them or anything. Highway 1 is dangerous enough without this sort of thing."

Bonnie smiled, nodded. She knew she was in very good hands with her daughter driving.

By the time they approached Big Sur, the winter sun touched the edge of the horizon. As the shadows lengthened, the stark cliffs, the black-green trees, and half-hidden resort buildings took on an unreal quality for Bonnie. Then suddenly, there was the little resort they had stayed at for those brief few days—she and Carl. The cabins were the same, the twinkling lights through the trees made her remember…things. Things as they were, emphasizing the *were* as she was coming to terms with Carl's death. How cruel fate could be, she thought, a red surge of anger slipping through to color her mind's flashing images. She wondered what the title of her life story would be: *The Sunset of Our Lives* or *How Many Roads Must a Woman Walk Down?* It certainly wasn't the *Casablanca* her parents' life had been.

"Want to stop, Mom? Want a snack or a cup of tea?"

"How's our time, kiddo?"

"We're fine."

Bonnie considered, and then thought, if we stop here, I'll remember more. She shook her head. "No, let's get on into San Francisco. I'll save my appetite for dinner."

"Okay," Trish looked in the mirror, chuckled. "The black secret agent is in front of the Arab now."

"Wonder if they'll have dinner with us?" Bonnie glanced back.

"We should pick a good restaurant."

"Yes, we should," laughed Bonnie. "And what is it Muslims can't eat?"

"Sorta like Jews, I think," said Trisha, "no pork, no crabs, or shrimp."

"Right, then may I tender the suggestion that we eat on the wharf?"

"Ha! Great!" Trisha laughed out loud.

Two-and-a-half hours later, they pulled into the parking area under the small hotel, the Franciscan, checked in, and gleefully, like a couple of wayward teenagers, took off walking to Ghirardelli Square. They picked the one restaurant that promised only fish dinners and took immense enjoyment at the fact that the Arab agent stayed out on the sidewalk in the chilly foggy night. The black agent took a seat at a distance furthest from them and seemed to appreciate their choice of restaurant.

After two glasses of wine, Trisha leaned over to her mother and whispered, "I wanna walk past him and just say hi."

Bonnie giggled. She too had had some wine. "Tempting, isn't it?"

Trish sat up, looked directly at the agent, then back at her mom, "Better not. I mean, we really don't know how serious this all is."

"True," sighed Bonnie and at that moment, the black agent was joined by the woman agent they'd noticed arrive at the farm each night. The two chatted quietly to each other, then the black agent finished his dinner and discreetly slipped out the front door.

"Change of guard," said Trisha.

Bonnie nodded. "What happens when we get on the plane, I wonder?"

"That will be interesting." Trish cleaned her plate, deliberately staring at the woman agent. "Hey, I've got a super idea. Why don't we walk up to Ghirardelli Square and pig out on a chocolate sundae?"

Bonnie glanced at the woman agent who was built very solidly. "Bet she has to really watch her weight. Yes, let's do it."

"Let me know the Ixey itinerary soon as you get it," Tidewater said to Russ as the older man headed for his office.

Russ jumped to his feet, moving quickly after him. "They got to San Francisco last night, their plane leaves for New York this afternoon at 4:15. Arrives in New York at 7 35. At Kennedy."

Tidewater, taking his cup of coffee from Lily, nodded as he sipped. "You're one hot son-uv-a-be-hive, young man. Okay, get us a chopper into Kennedy in time to be there. I want access into Passport Control. She'll have to move all the way from their national flight to the SAS International flight. Which national carrier are they on?"

"Delta, sir," Russ replied.

"Okay. And pack your weapon." Tidewater patted his waist where he kept his pistol tucked away.

Hoping that his knife would count, Russ nodded. He had decided, after carefully reading his transfer papers, that carrying the pistol he'd been assigned this morning was not part of his job description. "Are we interviewing Ixey? Or holding her? Or...what?"

Tidewater paused as he was putting his butt into the chair, "I'm gonna see if we can hold her up on some sort of passport violation thing. That should give the EW some fluttery heartbeats!"

"Yessir," said Russ, being wise enough not to shake his head in frustration until he'd made it back into his cubby. He was having a very difficult time with this. What was it in Tidewater that made the man hate EW with such fervor that he would destroy it? Why did the rescue of terrified, endangered, battered women make him crazy? The Native American drew in a calming breath and ordered up the helicopter, sent an e-mail to Kennedy Airport Customs and Immigration Passport Control, and accessed SAS to see which gate the flight to Stockholm would be departing.

The tap on his door by Tidewater came as he scribbled down the latter number.

"Are we ready?" the older man asked.

Russ nodded, held up the slip of paper. "Everything online." He grabbed up his leather jacket and bundled into it as he followed Tidewater to the elevator.

As the elevator shot to the roof, Tidewater smirked at Russ, "Ever ride in a chopper?"

Images, one upon another, stormed through Russ's mind: smoke, fire, leaping into the unknown, flames licking at his boots trying to pull him in, or so it seemed as he and his crew dropped into hell. This boss, thought Russ, must not have read his résumé very carefully.

"More times than I care to remember," said Russ softly.

Almost disappointed, Tidewater mumbled, "Oh. Doing what?"

"Earned money for college as a smoke jumper, sir."

"Well, I'll be damned." Tidewater ducked off the elevator onto the roof ahead of him. "You're a man of many talents."

"Yessir," was all Russ said. More words would have been wasted in the drone of the chopper blades starting their warm-up. The pilot motioned them onboard.

"Kennedy?" he shouted. Tidewater nodded. The pilot pointed to their seat belts. "Make yourself comfortable. It'll take me a while to get clearance."

Tidewater wrapped his belt tightly around himself. "Why? Just tell 'em it's FBI business."

"That won't go for squat," said the pilot. "Sunday's their busiest travel day. Squeezing us into a landing area will be like doing it without K-Y, boss." He chuckled and adjusted his radio headset.

Tidewater clenched a fist even while he laughed. Russ, too, had to smile. He put his belt on loosely, not comfortable with being locked in tightly. After all, when you'd jumped from these damned machines, what did seat belts mean? While the pilot negotiated with ground control, Russ watched the winter traffic far below, crawling along on the throughway. He was going to see Mrs. Ixey very soon, and her daughter, Trish. And what would he say? Probably nothing, probably he would be as still as his ancestors had drilled into him for dangerous situations…make no move, listen, put no words in, take no words out, always do your best to walk in peace. That was the crux of the dilemma on him, wasn't it? He was out of harmony. He was *koyaanisqatsi* as the Hopis put it.

"Got it," said the pilot and started the check off on his engines. "You all belted in? Okay, here goes."

The familiar whine and jerk of the rotors made Russ instantly sleepy. An old habit—if you were riding into danger, sleep while you could.

CHAPTER 8: TIDE COMES IN, THE TIDE GOES OUT

The bitter cold wind whipped Tahireh's black abba as she came demurely from the hotel lobby to the Land Cruiser. Habib held open the door. She pulled her hood tightly over her head as she stepped up and in. Habib got behind the wheel and they started off.

"I've got the heater on," said Habib, "you can take the hood off."

"Thank you," she grumbled, pulling the hood back. She was dressed completely in Muslim mufti: black dress, black scarf, even the black face covering. "Stupid, stupid, stupid, making women dress this way. I hope that hell for Muslim men means mufti forever."

"You are a spoiled young lady!" laughed Habib Mansur, teasing her.

"Yes!" she exclaimed, "And I intend to stay spoiled. How can I do adventures totally wrapped up in hideous coverings? Eh? Eh? Bah!"

He laughed, honked at a donkey cart, and swerved around it. Most of the slower conveyances had left the road, a wise precaution at night in Lebanon. The roads here made the Israeli roads seem like freeways. They were soon into the suburbs of Beirut, which consisted of miles and miles of plaster and daub houses, many only partially constructed. In good Mid-Eastern tradition, the houses were constructed as the money came in, a living room now, a kitchen tomorrow. Slowly, improvements were being made in the suburbs of Beirut. The shelled out buildings were piece by piece being replaced by these half-constructed homes. People were getting more animals. More cotton and orchards were being planted in the stony fields.

Slowly, slowly, Habib thought as he negotiated some tight turns to double back at a place where a shopkeeper still had a lantern out. He checked his mirror. As he'd suspected, a small jeep without lights quickly turned the same way.

"Who is it?" asked Tahireh.

Habib shrugged. "Hard to say. Could be anyone from the Hezbollah to the Iranian secret police."

"It would be the ultimate irony," she muttered, "if we were taken hostage before we even got out of Beirut."

"No, no, whoever these people in the little jeep are, they will not bother us yet."

"How can you be so sure?" she asked.

"Because I still have my haji robes on, they will not molest a haji in front of witnesses. My status counts for something!" he insisted.

"Optimist," said Tahireh, reaching up under her mask and scratching her nose. "Damn this outfit."

"But you will have to wait to take off your abba a little while longer."

"Merde!" she swore again, only this time in vulgar French.

"I will do my best to lose these buggers," said Habib and turned into, and promptly out of another alley. No luck. He flicked off his lights, drove through a small shop's tiny parking area, pulled around back, squeezed the Cruiser through someone's driveway, and slowly peeked the hood back onto the road. The jeep was nowhere to be seen. He let the Cruiser roll onto another alleyway, and taking some giant potholes with gusto, maneuvered back onto a road.

Tahireh looked around, and around again. "I think you've lost them."

"I hope I have not lost us," he moaned, "oh, my!"

"Great! Our mission gets stranded in the alleys of Beirut!" she laughed.

"Don't worry," he assured her, "do not worry. I will find our way!" He stopped the Cruiser, got out, and looked at the stars, brilliant in the cleanly wind-swept night.

Tahireh also jumped out and jerked off the heavy wool cape. "Ahhh," she sighed with relief, folded the thick garment and put it neatly into the back seat. With a light step, despite the thick layer of skirts, she walked over to Habib's side. "Okay, so you are now going to navigate by the stars?"

"They served many men well," he said and pointed, "there is the North Star, there is Jupiter, we are merely turned slightly around. Yes, I know where to go." He took her hand and lifted it toward the heavens. "Remember them, in case you need to find your way."

She laughed a soft, gentle laugh, relaxing a bit, "What need have I of stars to guide me, old man, in Paris there are street signs and gendarmes to give directions."

"For the next week," he responded in a serious voice as he let her hand drop, "you will be on the desert, my child, and the desert's roads are better found by starlight."

"On the desert, I have you." She hugged him.

"That may not always be the case," he admonished her.

Tahireh felt a chill go through her. She pulled her abba around her. "I'll remember your stars then. Come on, let's get out of this city and onto the desert."

"Yes, my dear." He too laughed and filled with the anticipation of more danger to come, they climbed into their respective sides of the Cruiser, and Habib set out through the small side roads until the big vehicle could get up onto the highway again. There was absolutely no sign of the little jeep, nor sign, really of anything on the long, empty road, except an occasional feral cat, slinking away into the blackness or a rabbit whisking its tail as it fled their approach.

"How long to the Jordanian border?" inquired Tahireh.

"Same as always, three hours. Sleep if you want."

"Maybe," she responded, "maybe I will."

Habib settled into the drive.

Tahireh said as an afterthought, "You got the message off to Princess Zhara? It is okay?"

"Yes, she knows when to expect us," he hesitated, "did I tell you she wants us to bring her mother out also?"

"Is that possible?"

She saw his head shake doubtfully. He shrugged. "I couldn't promise her anything. It's another whole set of logistics we hadn't counted on. We don't have the paperwork, the costumes, anything. Maxwell in Kuwait needs a lot more advance notice to help in this sort of rescue."

"That's too bad," said Tahireh, "I know the sheikh will use the daughter's escape to terrorize the mother."

"Perhaps even condemn her to death." Habib was silent a long while. Finally, as they crested the hills where the once famous Cedars of Lebanon groves stood, now mostly the cedar stumps of Lebanon, Habib whispered, "We can only do so much, just so much, no more."

Another several kilometers went by before Tahireh asked, so softly she was barely audible, "I wonder if the baron has met his amour yet?"

"Probably not, my dear, he is so shy, that one." Habib stole a glance at his companion. Her head was nodding with exhaustion. He would get his sleep once they reached the oasis. He would feel much, much safer in the company of the camel herders. These people would not betray him, or Tahireh. The nomad code still held and he, as a very young child, had been part of that tradition. But that was another era, another time. He breathed deeply of the cold wind that seeped into the vent and let the subtle smells of brush and sand bring back the memories, such memories...

His companion took her thick wooly abba and stuffed it between the seat and the window to make a pillow and her head was now nestled against it. Almost instantly, she began to snore lightly, oblivious to the dark desolation around them.

It was as if they had dropped off the face of the earth. Each hillcrest seemed to end in the star-filled sky, each rock seemed to be from another planet. A very familiar deja vu sensation enclosed him like a warm quilt. He was going home.

Baron Carl-Joran Hermelin had arrived at the Ixey farm just after dawn. He'd had to ask directions at a gas station in Morro Bay where a sleepy attendant at first shrugged and told him to look on their local map, on the office wall. Carl-Joran noticed the poor lad gulping down coffee and after a moment, the boy came into the office, much less grumpy, and said, "You mean the Ixey Posey Farm, right?"

"Yes."

"Yeah," said the lad, "well, they raise more ginseng than flowers now. The easiest way is..." The directions were then forthcoming.

But Bonnie had left the night before Carl-Joran discovered when he braved the barking dog enough to lower his window to ask the little Japanese lady working in a greenhouse.

She only glanced at him while mumbling, "Gone, she gone to San Flancisco."

When he'd asked further, "San Francisco? Where in San Francisco?" she suddenly lost her ability to speak English at all. She waved at a young man coming quickly out of the house toward them. Carl-Joran had instantly decided it was time to leave. The big shaggy dog barked behind the car all the way down the drive. That was okay, he knew which plane Bonnie would be on. All he would have to do was wait.

Wait. Had Bonnie waited for him? Those months after he'd left her so suddenly, with no word coming from him? Had she tried to find him? The realization that she could have felt very lost and abandoned surged through him like a spurt of icy cold water. Toby had told him she was already dating someone else, that she had brushed off his leaving without much care. For the first time in all these many years, the shock of imagining that Toby may not have told the truth drove him mad. His teeth gritted shut.

Luckily, the wrinkles in the road gave his mind something to deal with as he wound through the San Simeon countryside. He stared with hard eyes at the golden hills and wondered with bitterness if any of Hearst's zebras still survived, or the buffalo? Hearst had had an entire free-ranging zoo on his vast property back when Carl Mink and Bonnie had driven by, but all that seemed to remain were boring cows and an occasional hawk or vulture soaring across the scrub. Almost unnoticed, the scenery began to grow strangely shaped pine trees, bent and twisted from the offshore wind. He was coming into the wilderness of Big Sur.

His stomach notified him that he needed breakfast. With an almost hallucinogenic sense of loss of time, his hands turned the steering wheel dragging the car into the parking lot of an isolated little coffee shop. Surrounded by trees, it was virtually invisible from the road. No change...no change at all, the same as the day he and Bonnie had come for breakfast, come out of the Big Sur woods to meet Toby. He stumbled as he got out of the little car and stumbled as he climbed the steps to the door. The smell of oiled table cloths, of smoky lamps, of old cigarette smoke...the same, the same, the same...he put a hand on the counter. They had sat in that far table.

He went to a table slowly, with the proprietor watching warily.

"Hey, bud, it's past breakfast serving, why don't you sit up here, at the counter?"

Carl-Joran shook his head. "Serve me here," he insisted, "don't worry, I'll tip you enough."

"Sure, whadda I care?" The man wiped his hands on his apron and came over, dropping a menu in front of the big patron. "You want a cuppa coffee?

"No. Iced tea?"

"Don't usually have that in the winter, but sure," the man shuffled back to the counter area.

Carl-Joran looked intently at the menu, not seeing anything in it. His mind was counting the years; he held up fingers, ticked off the months in that year. Yes, it would have been September or October, no, earlier because he remembered the smell of the eucalyptus.

The iced tea plunked onto the table. "You ready to order?"

"Uh, yes," Carl-Joran responded. "A sandwich, if you have turkey."

"You don't wanna look in the menu, or what?" the man asked and then noted the big patron's confused expression, "Sure, yeah, turkey, and you wanna bowl of soup too? I got some great homemade mushroom soup."

"Yes, that's fine," said Carl-Joran, relieved, and as the man turned away, he added, "Do you have pie, that really good pie I had here a long time ago?"

"Got a couple different pies—apple, pumpkin, raisin-mince?"

"No peach?"

The man let a small smile flick over his face, "Not in the winter. Hey, got a new one, a cranberry pie. It's delicious a la mode."

"I take that." He sipped his tea and returned to counting off something with his fingers.

Somehow his memories were stuck on the frantic Toby shoving him into the VW bug, not even letting him give Bonnie a last kiss goodbye. Tires screeching along the cliff edge as they sped up Highway 1 into Monterey, winding through the back streets of the little fishing village to shake off their pursuers. Hiding behind some wealthy man's house until darkness when they dropped back down into the fishy stench of the warehouses along Cannery Row to a small dock and a motorboat that had ferried him to the tanker. His new life had begun. The terribly hard work on the evil-smelling old ship had mercifully left him no time for reflection. When he'd jumped ship in New Zealand, he had pushed much of that history out of his mind.

Here he was, back in the restaurant. But like a movie flashing before him, in reverse, there was Bonnie reading the menu, ordering for them. He could see the tears in her eyes, see her struggling not to let them show, her tiny hand reaching for him as he turned away when Toby drove into the gravel parking lot. "I must go," the then Carl had said, "the CIA has found me, that is what Toby tells me. You will be in danger. I must go."

"I don't care," she'd insisted. "Stay! We'll fight it. You're married. We're married."

"Toby says I must go because our marriage has no effect," Carl had put his big hand over hers.

As if the years had suddenly evaporated, he suddenly saw the weeks before the moments in this coffee shop, before Toby had taken him away. It had been summer. The nights they had made love on the beach in front of the driftwood fires, the nights in the cabin, the days spent talking, designing a world where suffering did not exist, where children were loved, where these two young people could be in love without worry. This woman, this tiny woman had been only a few years older than him, but years and years more mature. He owed every sense of moral structure that guided his entire life to her. Bonnie Seastrand.

Bonnie...Mink. He had given her the name Mink. And she had not known, until this last week that it was a real name, that she was and had always been, a baroness.

As the turkey sandwich and bowl of soup were laid in front of him, he nodded to himself. She did deserve his estate. All of what his life became was because of her. They would talk soon and Sture would come to accept her. Carl-Joran knew the boy would be okay. His upbringing had been good. His mother had been a wonderful mother and Carl-Joran had loved her, differently from Bonnie, to be sure, but the love had existed for his family.

A peacefulness settled around the big man as he ate. Finally, he paid his bill and got back into the rental car. It was time to catch up, he thought, in many ways. The car grumbled over the parking lot gravel and jumped onto Highway 1. He wanted to get into San Francisco as quickly as possible.

There is nothing as agonizing as having to wait. He checked into a hotel near the airport and managed to get a few hours' sleep. Yet, he had dreamed uncomfortable, unhappy, tense dreams that made his jaw ache from clenching so hard.

He was absolutely certain there were Iranian agents after Bonnie and there he had been napping. He jumped awake at two p.m., had a quick shower, and trimmed his now bushy beard, ate a quick late lunch and hopped the shuttle to the departure terminal. He had coach seating on the big plane to New York.

He was standing behind a pillar where he could observe the incoming travelers when he saw first what was probably an FBI agent. What else could the tall black man in the brown suit with the almost invisible hearing aid-style transponder be? Yes, he even had the requisite trench coat over one arm. The presence of the United States security agency did not make Carl-Joran any less anxious. How could he know if they were any less hostile than the Iranian security agency?

Speaking of which, he spotted the ISF agent, a small weasel of a man, lurking by the espresso coffee stand. The two agents were blatantly aware of each other, glancing past each other, pretending not to notice the other's presence.

A tall, gawky young woman, whose wild red hair could only barely be contained by a rubber band, stumbled over another passenger's feet as she hefted two carryon bags into a chair. Behind the tall woman was a short, white-haired older woman whose beautiful blue eyes made Carl-Joran's heart race. Bonnie Seastrand. It was she. He had no doubts whatever. She had become a very lovely woman. The mousy little girl he had known those many years ago had matured into a fine lady. *Min gud*, he whispered, and I missed this. I missed all those years. He eased further around the post.

Who was the tall gawky young woman with her? A friend? He peeked at her. No, the family resemblance was there despite the height difference. It must be the daughter, Trisha.

The probable FBI agent sat near them. Carl-Joran's whole attention focused on this person, every protective instinct in his body aligned. The agent flipped open a newspaper in front of his face in an attempt to hide.

The tall young woman with bright red hair laughed and it could be heard all the way across the room. So they knew they were being tailed. Did they know about the Iranian?

Carl-Joran slouched as much as he could and made his way behind other people to the coffee stand. The ISF man was just being handed his espresso. With amazing deftness, the big man slid close enough to put a hand under the paper cup and tap it. Despite the cap on the cup, it popped and the thick, black really hot liquid poured down the front of the agent who yelled with the sudden pain. The little man, an utterly vicious expression on his face, scowled up at…no one was there. Carl-Joran was back behind the pillar. The ISF agent futilely brushed at his soaked and steaming shirt and pants. He glanced at the milling group of people being herded toward the boarding ramp. He glanced at the distant men's room and made the fatal decision to take care of his burning skin. He half ran toward the men's room and to Carl-Joran's relief, Bonnie nudged Trisha and the two shook their heads in unison, giggling. Yes, they were aware of the Arab. The probable FBI agent hid deeper behind his newspaper and Carl-Joran took the opportunity to hurry after the ISF man.

"First class boarding," came the announcement as Carl-Joran emerged moments later from the men's room, "please present your boarding passes."

The tall, red-haired woman, a massive grin on her face, grabbed up the carryon bags and nudged her mom. "That's us."

"Yes, dear, let's go."

Carl-Joran, also a smile on his face, watched the two women hold out their passes. His smile vanished though as the American agent pulled out his cell phone and, with one or two glimpses at the women, called someone. Carl-Joran guessed it was the man's superior, probably telling him that the women were on board and out of his jurisdiction, or simply that the next agent could pick up the trail at the plane's destination. When the agent turned and walked from the area, the latter guess was confirmed in Carl-Joran's mind. He mentally assessed how many people were left to board the huge jet, and then hurried after the departing agent.

At the next boarding area which was empty and out of view of the group he had just left, Carl-Joran slid up behind the black man and neatly, cleanly, snapped a quick stroke across the side of his neck. The blow instantly stopped the flow of blood to the man's brain for a moment and he folded softly into Carl-Joran's arms. Seating the man gently, the big man reached into his pocket and extracted the black man's ID; he was Agency, well, well—and also the phone. Punching redial, he noted the number, wrote it down on a piece of scrap paper. Someone answered the ring.

"Agent Tidewater's office," said a woman who must have looked at the caller ID because there was instant surprise in her voice, "oh, hello again, Agent Claybourne."

Carl-Joran scratched the phone to imitate static. "I need to get that information again," he mumbled.

"I can barely hear you," said the woman. "Did you find the ISF man? Is that what you're saying?"

Carl-Joran looked around anxiously at the lessening numbers of people waiting to board way down the hall. "Yes, he is in the men's room. He won't be on the plane."

"Right, good, I'll tell Agent Tidewater," the woman said.

Scratching the phone again, Carl-Joran asked, "When can I speak to Mr. Tidewater?"

"I told you, Mr. Tidewater just left along with his assistant, Mr. Snow. Do you want me to connect you to the helicopter?"

"No," said Carl-Joran twiddling the volume dial, "I will contact him at the destination. When will he arrive there?"

"Ummm, they should be landing at Kennedy any minute and I believe going straight to Immigration."

"Okay. I will call Immigration."

"Sure thing, Agent Claybourne."

Carl-Joran clicked off, wiped the phone and ID clean of prints, and slipped them back into the correct pocket. Agent Claybourne went on sleeping as the baron hurried back down the hall to the tail end of the boarding queue. He grabbed up his briefcase and duffel, dug out his boarding pass, and breathed a sigh of relief as he went down the ramp and into the plane. Then he saw Bonnie and her daughter sitting in first class. He would have to pass right by them. Twisting around, he managed to squeeze along the aisle with a chunky male passenger in front of him. Putting the duffel on his shoulder as he passed Bonnie, his entry went unnoticed. He did wish though, really wish, he were in one of those first class seats. His assigned seat, back in the cattle-car section, barely was able to contain his long, long legs. New York City and Kennedy Airport seemed forever away. He groaned and fastened his seat belt. The only good part of this whole flight was the fact that the Iranian was taken care of. Carl-Joran would, as soon as the seat belt sign went off, call Barbara Monday and see if she could find out who this Tidewater person was and which department he worked for and if there was anything to fear about his being at Kennedy when they arrived.

The soft Mediterranean night wind moved with little puffs in and out of the byways of Haifa and in through the barred, heavily screened windows of the big EW building near the docks. Dr. Legesse could smell the rich mix of wharf pilings, creosote, kelp, seaweed, and harbor mud left by the retreating low tide. Smells of women and children, packed in closely together, assailed her as she hurried through the sleeping hallways of the shelter area. She reached the front office just as a timid knock on the double front doors announced the arrival of Taqi's big Mercedes and Devi with the latest arrivals.

Dr. Legesse opened one of the creaky double doors and smiled at the khaki-dressed Devi who had one arm over the shoulder of a small black girl. Behind her stood the mom, a solid African woman in glorious long skirts and colorful blouse and Mom had an older girl in tow. Taqi stood right behind them, bags in hand. Devi pushed the little girl through the door.

"Judge Moabi wants you to call her right away," said Devi.

"Right now, at night?" asked Dr. Legesse.

"Yep," replied Devi already down the hallway.

Halima Legesse turned back to the stocky black woman, held out her big knobby hand, and gently took her arm to guide her in. "Welcome, Mrs. Makwaia."

"Thank you, thank you," said the woman, shaking with pent-up anxiety. "This daughter is Jo." She made the older girl shake hands with Dr. Legesse, "and the other is Esie. Okay? Is it okay?"

"Yes, everything is okay. You are safe now. Come in, let us serve you some warm tea and good food, or do you want to go straight to your beds and sleep?"

"Tea would be wonderful," said Fumilao Makwaia.

The older girl, Jo, spoke up as she passed the tall doctor, "I wanna go to the toilet."

"Please, say please," said Fumilao.

"Please," said the girl.

"Go catch up to Devi, she will show you." Dr. Legesse motioned to Taqi, "Their bags go into the fourth family room."

The small man, smiling happily, nodded and carted the heavy bags down the broad hallway. He was this way every time he brought women in, happy, satisfied, and proud.

"Devi," called Dr. Legesse, "I leave them in your hands."

"No problem," came Devi's voice, and Dr. Legesse waved the family on past her. She had better get that phone call made to the judge.

As Mrs. Fumilao Makwaia sat her bulk down at the dining room table, Devi hurried out with a pot of steaming tea, warm milk, and a stack of sandwiches left from lunch. "This okay, Mrs. Makwaia? Until breakfast? We don't know your diet needs yet."

"This is more than I could ever wish for," said Fumilao as a giant sigh came from the very bottom of her feet all the way up through her substantial bosom and round face. The two girls came bounding over to her and sat, digging into the leftover sandwiches as if this were a feast from heaven.

"Mom," said Esie, "the room is very small. Can I sleep with you in the big bed? I hate sleeping with Jo. She kicks hard when she dreams."

"Yes, little child," replied the Mom, pouring the strong tea.

Devi hovered for a moment, then smiling at the small family, left the room to go to Dr. Legesse's office. Taqi waved at her as he departed.

The tall, black doctor was seated behind her desk, phone to her ear. She looked up at Devi, "Everything okay? If it is, go on home, get some sleep. The house matron can take over from here."

"It is and I will," said Devi.

Dr. Legesse pointed at the phone, "Kendalla Moabi," and into the phone, Dr. Legesse said, "They're tired, but just fine. Yes, everything is fine. You're right, the Valentine woman has to make her skin blacker and get her hair dyed. Barbara can do that in Miami. Remember, Valentine was an actress so the Jamaican accent should be no problem. Yes, it's all arranged." Dr. Legesse looked down at her phone board, "Can you wait a minute, Kendalla? I've got another call coming in on my private line. Hold on." Halima punched the buttons, "Yes? Baron. Where are you?"

Devi, at the door, heard and stopped.

"Yes, yes, I understand. I'll have Siddhu on it immediately. No, I haven't heard from Barbara Monday. Yes, I'll take care of it. Say the name of that supervising agent again. Interesting. Tidewater. And his assistant is Snow and their office is in Washington, DC. When do you land in Kennedy? Yes, I'll have Siddhu find out everything before you land. Mrs. Ixey and her daughter are safely on the plane? That is good. Yes, everyone is fine here. The woman and her daughters arrived from Uganda just moments ago. Judge Moabi is ready to receive Valentine. It is working well. No, I have had no word from Habib Mansur. Not since he went through the Good Gate into Lebanon. Yes. Goodbye. Safe journey."

Dr. Legesse punched a button and waved at Devi.

"I heard," said the young woman, "I'll go wake Siddhu." She trotted purposefully down the hallway to her own desk in the front office.

"Now, Kendalla, where were we?" Halima Legesse said into the phone. "They will be here only a week at most. I believe Dr. Bar-Fischer will house them in her hospital until they can be sent to Sweden. Everything is fine."

Devi poked her head back into Dr. Legesse's office. "Siddhu is on it, Boss."

Dr. Legesse nodded. "Go get some sleep."

"Yes'm." Devi saluted and left.

Muhit, strong old legs shuffling as fast as possible, hurried right past Walid, the secretary, who jumped to his feet, screeching, "Stop, stop!" but Ali Muhit was already pushing the big door open. Sadiq-Fath, busily writing a report to the assembly, straightened in surprise.

"He didn't make the plane."

"Who...?"

"Our agent tailing Mrs. Ixey and her daughter." Muhit slammed a fist against the wall, "He was put to sleep. Knocked out, something! I don't know. All I know is he woke up a minute ago with a terrible headache and called his superior in San Francisco."

"May Allah curse him!" growled the darughih.

"It wasn't his fault, sir," Muhit tried to apologize and Sadiq-Fath howled with rage.

"Yes it was, however it happened, he should not have been so incompetent as to get *put to sleep*. What's going on over there?" the Iranian commander stormed as he jumped to his feet. "Who took him out? The Agency? Get me Tidewater. Now!" Sadiq-Fath punched the intercom and shouted at Walid. "Get me a direct line to Marion Tidewater's office."

"I assure you," said Muhit, trying to placate the infuriated commander, "it was not an American agent. You will want to talk to Tidewater. He may not know that his man was also taken out."

Sadiq-Fath's storm blew cold. "What?"

"Tidewater may not know that Agent Claybourne, the black agent assigned to Mrs. Ixey in California, was put to sleep in the San Francisco airport also. Our agent found him when he woke up and came out of the men's room."

"Found him?"

"Unconscious in an adjoining boarding area." Muhit let a tiny smile cross his aged features.

"May Allah praise us!" Sadiq-Fath said in shock. The intercom buzzed. It was Walid.

"Mr. Tidewater's secretary on the line, sir."

"Put her on," he ordered.

"Hello, hello?" came Lily's voice. "Uh, both Mr. Tidewater and Mr. Snow are out of the office," she said insistently.

Reeking with contempt, Sadiq-Fath inquired, "Do you know where your Agent Claybourne is?"

"Commander Fath, sir," Lily replied being as diplomatic as possible, "I have no idea who you are talking about."

Sadiq-Fath paid no attention. "Tell Marion that his west coast agent is asleep in the San Francisco airport."

Lily sputtered, "You shouldn't know anything about...'

"But I do and you are found out, aren't you? The man's cover was blown." He laughed cruelly and hung up.

Muhit was nodding. "I'm sure you are right."

"I know I am right. I would love to see Marion's face when his secretary tells him. Ha!" Quddus Sadiq-Fath clapped his hands twice. "I would die a happy man believing that Marion Tidewater has just had his whole EW operation completely broken open."

The old warrior in front of him grinned, then said, "I will tell our New York office to get an agent to Kennedy immediately."

"Yes, do that and make sure *he* is at least competent enough to stay on the Ixeys this time!"

"It will be done," promised Muhit, still smiling.

At the very moment Lily was frantically trying to explain something she did not at all understand to Russ Snow, who was madly waving to Tidewater to come to the Immigration desk phone, a sleepy Siddhu Singh Prakash in Haifa, Israel was calling the airplane carrying the baron to Kennedy Airport.

A flight attendant gently shook him until he awoke. "You have a call, Mr. Mink."

"Yes," said Carl-Joran, "where do I use the telephone?"

"Either up front or in the tail section, sir," she smiled.

Extracting himself from the cramped seat, the big man made his way back to the tail section and picked up the receiver. "Yes, this is Mink."

Siddhu laughed. "Baron, you will not be so surprised to find out who Agent Marion Tidewater is."

"Eh? I won't?"

"He is very high ranking Agency man."

"He? His name is Marian?"

"Yes. M-A-R-I-O-N," Siddhu spelled it out, "and the Mr. Russell Snow is his assistant, a new man, in Agent Tidewater's office only for the last week. He was transferred from the Computer Records office. He is American Indian."

"I see." Carl-Joran yawned. "So these two men are waiting for Bonnie and Trisha at Kennedy. Why? What does the Agency want with the Ixeys?"

"Do not ask me! I cannot help you on that," replied Siddhu. "I can only access the employee tax and payroll information."

"Thank you, my friend."

An announcement came over the plane's speakers, "Please take your seats and fasten your seat belts, we are starting our descent into Kennedy Airport."

"I have to go," said Carl-Joran.

"Be careful," warned the Sikh, "these men could be very dangerous. I have sent help."

"I am always careful," said the big man. "Always." He hung up and made his way dutifully back to the cramped seat, vaguely wondering as he stuffed himself back into a seat belt, who Siddhu would have called to help.

It took forever, seemingly, for the passengers to file off the big jet and by the time Carl-Joran hurried down the ramp, Bonnie and Trisha were walking quickly toward the moving walkway that would take them to the international flight departure area and the Swedish plane. As the baron hefted his duffel bag under one arm, he spotted a robust man with long black hair pulled back into a ponytail step away from the bookstall and walk the same direction as the Ixeys. Carl-Joran moved quickly to get behind him. He didn't look Middle Eastern. Irish maybe, but not Arab...unless...perhaps one of the Iranian-American fellows born from an American Marine father during the Shah's regime. The man was definitely following Bonnie and Trish.

Suddenly, an ugly little man, partly balding and with beady black eyes and dressed in the requisite well-tailored suit, popped out of a side hallway right next to Bonnie and Trish and almost arm-to-arm with them, though not saying anything, walked alongside them. This was the Agency, thought Carl-Joran, perhaps Mr. Tidewater himself. The robust man with the ponytail held back a couple paces more, which further confirmed Carl-Joran's assumption.

The long group came to the guards and metal detectors at the head of the international departures boarding area. Trisha put the two handbags in the x-ray machine and the two women stepped through the metal detectors without problem. The agent flashed a badge and stepped hurriedly through, signaling to a tall, darker man on the other side.

Ponytail man hesitated. Carl-Joran ducked behind a column, then into a tax-free shop. From there he watched helplessly as darker man, whom Carl-Joran was guessing was Mr. Russ Snow, came closer and closer to Bonnie and Trisha, as they picked up their handbags from the x-ray table.

Suddenly, from a boarding area behind Mr. Snow, hustling at great speed, came Barbara Monday. Carl-Joran stared. How the hell did she get here? Oh, he remembered—Siddhu's "help."

She half-shoved Mr. Snow to one side, which put her face to face with Bonnie Ixey. Barbara, a very serious expression on her face, said something to the small woman, flashed an ID card and taking her elbow, stuffed the ID card back in a pocket before grabbing Trisha with the other hand. Barbara pulled them forward, right past Snow.

The man Carl-Joran assumed was Marion Tidewater waved frantically at Snow. Both of them rushed after the women. Ponytail man now made his move, going quickly and uneventfully through the metal detector and after the now even longer group.

Carl-Joran went through next. He quickly caught up with ponytail and just as they passed a men's room, Carl-Joran quietly tripped ponytail so that he fell sideways into the tiled entryway. In a flash, ponytail recovered his balance and struck out with a pinpoint accurate kung-fu punch to Carl-Joran's midsection. Carl-Joran felt the wind suck out of his lungs and several impressions flashed at light speed through his mind; first, that this man whose eyes were as green as any Irishman's was most probably not Arab but Irish and secondly, he was a worthy and dangerous opponent.

A second blow, a karate chop was coming for Carl-Joran's neck. The big man straightened despite the pain in his chest, and diverted the chop into the tiled wall. It must have hurt, but ponytail showed no pain, rather he struck quickly with the other hand just as a man coming from inside the men's room shouted and ducked back in. Carl-Joran neatly caught the strike with a *katatori sankyo* grab that brought a muffled scream from ponytail as his wrist snapped while he flew on his own momentum into the men's room. Carl-Joran knew Airport Security would soon arrive. With the grace of a ballerina, the giant of a man leapt into the men's room and snapped his fingers across the upper bridge of ponytail's nose spewing blood across the floor and the man soundlessly went limp. Carl-Joran turned to his unwilling audience who had watched in horror.

"Excuse me, but he is a terrorist. You will watch him until Security arrives and tell them all about it?"

"I gotta get a plane, buddy," said one man, quickly sidling past the bleeding hump on the floor.

"Yeah, me too," the other squealed as he followed the first. "Didn't see nothing. Don't wanna be held up. Gotta be in Paris tomorrow. Hey, I'm outta here."

Carl-Joran laughed. He'd counted on that. "*Kom, slofock,*" he insulted the unconscious man in Swedish, and stuffed him into a stall. Back in the hallway, there was no sign of the women or the American agents. He sighed with anxiety. Cautiously he moved along the edge of the hallway toward the SAS International boarding area. After all, Bonnie's plane was not supposed to leave for Stockholm for another two hours. What was Barbara going to do with the women until then?

He saw the Agency men at the doorway to the Diplomats Lounge on the other side of the SAS boarding area, talking animatedly with an immense black fellow in African dress. Only those with diplomatic passes got into that area. The huge black fellow ferociously shook his head and Tidewater was snarling back, his voice carried.

"This is official business, I want to talk to someone in this area."

"You cannot!" responded the African.

Tidewater turned to Snow, "Go get Security."

"Yessir," said the Native American and turned away to hurry toward where Carl-Joran was hiding.

The huge black man smiled nastily and shut the door in Tidewater's face.

As Carl-Joran stepped aside in order to keep his face from being seen by Russ Snow, Barbara Monday's voice softly said, "I need you in Miami."

He couldn't see her until he looked back toward the women's room. "How did you get here?" he whispered loudly.

"I was in my office at the UN when Siddhu called. So here I am. You should be thankful."

"So, I am thankful. But," he shook his head, motioned toward the Diplomats Lounge, "I cannot go to Miami with you."

Russ Snow passed, hurried on toward a phone. Once he was gone, Barbara peeked out. "That Agency man knows who I am, he said so right to my face. He'll have someone on my tail. You have to go to Miami—now! And help them get Valentine onto the plane to Africa."

"Oh, jeez!" cursed the baron, "Now I must go to Sweden, I must stay with Bonnie."

"She's safe. My buddy LaFoon will see to that. He's a prince."

"A prince of a guy? Eh?" The note of jealousy made Barbara smile, which made Carl-Joran Hermelin lean back against the wall in defeat. "Which plane?"

"American Flight 122, leaves in half an hour. Someone will meet you at the airport."

"Skitskrap!"

"Ooo, naughty language," the fine lady in the pink suit scolded. "I promise, you'll be on the next flight out of Miami to Stockholm. Promise, promise. You better call Sture and tell him to get Bonnie and her daughter." The woman glanced around at the returning Russ Snow who had Airport Security in tow. She ducked back into the women's room. Carl-Joran turned his back to the security entourage.

The next words he heard were swear words from Agent Tidewater as Security informed him that his quarry had been officially taken into Prince LaFoon's protection.

"Prince of what! Which country?" screamed Agent Tidewater.

A Security officer shrugged, "Who knows? But he's a diplomat and diplomats got immunity."

Carl-Joran peeked out in time to see Tidewater jerk his hand toward Snow. As they walked down the hallway past Carl-Joran, Tidewater growled, "Get us an agent in Sweden, get someone on Monday's tail, and find out what the hell country LaFoon is prince of. God damn them all to hell!"

"Yessir," was Snow's meek response.

Very, very reluctantly, Baron Hermelin pulled himself away from the wall, and from the SAS boarding area, and hefting up his duffel and briefcase, moved along toward the domestic flights departure area. He did not want to go to Miami. He really didn't. Just before he boarded the Miami-bound plane, at least he was flying First Class this time, he phoned Sture. Actually, Carl-Joran was amazed that his son knew that many vulgar Swedish words. He must have learned them in medical school. Yet, what choice did the boy have? He and Krister would pick up the women in Stockholm and stall: take them shopping, see the Vasaskjept, the palace, anything they wanted before finally taking them out to the castle, and, Carl-Joran insisted, tell them nothing until the baron arrived. When? He didn't know. At least Miami would be nice and warm.

Their instant and strange African benefactor with the pitch-black skin and gloriously colored robes had accompanied them hand-in-hand to the boarding ramp and made sure they were safely onto the Swedish plane before bowing ever so politely and bidding them a very *gentile adieu*. A flight attendant guided them to their first class seats. He almost had to wrestle the hand baggage from Trisha to put it in the overhead bins. With a sigh, Trish sank into her seat and accepted the glass of champagne that he put into her hand.

"If you wish more drink, tell me," he insisted, smiling at the tall, anxious redhead.

Trisha nodded, sipping the champagne. Her mom slipped into her seat and grinned at him. "I'd like something warm to drink, please."

"*Ja so*," he smiled, helping Bonnie to fasten her seat belt. "Tea, coffee, *choklad mjolk*?"

"Oh, the milk please." Bonnie turned to her daughter. Trisha had set the glass on the armrest and had leaned her head back against the seat. Her eyes were closing. She sighed again.

As the milling passengers filed onto the giant plane, the attendant somehow managed to bring Bonnie a tall cup of hot chocolate. "This is wonderful, thank you," said Bonnie.

"You are welcome," he reached across and nabbed Trisha's empty glass before it fell over. "Anything you want, let us know." Immediately, other passengers demanded the man's attention and he vanished into the herd of people trying to find seats and store baggage.

It seemed only moments passed before they were airborne. The image of the young woman in the very expensive and sleekly tailored pink suit appearing out of nowhere and commandeering them at the x-ray table could be thought about again and Bonnie did so. She was from the UN Diplomat Corps or the Women's IHO and her name was Barbara? Right? Was it Barbara Nonady, or Monady, something like that. Bonnie mentally shook her head. She wished she had written it down. She dug into her pocket and pulled out the business card but the print was way too small for her to read without her glasses, which were in her handbag. She held it out at full arm's length—no luck.

A soft chuckle from the man across the aisle made Bonnie's head turn. A plump, older man, who had a lap full of papers he was sorting through, gently took the card and peering through his bifocals, read aloud: Barbara Monday, Administrative Assistant, International Health Organization, Women's Division, United Nations, and a phone number and e-mail address.

"Thank you so much," laughed Bonnie, embarrassed.

"Well, comes this age, you either gotta get longer arms or permanent glasses." He handed the card back to Bonnie.

This Barbara Monday had not explained anything to Bonnie and Trisha, not a word more than "Come here" and "Go with him" as she had hurried them down the hallway to the Diplomats Lounge. Who were those men on either side of them? The short, stocky, beady-eyed one that shouted into the Diplomats Lounge, who had been addressed as Mr. Tidewater by Prince LaFoon? The tall, darker man that had been called Russ Snow by the beady-eyed one? And Bonnie was sure there had been others. Like stars seen more clearly out of the side of one's eyes, she had noted early on at the airport a hunky fellow with a ponytail. He had mysteriously vanished. And a giant man with bushy dark hair and beard who kept his back turned to them, always. He seemed to hang like a strange night creature against the farthest wall. The tension had been so thick it was epidemic. The screaming, the shouting, Barbara's amazing calmness as she literally shoved Bonnie and Trisha into the Diplomats Lounge and pulled Prince LaFoon from his comfortable seat, and told him in French to—what? Guard them? Obviously that was the intention because LaFoon had kept that ugly Tidewater guy at bay, as well as Airport Security. So who was Tidewater and what did he want with her and Trish? Who was Snow? Who was the man with the ponytail? Who was the giant? Who? Who? Bonnie let her eyes close. She was as worn out as her daughter, undeniably from the rush and tension and confusion. They had six hours of flying time until Stockholm. Perhaps she would sleep the entire way.

In that moment before sleep overtook her, a vivid memory of being seventeen-years-old and waiting for a bus on a dark street corner in San Francisco appeared in her mind's eye. She had gone to a concert, she had missed the bus home to Morro Bay, and her parents would be furious. Her whole teenage self had been cringing from the anticipated response of her father when she arrived home so late, cringing so much that only from the side of her eyes had she noticed, but noticed clearly, the older, proper-looking man hovering around her at the outer edge of the dimly lighted bus stop. What caught her attention was the incongruity of the very big monkey wrench peeking from his suit coat pocket and his hand rested on it as he stood about three feet from her. Then the bus arrived. This man, whose intentions she had begun to worry about, half whispered to her, "A pretty girl like you should not be standing alone at night." He had motioned with his head toward the inky shadows, "there's all sorts of men not as nice as I am, remember that." As she stepped up, into the bus, her vision caught the movement of a skinny, leather-coated man slinking away. The proper man, an extremely relieved look on his face, had waved goodbye to her as she took a seat in the bus. As sleep overcame her here, many years later on the plane to Sweden, she became absolutely certain that Barbara Monday had served the same purpose as that man at the bus stop in San Francisco.

CHAPTER 9: MINK CASTLE

Marion Tidewater stepped quietly into his assistant's office. "Snow?"

The man jumped, startled, "Yes, Mr. Tidewater." He had been completely absorbed by what was on the computer screen.

"Waiting for that information," the agent demanded softly. He had an expression on his face that the Indian hadn't seen before, sort of a cross between hatred and numb shock, with a fleeting coarse little smile thrown in. Marion Tidewater had not been in a good frame of mind since yesterday, but the moment Russ had come within sight of him this morning, the agent had turned uglier than usual.

"Right, yessir," Russ Snow shook his head, put a finger on the screen. "As far as I can see from airline bookings and her credit card use, Barbara Monday is still in New York. She had a reservation yesterday on American Airlines to Miami, Florida, but she cancelled it right after our meeting at Kennedy."

"Miami?" Tidewater's voice didn't have the usual clipped terseness. It seemed to reek of caution. "Wonder if she cancelled because of us?"

Was it something he had, or had not, done, Russ mused. In a nervous movement, he lifted the feathery beaded headband and swept his black hair back across his head. "Yep. And I've tapped into the women's shelters in Miami, their encryption is minimal." He shook his head. "No listing of rescued women though. Their computers may be second-rate, but they aren't stupid about what files to leave open." He sat back in his chair and sighed. "And nothing, absolutely nothing from San Diego. Claybourne was taken to the hospital. He has a dislocated shoulder and a really bad bruise on the back of his neck, plus continuing dizzy spells. Hasn't a clue who knocked him out or how." Russell held up both hands and shrugged.

Gingerly, as if approaching something dangerous, the ugly little agent sat on the metal chair next to Russ's computer array. He said, "I had a phone call from Commander Yusef in Saudi Arabia just now. He's received word from his contact at the women's jail that a man named Shamsi Granfa is paying all sorts of bribe money around. The suspicion is that it's for a Thai girl about to go to trial on assault."

"What'd she do?" Russ casually asked while tapping on the keyboard. Definitely, his boss's eyes were constantly snapping back to the headband. Was it against some Agency dress code to wear native handiwork? He'd received it in the mail yesterday from his mother with a note saying he had to wear it to keep the evil spirits away. Mom said she'd been having dreams lately that he was walking close to darkness. That was Mom, a walker in the old ways, but Russ never made the mistake of dismissing her clairvoyant abilities. Russ would be calling her later today and nothing on Earth could make him lie to his mom. So he had to wear the headband.

"Huh, oh, the Thai girl?" Marion Tidewater shifted in his chair, "she's one of those indentured servants brought in from Asia."

"Yes, but what was her crime?" the Native American insisted without taking his eyes from the screen.

"Assault, I said that didn't I?" Tidewater growled. "I don't know. Find out for yourself."

Russ nodded, looked around. "Sure, sure."

Tidewater went on, "Now, there's no evidence that this Shamsi is any way tied in with Habib Mansur or the EW. This is their style though. Do Yusef a favor and get some dope on Mr. Granfa? See if you can backtrack his financing."

"Um," said Snow, "I can try." His thoughts went to the girl, locked away in the Arab prison.

"If we can do Yusef that favor, we'll have something to collect on him later." Tidewater suddenly looked very despondent. He wrapped his hands together and wrung them as if washing the backs of his fingers. "Who took out Claybourne and the Iranian agent? Who the hell has the expertise? Clean, efficient." Marion Tidewater let his eyes drop.

"Well, you might like to know," said Russ, with a little smile, "that just after we left the airport, a known Irish operative was found unconscious in the men's bathroom..."

Tidewater perked up. "Where?"

Snow grimaced, "...about fifty feet down the hall from the Diplomats Lounge."

The corners of Tidewater's mouth flicked. "Really? Tall, nasty asshole named McCranny?"

"That's him. He's in police custody. That's how I found out. Came over the police booking monitor." Russ tapped some keys and a booking photo of McCranny blinked onto the screen. The man's face was puffed up with bruises.

"Damn." The agent nodded, slightly mollified.

Russ tapped a few more keys to bring up the booking report. "Found a couple plastic weapons on him, which didn't seem to have stopped his assailant. A wad of money, no ID. Interpol ID'd him from fingerprints."

"Well, well, well. Someone's bringing in big guns to track the Ixeys."

"You think so?" Russ asked the agent.

Tidewater slowly got to his feet, "Why else would a high-flying asshole like McCranny be that close to us? Hmm? Taking that kind of chance?" Tidewater turned, "Get that info for Yusef, okay? And if you can find out who hired McCranny, all the better." The agent slouched out of the cubbyhole.

"Yessir," Snow replied and tapped up the you've-got-mail button to access the new downloads that had come in from the Paris gendarmerie. It was going to take some time. There were several jpg and gif files, meaning photos. His eyes strayed back to the McCranny file. Although not proven, McCranny was suspected in several assassinations, two bombings, and four robberies. Russ Snow felt a deep discomfort. Someone was so eager to keep the Ixeys under surveillance that they had hired an assassin to do it. A sociopath who'd have not the slightest hesitancy to eliminate a fifty-year-old librarian or a twenty-six-year-old PE teacher on a mere word. Who…?

As the photo of a very beautiful woman began appearing from the Paris downloads, Russ suddenly recalled that there had been not one Arab-looking person in the SAS waiting area when they were there. Not one. Of course, he thought, the Iranians had lost two agents tracking Bonnie Ixey so far that he knew of, one to a dog bite, the other to this person who was taking out any potential threats to Bonnie Ixey. Two of their own, so Sadiq-Fath must have decided to let someone else try tracking, someone even more sinister than ISF men.

Russ tensed his legs, moving to get up, to go tell Agent Tidewater what he suspected, when a great invisible hand pressed down on him. Russ sat back down. A howl of conscience went up from his throat but never surfaced to sound. Another level of conscience had emerged, a warning like the internal shockwave of thunder after lightning. A great battle stormed through his body, into his mind, deep, deep into his soul. He fell forward toward the desk, caught himself with outstretched hands, and muffled a scream. Then his eyes looked into the big computer screen and saw the stunning woman with café-au-lait skin, sleek black hair pulled into a tight bun, eyes the shade of Apache tears, glinting in the runway lights. The dress she was modeling was a tiny thing of shimmering ivory-cream that left long, long legs in the bright lights. A soft olive jacket was slung over her shoulder. Yet this was no frail, underfed model. Muscles rippled under that beautiful skin. A runner? Bike rider?

Russ pulled up the next page. Tahireh Guillé Ibrahim. Guillé was her stage name....”The *advant femme* Guillé in the little silk frock from the genius of...” Russ Snow gulped. His face got hot. He read through her entire biographical sketch. How much had her modeling agency put in there and how much was real, who could say, except Tahireh and the agency. Yet it seemed she was an amazing contrast to other women of her culture. Put into school in Paris for safekeeping by her Iranian parents at the age of six, she had escaped the purge of Baha'is in Iran, only to lose her parents, her brother, most of her relatives over the next few years. She volunteered with the Torture Treatment Centre in Paris beginning as a teenager and somehow continued her humanitarian work while establishing her career as one of Paris's most glamorous models. The clothes designers loved the shade of her skin. It was perfect to show off their whites and creams and pastels.

The tall Native American stared at the photo. This was the woman Tidewater, his boss, wanted him to report on to the most heinous security chief in the world. This was the woman whose life would be severely terminated if ever caught back in Iran. How could it be?

With great exertion, Russ tapped the save key and let the photo go away into some sparkling electronic file in the bowels of his computer.

He set to work on the other assignment: Shamsi Granfa and the Thai girl in the Arab prison. It took about an hour of searching. As he was about to take a break for lunch, the computer binged and up came two files on women prisoners in Arab countries, one from Interpol and the other from Amnesty International. He read the Interpol report first. She was not in Saudi Arabia, she was in a Kuwaiti jail. Her name was Milind Pandharpurkar, she was...Russ sucked in his breath, fifteen-years-old, no, she'd have just turned sixteen. Sold into servitude by her parents to help support her ten brothers and sisters in Thailand. She was, had been, employed in the Syrian embassy kitchen. Her crime? She'd knifed the son of a Saudi diplomat. Okay, thought Russ, that was assault all right.

He set about downloading the preliminary investigation reports. They were all in Arabic. He programmed them to go to the translator. He'd retrieve them after lunch. As he stood, the booking photo of Milind Pandharpurkar flashed across the screen. A tiny, terrified girl whose face and obviously naked shoulders were striped with welts of some sort. Russ was on his feet though, and determined to get out and get some food. It was almost two p.m. and he was starving. He'd read the translations and the Amnesty report when he returned and he started the research on Granfa.

Tahireh, at this very moment, bore no resemblance to the sexy, gorgeous Parisian model in the photo in Russ's computer file. Not unless grunge had suddenly come into style. The bright ruddy light of the big central campfire sent sparks into the desert night sky. The women of the Bedouin camp were gleefully patting Tahireh's heavy cotton shirt and pants to make the dust swirl. Her face was streaked with grime and she, too, was giggling. The tribe was turning her into a camel boy. The men and boys in charge of the donkey and camel caravans were squatting in the dark outside the circle of women, critically observing the process To them it was a life or death operation and they felt entitled to their occasional shouts of advice and teasing.

The elders of the tribe were huddled with Haji Habib Mansur. There would be rituals to take care of in the morning before the men and boys set out with the camels and donkeys to the i-Shibl compound. Habib was obligated to pay his respects to the other hajis and wise old men. He would bless their wives and children and receive in return the Bedouin assurance of protection. Habib, though, was well aware that the only real protection these remnants from a time in history long, long past, could afford him and Tahireh, was temporary invisibility. Even that was not what it used to be, what with the way satellites could pick out even individual people in the remotest locale. Luckily, at this moment, it was highly unlikely that any military observer cared about a wandering tribe of Bedouins.

It was muggy in Miami, like walking into a glass-covered arboretum. The reflected lights on the surrounding black water had been beautiful. The night sky had been misty. Carl-Joran slung his duffel over his shoulder and trudged, dog-tired from the plane. His eyes did the cursory scan of people waiting in the nearly empty boarding area. Mostly Latino people, no one obviously Iranian, no one obviously FBI or Agency. Two women, dressed alike in tank tops, mussed shirts and blue jeans, one skinny with clipped blonde hair, the other thickset, black-skinned and very serious, both not much more than teenagers, disengaged themselves from their chairs and caught his glance. He gave a little nod.

They walked quickly out of the boarding area and down the long hallway. He followed. They went through the large terminal, onto the arrival pick-up sidewalk, across a pedestrian zone, and hurriedly into a large parking area. The sky was lit by the reflection of the airport landing lights on the lowering mist. It wasn't raining, but the threat was there. The humidity was so high it condensed on Carl-Joran's skin.

The women unlocked and got into an old purple van. Carl-Joran hung back. The engine started up, it pulled forward, the sliding door opened, and he jumped in. The skinny blonde slammed the door shut as the black girl accelerated out of the lot. Gratefully, the baron fell into the bench seat. The skinny blonde held out her hand, "I'm Tammy. That's Sherralyn."

The driver held up one hand in a semisalute. "Bet you're jes skunked."

"Um, if you mean, am I exhausted," Carl-Joran said, "yes, I am. Very."

"We get you to bed real soon." Her seriousness evaporated into a broad grin reflected in the mirror. Tammy wriggled into the front passenger seat. "Then we get to work on Ms. Valentine. She safe by the way. An' doin' fine. Learnin' to speak Jamaican dialect real quick."

"Excellent," said the big man, barely able to keep his eyes from closing.

Tammy glanced back at him, "Go ahead and sleep if you want. It's a ways to the shelter."

"Thank you," said Carl-Joran and promptly passed out.

It was late in the evening when Russ Snow sat down at his desk at home to read the translations and the Amnesty report. He'd stopped off at a little restaurant on the way home, a place run by an old Cheyenne friend of his. Russ needed to talk to someone and Lost-in-Clouds, whose white name was Freddie, was a good listener.

"So what'd you expect?" was Freddie's summation of Russ's complaint. The tall Native American with the cook's apron around his middle shrugged his broad shoulders and slumped into his chair. "Hey, my grandfather was a sniper during WWII. Got wounded on Iwo Jima, got all sorts of medals and was treated like crap after being de-mobbed. Like, prejudice still happens."

Freddie put some plates of excellent enchiladas con frijoles y cheso in front of the two of them. Though the aged Cheyenne kept keen attention on his two cooks in back, he pointed his fork at Russ. "You lucky you still in the man's office, you lucky he didn't find some way to fire you on the spot."

"Maybe he will and it's taking him time to come up with something that'll prevent me from suing his butt." Russ dabbled in the food.

"Eat!" ordered Freddie. "So tell me what the secretary said again."

"Lily. Yeah," Russ tried a bite of the enchilada. It was heavenly and delicious and outstanding! He dug in and between mouthfuls, reviewed Lily's remarks. "She waved at me when I came in from lunch. Waved me over to her desk, and out of god-knows-where asks me to spell my name. Which I do. S-N-O-W. And she gives me this strange look and asks if that's my real name, did I get it from my family? And were they the Arizona Snows. And I say my folks are north country Snows from up against the Minnesota Canadian border. Snow's the name I use for my records and my job, and for when I was in school, but no, it's not my family's name. Oh, she says all sweet, and what was your birth name? So I get some pride in me and I tell her: Snow-from-Night-Sky. This is my mother's clan name. Like it should be if you're from a tribe of the Iroquois nation."

"You only half Menomonee, why not pass and use your father's white name?"

"Didn't know my dad. He left so quick. Mom said he was a kid her age and he got killed in 'Nam. Maybe so, maybe not. No records, nothing left. Maybe if I ever have kids I'll go look up the guy's history, you know, for medical purposes. Make sure he had good genes, mostly white from what Mom knew. I got his name written in my baby book." Russ finished off the plate of Mexican food and sighed. "So my genes are half and half, but my soul is Iroquois."

Freddie kept his respectful silence for a long moment, and then sagely nodded. "Yep, I'm almost all Cheyenne. I don't even know what the rest is, maybe black. Happened in Oklahoma a lot after the Civil War, slaves hiding out with our tribe. We understood, we helped when it was possible. And our women weren't so prejudiced like the white society." He refilled Russ's cup with decaf. "What else did this Lily woman say?"

"Not much, like, oh, that's interesting and you're so good at computers..." Russ laughed in pain, "Like I'm supposed to weave baskets or something?"

"You'll be back in the Intelligence Section by tomorrow. Watch what I say." Freddie cleaned the last few bites off his plate, then wiped his hands on his apron and glanced around the busy kitchen. Satisfied, he picked up his and Russ's empty plates and considered the fact that he ran a competent crew. He put the plates in the wash sink and helped himself to several dessert dulches—a cross between cookies and doughnuts, some pink ones, and put them on a napkin in front of Russ, who had shrugged again, muttering, "Like I need this job?" and ate one of the dulches.

So an hour later, sleepy with his full stomach, he was sitting at his desk, reading the reports he had forwarded from his office computer. All he could think was that his mom had sensed the future again. The darkness was closing in fast. The Thai girl was up for assault all right, but Amnesty International made it very clear that it was self-defense. She'd been fending off the son of a Saudi diplomat who was trying to rape her in the kitchen where she worked, of all places, and she'd stabbed him with a butcher knife. Although there was to be an official trial, the outcome was already on the books, that the punishment was execution by garroting. Women simply didn't strike back in conservative Muslim culture.

Russ knew for certain, with the conviction born of his mother's brother's honor as a warrior, that Russ Snow-from-Night-Sky would not pass on any more helpful information to Yusef or Sadiq-Fath or the not-so-honorable Marion Tidewater. For example, the bits and pieces he'd pulled up on Mr. Granfa, the man who was trying to bribe the guards to get Milind out? Why should Russ condemn a man who was trying to do something good? No more. Russ printed out the material on Tahireh to read in bed. She was on his mind a lot.

Sture wanted to pace the waiting area outside the passport and immigration check-in room, but there was a huge crowd milling around the big double doors that would soon open to let the recently arrived passengers out. He felt overdressed in his expensive wool slacks and trendy pullover sweater. He carried his matching jacket over one arm.

Krister, in his uniform, calmly flicked the sign above the heads of the crowd. He had neatly printed in big letters: BONNIE und TRISHA IXEY, copying the spelling of their names carefully from the official documents.

Sture brushed imaginary lint off his wool slacks for the umpteenth time. He was not happy with his father's demand that he and Krister entertain the Ixeys in Stockholm for the day. Why not just take them to the castle and turn them loose? Surely his father was not going to be so long in Miami that Bonnie's being at the castle would do any harm? Yes, Sture did realize that the moment Bonnie arrived in Norrkoping, Miss Algbak from the Pastorkirche would have a right to interview her, demanding that papers be signed, and Ms. Person would come to defend the Hermelin estate and things could get crazy fast. Sture brushed his pants again and Krister, very respectfully, harrumphed at him.

Inside the immigration terminal, Trisha was pushing the baggage cart containing their two big suitcases, plus the carryon luggage past the nothing-to-declare sign and toward the door. They had sped through the passport stamping section with no more than a casual "Why are you in Sweden? How long will you be staying?"

"It's not as cold as I expected," said her mother and Trisha nodded. "Yeah, I thought we'd have to put on our new jackets by now," Trish said, almost disappointed.

They pushed through the big double doors with a phalanx of other people and Trisha instantly saw a small man with thin face and pale skin, in a chauffeur's uniform hold up a sign with their names on it. "Look, Mom, that must be them." Next to the chauffeur was a very tall young man with untamed, ruddy hair and startlingly blue eyes.

Bonnie strained to her tiptoes, but could not see over the crowd.

"Come on," Trisha pushed the cart in that direction and flung her hand in the air in a semaphore motion. "Wow, Mom, a chauffeur and everything!" Bonnie felt the sadness leap into her throat again. She still did not know what she should say to the son, the stepson she had never met, never even known had existed. How would he react to her? She deliberately kept a few feet behind her large and enthusiastic daughter.

The chauffeur was the first to reach them. He had slipped through the throngs of mostly tall, blonde people and gently, but firmly took the cart from Trisha. He bowed politely. *"God dag, mina damer."*

"Hello," said Trisha, half bowing in response.

"You don't have to do that," said the young man tensely. He stepped past Trisha and very formally held out his massive hand to Bonnie. "I am Sture Nojd Hermelin."

Bonnie put her tiny hand in the great big one. It brought back an instant picture of the boy's father, at the same age. "I'm your stepmother, Sture," she said softly.

"Ja so," he melted a tiny bit and overcoming his reluctance, smiled at the pretty little lady, "I guess it is true." He turned stiffly to Trisha and proffered a hand.

Trisha's clumsy big hand almost matched his in size. "Hi, I'm your stepsister. I'm Trisha."

Sture did not acknowledge this comment, but rather said, "This is Krister." He waved at the chauffeur, who touched his cap and, motioning them to follow, set off, pushing the cart ahead of them, clearing a path through the crowd. The lanky young man, struggling with the English words, blurted out as they came to the front of the terminal, "My father wants..." he blushed bright red and coughed, "he wanted you to be comfortable, I am sure. *Ja so?* And you must be hungry for breakfast? Krister can take us to a good restaurant."

"That sounds wonderful," Bonnie agreed, doing her best to make the young man comfortable. They stepped outside and the intense darkness at six in the morning, plus the bitter cold hit her like a brick to the face. She quickly put on her new, extra-warm coat.

Sture had paid no attention to her words. Slipping into his suit coat, he stood at the edge of the sidewalk and scanned the throng bustling toward their cars.

Trish laughed her loud, very American bray, "Yeah, I'm really hungry for a decent meal." She either didn't notice, or simply was not paying attention to his discomfort. She too, was slipping into her coat, pulling up the high collar to ward off the deep-freeze chill. Sture motioned to Krister to get the car and the small man hurried off, pulling on his gloves as he trotted down the sidewalk, leaving the two women and Sture waiting at the curb.

The wind blew fitfully, carrying what felt like shards of glass. Trisha looked around and commented, "How come there's no snow on the ground and what's this hitting my face?"

"Dat is snow," said Sture, almost as an aside. "You see snow on the ground very soon. Here there is pipes under the road? Right? Hot water from the electric plant? So, no ice, no snow."

"That's an excellent plan," said Trisha, standing on tiptoes to watch Krister's progress to the parking lot.

"And this snow?" Bonnie brushed at her face, "It feels like ice."

Sture's flitting gaze had stopped on a small, dark man getting into a white Mercedes at the far end of the terminal roadway. "*Ja so. Da ga det,*" he muttered, and then glanced at Bonnie. "It is dry snow. Because it is so *kalt.*" He started anxiously shuffling his feet.

Trisha did notice this. She turned to him, "Aren't you cold without a big coat?"

"*Nej*," he tried to smile. It came out as a grimace. "It is warm right here, maybe only ten below freezing point?" His head went up as a big, black Saab pulled into the roadway and drove past the Mercedes and up to them. Even before it completely stopped, he had jerked open the back door. "You, *fru* Ixey and *froken* Ixey, you get in, please. Quickly."

Krister had hopped out and as he came to take over the door-holding job, Bonnie—Trisha had already climbed in—saw Sture nod toward the white Mercedes idling some yards behind them and Krister return the nod. Krister firmly took Bonnie's elbow and bowed, almost forcing her into the back seat. As soon as the door closed behind her, Sture jumped into the passenger seat and Krister literally ran to the driver's side. He said something in Swedish as he fastened his seat belt and Sture turned to the women, motioning his own seat belt fastening.

"It is the law," said Sture, again trying to smile, but his eyes flicked up, past Trisha's head, and out the back window. He exclaimed a string of words in Swedish to Krister, who immediately released the parking brake and sped down the roadway.

Trisha, as she locked her seat belt, turned her head to see what Sture was watching. She whispered, "Mom…"

Bonnie looked around. "The Mercedes?"

Trisha nodded, then asked Sture, "Are there secret agents after us here too?"

"Too?" He finally looked directly at the two women. "You mean, they are after you before?"

"Back at the farm," said Bonnie slowly so the boy would understand, "we had two agents watching us. In San Francisco, at the airport there was a black man, sometimes a woman, and some Arab guys. At Kennedy Airport several agents, I guess they were agents, came after us and a woman from the UN helped us get past them."

Sture sat back into his seat, sighed, said something in Swedish to Krister, who shook his head, resignedly it seemed. They carried on a terse conversation in Swedish for several minutes, of which Bonnie only understood the words *far*, *slott*, *fru*, *froken*, and some liberally used swear words such as *fy fan*. Funny how she remembered the words her father had told her never to repeat. The chauffeur and the young man became mostly silent as the busy-ness of the airport approach road turned into a long, empty, dark highway. Far off, on the horizon, were sparkling bright city lights. In the sub-zero cold, they looked like crystals glowing. Bonnie assumed that was Stockholm.

Trisha began to squirm in her warm leather seat and turned to her mom, "I gotta go."

"I will have to in a few minutes too." Bonnie leaned forward. "Sture, were we going to stop for breakfast?"

Instead of immediately answering, both Sture and Krister glanced in the rearview mirror. Trisha craned her head around also. Sture muttered, "*Nu! Tva!*"

"*Ja!*" the chauffeur responded.

"Two?" Trish asked.

"Yes," said Sture, "two cars are behind us."

"Shit," growled Trish, then, "I really gotta go."

"We are going," Sture said back to her in a similar growl.

"No! I mean I gotta *go*."

Bonnie laid a hand on her daughter's arm. "That's slang for having to go to the bathroom, Sture."

"*Bad?* You need a *bad*!" The boy was frantic. "You cannot wait until we get to the castle?"

"*Bad*, Mom," whispered Trisha urgently, "what's a *bad*!"

"No, Sture," Bonnie tried to be pleasant, "she meant she has to find a WC."

"Oh," Sture sighed and repeated WC to Krister in Swedish. The chauffeur laughed out loud.

"What the hell's a WC?" insisted Trish.

"Toilet," Bonnie told her.

"Oh, jeez, why double-u see?" The tall woman squirmed again.

"It means water closet, dear—toilet." Bonnie was getting anxious herself. "Sture, could we…?"

"*Ja so*," he actually turned and smiled at them. "There is good restaurant near. We stop. Eat breakfast? She can use the WC."

"*Jag ocksa*," Krister added, a grin in his voice.

"Him too," Sture pointed a thumb at the driver. "It is busy restaurant, all times of the day. We will be safe there. And I can call my…I can make a phone call." He held up a cell phone.

"Can't you just call from here?" asked Trisha.

"We are not close enough," the boy pointed toward the lights of Stockholm. "And the police, they not like people to phone in a car."

Within minutes, they came to a huge complex of lighted buildings, including a gas station, restaurant, and motel. Krister pulled in and up to the restaurant. At seven a.m., it was packed. Krister, Sture, Trish, and then reluctantly, Bonnie turned to look out the back window. The white

Mercedes was just coming in the parking lot and behind it, was a strikingly obvious maroon Ford Taurus, with not one, but two very American looking men in the front seat. Their hair was cut in so above-the-ears-proper-style it shouted American agents!

"So, we have company while we eat." Sture opened his door, "The restaurant, it should give us free food because we bring business." Yet, despite the humor, he was very nervous. He stuffed the cell phone into his pocket.

Krister asked him something in Swedish and the boy shook his head, replying something. Krister got out and ran around the side of the building toward the WC sign. In moments, he was back and opened the door for Trisha while Sture held Bonnie's. As the two women and Sture headed for the restaurant entrance, Krister got back into the Saab.

Bonnie was going to ask about that, when Sture, holding open the restaurant door, supplied, "He must protect the car." They stepped into the warmth of the big room and a waitress immediately approached to lead them to a table. She indicated a spot where three other people took up one side and Trisha opened her mouth to object. Her mother hushed her. "This is Europe, dear, we share."

They smiled at the other sleepy, weary people and sat as the waitress handed them menus. It took only moments to order plates of pancakes and sausage and boiled eggs. The older man of the three original occupants of the table held up a thermos pot of coffee, offering it to them. All three stuck out their cups and coffee as pale as tea was poured in. Trisha looked at it askance.

"Don't judge it by the color," warned Bonnie, who remembered the Swedish coffee at Lena's. "It's very strong. I think it comes from Indonesia."

"The coffee?" asked Sture. "Yes, and Africa." He nodded to the older man, "*Tack so mycket.*"

"*Garna,*" the man replied, stifling a yawn.

Trisha quickly went to the ladies' WC and came back. Bonnie took her turn.

"I take out food for Krister," said Sture as Bonnie sat and the waitress brought their breakfast. He looked around, out toward the Saab and Trish and Bonnie followed his gaze. The small dark man from the Mercedes was seated near the door, ordering breakfast and the two Americans were at the counter, just pouring their coffee. "So I say," muttered Sture, "we bring in much business." He grabbed up a cup of coffee to go, a package of smorgas, and patted his pocket. Both women smiled in acknowledgement as he stood, walked to the door, then out. The agents all started up, then noticed the women in their seats, and sat back down.

Krister accepted his breakfast sandwiches through an open car window and Sture made his phone call. He paced back and forth, conversing with gestures, his breath making big clouds of steam. It didn't take long. He snapped the phone shut, said some words to Krister, and reentered to sit back down at the table. "Do you want to see sights in Stockholm?" he asked in a depressed voice with words that came one by one as if rehearsed.

Trisha regarded her mother for a moment. "I have the energy, but I don't know about Mom."

"I'm a bit bushed," she said.

"Eh...tired?" the boy's voice asked hopefully.

"Yes, quite."

"Good," he exclaimed, the delight evident, "then we go directly home, to the castle. You can see Vasaskjept, and other famous things another day." His whole body relaxed. He dove into the pancakes with fork and knife flying. His mouth full, he stated with assured finality, "We will be much safer in the castle."

By eight a.m. they were back on the road, their little entourage behind them. The miles, or kilometers rather, flew by. They drove very fast; Bonnie figured around ninety miles an hour in the straightaways. Even with the moments of worrying about the black ice and packed snow, she did sleep, though fitfully, awaking to find them going much slower along a narrow road bordered by broad, flat expanses of sparkling snow. Dawn was breaking. She glanced at Trisha's wristwatch; it was ten thirty. She'd forgotten that so far north the sun would stay up only a couple hours this time of year. And a bleak sun it was, though the faint light made the entire world around them a fantasy of white: white trees, white fences, white roads and trails. Only the occasional passing car or person on cross-country skis had color, and then not much as the car would have snow on it and the person would be covered with frost from frozen breath. Trisha pointed out the big dogs in harnesses, guarding their sleds in front of a small grocery store.

About fifteen minutes later, the Saab slowed to a crawl to negotiate a turn into a very small lane, through a huge gate that opened by Krister's electronic command and closed after them. Bonnie noticed on the wrought iron of the gate a large circular coat-of-arms, the same one that had been on the official letter that had brought her here. This was the entrance to the Hermelin castle. Her castle. She owned a whole castle. The jet lag was making her feel lightheaded and silly, and perhaps also, it could be the most unusual circumstances.

Bonnie couldn't see any cars behind them. No, there they were—far, far behind, holding back, trying to be as invisible as possible. They would have to stop at the gate. Down the tiny lane the Saab went, huge snowdrifts as high as the car on each side, up to where the drifts parted and a small roundabout allowed the car to park at the entrance of an immense mansion. The face of the building was flat, even the twin front doors, exactly in the middle, opened onto the gravel drive with only the smallest of steps between the ground and the jamb. Windows, the same width and height as the doors, paraded outward on both sides, and each window had the exact same curtains, same color, same eighteenth century style. Drear was the only word to describe the shade of the natural yellow-gray stone. The roof, almost free of snow because of its steep peak, was of black slate. Except for the crystal glitter of the original glass in the windows and gaslight fixtures on the entrance, Hermelin Slott was ugly. Far to the right near a small door at the end of one wing, two cars were parked and plugged into heating posts.

"Welcome to the Hermelin Slott," Sture smiled. "This is where we live and," he nodded his head toward the right, "that is the birdwatchers' hostel. Not so busy this time of year."

Krister jumped from the car to open the doors for the women. Sture, without pausing, slid out and went ahead. The huge front doors opened and an old man in dark wool trousers and white wool shirt, stepped out, coatless. He saluted Sture who said something in Swedish and motioned toward the trunk of the Saab. As if in second thought, Sture turned and said loudly to Bonnie and Trisha, "Here is Gustav. He takes your baggage. Okay?" And the young man dashed into the castle. Krister was pulling out suitcases and Gustav was easily picking them up.

Bonnie and Trisha, freezing, shrugged at each other, grabbed up their jackets and half slid, half walked to the doors where a girl of about eighteen dressed in a dark blue uniform with white apron, met them and smiling, motioned them in. The vestibule was large, chilly, and lined with what looked like wooden pews. A steam heater in the corner burped and grumbled. Sture's recently worn boots lay next to the heater, along with rows and rows of other boots and shoes.

"*Din skon, har, tack?*" The girl pointed to a pair of boots which looked like they could be hers, then pointed to the slippers on her feet, then to Bonnie and Trisha's feet. "*Ja?*"

"Sure, yes," said Trisha as the girl took their jackets to hang up on a wooden peg. Trisha slipped off her new boots. Bonnie looked around first, at the well-worn heavy wooden furniture, the exquisitely carved inner doors, the slate floor. An outer door opened and Gustav stepped in with the first load of baggage. Bonnie could hear the Saab drive off, crunching on the icy gravel, going toward the back of the castle. The old man saluted her.

She nodded in return as she set to work taking her new boots off. Of a sudden, the memory of her father religiously putting his shoes and boots by the front door came back, and how her mother would carefully clean them before putting them into the hall closet. It was their unspoken negotiated settlement, like so much else in their lives; unspoken, loving compromises. So now Bonnie was in a real Swedish home and now she saw how shoes and boots were left at the door, not put in a closet. And the shoes and boots were all clean, probably cleaned by the maid, Bonnie guessed and smiled at the girl.

"I am Mrs. Ixey," said Bonnie slowly.

"*Hej*," said the girl, curtseying again and blushing, touched her bosom, "*Frida.*" Turning, she led them into a huge hallway that immediately opened into a giant entry room. Plush carpets covered the floor and went up the two curving staircases. A vast and delicate chandelier filled the room with soft light. It was now electric but was obviously made for candles. Imagine, thought Bonnie, the time it took to lower the chandelier and light all the candles and raise it back up again.

Large dark paintings of, Bonnie assumed, Hermelin ancestors lined the walls. This room was little warmer than the entryway.

Frida hurried along and guided them around the staircase and down a short hallway to a small room that was a den made into an office. It was warm, toasty in fact. Sture, sitting at the desk, hung up the black dial phone. The maid bowed and was about to back out, when Sture said something to her in Swedish. She stopped, waiting patiently, hands folded on her apron.

To Bonnie and Trish, he said, "You would like food? Astrid makes lunch soon. You want to rest?" He smiled tensely at Trisha, "Now you want a bath?"

"Yep, a bath would be great," said Trish, "and a nap, 'cause my body says it's evening."

"Yes, a nap," Bonnie agreed, "and a bath. Could we wait for lunch until your dinner hour? Then our jet lag will be better."

"*Ja so*," Sture nodded and made it clear to the maid that they were to go to their rooms.

Bonnie came closer to the desk, "When can I talk with that attorney, Ms. Person? I would really like to get the paperwork finished as quickly as possible."

As if he didn't expect this, Sture slid the big chair back, "My father says to wait for...it is rather, you must wait until tomorrow? That is better."

Bonnie noted Sture's use of the present tense again. Internally, she shook her head. Surely, it was just a language problem on the boy's part; he didn't know the past tense of English verbs, right? She continued to Sture, "Tomorrow? We couldn't see Ms. Person later this afternoon?"

"No, no. We will wait," Sture insisted.

"Wait for what?" Bonnie leaned over the desk making the young man very uncomfortable. He knew future tense, that was for sure, she thought. On the desk, she noticed the stacks of papers addressed to Carl-Joran, the bank statements and sympathy cards. There was a puzzle here, she was certain. "If I insist on seeing Ms. Person today, what would you do?"

The big shoulders shrugged, "It is a long walk to Norrkoping."

"She can't come here?" Bonnie picked up some of the papers. They were all in Swedish.

Sture reached forward and not too gently, but carefully, extracted them from her hands.

"If my mom decides she's gonna do something," Trisha volunteered, "you can bet she'll do it quick."

"Your mother does not know what this is all about," Sture shot back, "there is much she does not know, much to explain. I do not explain it. You will wait. And we must stay in the castle. It is dangerous to go."

"You mean the agents out on the road?" Trisha laughed, "They won't stay out there long in that cold."

The tall young man shook his head, "But they will wait in Norrkoping. And Krister is tired now. He must drive, he must protect the car." He held up the phone receiver, "You can call Ms. Person?" His tone was hopeful.

Bonnie nodded, "I will call her. Later, after my nap." Sture sighed with relief and set the receiver back in its hook as Bonnie went on, "Why must Krister protect the car?"

"This car today, it is a new car." Sture grimaced, "No, we stay in the castle until, until tomorrow."

Perhaps it was the jet lag, perhaps her own irritation and anger at being followed and harassed, but Bonnie put her hands on her hips and said, "Tomorrow and no postponing it. Sture, I know you are grieving for your father, but I want to see the attorney and I want to get the paperwork out of the way. That will make things easier for you too, won't it?"

"Also must you talk with the *tik* Algbak." Sture scowled. "Old moose's behind."

"What?" Trish interrupted.

"Algbak, the woman at the Pastorkirche. Her name means moose's behind," the young man explained, a smirk starting at the corner of his thin lips.

As one, suddenly, they laughed, all three of them, even Frida giggled. It broke the confrontational mood and Sture's face lightened.

"Okay." Bonnie stood up straight again, taking her hands off the desk, "Trish and I will try to relax. And wait."

"Yes, good." Sture spoke Swedish to the maid, then English to the women, "Frida will take you to your rooms. You must share a *badrum*. But you have hot water and the rooms have heat."

"Oh," said Trisha as she turned with her mom to follow Frida out. "You mean some rooms don't?"

The young baron said after them, "Most have no heat, only fireplaces. You will see. Later, we will have a tour."

Up the long stairway to the left they went, into a narrow, long, and chilly hall. About halfway down the hall, Frida opened two doors and indicated that these were their rooms. She pointed to an adjoining door and said, "*Bad, toilet, ja?*"

"Sure," Trisha agreed and went into her room. Bonnie, grateful to be where she could strip off her clothes and get comfortable, closed her door behind her. The room was about middling large and it was wonderfully warm. Her luggage was there. The furniture consisted of a high, four-poster, a ceiling-high wardrobe, a nightstand topped in silvery gray slate, a small washstand and intricately carved bureau, a brightly painted hope chest at the foot of the bed and all spoke of centuries of age. Not so the bedcovers, which were fresh and clean. The duvet of goose down had a creamy damask envelope and the sheet was of crisp linen in a brown stripe. A set of towels, as creamy as the duvet, was set on the washstand next to a white porcelain bowl and water jug. She opened the closet section of the wardrobe to find coat hangers. The shelves were empty, lined with scented paper ready for her things.

The steam heater in the corner burped and chugged happily. Her bags sat against the bureau. This would be home for a while, she thought, as she hefted the big bag onto the bed. She was glad she'd packed her bathrobe and slippers right on top. As she turned, she glanced toward the French windows and the scene outside pulled her to them.

This was hers now. Long meadows of snow, surrounded by black-green firs and naked maples. A river, thick with ice and rime, meandered through the moguls and she suddenly noticed three well-bundled hikers trudging through the man-high drifts. They carried bird binoculars. Ahead of them trotted deer. She could see no fence, no walls, just wilderness. A fat, furry bunny hopped away from the deer and hikers. Neither the bunny nor the deer had the least fear of the humans. Far to her right was a long wooden building painted dark red with several wide doors. In front were more deer and a couple of small moose eating hay; underfoot were wild birds, a few geese, and ducks. Was this building once the stable? Yes, there was the Saab they'd arrived in, barely visible through an open door. She watched Krister plug in the engine warmer.

A small knock came at the door. She opened it. Frida had a tray covered with a decorated cotton napkin in her hand. "*Varm mjolk? Ja? Bra at somna.*"

"*Uh, tack.*" Bonnie felt any effort at more Swedish would not be in her best interest.

The maid set the tray down and backed out quickly. On the tray was hot milk and rich Swedish cookies composed mostly, she was certain, of real butter and sugar. Well, thought Bonnie, keeping my girlish form will be difficult here. She sighed and started taking off her clothes. A bath would be wonderful.

"Mom!" came Trisha's voice, "there's no shower!"

"Yes, dear, I expected as much," Bonnie replied.

"You go first," Trisha grouched. "At least I can soak after you're through. Oh, yummy, snacks!" And in moments, all but one cookie vanished.

Bonnie smiled. Well, she thought, that takes care of those pesky extra calories. In her tired mind, she wondered how Trisha would take the news. Later, perhaps after dinner. And what about the fact that Sture conjugated his English verbs with enough skill to use future tense? She picked up a fluffy towel and her bathroom supplies. So was he just not accepting his father's death? Was he unable to come to terms with it? Bonnie sighed. Far off in the depths of the castle, she heard a phone ring.

***

Carl-Joran punched off the phone and then on again. Siddhu had finally reached him. The women in the Miami shelter had let him sleep even though Siddhu had called three times wanting to pass on the message that Sture had called him three times. The baron groaned. His phone bill would equal the national debt of a small country. Never before had that sort of thing meant anything to him. His accountant and Inge Person dealt with such mundane affairs. He sighed. The women had awakened him with breakfast. He had slept the entire night and into the day. It would be early afternoon in Sweden. He dialed. Sture answered.

It took some doing to calm the boy down. Yes, Bonnie and Trish were sleeping off their jet lag. So Bonnie wanted to see Inge? Well, no. Because Krister would have to drive to the airport for him. Yes, he would be home tomorrow afternoon and he would get rid of the agents. No more siege on the castle. *Tack gud.* And Astrid could fix a big dinner tomorrow, a real Swedish dinner, boiled potatoes and codfish and sugared carrots, yes. Wonderful. It would all be better tomorrow, he assured Sture. As he hung up, Carl-Joran wondered if that was so. There was a lot to do.

Tammy, grinning with pride and affection, took the giant Carl-Joran by the hand as he came from the room and pulled him along to the dining area. The women they passed all greeted him with sincere respect. He was inside a women's shelter and he was okay. It was a very good feeling. The dining room had been turned into a makeshift staging area for Polly Marie's conversion. The tables had cutout pieces of costume and padding which were being fitted together by a bevy of volunteers. Sherralyn, looking for all the world like a pugnacious black bulldog, hovered around the tall and strikingly beautiful Polly Marie, coaching her in Jamaican.

Hearing him enter, the woman turned to face him, her savior, and smiled all very white teeth. "D'ya like what ya see?" she said, her new Jamaican accent nearly perfect.

"Beautiful!" the baron responded.

"Isn't she great!" the women around her insisted, "she's got it so quick! You'd think she was native."

Sherralyn pointed to the table full of materials. "Next we make her fat."

"And she must be blacker," said Carl-Joran, "and squash her nose, make it wider. And her hair?"

Polly Marie groaned, putting one hand to her nose. "To think I paid several thousand dollars for this nose! What a laugh!"

A woman held up a box full of stage makeup. "She will be a real black mama by the time we're finished!" Another woman shook a large Afro wig loose from its box.

"Okay, back to work," Sherralyn ordered and Polly Marie, laughing, complied.

"What time is her plane?" asked Carl-Joran of Tammy.

"Ten o'clock tonight. She flies directly to Kampala," Tammy said," and she becomes African. But she will have to learn Swahili there. Or whatever language Judge Moabi decides she needs. Luckily, this woman can really learn fast."

"I *was* an actress," came Polly Marie's voice.

"No, my dear," the baron told her, "you are one, still. And you will be the best in Africa."

Breaking away from Sherralyn, the tall woman grabbed Carl-Joran and hugged him. "Do you know how it feels to be free? And safe! Oh, I cannot tell you how good it is. How grateful I am."

He gave her a fatherly hug back and patted her shoulders. He noted that the bruises on her face were fading fast. "We still must get through the Miami airport. I think we will be fine. You have truly become Eauso Valentine."

"Dat right, I'm de woman who jes came from de big island," she said in perfect accent. Everybody clapped.

"I'll put you on the plane," the giant man assured her.

Habib sat comfortably on the rocking old camel while Tahireh scurried on foot to keep up with the donkeys. She applied the switch to the little creatures' behinds with as much energy as any of the boys. When evening set in, they had crested the last sand dune before the rocky plain that surrounded the i-Shibl compound. The high stucco walls of the structure glistened orange from the last of the sunlight. The oasis behind the far corner was surrounded by a busy assortment of traders, nomads, and merchants, some of whom greeted their group as they came to their spot next to the wall. Habib shouted his camel to kneeling. Tahireh did exactly the same as the other donkey boys, getting the beasts to water, unloading, helping to set up camp.

Habib noticed only out of the corner of his eye when she scooped up a large bundle and trotted along with a half-dozen of the boys as they headed for the servants' entrance. It was expected that once a week, the boys were allowed into the compound to get baths and medical care, if needed, and hand-me-down clothes. They'd counted on this. Tahireh disappeared behind the gates and the armed guards. Habib's heart skipped a beat. Now came the real danger.

On the other side of the wall, Princess Zhara, her heart dancing with excitement, looked across the bunch of raggedy donkey boys streaming through the gate. Sweeping majestically along, Zhara came down the courtyard stairs and past the fountain. As she had done for the last six months, she stood beside the nurse and passed out vitamins, checked little heads for lice, pushed clothing into grubby hands and took old clothes from the kids for disposal.

A handsome boy, tall for his age, handed her a bundle. Zhara knew, even before the boy said, "I am from the haji," that this was her rescuer.

"Nurse," Zhara said loudly, "this one has lice. I will take him into the bath and make sure the men scrub him."

The nurse nodded and handed her more lice killer. She was completely uninterested in another urchin. There were so many and she had given up caring.

The princess grabbed the tall boy's shirt and dragged him along until they were out of sight in the hallway. "Come on," urged Zhara, "my rooms are upstairs. I can change there."

Tahireh nodded.

"Did you bring two sets of clothes?" the princess whispered as they entered her room.

"Two sets?" Tahireh asked.

Zhara shook out the bundle of raggedy, dirty clothes. The grimace on her face said it all. "Yes, one for my mother?"

Tahireh put her fingers in front of her mouth, signaling to be quiet and cautious. With extreme diligence, she searched around the large suite of rooms, examining under tables, tapping lights. She could see no obvious microphones, but that meant nothing. She went up to the princess and helped her get the fancy clothes off. "Here," Tahireh found the makeup hidden in the pockets of the scruffy pants. "Every inch of exposed skin must be dark and look dirty. Did you get something with mud in it like we told you?"

"Yes, there are several potted plants. I made their soil from mud," the princess pointed to them over by the window.

Tahireh went to the one whose soil looked the muddiest and smashed the plant onto the floor. She motioned to the princess. It took only moments to cut off most of the girl's long hair and rub the dirt into what was left.

Suddenly the inside door to the suite opened and Tahireh jumped up, pulling her small knife from its scabbard. But it was Jani, the mother, who, upon seeing her daughter now garbed like a boy and as dirty as any other nomad urchin, sucked in her breath and cried, "Oh, oh! What if you are caught! Oh, my precious child."

"You must come with us," said Zhara, who turned accusingly to Tahireh, "she must. Father will have her killed. He will. As soon as he finds out I am gone my mother will have a fatal accident." Zhara grabbed Tahireh's hands and pleading, kneeled before her. "Please, please!"

Tahireh threw back her head. "We have no more clothing. Only so much makeup. And could she…" Tahireh glared at Jani, "can you run alongside the donkeys? Or will you have to ride on a camel?" Tahireh looked directly at the mother who had collapsed onto the bed in sobs.

"Mama!" Zhara shifted her attention to her. "Mama!"

"I could not run very far. I have not been able to be so rebellious as to exercise like my daughter. I am in no condition to be a donkey boy." The woman whimpered.

"Then we'll put you on a camel. We will. I won't have my mother murdered!" Zhara's voice was rising.

"Shhhh," said Jani. "You go. You live. Emil is waiting for you. I will be okay."

"We both know you will be dead in a month," the princess insisted and shook her head at Tahireh, who could only shrug in agreement.

"Your daughter is right." Tahireh knelt down near the princess and finished rubbing dirt into the girl's now bare feet, then into the old, torn tennis shoes before they were put on the little feet. "Do you have any money? Any coins, any jewelry stashed away that you can use to pay the nomads? We simply don't have anything more we can pay them."

Jani was shaking her head. "The vizier cleaned my rooms of anything valuable two days ago. I am sure he suspects we will try to leave. Did he clean your suite, Zhara?"

"Yes." She sighed, "But I have something hidden. It…it was to be a present for Emil. No matter. It will be enough for the tribesmen and it cannot be traced." Zhara went to another, very large potted plant and ripped the entire tree out. From deep inside the dirt, she extracted a leather pouch and handed it to Tahireh who carefully unwrapped it. About four inches across, it was a magnificent American Indian silver belt buckle and it surely was worth more than enough to bribe the Bedouin chief.

"Where...?" Tahireh started to ask.

"In Berlin, before I came home. There are very fine Native American shops there. It was to be an anniversary present for Emil but, well, the school was raided and there I was."

"How did you get to keep it?" her mother asked.

"It was on a belt that was on a crummy pair of jeans in my suitcase. I guess the vizier didn't know what it was, so he left it in the suitcase. I thought I'd better hide it."

A buzzer sounded twice, three times and Jani jumped. "Fifteen minutes to dinner."

"You must go to dinner," said Tahireh, "you must say your daughter is being stubborn and rebellious and that..."

"Tell them I'm on my period," Zhara laughed, "that'll shock them silent."

"Zhara!" Jani did smile though.

"Then come right back here to her rooms." Tahireh grabbed the princess by a shoulder. "Can you take my place with the donkey boys that are leaving right now?"

"Yes, I can." The princess did not hesitate and she smiled, "You have a plan for my mother?"

Tahireh nodded. "As soon as you are outside, find the Haji Mansur. He will be with the Bedouins closest to the fountain. Tell him he will have a wife on the way back. Give him the belt buckle so he can pay the chief. Okay?"

"How do I get the buckle out? The guards often search the boys." Zhara was beginning to think like the rebel she was.

"Do you have tape?" Tahireh asked.

Jani jumped up, "There, on her desk."

"You better go to dinner, Mama," said Zhara, pulling down her pants. Tahireh immediately taped the buckle into the girl's groin. "Owww!" she winced.

"Wait until you rip it off. *That* will be painful!" said Tahireh and pulled Zhara's grubby trousers up over the tape. To Jani, she said urgently, "Go! And come back as soon as you can. I don't relish staying in this room very long. While you're gone, I'll do my best to make a costume for you. Go, hurry."

The woman sucked in her breath, and trembling with anxiety, pulled her veil completely around her face and dashed out.

"Okay, Princess. Your new name is Kahman Ferook. Here is an ID card." Tahireh pulled out a battered little piece of cardboard. It was a costly imitation of the Saudi equivalent of an identi-card. "Remember that you cannot read, so you only know what the haji of your tribe has told you about it. Don't elaborate if you're stopped and questioned, don't say any more than you need to and keep your grammar poor. Okay? Ready?"

"Yes."

They went to the door. Tahireh made her slouch and gave her a heavy slap to both cheeks, turning her face a beet red. "There, that will make you look sunburned under the dirt. Whatever you do, don't mouth off to the guards like the other boys sometimes do. Don't run. You can hurry, but don't be obvious. Blend in and get out."

"I will." Zhara rubbed the back of her now ugly fingernails deeper into the grimy pants. "I'm ready. I can do this." She slipped away down the hallway.

Tahireh, trying very hard to maintain the cool, unperturbed demeanor of the model she was, stepped back into the princess's suite and quickly opened one wardrobe after another. There were many. She chose the oldest robes and the worst T-shirts, some old scarves and long black socks. All of these she rubbed in the dirt of the tipped-over potted plants. Shoes would be a problem. She hoped Zhara would have some old tennis shoes that could be ripped and muddied.

Meanwhile, Zhara slouched past two sets of guards who glanced at her just enough to see that she was headed from the baths with the other boys who had been deloused, and that she was sticking to the path. As she went out the gate, she had a very frightening moment when one ugly guard patted her down. Luckily these old clothes were thick enough to cover her small breasts. She was waved on. She trotted clumsily after the urchins.

Although it seemed to take forever to run the distance around the outside of the compound, it was probably no more than five minutes before she was asking for the haji. A sunburned old Bedouin camel driver pointed to the man in the black abba who sat tending a little campfire of dried dung and roasting his own pot of food. She approached the venerable man and shyly said, "I am Kahman."

"Good," he said, "and where is my donkey boy?"

She shook her head. "Still in my room. He said to tell you that you will have a wife going home with you."

"Ahhh, I will?" the haji nodded with just a hint of surprise in his soft smile. "How will we pay for this wife?"

"I have something." Zhara looked around, saw a tent nearby. "Can I go in there?"

"Of course. And when you come back, you must join the boys over there and eat with them."

She hurried into the tent. The "boy" who'd rescued her was right. It hurt far worse coming off.

Jani i-Shibl ate very little. She simply could not overcome her nervousness. The other women had no such anxiety. They had so much to gossip about no one even asked about Zhara. A casual glance from one of the matrons was all Jani noticed of any merit and as soon as was proper, she slipped away. When she reentered her daughter's rooms, the tall boy, who had jumped into a wardrobe as she entered, came out. He held up a bundle of Zhara's old clothes, now ripped and dirty.

"I was able to find some well-used sandals in here, can you fit in them?" asked the boy, holding up a pair of Zhara's. "We can cut them if you can't."

It took not more than half an hour for Jani to change from a rich Arab woman to a Bedouin hag. Even her teeth got colored. Her posture slumped, she practiced limping. Her entire body and face were covered with rags. Finally she nodded. "I'm ready."

"Yes," agreed Tahireh. "You will be my mother, you will drag me out past the guards. My name is Hussein Amir, you can be Mariah Amir. Let's go. I don't have a card for you. I have one for me, so say you lost yours if the guards stop you. I think if you act it up well enough, that you're angry enough at me for running away from you and hiding here in the compound, you won't be bothered."

"Don't worry, I know what it is to be angry with a stubborn child," she laughed ruefully.

Lights were coming on throughout the compound making the shadows deeper than the darkness filling the bitterly cold sky. Jani really did take Tahireh's arm and really did drag her along, fussing at her in vulgar camp language. A guard at the servants' gate motioned the hag-woman to stop and she bravely cussed him out, cussed all men in general and her son and husband especially. The guard, snorting in derision, let the old woman through.

Tahireh took the lead, filing between the nomads' small campfires. Zhara, sitting with the donkey boys, jumped to her feet, then pretended she'd made a mistake and sat back down.

"Here is your wife, Habib," muttered Tahireh, as they arrived at the haji's little area. "Meet Mariah Amir."

"Delighted," said Habib, "I hope you know how to cook over a campfire and pitch a tent, wife."

"Not since I went camping with the Girl Guides as a child," said Jani, "in the wilds of Wales! I'll do my best though."

"And how are you, Tahireh, my dear?" asked Habib with great concern. Jani looked up at the boy in stunned surprise. She had not suspected for one moment that this urchin was a young woman.

"I'm fine," responded Tahireh in her own voice. "It's time to be a donkey boy again. I'd best go. Happy camel ride!" she said to Jani and walked away.

"Do you want to meet our camel?" Habib asked with a grin.

"Must I, at this moment?"

"No, you will have ample time to be acquainted with the big fellow," laughed Habib and poured them both a cup of campfire chai that steamed in the gusts of sand-filled wind. "And it would be wise if we started to pack him right away. Our group will be leaving in an hour or so. The chief accepted the silver buckle." Habib laughed sharply, "In fact, he knew its exact value. So much for international trade. Your daughter found a bargain, it is quite valuable. Anyway, we will be heading into the desert quickly now."

"We, Zhara and I, won't be missed until morning when we don't show up for breakfast." Jani eyed the tent with wishful eyes. Her soft skin was crinkling already under the brutal desert wind.

"Perhaps, I hope so, and if so, that is good. We will have plenty of time to become one with the sand dunes. Enjoy your hot tea while you can." Habib glanced around and motioned to the chief standing near the camel herd. The ferocious looking man walked up and down the ranks of his tribe, cursing them, pushing some of them and they, in turn, urged the boys to pack the beasts and line up the donkeys.

Inside the compound, Vizier Radi had just gotten around to taking the matron's daily report on the women. He stroked his pointy beard and thought about the fact that the princess had not come to dinner. Was that important? Or merely her usual ploy to upset the status quo? He debated stopping by her rooms. It would be a wise thing to do. At that very moment, the falconer knocked on the office door and announced that his majesty wanted to see how the new owl from Belize would perform. Could the vizier come to the courtyard?

Radi decided that watching a beautiful yellow owl fly would be much more enjoyable than facing down a rebellious girl.

Russ came into the office late. It was not intended, but a multi-car pileup on the icy interchange kept traffic blocked for almost an hour. Most of the secretaries hardly glanced at him. One though, an older woman who sat near the back of the room, waved at him. He had noticed the imitation dreamcatcher on her wall some time ago. One of those Native American wannabes, he sighed. That's all he needed was a woman who wanted to run with the wolves but couldn't or wouldn't lose enough weight to walk to the corner grocer. It just never made sense to Russ. If you knew that by changing some particular behavior you could improve who you were, why would you not do it? Yet, so few made any attempt to do that one thing.

The inner offices were buzzing. Lily held up a sheaf of interoffice memos for him and then leaned over her intercom and said, "Agent Tidewater, Mr. Snow is here."

"Where have you been?" the ugly man's throaty voice preceded his appearance. He stormed out of his office.

"Caught on an overpass, sir, with a lot of other vehicles..."

Shaking his head in frustration, Tidewater pointed to Russ's cubbyhole, "Get in there and get us more information. Los Angeles office just called me. They picked up a police report on a missing or kidnapped woman. The husband's a famous guy and he's sure a shelter in Malibu has his wife. The private investigator he had tailing her was taken out the other night, just like Claybourne was. And the ISF tail."

"Yessir," Russ was very aware that there was no longer any of the proffered camaraderie from his boss, no sign of mentorship, Russ had become merely an employee. "Is there anything further? I mean, how does that missing woman tie into EW or the Ixeys?"

"Nothing on the Ixeys except they're locked away in the Hermelin castle in Norrkoping, Sweden and the agents are freezing their behinds." Tidewater pointed to the messages in Russ's hand. "Look through those. Everything the LA office has dug up is there: a tall black woman being put on a plane from LA to Miami the day after the PI got conked, that Barbara Monday paid for the woman's ticket and got the airline to fly the woman under Monday's name."

"And we know that Monday cancelled her ticket from New York to Miami," Russ couldn't help but say. "Right, I'll go do some digging."

As he entered his cubbyhole, he groaned. This would take some very fancy footwork. He would have to give Tidewater enough information for it to appear that he was fulfilling his job requirements, yet keep the important stuff safe.

"Search," he said to his sleeping computer. "Search air line reservations." By noon, Russ had discovered that although Monday had cancelled her flight to Miami, there existed a flight reservation by the EW from Miami to Stockholm late tonight. While this search was going on, he picked up an instant message that the Agency office in Miami had tracked the black woman's arrival and that she, under the name Monday, had been met by several women. It was the Miami agent's contention that these women had probably been connected to a local shelter, which one he hadn't any idea. There were quite a few shelters in the Miami area alone, not to mention in nearby towns.

So Russ thought and thought. His mind worked furiously. What could he tell Tidewater? He had to tell him what the Miami agent had reported. The reservation to Stockholm? Would the black woman be leaving on that flight? To Sweden? Russ suddenly grinned. No, he told himself. Emigrant Women would not ship a black woman to Stockholm, Sweden. From all indications, the personnel at EW were very, very cunning. If he were they, with their connections, to make sure a tall woman, six feet tall he'd read, was safe from her husband, Russ would have her shipped to Africa. He said aloud, "Search airline reservations to Africa on today's flights for single female passengers."

It took only moments before the computer came up with a half-dozen matches. One to South Africa this morning, four to Nairobi as part of a tour group and one to Kampala nonstop via Cairo and who made the original reservations? Yep, it was as he guessed. Siddhu Singh Prakash. The accountant for EW. Smart. Not that many people, even in the Agency would recognize that that name was a man's name, an Indian man's name, being used for a single woman.

Okay.

After several minutes of serious consideration, Russ decided what to do and what to tell his boss. Within an hour, he and Tidewater were on a plane to Miami.

CHAPTER 10: MAN'S DEATH

A courier, female, in bike togs and helmet, stood by the ticket counter and as the tall black woman in African robes swept up, the helmeted girl asked, "Valentine?"

"Yes." Polly Marie accepted the envelope without a blink and tipped the messenger very well. It was a good exchange. She had now officially become a Ugandan woman, with a Jamaican mother, flying home from Jamaica to be with her dying father. Just like that. The new Eauso Valentine presented her passport and ticket at the counter. Behind her, Sherralyn, dressed in a wildly Jamaican style wrapdress looked like the personal assistant she was supposed to be, pushed a suitcase onto the scale.

"Thank you," Eauso Valentine haughtily said. "I see you when I return."

"Yes'm," responded Sherralyn, playing the part beautifully. She backed away past the waiting passengers and smiling quirkily, glanced toward the potted palms.

Carl-Joran smiled back So far there was no sign of agents. He slid along the walkway and stood by the entry to the big lounge. Valentine, putting her papers into her large shoulder bag, strode past him. He fell in behind her at a discreet distance. One by one everyone passed through the guard stations with the x-rays and metal detectors. Almost there, thought Carl-Joran, almost done and then he could get on the airplane home, he would be in Sweden, be with Bonnie.

It was at that moment he saw Tidewater striding from the other end of the walkway. Did he know? Did he? Carl-Joran stopped behind a kiosk. The American Indian, Snow, came quickly along after Tidewater waving a photo. They paused to look at the photo and Valentine, calm and deliberate, strode right past them. Russ Snow glanced at her and returned his attention to Tidewater and the photo. Tidewater gazed around the long, long room full of people and shook his head. He pointed in the direction that Valentine had gone, although not at her. They started in that direction, Snow lagging behind.

Carl-Joran, quietly as a cat, pounced on Snow, grabbing him, muffling his cry. The very tall man pulled him into a men's room, keeping his wrist locked in an *ikkyo* twist. Snow's face was a mask of terror as Carl-Joran lifted an open palm hissing at him to be still.

Russ did not fight at all. He smiled all teeth as he managed to squeak, "Are you with EW?"

The broad smile on the tall man's face said it all. "Like you are with the Agency."

Russ shook his head emphatically. "No more, I want no more of this. I want out. Let me help you. Please," he begged, "I believe in what you are doing."

The expression on Carl-Joran's face could hardly be more enigmatic. "Help?"

"Yes," Russ tried to squirm and the wrist hold felt like an electric shock up his arm. He gave a soft moan. Carl-Joran let the hold up just slightly.

"How to help?"

Russ grunted with pain. "I know Tidewater's contacts in Saudi and Iran. I know he wants to wipe out EW."

The big man looked very skeptical.

"I have no idea why," continued Russ, his words hurrying, "and he has at least one agent watching Hermelin's castle in Norrkoping, Sweden."

Carl-Joran released Russ's wrist and Russ shook the blood back into his numb, tingling fingers. Slowly, warily, he stood up straight. "I want to join up with you guys."

"With EW?"

"Yes."

"You must prove this," Carl-Joran looked around the edge of the door toward where Valentine, at the boarding gate, was presenting her ticket. Tidewater was nowhere in sight. "How can you prove this?"

"I can help you rescue the Thai girl, maybe."

"You know very much!" Carl-Joran snarled.

"Just about everything," said Russ and again, held up his hands in supplication, "but I haven't told Tidewater much, not since I found out about Milind, the poor little Thai girl in prison. Look, I do want to help."

"I must go find Mr. Tidewater," said Carl-Joran. Towering over Russ, he said down to him, "I will have someone check you out. When he says you are okay, we will tell you." Carl-Joran turned away and started out.

"You mean when Siddhu Singh Prakash says I'm okay?"

The giant man stopped, glanced back. "Yes."

"And if I go to Israel or Kuwait before that?"

"You would end up in Haifa, again waiting, until we are sure." Carl-Joran glared at the man. "You will lose your job here. You will have to pay for your own ticket!'

"Screw the job," Russ insisted, "I've got Indian money out the gazoo. I don't need a damned job with the Agency."

"Okay. Get us all the information you can get, first, before you come to us. Prove your intentions and we will welcome you. Siddhu will be very relieved to have a computer expert on the team."

"You got it." Russ stood up straighter and suddenly laughed out loud. "So you know about me too?"

Carl-Joran merely snorted as he slipped out the door and down the long hall. The KLM plane bound for Cairo and Kampala was already pulling away from the ramp. Valentine was now safe. It was done. He turned back to see Russ Snow hurrying ahead of him, catching up to Tidewater and Tidewater fussing at him as he shrugged, obviously giving some excuse for not finding Polly Marie. Beyond them were Sherralyn and Tammy anxiously watching for Carl-Joran's signal. With a grin, he gave them the okay sign. The two women turned around just ahead of the American agents and arm-in-arm walked away with a light skip in their step.

In an hour, Carl-Joran would be on another plane, destination Amsterdam, then Stockholm. He sighed as he walked toward the SAS gate. He did not want to think about how many hours he'd been airborne during the last week.

Russ Snow, oddly relieved and calm, walked casually behind Tidewater as the little man rampaged around the international departure gates, the HS offices, the check-in counters, and finally the security offices. Tidewater was not a happy man. Hours went by. The whole while, Russ's mind click-clicked over one question, over and over. Who was the giant man with the black hair and beard who could so easily have killed him, or left him incapacitated like the other agents?

Very late, actually early the next morning when he finally stumbled into his apartment, he managed to extend enough energy to pull up the employee list for EW. No one matched. No one. Except, no! He was blonde, and more importantly, he was dead. Baron Carl-Joran Hermelin, the godfather of EW, whose death by car bomb in Cairo was the cause of all the problems now being faced by EW. Six foot six inches tall, forty-eight years old, blonde with bright blue eyes, trained in guerilla warfare in Central America, severely dyslexic, wife deceased, twenty-two-year old son named Sture Nojd Hermelin...

Damn, thought Russ, if this photo had some age lines around the eyes and the hair was dyed black and there was a beard: yes, by the gods, it was Carl-Joran Hermelin, the baron. He was alive. Why the charade? Why pretend to be dead? It seemed a complicated way to get rid of the fatwa that had hung over his head.

Maybe they didn't expect the financial problems. Maybe the crisis with the Swiss banks was not part of the plan. If so, then the EW really was on the edge of disaster. Their agents were strung out on tightrope wires.

Russ fell into bed. He dreamed wild, escape-filled dreams. He dreamed about a land he had never seen. He dreamed about his mother's brother racing a pinto horse across the prairie and as the wind whipped his braid, he said to Russ, who seemed to also be riding a horse, galloping alongside, he said, "The creatures know the way."

Tahireh did the best she could with Zhara, who got frustrated easily. After dropping the third rope when a donkey nibbled at her arm, Zhara went stiff, fists clenched, teeth gritting, stifling a scream.

"Either you behave like a donkey boy or you will die," Tahireh spoke harshly, "and many of us along with you."

The donkey boys all nodded and began railing at the princess, slapping their thighs, pointing, and shaking their hands. Zhara's eyes clouded up with tears.

"No!" said Tahireh and the boys chorused that.

With great effort, the slight girl, shaking with stress and fear, began doing her assigned chore again. Slowly, deliberately, she tied the third donkey's rope to the second donkey's tail. One or two tears started down her cheeks, but blew quickly away in the wind. She moved on to the fourth donkey and Tahireh and the boys nodded and smiled and went back to their own chores.

The tribe's brief market visit had been a good one, profitable, and all the trade goods had to be sorted as to which beast would carry them. The tents had to be struck and personal belongings stowed. Yet, all this work was familiar to the group and it was done in a rhythm that made it go quickly. In less than an hour, the donkeys started out across the sand urged on by the boys, including Zhara. Not far behind, the camels followed.

Jani sat sidesaddle on Habib's beast, her face wrapped as tightly as possible against the fine sand that, kicked up by the animals, was caught by the night wind and twirled around like small tornadoes.

The hours rolled by. Habib walked steadily on and Jani marveled at the strength in the old man. Well, he wasn't that old, Jani mused, maybe in his late forties, but one ages faster out here in the desert, one truly does. The dunes, the brush, the stars wavering, shimmering in the wind…her eyes were so heavy. Abruptly, Habib was picking her up from the soft, warm sand, shaking her gently from a dream.

"Oh my God!" she laughed aloud. "I fell asleep. On a camel, I fell sound asleep!"

"If the camel had not jumped a little at that moment, I would not have known you'd left my company." Habib brushed sand from the rags covering her head. "Will you walk for a while?"

Jani looked at the saddle and laughed again. "Lucky I landed where I did, in a heap of sand. Yes, I'll walk with you."

Habib took her hand and, his eyes smiling, said, "It is common to relax profoundly at this stage of the journey, of your journey to freedom. You could have landed on rocks and merely bounced. You must not let your guard down though. You must stay alert. Come along, it is time to hurry and catch up to the group."

They moved on, falling into place in the long parade of camels and donkeys and Bedouins. Into the night they trekked, following an ancient trail, guided by the icy bright stars, on and on. Jani grew amazed at her own energy. She thought how she would probably be stiff and sore tomorrow. Yet there was no doubt she was now awake and striding along like Habib. What affection she had for this man, this haji. In her whole life, she had never met a truly brave man. She had doubted such men even existed and here one was rescuing her. Her life was in his hands.

A donkey brayed, reminding her that Zhara was somewhere near the front. Jani hoped her daughter was doing as well as she, that Tahireh was watching over her, urging her on, keeping her focused. Out of all this, perhaps her Princess daughter would be transformed. Perhaps this real danger, these real heroes, would give the spoiled child the shock of reality she had always needed. The troop was coming to a heavily graveled path between cliffs. She felt Habib's gentle, rough-skinned hand slip out of hers. He took the camel rope with both hands to urge the beast along.

"A stream bed millennia ago," he explained, "sometimes there are sharp stones and the beasts balk."

She didn't care. She knew she wouldn't stumble. "How far?" she asked.

"Until we reach the Land Cruiser at the oasis."

"Is that what awaits us?"

He nodded, "If we proceed as we are, I would say just after dawn."

"And then?"

"To the American air base in Kuwait," said Habib. "By tomorrow night you will be a lieutenant's wife on her way to Switzerland."

"Amazing," whispered the woman covered in rags. "Amazing."

The blackness outside was absolute. Only ice-bright stars and a pale, timid new moon gave any light and it seemed circumspect and selfish. Bonnie's glance at the bedside clock told her she had napped for almost an hour and a half and in that time, the sun had slipped behind the world and night had returned. Five p.m. and her stomach was insisting it be fed breakfast. Really insisting.

She put on one of the pair of new wool slacks she'd bought in San Francisco, the brown pair and a soft yellow turtleneck pullover and a knitted vest. Time to search out the kitchen, she thought and wondered if she should wake Trisha. She opened Trish's door a crack. No sign of her. Knowing her appetite, her stomach had probably already awakened her and sent her in search of food.

Down the big stairs, along the wide corridors, and suddenly delicious smells pointed Bonnie's nose in the right direction. In a giant dining room, she found Trisha standing next to a long banquet table, looking forlorn and lost.

"Hey, Mom." Her eyes moved to a big door that, by best guess, led to a kitchen. "I got this far. I don't know if we're supposed to knock, or shout or just go in there."

"My extensive experience with servants says we just go in," said Bonnie.

"Mom, the only servant you ever had in your life was a Mexican cleaning woman who made you help her move the furniture so she could vacuum." Trisha leaned toward the big door.

Bonnie shrugged, "Yes. Well. Come on, I'm starving." Bonnie opened the big door. The wonderful odors of dinner flooded out and Trisha groaned. Bonnie stepped in, followed closely by her daughter who hovered like a basketball guard. The kitchen was huge. The left side of the room was dominated by a fireplace obviously designed for cooking for large crowds. A small cow could have been spitted in there and there would be room left for the soup pot. Modernity was in evidence though with the lovely giant gas chef stove and oven taking up the center of the room. Around it, from a metal strip attached to the high ceiling, hung pots and pans and numerous utensils. On the stove were several pots, bubbling. The two women eased past the refrigerators and walk-in freezer toward the long prep table. Behind it was a nook table with bench seats. Standing at the prep table, lining up plates, was a sturdy woman, aproned, her white-blonde hair braided onto her head in two rings covered by a net.

"*Ah, velkommen!*" said the woman, "*Sie ar den Amerikanishers, jo?*" She waved a massive, callused hand at them.

"*Ja,*" said Bonnie.

"*Ja, so.*" The woman wiped her hands on her apron and held out the right one. "*Jag heter Astrid.*"

"Astrid, the cook." Bonnie confirmed.

"*Ja,*" the woman pointed a plate at the nook. "*Aten sie middag?*"

"*Ja!*" exclaimed Trisha and sat promptly. Bonnie sat next to her and Astrid served up plates of steaming noodles with slices of meatloaf-looking stuff. The vegetable was Brussels sprouts, and to Bonnie's amazement, Trisha devoured them, cleaning her plate in a flash and asking for seconds.

"Really good, Mom, really good," she said between bites.

Astrid smiled, pleased and, reaching into the bigger refrigerator, pulled out a bowl of what looked like trifle. Bonnie, inwardly, groaned. She definitely was going to have to take up indoor tennis or cross-country skiing and both in the same day, anything that was very, very energetic.

The maid, Marie, came into the kitchen and told Astrid something, at which the large woman retrieved a serving tray and served up a meal for Marie to take away. Noticing Bonnie's gaze, Astrid said, "*Fur den ung herre.*"

Trish looked at her mother. Bonnie translated, "For the young lord." Trish said, "Ahhh."

Astrid nodded and said in a level of Swedish meant perhaps for a child, "*Han lasa bokker. Han studera den kvall. Han sager er vilyan television bevittna? Eh, television?*" With a flourish, she grabbed out another serving tray and put two bowls of the trifle-like dessert onto it, with spoons and napkins. "*Kaffee?*" She held up a cup.

"*Nej fur me, tack,*" Bonnie responded. "Coffee, Trish?"

"No," she shook her head. "Beer?"

"Be-er?" Astrid shook her head, shrugging. Trish went to the refrigerator and looked inside. Not there.

"Look in the pantry," suggested Bonnie. "No one in Europe drinks cold beer."

"*Warm* beer?" said Trish and went to the pantry. She held up a can. "Could this be it? It says *ol.*"

"Ahh," nodded Astrid, "*Jo! Ol.*" She pronounced it like oil. She took the can from Trisha, found a glass beer mug and poured out the can of pale beer and handed it to Trish. "*Ol.*"

Trish sipped it. "Yep, beer. Not bad tasting either."

"Television?" Astrid asked again, picking up the tray.

"Sure," said Trish.

Bonnie said, "I really wanted to talk to Sture tonight, about the papers." She got up and followed Trish and Astrid down the hall.

Astrid looked around at Sture's name, "*Den herre studera.*"

"Studying?" Trish guessed and Bonnie nodded, "Yes, well, he is in medical school."

They were led to a small room about halfway down the hall. Warm and comfortable, with a big cushy sofa and two reclining chairs, the room was strictly modern. The television was actually a small movie screen and, after setting down the dessert tray, Astrid indicated where the controls were and pointed to a shelf full of videotapes. "Film? Okay?"

"Sure," Trish agreed, "thank you."

"*Tack so mycket,*" said Bonnie and Astrid, bowing a couple times, backed out of the rooms. It took Trisha only moments to figure out how to get the set on and where the channels were.

"Must be satellite," she said and flipped through the offerings. Every conceivable language came at them. "Oh!" said Trish as the Finnish channel came through, "are they doing what I think they're doing?"

"Looks like it, kiddo," laughed Bonnie.

"Right at dinner time, with no warnings on the channel info."

"The Scandinavian countries have a much more relaxed attitude about sex," Bonnie explained.

Trisha clicked through a bunch more channels with the same activities. "Guess so. Boy, the moral right in the US would have kitten-conniptions and then some."

Bonnie ate a few bites of her trifle, then made a decision. "I'm going to see if I can find *den herre.* You stay and enjoy."

"Notice something, Mom? Notice that there isn't one single violent movie on? Not one. It's like Lassie reigns. Lassie on half the channels and fun and games in saunas on the others."

"Interestingly enough," said Bonnie as she headed for the door, "I read an article some months ago that quoted statistics on teenage pregnancy in relation to sexual attitudes and the teens in Scandinavia have, by far, the smallest percentage of teen pregnancy, the fewest abortions per girl, and the healthiest babies of those who are born to teen moms."

Trish looked up at her, "Really? Early sex education does that?"

"Probably more than mere sex education," said Bonnie, "the entire society itself has different expectations for their kids, for example, there has been equality for women, and men, insisted upon for over seventy years. Men take paid child-care leave as easily as a woman, for up to two years. Plus, well, a lot of things contribute, and underlying it all, an excellent health care system which insists on preventive medicine first."

"If I even hinted to my high school health class that we were going to show porno, my butt would be fried and fired so fast! The powers-that-be wouldn't give me time to clean my desk!" Trisha went back to channel surfing. "You're off to find Sture?"

Bonnie nodded. Her original intention of getting Trisha and Sture together would not happen this evening, she was certain, and it was for the best. They should have an opportunity to at least get to know each other better, to come to more familiar terms. So, barring that goal being reached in one evening, the first evening, Bonnie thought it likely she could get into the den and use some of her expertise in information research. She was completely intrigued over Sture's use of English verb tenses.

"Actually, I'm going to look into the family history if I can." She smiled, thinking, that was one way to put it, and closed the door behind her. First she would have to get a sweater. The castle was quite cold. As she ascended the grand stairs, the ancestors in the portraits looked down on her. These were not angry people, nor overly proud and arrogant people. The Hermelins had expressions, for the most part, of contentment and satisfaction. The dates on the plaques on the paintings ran oldest at the bottom of the stairs to most recent at the top. In the alcove on the top landing were two she hadn't noticed her first time up the stairs, but then she was very jet lagged and wanting only a bath and a nap. The one was of Carl-Joran at about forty-five, tall and blond, with the slightly off-center features of his ancestors. His eyes held a sadness she would not have expected, like the grief of millennia had lodged in them. Next to him, and much younger when she was painted, was, Bonnie read the plaque: Heda Lind Hermelin, nee Bergshem, wife of Carl-Joran, Baron Hermelin, with the dates of birth and death. But Carl-Joran's gave only the date of birth. Had Sture not got to this yet?

Feeling the chill of the hallway, Bonnie moved on toward her room. The fleeting question of whether or not she should have her portrait put up was only momentary, more as a private joke. She truly felt an outsider. Sture was the natural inheritor here, and she did not want all of this on her conscience.

As for Sture, she heard music coming from the first door on the left after the alcove and was assured that the young man was diligently memorizing medical terms or figuring out how to cut open a patient. She hurried on and retrieved the thick sweater she'd packed in the duffel and headed back down the grand stairway. As she had guessed, the door to the den was not only not locked, it was standing open and one of the soft, indirect lights above the giant bookcases was on. Sture was not a naturally suspicious person, nor was the castle staff accustomed to security needs. Bonnie slipped into the den, let her eyes adjust and set about learning the filing system of the room.

It was what she, being a skilled librarian and researcher, generously called informal. No secretary had ever touched this collection of papers and bills and letters. One out box was labeled *bokforare*, and from what was stacked high there, she could assume was for an accountant. Another outbox read *advokat*, and she knew that meant attorney. Next to the telephone was a largish phone-memo-calendar book. In it were scribbled notations in various dates, plus phone numbers. She saw her and Trish's arrival noted, she saw on previous dates appointments for Sture with advokat Person and with other people—his professors possibly? And her eye caught the notation for tomorrow: one p.m. Krister *pa flygplats*. Krister had to be at the airport at one p.m.? Why? Who for? She gently rifled through the other papers scattered on the big desk. Sture's handwriting gave full evidence that he was to be a physician. It was barely legible. Stick-em notes to call Person, notes about Algbakdel, notes about the Ixeys with exclamation points after, notes about things that must be done in the castle and notes regarding the EW and...*far*. What about *far*, his father? The little she could interpret had to do with kronor and Swiss accounts. Not surprising, but not illuminating. She sighed. There was nothing that would explain the boy's English language quirks that she could decipher anyway.

Faintly, along the hallway, came the sound of footsteps. She slipped quickly to the door and peeked out. Her daughter, Trisha, was headed back to the kitchen. Bonnie smiled. She ducked out, leaving the light and the door as she had found them, and went back to watch the night's offering of Swedish television. Trisha appeared to have settled on a satellite channel of English programs with Swedish subtitles. Hercule Poirot was busy solving a case that she, Bonnie, already had read the ending to years ago. Oh, well, she liked the actor, she enjoyed the British accents, and she decided it wouldn't hurt to finish her bowl of trifle.

The beautiful yellow owl from Belize had enjoyed its moments of comparative freedom. It had flown well in the cool of the late evening. Everyone had enjoyed the sight, including Vizier Rida. Later as he left his duties behind him and headed for his quarters and his wives, he had only a momentary glitch of conscience about the plight of a tropical owl in the heat of the desert. Rarely did these magnificent birds live longer than three months at most. Air-conditioned and luxuriant cage-mews merely postponed the inevitable.

He paused at the back stairs, wondering if he had forgotten something. Whatever it was nagging at him would have to wait. He was hungry and he wanted to go home and he had had enough of the sultan's demands and family squabbles.

It was early morning, still dark, when Russ tossed a ring of duplicate keys onto the counter and Freddie, slowly, with deliberation as he did so, picked them up. Next, Russ pushed an addressed messenger delivery envelope across the counter. "At noon tomorrow exactly. That way it'll be delivered minutes before five p.m."

"You really doing this? You really flying off to Israel?"

"Yep." Russ slid onto a seat at the counter, patted his pocket where his official papers and passport were hiding.

Freddie took the ring of keys and put them in his pants pocket. He took the envelope and stuck it in the slot under the cash register. "Okay. I think you burning your bridges. One great conflagration. Whoom! All gone." He poured Russ a cup of coffee. "The Agency don't take kindly to guys trying to burn their bridges with them. I doubt you can do it, completely."

"How about some breakfast before my cab comes?" asked Russ, the butterflies in his stomach more obvious than he'd care to admit. He sipped his coffee.

"Sure thing. What you want?"

"Big bowl of oatmeal, toast."

Freddie hollered the order back to the lone breakfast cook, then sat across from Russ. "How'd you get onto an El Al flight so quick anyway? My cousin and his church group took them a month just to get reservations."

"Computer stuff," smiled Russ. "Besides, I'm not going El Al. I'm taking another route that puts me in Geneva first. It's okay, don't worry. Israeli security will let me in. I got a high level passport."

"Yeah, until your boss reads your letter of resignation this evening." Freddie reached around and got the bowl of oatmeal and the plate of toast and put it in front of Russ. "There gonna be fireworks in that office like you never saw! You gonna be lucky if the man doesn't put a hit out on you."

"The Agency doesn't do that sort of stuff anymore." Russ made an effort to eat.

"Yeah, sure." Freddie poured himself some coffee. "An' my Aunt Tillie still don't smoke cigars."

"They don't," Russ insisted.

"You watch, someone'll catch up to you about when you land in Tel Aviv. More 'an that, inside a month, the IRS'll be auditing your Indian money accounts…"

"They can't. The accounts are in Canada and I got access with British banks as well as Canadian. Hey, my mom knew what she was doing both when the tribe was paid reparations and when they bought their land back with casino profits. Mom put almost every penny in long-term bonds and Canadian investments."

"Smart move." Freddie nodded, "Maybe you'll do all right, Injun. Maybe you'll rescue the girl and do all right."

Russ pulled the picture of Tahireh out of his coat pocket. "Think she's worth all this?" He slid the computer printout across the counter.

The older man put the fingers of one hand delicately on the edge of the printout. "You going halfway round the world to rescue this lady? You either nuts or some crazed warrior on his vision quest. That's what I say."

"Didn't think of it that way before," said Russ, his stomach suddenly calming down. "Yeah, this is like a vision quest. Never been on one, really, maybe this is what it is."

"Seems like it to me," said Freddie.

A taxi horn beep-beeped out in front of the cafe and Freddie pointed with his jaw, "You gotta go."

"Yes," Russ Snow-from-Night-Sky agreed, "I gotta go. Take care of my place and my jeep, okay?"

"Sure, 'course I will. You be careful. Send me a postcard. Or two.' The tall Cheyenne clasped Russ's arm in a mutual farewell. "I envy you. I know inside here," he clapped the palm of his right hand onto his left breast, "you're doin' the right thing."

"Thank you, Fred. You're a good friend." Russ pulled away and grabbing up his big suitcase and shoulder bag, dashed out the door to the waiting taxi.

The night flight from Miami to Frankfurt passed uneventfully for the baron. He awoke as the tires screeched on the tarmac. He had only a two-hour wait until the connecting flight left for Stockholm, enough time for some breakfast and a good cup of German coffee. Before the seat belt sign turned off, he had his gear from the overhead and was ready to disembark. The attendants were too busy with some small children at the back of the plane to notice the big man who was leading the passengers to the airlock.

As the gate extension clunked into place and the airlock opened, Carl-Joran wondered if he needed to call his son again and he decided it wasn't necessary. The boy would be anxious enough and Krister certainly would not dream of being late arriving at the airport. Unless the car broke down or the snow closed the roads or...No, he thought, everything will go fine. Then he would be at the castle and he would face Bonnie.

About the time Bonnie and Trisha were peeking out from under their snuggly duvets and facing an icy cold morning, and Russ's first leg of his journey was landing him in Geneva, and Carl-Joran was pacing back and forth in the waiting area for the SAS flight out of Frankfurt, the vizier of Sheikh Sultan i-Shibl's compound was adjusting his gold turban as he hurriedly strode toward the women's dining area. He had been rudely awakened not twenty minutes before by a guard who had been told by the women's matron that the first wife and oldest daughter had not appeared for breakfast and neither responded to knocks on their doors.

Rida had brushed off the guard with a they-probably-went-riding-very-early.

"Yessir," the guard replied, not caring one way or another, and ambled back to his patrol duties. But deep inside, Rida knew he had slipped up. He had not looked in on those two last night. He felt that awful sinking feeling in his gut that prefaced something bad, very, very bad. He brushed some lint off his coat, the simple white one as he did not want to bother with all the buttons on the purple one, and composing himself into the strong ogre his role called on him to be, he went into the women's dining area.

The babble of women's voices stilled instantly. Second wife held her breath and looked at the pillows where Jani and Zhara should be sitting at the long table, and weren't. Rida did not say a word. As he turned to leave, he heard a couple of the women giggle. They had no pity, those women. It was as cruel in there as out on a battlefield, as cutthroat as politics. The women showed no gratitude at all for their luxury and protection. He shook his head in censure. What further proof could there be of the inferior personality of women? He hurried down the hall, past the many bedrooms, and to Jani's room.

He called out her name, as he was supposed to do, and when no answer came, he knocked and waited. Nothing. He pushed open the door. The bed had not been slept in, the room was a disaster—clothes and shoes pulled from the closet, tossed on chairs and the bed. At Zhara's room, he didn't bother to call out her name or even knock. He went directly in. Neither had her bed had been slept in. Most telling was the astounding chaos of clothes and tipped over potted plants and ripped rags and piles of shoes. For one fraction of a second, he had hopes that the women had been taken against their will. That idea was squashed quickly. They had been taken all right, but they had gone in disguise and they had gone most willingly. This would cost him his job, perhaps his life. He was doomed.

Thinking on his feet, he decided that before awaking the sheikh, he would mobilize the guards to canvas the merchants and travelers outside the compound wall. Some mitigation in his punishment could come from obtaining every bit of information possible before laying his neck on the block. At the top of his lungs, he shouted for the guards, then he pulled the cell phone from his pocket and called his lieutenant of security.

Within an hour, he knew who had come and gone from the compound yesterday and last night. No motor vehicles, except for the grocery transport, had entered and left the compound. Three caravans—two merchant groups with both jeeps and camels and one nomadic Bedouin group with a camel and donkey caravan had departed. None of the merchants and no Bedouin had entered the compound, or so yesterday's gate guards reported. The last caravan to depart, as night was falling, was the nomadic Bedouin and they had struck out across the roughest terrain toward the northeast. He very much doubted that two very spoiled and pampered women would be riding camels into that territory with wild Bedouin. Thus it had to be one of the two merchant groups with jeeps.

Back in the compound, he went to his office. For almost fifteen minutes he debated whether to tell the sheikh first or call Commander Yusef. Finally, the worried man raised his voice to Allah and begging forgiveness, he also cried, *"Allah u abha!"* (God the magnificent!) hoping such praise would save his butt. Then he called Commander Gurgin Yusef.

Tidewater struggled out of a very intense dream that included powerful strobe lights, hovering helicopters whose rotors buffeted him in the backwash…

"Wake up, Marion!" Arletta, his wife ordered in her most demanding tone of voice. "You have a call coming in."

"What the hell time is?" he mumbled, sitting up, running his hands across the bald top of his head. "Uhhhh."

"Quarter after midnight." She pulled her old terry cloth robe around her with one hand while she pushed the phone into his face with the other. "Your secretary?"

"Fuck. Why did she get a long distance call meant for me? At midnight?" Tidewater grabbed the phone, clicking the talk button as he walked into the bathroom. He took a long piss while Lily frantically explained that Commander Gurgin Yusef in Saudi Arabia was insisting on satellite surveillance now! "Wait, wait," said Tidewater, stumbling back to sit on the edge of the bed.

Lily did not wait, she went on, "Yusef connected to us by cell phone and radio transmission that always gets shunted to me. Yusef has mobilized an elite search team and they're headed for the i-Shibl compound. He's calling from his Humvee."

"i-Shibl. The sheikh with the daughter who was taken out of that school in Paris and brought back to Saudi. Okay. I'm with you. And?" Tidewater shook the recumbent form of his wife and, covering the mouthpiece of his phone, barked at her, "Get me a cup of coffee. Strong."

"Get your own damned coffee, I have to be at a Republican Women's breakfast meeting at six a.m." Arletta turned further away from her husband.

"Damn it," the man snarled and finding he was awake enough to walk without stumbling, he headed toward the kitchen as Lily continued, "Both the mother and daughter have disappeared. The vizier, the sultan's vizier, believes they were taken away last night by a merchant caravan. Yusef is certain Emigrant Women had something to do with their kidnapping."

Uncovering the mouthpiece, calming his voice as he fumbled for a cup and the instant coffee, Tidewater interrupted her monologue and declared firmly, "Patch me through to the commander, Lily."

"Yessir. Shall I put it onto this phone or your cell phone, sir?"

"My cell phone. As soon as I have clothes on, I'm headed for the office."

"What should I tell Commander Yusef, sir? About using satellite surveillance?" Lily inquired.

Tidewater punched minutes into the microwave control and pushed the start button. "Should be able to get a linkup. Tell him I'll know more once I'm in the office. I'll need the exact latitude and longitudinal coordinates. Oh, and call Snow. I want that Injun on the computers. He may be a heathen, but he's damned smart. Right? Anything else?"

Lily yawned over the phone, "No sir, 'cept, do I get overtime for all this?"

"Yes, Lily, yes." He clicked off the phone and dropped it into its cradle. The microwave buzzer went off and Tidewater grabbed up the coffee and headed back to the bedroom to put on clothes. Jeans, a long-sleeved shirt, and his black SWAT team jacket would be best. Without compunction, he flicked on the bedroom overhead light.

"You pig," muttered Arletta and pulled the covers over her head.

Tidewater's only consideration as he rummaged for his jeans was: should he call the Darughih of Iran yet? Or savor for a while longer the powerful man's ignorance of what was transpiring there on the Saudi desert, almost under his nose? Nothing would make Marion Tidewater happier than to dangle some EW people in front of Sadiq-Fath and out of his reach. Why not? Tidewater put on deodorant, scrubbed his teeth, and brushed the friar's ring of remaining hair. He pulled on a pair of thick socks. He found the SWAT jacket in the hallway, slipped it on, zipped it up. Found his tennis shoes by the back door, pulled them onto his feet and velcroed them shut. Leaving the coffee untouched on the bureau and the bedroom light on to deliberately provoke Arletta, Tidewater hastened out the front door to the Agency car parked in his driveway.

Dr. Legesse had her hands full. Devi sat across from her desk griping the arms of the chair tightly. "It's the same, Doc, we get them in here and then they freak out and want to go home. Fumilao is going nutso. She thinks her husband's brothers are on their way here to kill her and take her daughters."

"She could be right, Devi," said Halima, "you know that, you know we *never* underestimate the potential of these men for violence." Halima leaned forward, "I thought though, that Fumilao and her daughters were doing okay, that they were ready to go with Rachel to the drug treatment center today."

"They are," said Devi, "Dr. Bar-Fischer will be here around noon. I mean, these girls can't be any safer than they will be up there on the hill. That treatment center was designed to keep in even the meanest Israeli Defense Force vets with posttraumatic stress and high on speed. It's very tight security."

"Then let's take a look at what's going on with Fumilao. Is it just her," asked Halima, "or are the girls upset too?"

"The girls are upset 'cause the mom's upset, but only Mom wants to go home."

Dr. Legesse nodded and rose, "Come on, we'll talk with them."

Esie and Jo, the two Makwaia girls, sat, legs dangling, on the high serving counter in the nearly empty dining room. Another mom, with three kids, was cleaning lunch dishes from her table and getting ready to take the kids to the playroom. She glanced now and then at Mrs. Makwaia, and smiled. She knew that nothing she could say or do would help, although she had been in that exact same emotional crisis herself, back at the beginning of her stay. The doctor would help, that she did know. She gathered up her children and left as Dr. Legesse and Devi entered.

Esie, Fumilao's younger daughter, was crying, sobbing, her tiny pixie face wracked with tremulous shivers. "Don't go back, Mom, don't go back. Jo will be cut, Jo will be cut! You can't do that, Mom!"

Jo's face was of stone, her entire body seemed in rigor mortis, perhaps preparing herself for the ordeal of circumcision that she had, ever so briefly, thought she'd escaped. No words came from her. Her lips were stretched taut in fear.

Fumilao Makwaia, her stout form quaking, paced back and forth, back and forth, brushing aside chairs. "What can I do? Your father's brothers will kill me. They could kill you, kill you both. They will be so angry because I take you away. You will not marry properly, you have been taken from the family, you will be…"

"Gone!" exclaimed Esie, "Gone far away! We wanted that, Mom, Jo wants that. She doesn't want her private parts cut off. She wants to be a real woman. Don't you, Jo?" The young girl screeched, "Not like you, Mom, she wants to be a whole woman!"

Jo frozen mute nodded and at Esie's words, Fumilao shuddered, hugging herself in pain.

Dr. Legesse stepped in front of the pacing Fumilao. "Stop."

The Ugandan woman stopped, clenched her fists.

"Sit," ordered Dr. Legesse.

Slowly, in profound emotional turmoil, Fumilao sat on a chair. Both Halima Legesse and Devi pulled up chairs and sat next to her. Halima looked at her watch, then looked at the clock on the wall. Both read ten minutes to one. Firmly, but with utmost kindness, the very tall black doctor took Fumilao's black hands, "When you were back in the village, what happened at noon?"

Gasping for a breath, Fumilao shrugged, "Oh, it is noon in Uganda. I…I…we…go to the mine, we take the men lunch."

"So," continued the doctor, "about fifteen minutes ago, you suddenly panicked. The habit of going to the mines is strong, your body and mind were telling you it was time for the women to take lunch to the men. Is that right?"

Comprehension seeped into the terrified woman's soul. "Oh, oh, oh! Yes. Yes. Is that it? I feel I must go to the men, if I don't go, I will be beaten."

"How many years has this happened?" asked Devi quietly.

"Since I was a small child, for my father, now for my husband and his brothers. Thirty years." Fumilao shivered. "Thirty years I have walked that path to the mine, taking lunches. Here I am, I cannot go. They will be furious and they will come after me and they will beat us."

"If you were there, that is what would happen," Halima said softly. "But you are here and you are safe."

"Yes, I am here. Esie and Jo are here. The men do not know where we are. They cannot know. We were so careful to escape undetected. Judge Moabi disguised us." She breathed. Long sighs of breath began to relax her.

Devi scooted her chair closer and put an arm over the woman's shoulders, "You must realize that this can happen for a long time, that you can have reactions like this. It's called a flashback, okay?"

"Fumilao," said Halima, "sometimes these sensations can be so strong you can actually imagine your husband right here in the room. We will show you a technique tonight to help you through these moments. As soon as you get into the treatment center, Dr. Bar-Fischer will teach you. It's called a desensitization procedure."

"Anything," wailed Fumilao, "anything to make this fear go away. I cannot believe I considered going back. Oh, God!"

Esie climbed off the serving shelf and threw her arms around her mom. "Mom, don't scare us like that again. You gotta know, we wouldn't have gone with you. Right, Jo?" She glanced at her sister who mutely nodded. "But we'll stay with you here, we'll be by your side."

Fumilao broke into sobs, hugging Esie. "I'm okay now. We're okay." Between sobs, she asked Dr. Legesse, "When do we go to the treatment center?"

"In about an hour. Then, as soon as you learn how to do that desensitization technique, probably in a couple days, maybe as long as a week, you'll be sent to Sweden."

"That will be a big shock!" laughed Devi.

"Why?" the mother stopped crying. "The weather? It is much colder, I know."

Dr. Legesse grinned, "Nah. Because in Sweden women are equal to men. It will take some getting used to."

Jo timidly spoke up, "You mean I can continue with school? Both Esie and I?"

"All the way through college if you want," replied Devi.

"Wow," said Jo, the rigid face melting into a smile. "I want to be wildlife biologist. That's what I'm gonna be."

"I'm gonna be an actress," said Esie proudly. "I really am!"

The tall black doctor got to her feet, "And so you shall." She turned to Devi, "I must return to my office. Baron Hermelin should be calling in and I'm becoming worried about Mansur. He should check in with us soon to make arrangements for later this afternoon when they reach the American air force base in Kuwait."

"Nothing from him or Tahireh yet?" asked Devi.

"No," Halima shook her head. "Nothing."

At first she wasn't sure whether the wind or the stillness was worse. Above, on the dunes, the wind screamed. The spitting sand tore at everything making it impossible to see the front camel of the caravan or the donkey at the end behind them. For hours, Jani had walked step-by-step in the haji's wake, so close to him, she could smell the sandalwood fragrance of his robes. All around them the dunes moved, shifting like giant snakes. What little of her skin was exposed had been scraped raw. Entering the wadi was a shock. A silence as solid as the forty-meter high walls on each side of them descended like a thick golden-brown theatre curtain. The camels had to pass one by one through the narrow gorge and the walls grew higher and higher. The front camels began to scramble faster and their camel tugged on the rope in Habib's hands.

"Can you feel the moisture?" he asked Jani.

She let the scarf and hood fall from her face. The water in the air was like perfume. "Ahhh, yes. It's heavenly!"

"Get ready, our camel knows its there. We may have to trot to keep up." He smiled at her.

Five minutes ago, she would have collapsed if he'd told her that. "I'm ready. Can we all jump in the water?"

Habib's laughter echoed along the canyon, "I wouldn't recommend it. The camels all go in first."

"I might have known," said Jani and skipped along faster.

They came out of the narrow passageway as suddenly as they entered. The walls soared to the sky in glorious shades of red and gold and ochre and yellow and covering nearly the entire lowest part of the great chasm was a vast pool of sheer green water. Sounds bounced from one wall to the other in a symphony of noisy camels yowling, donkeys braying, men shouting, women singing. Another group of Bedouins was at the far end of the canyon, settled, camels and donkeys lazing in the water, tents and cooking fires all organized. Women washing clothes in the higher streams. The greetings were joyous and uncomplicated. Before long the newly arrived group was comfortably arranged. It was all Jani could do to not look around for her daughter. She knew she mustn't. She knew she must look exactly like the haji's wife. She kept her head down and began unloading their camel.

"Do we put up our tent?" she asked in a whisper.

Habib shook his head. "You and I, in a couple minutes, take the duffels, here," he handed her a heavy canvas bag, "and start walking toward that clump of palm trees. See them? Far up at the other opening to the wadi?"

She nodded.

"As we pass the donkey boys, Tahireh and Zhara will make their way along the same path. You three will go get the Land Cruiser started. I must make ritual farewells to the chief of the tribe. It is required to show our gratitude."

"I should imagine so," said Jani. "They risked their lives."

"It all comes round. One day they will need the EW's services and we will be obligated to help, which we will do gladly. The Bedouin are resilient people, but their culture is under a lot of pressure to change from nomadic to urban. Those tribespeople who have given up and gone into the cities usually perish quickly." Habib carefully finished unloading the camel and covered the tent and equipment for retrieval by the tribespeople he'd borrowed them from. He grabbed up the second duffel, looked casually around, and began walking. Jani, staggering with her smaller canvas bag, did her best to keep up.

Habib was taking one of the many grooved paths leading along the edge of the water. Since her head was down, properly down, Jani did not realize they'd come to the donkey troupe until a sudden movement and Jani felt the weight of the bag lifted. Tahireh had taken it. Glancing furtively behind her, Jani saw the two dirty, waifish creatures and marveled at the calmness of her daughter. Not a hint of girlishness escaped from that little urchin with the matted hair and sand-bitten face. Her walk had become the splayfooted sandal stride of the donkey boys and on her belt were a knife, tin cup and bowl, a leather quirt, and a small bag. She had a long, woven tie-down rope neatly coiled and slung over her shoulder. If challenged to pick her daughter from other donkey boys, Jani would have failed. This is good, Jani thought.

Habib led them onto higher ground along the north wall. So many millennia of footsteps had gone along these paths that the grooves in the sandstone were often as much as a foot deep. They moved through the first Bedouin camp quite rapidly. Habib stopped only momentarily to ask the whereabouts of the chief and being told the man was in the second camp, the foursome moved on. Few Bedouins noticed them pass. Here and there, a woman looked up from cooking and raised a hand in acknowledgement. The rich smells of saffron rice, stew, and warm homemade beer made Jani's stomach growl with hunger.

They were almost to the end of the second encampment before Habib motioned Tahireh to his side and nodded, without a word, toward the grove of palm trees. He handed his duffel to Jani and Zhara reached out and grabbed it, smiling. The three women set off single file along one of the many sandstone grooves with Tahireh in the lead and Jani and Zhara doing their best to carry the heavier duffel. As they reached the sand along the shore of the water, they dropped the long duffel to the ground and dragged it. Their long journey was beginning to tell on soft muscles and untrained bodies.

Jani once looked over her shoulder. A glimpse was all she had of him there high up against the cliff edge. She felt a sudden chill and a giant rift as Habib, his dark brown abba billowing about him, hiked steadily toward the second camp and the chieftain's tent. More than anything, she wanted to clasp onto him, hold him with her, keep him from going up there. That's silly, she thought, we are within a mere kilometer of reaching the Land Cruiser. We'll be trundling across the desert toward Kuwait and headed for the air force base in another few moments.

On this end of the canyon, the cliffs were not so high, perhaps twenty meters, but the shade of the north wall already covered the palm trees in shadow so deep it seemed invisible when viewed from the bright sunlight. Not until they were inside the brushy perimeter and within arm's length of the Cruiser was a vehicle barely recognizable under the camouflage netting and layers of palm leaves and brush. It was almost chilly in the darkness of the grove. Birds squawked and scattered as the women beat through the tall brush. The green leaves closed behind them leaving not a trace of their passage. Here and there a stray goat scampered away. Insects hummed and an occasional lizard skittered into the leafy groundcover.

"Come help me," ordered Tahireh, sighing as she set the duffel down near one corner of the netting. Zhara and Jani dropped the larger duffel. Tahireh undid the thick rope holding the netting in place and motioned for the two women to start rolling the netting back. It took considerable effort as the netting had been intertwined with brush and palm fronds. "Pull the fronds out, put the brush to one side," Tahireh instructed, "we want to be able to fold up the net and take it with us."

Zhara did not hesitate, standing next to her mother, she jerked on the palm fronds as Jani held the net taut. Jani smiled at Zhara and with a gleam of fierce pride in her eyes, Zhara smiled back. Jani's heart soared. Her daughter had been transformed. In the space of twenty-four hours, Zhara had cast off her princess's arrogance. If the worst happens at this very moment, thought Jani, all the fear and terror will have been worth it. My daughter has grown up.

Meanwhile, Tahireh lay down in the sand and slid under the chassis. When she wriggled out, she had a magnetic key box in her hands. "We've got a go," she laughed, holding up the tiny box before opening it. "The Cruiser looks to be in good shape and the keys were right where we left them. Here," she said, grabbing the middle of the heavy roll of netting, "throw it onto the floor in back." She held the roll on one knee as she unlocked the back hatch door. They wrestled the netting into the Cruiser and then put the duffels on the jump seats. "There," said Tahireh, slamming the hatch door shut, "this way we have access to the net on a moment's notice. Now, deep breath everyone," she went to the driver side door and unlocked it, which unlatched the other doors, "while I get the engine started. You two, sit in back so I can sit up front with Haji Mansur. He'll want to drive."

She switched on the key. The engine coughed and sputtered in agonizing complaints. She tried again. And again.

"Damn," Tahireh swore loudly, shocking Jani. Zhara giggled. Tahireh tried again. And again. "God, I hope the battery is all right." She looked at the meters. "It seems to be fine. Water is fine. Damn, I hope we don't have a bad starter motor, I hope it didn't get sand in it!" She reached down and unlatched the hood and stepped out.

Jani grabbed her daughter's hand. Zhara looked up at her mom and said, "I've forgotten most of the words to most of the prayers we were supposed to learn."

"Me too," admitted Jani, "the thought better be what counts!"

As Tahireh tinkered under the hood, Jani peered out the side window. The smallest of holes in the brush allowed her to have a pinpoint, telescopic view and she was amazed at how far away the second encampment was, at least a kilometer away, perhaps closer to one and a half kilometers. She couldn't believe they'd walked so far in the last hour.

Just barely she could see, near the big tent on the edge of the encampment, three brown-robed men like little ants, tiny against the vast canyon wall. They were exiting the camp and starting toward the palm trees. She thought the middle figure was Habib, but the resemblance of one man to another was striking. All had brown abbas, all had gray beards and white turbans with white face scarves, and all walked with the slow deliberate gate of experienced desert dwellers. She thought the middle one was Habib because of the way he raised his head to glance toward where she and Zhara and Tahireh were hidden.

Abruptly, all three men jerked their heads upward to stare into the narrow slit of visible sky. Jani couldn't see anything because of their cover of heavy brush and palm trees, but she suddenly felt the powerful thumping of helicopter blades reverberating and echoing throughout the canyon. The three men turned and hurried back toward the camp.

"Tahireh!" Jani screamed out the window, "A helicopter!"

"Shhh," said Tahireh as Zhara clutched her mother's arm. Slowly, cautiously, Tahireh went to where the brush met the water and looked up. Jani, from her pinhole view saw a giant black shadow swoop over the camp. Tahireh rushed back and lowered the hood carefully, pushing it to latch it. She leaned into Cruiser and hissed, "Now! Get out, pull the camouflage back over and throw as much brush and palm fronds onto it as you can. Keep your heads down. Do it now!"

Without hesitation, both Jani and Zhara slid from the back seat and opening the hatch door only enough to pull the netting out, quickly doing as Tahireh ordered.

"Who is it," asked Zhara, "in the helicopter?"

Tahireh shouted loudly enough for both women to hear, "Saudi military, probably an elite search team!" She ferociously jabbed the discarded pieces of brush and the palm fronds into the netting as fast as Jani and Zhara tied down the net ropes. No more than three minutes had passed before the Cruiser was invisible again.

"Inside," Tahireh said, motioning and the three women squirmed under the netting and into the Cruiser. "If we're very, very lucky, they won't know we're here." She twitched around in her seat, "Tracks...did we leave tracks?"

Jani put one hand to her mouth, "Oh! Oh! I don't believe so. We came down that sandstone gully and that little stretch of sand...? It was wet from the camels and donkeys..."

"...and we dragged the duffel, see?" Zhara blurted out, pointing to Habib's sandy-bottomed duffel.

Tahireh nodded and sighed. "Here's hoping. Jani," she noticed Jani looking out the window, "you can see the camp from there?"

"Only a little bit," she answered.

"Tell us what happens," said Tahireh and Jani, teeth clenched, nodded. Zhara bent down to get a view. What they saw was the black helicopter shadow swoop down again and this time point its nose toward the retreating figures of the three men. The staccato of gunfire filled the canyon, echoing endlessly. All three men were blasted to the ground. All three lay still.

CHAPTER 11: THE DUST AND THE WIND

The i-Shibl compound was in an uproar. Vizier Rida had mobilized every guard, on duty or not. It looked good, he told himself, although personally, in his most hidden thoughts, he felt it was gathering up rope to tie the camel after it had joined the wild ones. Rida was going through the motions. He did what appeared competent to do at this point. Anything, for he had been stunned by the sultan's response when he had told him about the absence of the women and what his suspicions were. Rida expected to be dead and here he was, busily working.

Sheikh Sultan Rassid i-Shibl, sitting up in bed with his third wife next to him, had listened patiently. He shook his head, shrugged, and said in a rather calm voice, "What could you do, Rida? Handcuff them to their beds each night? That's why I had Yusef out here, to see if there was any breach of security we'd overlooked. Obviously, if the head of Saudi security can't figure out EW's methods, how can we be expected to do better?"

"Your highness..." the vizier had attempted to repeat his apology.

"No, Rida, we did all we could do. You did the best you could. When Yusef gets here, we'll put it in his hands and see if he can find them. That's his job, right?" The sheikh seemed resigned. "Tell me when he arrives."

"Yes, sire," said Rida, and backed out of the bedroom.

A guard, breathless from running, met him in the hall. "Commander Yusef called. He expects to be here momentarily and asks to use a computer."

"Of course, which one?"

"He said the one with the fastest...something."

"That would be the one in the office, let's go make sure it's available for him," said the vizier and they headed for the other end of the compound.

Lily, her eyes not fully open yet, was unlocking the office door as Marion Tidewater came pounding down the hall. He pushed through the door and toward his office as she shut the door behind them.

"Where's Russ Snow?" he demanded.

"His home phone's been disconnected," Lily said in a loud enough voice to carry across the room and to his office.

"What?" he halted at his own door.

Lily hustled to her own desk. "I asked the phone service about it, they told me he ordered it disconnected with no forwarding number as of five p.m. last night."

"But...but..." Tidewater ran a hand over his head, "I don't know squat about computers, he has everything all set up in there."

The messenger delivery envelope lay on top of everything else on Lily's desk. Curious, she slit it open, took out the single sheet of writing paper, read it. Her eyes, full of amazement, looked up at her boss. "He's quit. He's gone."

"Who?"

"Russell Snow. He's quit the Agency and he's left town." Lily handed the letter to Tidewater, who, upon reading the letter, stood for a full minute with his mouth open.

"This has never happened before," he said in a whisper, "that I know of. Find me another computer geek, now. Right this minute. Tonight."

"Yes, sir," she responded and began pressing buttons.

Commander Gurgin Yusef did not receive the expected telephone call from Marion Tidewater until almost three-quarters the distance between Khalid Military City and the i-Shibl compound. His assistant handed him the cell phone.

"North and northwest quadrant, all the photos you want," said Tidewater, "that do you?"

"Excellently," said Yusef, "and what is on those photos?"

"Well, I'm not sure what you're looking for, Commander," replied Tidewater.

"Caravans. I must see who is in the three caravans that departed the i-Shibl residence yesterday afternoon and where they camped, if they did, and where they ended up. That is what I must have," Commander Yusef explained in a loud voice to compensate for the increasing noise of the fierce winds.

"Caravans you shall have," answered Tidewater, "and sorry about taking so long, had a little glitch here. We're back on track though. We'll have it on your computer screen in a flash."

"Good. When we arrive at the sheikh's compound, I will call you with his Internet address," Yusef confirmed.

"Does he have teleconferencing?" asked the Agency man.

"I imagine he has better equipment than you, Marion," he laughed. "Call you in about half an hour."

"I'll be here," said Tidewater and hung up.

The relief Carl-Joran felt as his American passport under the name of Carl Mink was stamped without comment could hardly be described. He was waved through immigration without a hitch. He contained himself enough to walk, not dance, through the big double doors into the waiting area. Like a giant balloon floating into the sky, like a stream breaking from a pond and falling into a chasm—whoosh, he was back in Sweden. The smiling face of Krister made the baron's arrival on home soil all the more pleasant. Home at last, he sighed.

"*Min herre,*" Krister acknowledged as he took the bags, "*valkommen!* It is so good to see you alive!"

"*Ga det bra?*" asked the baron, "and yes, it is good to be alive. But, we are safe like this, you were not followed?"

"We are safe," Krister assured him. "*Ja, aven om din son ar enslig.*"

"*Ja so,*" responded the baron, "I expected Sture to be anxious. Let me use the telephone first, before we head to the castle." It took only a moment to place the call to Haifa and Dr. Legesse, who answered before the phone rang. "I am fine," insisted Carl-Joran after listening to her entreaties to be careful. "Now, tell me the news of Habib and Tahireh." He listened some more. "Nothing? Nothing at all?" he interjected. "Shhh," he got her to be quiet for a second, "I must tell you about a young man who is coming to Israel to help with EW, someone Siddhu must check out thoroughly. His name is Russell Snow-from-Night-Sky, yes, that Snow, the young American Indian man who was working for Tidewater at the Agency. He is defecting and he has some idea of meeting up with Tahireh. Yes. Totally in love with her. Wait, wait," the baron insisted as Legesse's voice rose several octaves from its normal deep alto tone, "he could be very valuable to us. Just have Siddhu keep him isolated for a while and you all, each of you, interview him. Let him know his life is on the line if he's faking this. Okay?" There was a moment's silence as Dr. Legesse took in the baron's orders. She reluctantly agreed with him and Carl-Joran bid her adieu.

Hoping he had done the right thing, the baron followed Krister out of the building and to the new Saab. Krister put the bags in the trunk and within minutes they were maneuvering out of the airport congestion and into the fast lane of the highway traveling east.

"Krister?" the baron asked as they got up to highway speed and onto the road leading toward home, "is the castle still being watched? Are you absolutely certain you weren't followed?"

"I was not followed past downtown Norrkoping, sir, I lost them at the onramp," he answered. "The castle though, is still watched. You must hide as we go east out of Norrkoping. The American agents park near the ICA store and the Arabs drive back and forth along the road. It is all very strange."

"It is stupidity," the big man agreed. "God, I can't wait to come alive again."

"Yes, sir," smiled Krister. "Do you have any idea how much longer you must be dead, *min herre*?"

Carl-Joran shook his head. "Until we trap Darughih Quddus Sadiq-Fath and make sure he will not plot against us again." The big man adjusted the car seat to fit his legs. He turned his head to look at the comforting familiarity of the snow-white Swedish landscape whiz by. "Ah, Krister, at the castle, how are the women?"

The chauffeur discreetly grinned, "When I left this morning, the older one, Bonnie, was going for a hike to the river and the younger, Trisha, was preparing to cross-country ski. I made sure they were dressed warmly enough, sir."

"Thank you," was all Carl Joran said as he managed to get the car seat back a little more.

The guards waved Commander Gurgin Yusef and his elite search team through the i-Shibl compound gates. One young guard shouted, "Vizier Rida is in the office, you will find him there." Yusef nodded and pointed the way for the troop of men.

Rida greeted Yusef at the door of the i-Shibl business office with a salute and motioned him and his assistant, Faruq, into the large room. Gurgin smiled to himself as he regarded the expensive, up-to-date computer equipment. He had been correct.

Within moments, Faruq had reached Marion Tidewater and was downloading satellite images. They were so amazing in detail it almost took Yusef's breath away. He, with Rida looking over his shoulder, could watch each separate caravan pack up and leave. He could see individual jeeps and camels and make out the shapes of merchants and camp followers. He tracked both merchant caravans to their destinations. Then he went back over the action outside the i-Shibl compound as the caravans made preparations to leave. And again, he went over the images during that time slot.

He turned to look up at the vizier. "Do you notice that there is not one person coming from the compound to these caravans that did not originally go from the caravan into the compound?"

The vizier nodded. "You are right, every merchant can be accounted for."

"How did they get the women out if they did not bring more people out than went in?" Yusef asked and Rida shook his head.

Faruq was squinting closely at the screen. He had gone on with the surveillance photos not realizing the two men were only interested in the merchant caravans. Abruptly he stopped the flow of scenes. "Sir," he said to his boss, "look at this."

Yusef leaned forward. "That's the Bedouin tribe. Those women could not have gone with that bunch."

"But look, sir," insisted Faruq, "look at the boys coming from the compound."

"Boys?" Yusef questioned.

"Donkey boys," Faruq replied.

Yusef twisted his head around and looked directly at Rida. "Do donkey boys come into the compound? I mean, they obviously did. Look at the photos."

Rida slapped his palm against his forehead. "I didn't consider them. They are dirty waifs, urchins. No one pays attention to them, except...the sheikh's wives run a delousing and cleaning program for the little beggars whenever a Bedouin caravan comes."

"All the wives?"

Rida shook his head, understanding now, knowing for a certainty how it all had transpired. "No, just the first wife and Princess Zhara with the help of maids. After the health check-ups, the boys get new clothes and shoes, and they are fed a meal. Jani and Zhara have been doing this since we brought Zhara back from Paris, let's see, six months ago."

As photos clicked by, Faruq pointed to one specific boy who left the compound alone, before any of the others. This lone boy walked directly to the Bedouin camp and up to a man who stood in front of a tent. In subsequent photos, Faruq pointed to a shape that seemed to be an old woman with a teenage boy who also left the compound unaccompanied by donkey boys and who went straight to the Bedouin camp, stopping at the same tent, the same man. The teenage boy left the man and old woman and joined the Bedouin donkey boys who had stayed in camp and the donkeys. Fifteen minutes later, all the donkey boys who had gone into the compound two hours before came out.

"Enlarge those photos," Yusef ordered and Faruq complied. The shadows of the late afternoon made the figures very distorted, but Yusef slapped his fist into his hand and grinned. "Habib Mansur. That is he, I am certain. The woman with him, who joined up with him here, that is Jani i-Shibl. The first boy? I am certain that is Zhara. We have them." He almost shouted at his assistant, "Find where the caravan stopped."

"Yessir," said Faruq and continued the surveillance photos. "Hard to see in the dark, sir," he said, "and the sandstorm is covering their tracks." The minutes passed by. "Found it," he finally said. "They passed by Ras al Khafii and went on to here, about fifty miles outside of Rumah, staying on the high desert. Here, see, as the sun comes up, they're entering the Grand Wadi. The satellite can't see into the canyon well because of the angle of the cliffs. The cameras only pick up the water, but this is definitely where the caravan stops. This last photo? It was taken about an hour and a half ago. No one has come out of the canyon from either end. They're in there, in the wadi, at the oasis. They're camping there."

"Good work, Faruq," said Commander Yusef and jerked his cell phone from its holder. He pushed redial and got Tidewater, "We found them, yes, both women. They are with the Haji Habib Mansur. Yes, it is an Emigrant Women operation. I'm ordering up a helicopter and we are on the way."

As the baron was disembarking in Sweden, Russ Snow, in Tel Aviv, was retrieving his big suitcase and shoulder bag from Israeli Customs. Both suitcase and shoulder bag had been thoroughly searched. He, himself, had been gone over with sensing equipment. He had been interviewed again and again and again as to his intentions in Israel, his destination, if he had friends and/or business acquaintances. They would finish interviewing, he thought he could move on, and abruptly another interviewer would appear and start it all over again. Finally, suddenly, in mid-sentence, a person Russ assumed to be a supervisor or superior officer simply nodded to the present interviewer and with a sweep of the hand, he was motioned onto the painted pathway toward the immigration desks. All along the pathway, young Israeli soldiers stood on alert with rifles at the ready. Russell could not believe the level of security. These soldiers were not just bored guards, they were frontline troops ready to defend their home.

He ended up mixed into a flow of Japanese tourists, laden with cameras, who politely moved one by one toward the immigration desks. At the immigration desk he reached, a very tough young woman, backed by the requisite armed guard, questioned him again about why he was in Israel. When he said for the zillionth time that he was here to join the EW, she snapped at him, "Stay standing right there," and she turned around and motioned to another immigration officer. They conversed in Hebrew, briefly, seriously, and the other officer stepped into a guarded room behind the desks and came out with a short East Indian man, a Hindi by his turban, who hurried directly to the immigration woman. He pulled a passport wallet from his coat pocket and extracted several ID cards and a formal letter and handed them to the serious young woman. He glanced surreptitiously at Russ as the ID cards were scrutinized.

The serious woman handed the cards back to the man and actually smiled at Russ. In perfect British English she said, "Seems you have been telling the truth. Mr. Prakash here has come to collect you."

"Coll...collect me?" Russ's eyebrows raised.

The woman grinned and nodded and swept him by with her hand as Prakash took him by the elbow to guide him through. Russ had only seconds to grab up his baggage.

"You come with me," Siddhu said resolutely, and in a very adamant tone continued, "You are lucky, very, very lucky the baron called us and told us you were attempting to come to EW or otherwise you would be on your way to an Israeli jail. They are not nice. You do not want to go to Israeli jails. Now you come with me and you do just what I say or the soldiers will be on you in a heartbeat."

"Uhh...I take it you're Mr. Singh Siddhu Prakash?"

"No, I am Siddhu Singh Prakash. Do not talk too much. Be quick." They sped through the airport terminal and out into the warm sun. Siddhu did not release his elbow once. At the curb, the Indian man raised a hand to signal to a far-away Mercedes. Within minutes the car was in front of them and a small Arab man leaped from the driver's seat. He literally threw Russ's suitcase into the trunk before opening the back door.

"In," ordered Siddhu Singh Prakash. Russ slid in; the Arab man slammed the door shut and jumped in the driver's side. Off they went in and out of traffic and onto a highway.

Siddhu motioned toward the Arab man, "Russell Snow, you are meeting Taqi Nabil-Nasiri d'Din." The driver nodded without diverting his eyes from the road.

Smiling, Russ said, "Your name is longer than you are."

"Ha!" laughed Siddhu and translated for the driver who roared with laughter and responded with several sentences. Siddhu said to Russ, "He believes you are correct. He says your name, although very long, is not as long as you are tall."

"Right," said Russ and felt the atmosphere become instantly much friendlier.

"You may as well relax, Russ Snow-from-Night-Sky, it is a long journey to Haifa."

Siddhu settled back into his seat. "Are you hungry? Thirsty? We will stop along the way, perhaps at a cafe` near the water and get food and something to drink."

"Thank you, yes, the food on the plane was awful."

Siddhu said something to Taqi, probably translating this last sentence because Taqi laughed as he nodded in agreement. Turning to Russ again, Siddhu repeated, "Relax, Mr. Snow. Enjoy the ride."

Yusef ordered the pilot of the helicopter to land as close to the bodies as he could get. After several minutes of circling, the pilot managed to get the machine settled onto the sandstone area at the top of the slope mere feet from the edge of the encampment. Several tents bent almost to collapse in the backwash of the rotors.

The Bedouin men, silent and brutal, had surrounded the bodies. Each man bristled with guns. Yusef told the pilot to keep the rotors moving. For one brief second, he wondered whether his decision to kill the three hajis was a good one, but then he again considered the fact that if those men had reached the village, they'd have instantly become invisible. Only by the grace of Allah did he have the opportunity he did.

He signaled his squad of soldiers. Also heavily armed, they jumped from the helicopter and set up a perimeter. Commander Yusef, pistols in his belt, walked through the perimeter and flanked by his two top security agents, walked toward the Bedouin men.

One of those men stepped forward. "Allah shall strike you dead for killing hajis. It is enough, we now have blood war, you and two tribes of the desert."

Twenty meters from the man, Commander Yusef stopped. His entire body felt the prickle of guns aimed at him. Many guns. "One of the hajis is a wanted man, a man who steals Arab women. He is the one we came for."

"No haji steals women. You are mistaken. It was a bad mistake." The man growled.

"Haji Habib Mansur. He is one of those three dead men. I want his body." Yusef stepped forward and all of the Bedouin guns cocked. With an imperious shout, Yusef declared, "We can slaughter your entire village in one sweep of the helicopter's machine guns. Will you go that far to protect the body of a criminal?"

"You want the body of Haji Mansur?" asked the man. "No. You have done enough in killing him."

It was clear that this could turn into a very ugly standoff. Yusef glanced around at his lieutenant and inquired in a low voice, "Did we bring the camera?"

"Yessir. Shall I get it?"

Yusef nodded, then looked directly back at the Bedouin man, standing proudly in front of his tribesmen. Yusef shouted, "We can take photos. To prove it is Mansur."

"I will confer," said the man and stepped back into the crowd of men. After about five minutes, the man stepped forward again. "If you allow us to take our chiefs back to the tents so they will not be cursed by your camera. We take them immediately."

"You do that. Take them. Leave the body of Mansur," Yusef agreed.

Several Bedouin men slipped away from the group and quickly retrieved two bodies. They were gone so quickly that Yusef did not even have time to photograph their movements. The man in front motioned to Yusef to come forward. "Only you," he said firmly. "No one else."

Commander Yusef took the camera from his lieutenant. Slowly he made his way through the phalanx of Bedouin tribesmen who parted only inches from his path. He could smell their clothing, feel the heat of their skin as he passed.

Mansur's body in its bloody brown abba lay face down, which meant Yusef had to roll it over for the face to be seen by the cameras. Mansur's blood, still flowing from the half-dozen wounds, smeared his hands. At least one of the heavy machine-gun bullets had pierced the side of the face. Still, Yusef had no doubt, from the many photos he'd seen of Habib Mansur, that this was the man and the man was surely dead. The late afternoon shadow of the canyon wall meant he had to open the camera lens. He held the camera steady and snapped ten photos. It was a digital camera. It wouldn't take much to improve the quality of the photos once he had them back on the computer. The old warrior smirked. He'd done it. He'd stopped one of the prime movers of the EW.

Which brought up the issue of the women. He walked back through the Bedouin soldiers, stopping in front of the leader. "There were two, maybe three women with the haji. Women he stole from the compound of Sheikh Sultan i-Shibl."

The leader of the Bedouins had no expression at all on his face. "Do not ask us about women. You cannot keep your women at home, that is not our problem. Go now before we kill all of you."

"You fire on us and the helicopter wipes out this entire encampment. Completely. Nothing left," threatened Yusef, although he knew that actually, the powerful rifles the Bedouin carried were quite adequate to penetrate the side of the helicopter and disable it.

Perhaps the leader of the Bedouins was also aware of this because he did not stand down. Instead, he looked directly into Yusef's eyes, challenging him. "Search our camp if you will, we do not have your women. They were sent away long before we came to this camp. High on the desert in the middle of the sandstorm. Taken away by a jeep, may Allah protect them. Go find them yourself. That is all."

"Where on the high desert?" demanded Yusef.

The leader shrugged. "How should I know? The wind makes the stars dance, the sand swim. The night was very dark. Tell me, how can I describe where a map does not go?" He grinned and snarled, "You will leave now. Immediately."

For one long moment, Yusef considered fulfilling his threat to wipe out the village once they were airborne. He could land again to search every tent. But what would that gain him? An incident that could be taken to a higher court? No, it wasn't worth the effort. Chances were, since Haji Mansur was walking with two other hajis in broad daylight, unafraid of being seen, and not riding in a vehicle with the women, that the Bedouin leader was telling at least a partial truth. The women had been picked up last night. That explained how two soft, spoiled women could have disappeared so completely. Those women could never have made it this far, walking or on a camel. Of course, the man was lying about not knowing where. No nomadic Bedouin would ever say he did not know precisely where on the desert an event in his life happened. The man may have been in a complete blinding sandstorm, but he knew exactly where the sandstorm hit him and where he had holed up to wait it out. These nomads had not stopped, they had continued; thus last night's sandstorm was a mere ruffle in the sand to them and not a moment during that time did they lose their way. Yes, thought Yusef, the caravan was met by a jeep probably only a few miles from the compound and the swirling sand hid them and their tracks from the satellite surveillance cameras.

Yusef smiled. He had done enough. Let Tidewater deal with it from here because for certain, the women were already outside of Saudi by now. He spun on his heels and signaled to his lieutenant and the squadron to follow him back to the helicopter.

Moments later, high in the air above the deeply shadowed great wadi, he could just barely make out the Bedouin men carrying Mansur's body to the camp. Far to the west, Yusef saw the beginnings of a very nice sunset. It had been a good day, all told. It would please him, in a way, to give this over to Marion Tidewater. With a swift turn, the helicopter sped away toward the military city and Yusef's headquarters.

CHAPTER 12: THE VALUE OF WOMEN

The blindfold meant Russ lost track of time. It had been put on him as they entered the outskirts of Haifa. He'd sensed sharp twists in the road, felt the Mercedes slow, and heard the traffic get heavier. Before too long, there came the heavy, rich smell of an outgoing tide, of wharfing, oiled timbers, the hoooot of a big ship entering a harbor. Then the Mercedes parked and he was led into a building. As they walked along what seemed to be a hallway, he could hear children's voices, some women—most likely their moms—talking in several different languages and finally the whoosh of big doors opening and closing and silence.

His blindfold came off. In front of him, filling the room, was a giant black and white table, at the head of which stood an elegant black woman in a prim red suit. Although Russ noticed the dark Israeli woman seated to her right, his eyes were held tight by the black eyes of the woman in the red suit. Siddhu pulled him into a seat and sat next to him.

"Welcome to Emigrant Women. Let me introduce myself. I am Dr. Halima Legesse and this," she motioned toward the Israeli woman, "is Dr. Rachel Bar-Fischer from the Israeli Drug Treatment Centre." Dr. Legesse leaned onto her knuckles and with emphasis said, "You are very lucky, Mr. Snow, that we were made aware of your arrival."

"Mr. Prakash told me that," Russ nodded.

"He was right. You could be languishing in jail as we speak." Dr. Legesse sat down. "What to do with you? We have discussed this for most of the day. Baron Hermelin wants us to trust you, but keep a close eye on you. Siddhu, here, wants you locked away for a month or so."

"As a precaution," said Siddhu.

Dr. Legesse nodded toward Siddhu, "He could be right. I may be the boss of Emigrant Women, but I'm no dictator." She chuckled, "This is a group of chiefs without any Indians. Thus I've decided that a compromise would be in the best interest of everyone. After all, if you do have the computer skills Carl-Joran says you do, then we want to make use of them. But if you offer a threat, as Siddhu warns, we want to keep you under control. I've asked Dr. Bar-Fischer to let you occupy a room in her drug treatment center. Yes, it is a lockup. I will have Siddhu bring you here during the day and he can watch over your shoulder as you learn our computer system. That won't take much of your time. Our system is about as antiquated as you can find."

"That could be my first job," said Russ with enthusiasm, "to update your system. Put some firewalls up. You really need them."

"I wouldn't know what a computer firewall was if it popped up and said hello!" Shaking her head, Dr. Legesse stood again, "More likely, your first assignment will be to monitor reports coming in. They are the most important. Mind you, this is all dependent on your excellent behavior and total compliance with all our rules. So, we shall see." She nodded to Siddhu who rose to his feet and pulled Russ to his. "Make no mistake, Mr. Snow, you are on probation. Understood?"

"Yes ma'am," he curtly replied.

Dr. Legesse smiled at him. It was not a warm smile, but an obligatory one. "You probably could use a hot meal and a hot shower. Siddhu, you and Rachel get him settled at the treatment center." She started out the door. Siddhu put the blindfold over Russ's eyes and they went back the way they'd come.

Russ was aware that only he and Siddhu got into the Mercedes. He heard Taqi talking to Siddhu as they drove through the twisting streets and uphill. Steeply uphill, up and up until Russ's ears popped. The odors wafting in through the vent changed dramatically from ocean to dry, cold desert. When the car pulled to a stop, Siddhu got out first and, as Russ climbed out, Siddhu pulled off his blindfold.

"You might as well see where you're going," he said, "because once you are in this place, there is no way out."

During the drive, evening had set in. Lights were coming on. They had stopped in a large parking area in front of a two-story stucco building surrounded by high, barbed wire, electrified fencing. Beyond the fence was rocky desert. It occurred to Russ that the place could be a prison and he wondered why a drug treatment center would have such heavy security. Dr. Rachel Bar-Fischer's little car came zipping through the big gate and parked next to the Mercedes. Taqi opened her door for her.

She immediately walked to what looked like the front door, painted a violently bright blue. The men, except Taqi, followed. She held it open for Siddhu and Russ, and then led them down a long hallway. "Room ten," she told Siddhu and within moments, Russ was deposited into what would be his space. Dr. Bar-Fischer told him, "You have a toilet in the room, the bath is down the hall, and the cafeteria is all the way along the hall and to your right. I've told the cook to set out some supper for you.

Just ring when you're ready to go eat and an orderly will take you along. Okay?"

"Yes," replied Russ. "And tomorrow?"

"Tomorrow, we will see," Siddhu answered him. "If I do not get terribly busy with the Kuwaiti case, I will come get you in the morning."

"That's Milind, the Thai girl who's in prison?" Snow said and Siddhu shook his head, frustrated.

"You know a lot more than we care to have you know."

Russ shrugged, "Both Tidewater of the Agency and Sadiq-Fath of the Iranian Security Forces are aware you're interested in saving her. I think it's a trap."

"We think so too," was Siddhu's reply and he motioned Russ into the tiny room. "Sleep well. Rest."

The door closed and Russ looked around at his new quarters. Luckily, he'd packed a book because there was no TV, not even a radio, merely a cot, a toilet, and a porthole of a window. The view from the window was stunning. Russ could see the entire city of Haifa below him. They must be very high up on the cliffs. He watched the harbor lights come on. Across the bay, on the opposite cliff side, was an immense wooded area filled with magnificent buildings illuminated by spotlights. The top of one building had a brilliant gold dome. On the top of that cliff were a series of hotels.

He managed to get the window open a crack and in came soft Mediterranean breezes with incredibly exotic odors. Suddenly he felt exhausted to the bone. And hungry, and he needed a shower. He rang for the orderly and while waiting, pulled his toilet kit and a clean set of clothes from the big suitcase. He hoped he could stay awake long enough to both shower and eat.

"I...I really want to go to the toilet," whispered Zhara, her voice breaking the silence of hours. Her mother ssshhed her. For some reason at this, Tahireh began to laugh. It was not a funny ha-ha laugh. It was a gut-wrenching, sobbing laugh. Slowly, the tall model sat up. She and Zhara and Jani had lain flat, below the window level in the pitch-black dark for all this time. Tahireh's choking laughter filled the Cruiser. Zhara sat up, groaning.

"Please," begged Zhara, "I gotta go!"

"Go," said Tahireh between laughing sobs.

Jani tried to sit up and felt paralyzed in every muscle in her body. "Oh!" she moaned sharply, "I hurt. Oh, God, do we have any aspirin?"

Zhara pulled at her mother's shoulders, helping her.

"Look in the smaller duffel," Tahireh offered. "I packed some. I'm sure."

Once Jani was in an upright position, Zhara gave her mom a quick hug, then grabbed up a couple tissues and as quietly as possible, pushed the Cruiser door open which switched on the interior light, and slipped out. With effort, Jani turned first to rummage in the duffel for the aspirin. She found it, shook out two, and swallowed them with a swig of water from the canteen under her feet. Painfully, she swung her head around to look through the peephole of brush and trees. Tiny campfire lights could be seen like stars in the otherwise impenetrable darkness. She lowered her window to let the cold night air creep in. With it came muted sounds of bleating goats and keening voices. An occasional grunt of a camel carried across the water. The rustle of bushes signaled Zhara's duties finished. She climbed back in the Cruiser and took the canteen from her mother. The water tasted really good. It relieved the parched throat. She handed it to Tahireh who took it but put it in her lap.

The shock of what had happened was easing up. Jani, listening to Tahireh's laughing sobs, began to allow her own tears to flow. Her crying was in whimpers. The pain was too great for anything else. She was numb with fear and grief. He was dead. She'd watched him fall and be carried away. The man who was her savior was gone. Zhara, her face ruddy in the glow of the interior light, hugged her close. Her daughter smelled like donkeys.

A thump-thump-thump of small feet was felt before heard and a sharp rustle of brush against the Cruiser made all three women suck in breath and hold it. They stared to their left. A small, tousled black-haired head poked above the level of the driver's side window enough so that a pair of eyes, white surrounding black iris, peered curiously into the Cruiser. The little guy was one of the donkey boys. Seeing the women, he hissed and motioned for Tahireh to roll down her window, which she did.

"You must go now," he said in Arabic. "My mother says it is time. No one will see you. It is between moving stars. Okay?"

Tahireh shook her head. "What do you mean, between moving stars?"

With a big shrug, the youngster replied, "I, myself, I don't know. My mother tells me the men order me to tell you that the men say it is how the helicopter found the camp. It is the only way, say the men. The caravan tracks from the compound were covered by the wind and sand, so you could not have been followed. The men talk about the moving stars that take pictures. They were warned a year ago about these moving stars. Your haji warned them. It is all fantastical to me, but maybe you understand?"

"Yes," Tahireh responded. "I understand. Listen, little man, the haji was right. The moving stars do take pictures and they see everything. It is right to be careful when they are flying over. Thank you for being such a brave person and coming to us."

Jani leaned forward. "Ask him about Habib."

The boy hefted a bundle tied in roughly woven cloth through Tahireh's window. "Food for your journey," he said softly and turned to leave.

"Boy! Boy!" Tahireh shouted after him. He stopped and laid fingers across his mouth in a motion for silence. She whispered loudly, "Our friend, Mansur, was he killed?"

The boy shrugged. "This was not for me to know. I saw the hajis shot down. I saw the men take the bodies to the tents of the old women, but no one has told me of their fates. I cannot believe they lived. The gunfire from the helicopter was terrible. I have heard the women wailing tonight."

"The person who gave you this food, he didn't tell you anything?" Jani insisted.

"She. My mother. She said for me to hurry and to be very quiet and invisible. To stay in the grooves of sandstone. And to warn you of moving stars. I did all that."

"Yes you did, young one," Tahireh said. "What is your name that we may remember you and thank you with a prayer to Allah."

"Khalil Mahmoudi, kind sister."

"Khalil, you had better hurry back to your mother," Tahireh ordered, "before she worries herself sick."

"Good journey!" said the boy, "And be careful to cover yourself when the moving stars go over." Pointing to the heavens, he disappeared into the brush. The faint rustle of his passing could be heard for a moment then was quickly drowned out by the humming of locusts and flutter of a night bird's wings.

Tahireh put the stopper in the canteen and opened the bundle and the aroma of saffron rice, taboleh, hot pita bread, and chunks of meat, probably goat, wafted through the car. They ate like starving creatures, but only enough to kill the pangs of hunger. They had to take the boy's warnings seriously. It was time to travel.

Each with a flashlight, they jumped from the Cruiser. As one movement, all three hurried to clean the brush and palm fronds from the netting and drag the netting off the vehicle. It was quickly folded and stuffed into the rear of the Cruiser.

Zhara stood in front of the car with a flashlight lighting the heavily occluded path toward the water's edge. Two faint rows of broken and crushed underbrush were the only sign of where Habib had driven the Cruiser in. Jani, taking the front passenger seat, held the gearshift in first gear as Tahireh, her foot firmly on the clutch, turned the starter and pulled out the throttle. A few coughs and the engine, cool now in the night air, roared to life. All the women took deep breaths of relief. The motor's noise scattered creatures all around, birds, insects, lizards. The Cruiser jumped forward as Tahireh released the clutch and Tahireh held it in check only long enough for Zhara to climb aboard. Turning the headlights on, Tahireh put in the clutch again. Jani held it in gear while Tahireh shifted to four-wheel drive. Stuttering at first, slowly, the Cruiser began to plow at a snail's pace through the brush. It took about ten minutes, ten very long minutes, for them to break into the open at the edge of the water. Wrenching the wheel, Tahireh managed to turn the vehicle so it did not continue forward into the oasis. Instead, at an uncomfortable tilt, they bumped their way past the brush and palm trees and onto the sandy beach area that led toward the opening of the canyon opposite from which they had entered yesterday afternoon.

Careful not to hit any goats or camels, they picked up speed and were soon onto a rocky trail that climbed steeply around the outside edge of the wadi and onto the desert. At the top of the rise, Tahireh stopped the Cruiser, leaving it in idle, and stepped out. Jani and Zhara watched her stare into the night sky. Both of them got out and looked up. The stars were diamonds, brilliant beyond counting.

"What are you doing?" asked Zhara.

"Following directions," smiled Tahireh, "finding our map."

"There's the North Star," pointed Jani and Tahireh nodded, saying, "Yes, I know the way now."

She motioned them back into the Cruiser and they headed north by northwest, toward the Saudi-Kuwaiti border, toward the American air base, toward freedom for Jani and Zhara.

***

As athletic as Trisha was, still she was completely exhausted by the two-hour stint of cross-country skiing. Bonnie, lying on the long divan reading a book in front of the fireplace in the small living room, waved at her as she trudged past in the hall.

"Going to go take a nap, Mom," Trish called out and, pulling off her sweater, headed up the stairs.

Bonnie had been invigorated by her walk to the hot springs. She'd come very close to some small moose, had seen a huge flock of geese at the hot springs, and two small foxes ran briefly down the trail ahead of her as she hiked back. The bitter cold had taken its toll, however, and on arriving at the castle, she'd wanted nothing more than to curl up in a warm place with her book and a cup of hot chocolate. The last of the jet lag also took effect and the urge to nap washed over her. Her conscience nagged her to seek out Sture and move him along toward the promised meeting with Ms. Person, but drowsiness won. By the time Trisha had reached the top of the huge staircase, Bonnie's eyes closed.

She had a strange dream. Carl Mink was an old man and he and she were in a jet flying somewhere, which was totally ridiculous because Carl was dead and the dream came to an abrupt halt when Sture's voice gently called to her. "Mrs. Ixey? Mrs. Ixey? Bonnie?"

Her book fell from her hands with a thump onto the floor and she grabbed it up hoping not to lose her place. "Yes, Sture," she answered. It must be dinnertime. She glanced at the beautiful antique clock on the mantel. Yes, five-fifteen. She sat up.

The gangly young man was shifting uncomfortably from one foot to another, his large hands fluttering nervously. "Will you come with me, please? You are to see someone."

"I'm going to see Ms. Person now?" was the only thing Bonnie could think to say.

Sture shook his head, "No. Not her."

Stiffly, Bonnie got to her feet. The wonderful smells of salmon, dill, potatoes, and cheese floated across the room. "Is dinner served?"

"In about an hour," said the young man and turned on his heel, expecting her to follow. Completely puzzled, Bonnie tagged along behind him, hurrying to keep up with his long strides down the hall to the back stairs, up the cold stairs to the lower end of the hall and past Sture's room. At the beautiful cherry wood door to the grand master bedroom suite, Sture stopped, knocked firmly and a muffled male voice responded from inside, "*Komm in.*"

Sture turned the lion head brass doorknob, pushed the door open, and stood back, motioning for Bonnie to go in. Hesitating, she laid one hand on the door. The cherry wood was warm and smooth. The expression on Sture's face added to the puzzle. He had a cat with canary feathers in its mouth grin. Sture pushed the door open a little further and Bonnie stepped in.

The deep male voice insisted, "*Komm nu.*"

The door closed behind her and she was standing, seemingly alone, in a massive room one-half of which was filled with beautiful antiques: delicately inlaid bureaus and dressers and nightstands and wardrobes and a massive four-poster bed, all matching. By the fireplace filled with a roaring fire, were, in stark contrast, a modern couch and rollback chair, a panel television, sound equipment, and a large desk topped with computers. The draperies and hangings were dark red and thick. Four giant Persian carpets covered old cherry wood floors. From the tall, narrow windows could be seen the lights along the front drive and, in the distance, the iron gate with the Hermelin shield.

But there was no one except her in the room. Where had the voice come from, she wondered?

Abruptly, a man emerged from the adjoining bathroom suite. A very tall man, in fact, the very tall black-haired, black bearded man who had been at the airport, stepped into the bedroom, only he no longer had a black beard. He was wiping the last of the shaving cream from his face and toweling dry white-blond hair. He had on comfortable sweat pants and a white T-shirt, his feet were bare. He saw her. He stopped moving. She saw him breathe deeply and a wide smile came to his face. An oh! so familiar smile. In almost a whisper, he said, "Bonnie."

All she could do was shake her head in confusion.

"Yes, it is okay. I am alive," he assured her.

"Carl?" she queried, knowing full well that it was he. Her knees shook, her hands trembled. "How can this be?"

Before her knees collapsed completely, he had gently put arms around her and helped her into a seat at a small table where a tea service had been laid out and covered with a cloth. "You will be all right in a moment," he said, "when your mind accepts what is true." He sat in a chair next to her, pulled the cloth off the tea set to reveal not only teapot and cups, but tiny sandwiches and cakes as well. "Tea? Yes, that will help?" He poured her a cup. "Or something stronger?" He reached for a nearby bottle of fine brandy.

"No! No!" she insisted and put her tiny hand on his arm. "Tell me what is happening!"

"I did not really die," he said, grinning.

"You.you were at the airport. That was you? You are here!" Tears began to run down her cheeks. "You're not dead!" This was said with anger, anger and frustration. "You were dead and now you are not dead! You tricked me! You..." She began to cry in earnest.

Carl-Joran took her hands in his. "I am so sorry."

"Sorry does not even start to make up for all these years," she exclaimed, "not knowing, thinking maybe you had died in some god-awful crusade in some hideous war, dreading to find out, not wanting to know..."

"I was never sure," whispered Carl-Joran.

Jumping to her feet, Bonnie grasped his hands, "Sure? Sure of what? What did you need to be sure of?"

He pulled her hands to his face, "Sure you loved me enough for me to contact you. I was terrified that I had compromised your safety. I wanted only to hide away and become invisible so no one would trace me to you. Those were dangerous times and there was much work left to do. When I finally returned to Sweden after my father died, we...you and I, just seemed so far away. Then I was too embarrassed to contact you. You were married. You'd had a baby, in fact two children. You seemed happy with the old man."

Bonnie's face flushed with realization. "You kept track of me all these years."

He nodded. "If, at any time, you had been in danger, you would have had help immediately."

"Some consolation," she whimpered.

"You were not happy in your life?" he asked.

She stood looking down into the face exasperatingly familiar yet strange, strange because it had aged, as hers had. "I was happy, what can I say? Yes. I've had a good life."

"Then you did not need a wild, crazy man like me interfering." He nodded again, confident of being correct.

Slowly her hands let go of his and balled into small fists. "How can you say that? How could you leave me? I was so afraid, so alone."

"You had your parents," he tried to say.

"Fool!" she yelled at him and pounded his shoulders with her fists. He took her wrists in his hands and pulled her close. She was sobbing. Gently, he drew her into his lap and hugged her close.

"I do not understand," he whispered. "I stayed away because I loved you."

"I was pregnant with your child," she said into his chest.

He held her face up, "What do you say?"

"Trisha is your daughter."

"*Min Gud!*" he exclaimed, hugging her close again. "I did not know. This I did not even guess." The full impact of it made him ache all the way through his body. Carl-Joran put one big hand on Bonnie's soft white hair and laid his head on hers. There were no more words, not for some time. They sat huddled together, souls returning to the bond that had been ripped asunder so many years before. It was as if time had stood still and space had warped. The tea grew cold.

Tidewater leaned back in his chair with a satisfied smile on his face. He was ready to finish up his day and go home. He glanced at his secretary and noticed she was animatedly talking to someone on the phone. She pushed an extension button, put down the receiver and looked around toward him.

"Commander Gurgin Yusef for you," Lily said, motioning.

"Ahhh," said Tidewater jerking up the phone. "Yes, Commander, how's it going? Must be important 'cause it's about three in the morning there."

"It is two-thirty," responded Yusef, "and yes, it is important. I am having my computer person send you photos. You will be pleased. I have taken care of Habib Mansur. He is no longer alive."

"That is wonderful news," exclaimed Marion Tidewater, "and the photos are of..."

"The body. We could not take it away. But you can see for yourself it is the haji." Yusef was very proud.

Tidewater leaned out of his office and waved at Lily to get Norm, the new computer geek. "What about the women? Did you get them? Return them?" When Norm stuck his head into Tidewater's office, Tidewater covered the mouthpiece and whispered, "Check the e-mail files for photos coming in from Commander Yusef." Norm nodded and hurried back to his cubby.

Yusef, a tired note in his voice, explained, "I am afraid not. They leave the caravan before we find it, before it reached the Grand Wadi. I am certain though that they were picked up not far from the i-Shibl residence. I am also certain that Tahireh Ibrahim is the one who disguised the women and got them out of the compound. She is probably still with them."

"Where would they head for?"

"My guess is Kuwait," replied Yusef. "Perhaps you have contacts in Kuwait? Better than I have?"

"You betcha. I can get right on it." Tidewater heard the printer humming and turned as the computer expert handed him three photos. "Yep, that's Habib Mansur," Marion Tidewater said. "Looks like you really shot the hell out of him."

There was a shrug from the other end of the phone. "We used the helicopter machine guns. It was very good luck that the man was right out in the open. So you will take care of finding the women for Sheikh i-Shibl?"

"Right on it, old buddy. I'll have messages sent out before I leave work tonight." The grin on Tidewater's face was ear to ear. "I owe you one."

"Just find the women," Yusef insisted, "and send Ibrahim to me. Is that a deal?"

"That's a deal. Good night, Gurgin." Tidewater hung up. He stood and did a little two-step dance around the office. "Yessir, yessir!" He finished up the dance near the computer room door, "Norm, write up an e-mail to Darughih Sadiq-Fath's office. His assistant Ali Muhit will read it first thing in the morning, which will be about six hours from now. Send the photo files you just downloaded and tell the darughih he and I got to talk. I want his agents on the job in Kuwait within the hour he picks up this message. Got that?" Norm nodded, Marion Tidewater went on, "Say this exactly: You'll find Tahireh Ibrahim and the two women she stole, Princess Zhara i-Shibl and her mother, Jani Felice i-Shibl, in Kuwait. Then say if he needs any more information, call me at eight a.m. my time tomorrow morning. Got that?"

Norm nodded and was already setting up the e-mail. "No problem, Boss."

As Marion Tidewater passed Lily's desk, he gave her a little hug and she blushed. "Not tonight, but how about tomorrow, darling?"

"Oh, Marion, you're sure?" she cooed.

"You can count on it, I want to party, as my teenagers say." Tidewater laughed.

"I guess we can, okay, after work?"

"After work." His footsteps were light as he left the room.

Five hours later, Ali Muhit wrote back that his boss, Darughih Sadiq-Fath had set in motion a plan to trap Tahireh Ibrahim in Kuwait. He, Sadiq-Fath, had made sure the little Thai girl, Milind would not be freed, that her trial would go smoothly and her execution swiftly. No more women would be taken by the EW's agents, he promised and went on with: "Quddus Sadiq-Fath sends his personal congratulations to Commander Yusef via Tidewater on the elimination of their hated enemy, Haji Mansur." Muhit finished up the e-mail letter, writing, "When my agents pick up the sheikh's women, either in Kuwait or in Europe, where should they be delivered? This is assuming they've not died on the desert."

Tahireh had to drive. Neither Jani nor Zhara had ever learned to handle a 4X4 vehicle. The guiding stars turned in their vast celestial wheel until yellow-pink tendrils of dawn peeked over the flat rocky terrain in front of them. There was no wadi or cliff or rock shelter to hide them and Tahireh hesitated to stop out here in the open. Finally, as dawn evolved to bright, cold morning, tall date palm trees signaled an oasis on the horizon. A few ramshackle buildings and about a dozen tents huddled under the massive date palms. Further in the distance, lorries and petrol tankers could be seen speeding along a narrow highway. The women had crossed the desert all the way to the corner of northeast Saudi. Right where she had wanted them to arrive. With a sigh of relief, Tahireh pulled up behind the decrepit buildings and gratefully parked in the shadow of a broad, red and blue striped awning where tables and chairs awaited lunch customers.

"Wake up," she hollered at her two companions. "Breakfast! Who wants breakfast?"

Zhara held up her hand as she groggily opened her eyes. "Where are we?" She shook her mother who moaned and turned over in the back seat. "Come alive, Mom. Open your eyes."

Stretching, Jani sat up. "Oh," she said, looking out the window, "civilization!"

"Now we must face some problems," Tahireh began, "we have not had baths and Zhara and I look and smell like donkey boys."

"I don't," said Jani, grinning.

"You do smell," retorted her daughter holding her nose, "you stink like a camel."

"That can't be helped," Jani answered back. "Besides, I don't think my odor will keep me from doing business in there."

"Probably not," agreed Tahireh. "Why don't you go in and buy us some food and drink and Zhara and I will sneak into the restroom back here and become women again. We are to become wives of American air force men."

"Really?" asked Zhara.

"Yes," responded Tahireh, "and all because we were able to bring those duffels with us."

"How about me?" Jani queried.

Tahireh shook her head. "You will stay as an Arab woman. The identification Habib and I used to rent the Cruiser will have to do for you. We can only pray."

Jani opened the door of the Land Cruiser, then halted. "Damn, Tahireh! What do I use for money? I came…we came away with nothing. Not even jewelry."

Reaching into the glove compartment, Tahireh pulled out a billfold. "Habib's," she whispered. Inside was a wad of bills. "This came from EW. It is for our expenses, but we must be very cautious in how much we spend this because if anything goes wrong, if we can't reach the air force base as planned, we'll need to use a lot of it for bribes." She handed Jani several bills.

"I understand," said the older woman and dusting off her Bedouin style burqa; she pulled the scarf over her face and got out, disappearing quickly around the corner of the building.

Zhara and Tahireh locked the car doors after they pulled the smaller duffel from the back. No one saw them duck into the doorway marked WC. It was definitely a unisex toilet stinking of urine from the Turkish style hole in the floor. Each woman squatted to do her business. There was no hot water, but there was soap. Evil smelling stuff that had more grit than cleansing oil. It did the job though and in fifteen minutes, both Tahireh and Zhara exited the WC looking very different from when they had entered. Zhara was dressed in jeans and an embroidered white overshirt blouse that went to her knees. Around her hair and face she arranged a scarf. Tahireh had put on a woman's linen suit of knee-length skirt, long-sleeved gold blouse, and jacket. She'd even managed to get a necklace and earrings on. Every inch the Parisian model, except her hair had to be stuffed under a beret and scarf just in case she had to cover her face. Washing their hair in that restroom was out of the question so it was just as well they had to keep their tresses covered. There was even makeup in the duffel. Both women put it on to the hilt.

Jani was waiting by the Cruiser holding a large tray stacked with pita bread, hummus, yogurt, dates, and best of all, thick white porcelain cups of steaming Arabic black sweet coffee. They sat in the Cruiser and wolfed down the food. The coffee was so good it brought tears to their eyes. When Jani had finished, she took the small duffel and went back to the WC to change into Tahireh's black abba and scarf. She too applied makeup, but lightly. As per Tahireh's orders, she stuffed the Bedouin costume into the trash receptacle where the donkey boy outfits had gone.

"You look much better, Mom," said Zhara as she climbed back into the Cruiser. "Tahireh, how much further do we have to drive?"

"Only about an hour. We're nearly at the Kuwaiti border." Tahireh put her bowls into the stack, finished her coffee, and handed the whole mess to Jani. "It would be best if you take all this back in. I should be seen as little as possible. Also, tell the gentleman inside," Tahireh handed Jani more bills and Jani laughed sharply at the term gentleman, "that we wish to fill the petrol tank."

"Right," said Jani gathering up the plates and cups and trash and headed for the front of the store.

Zhara brushed crumbs from her lap. "Do you think we'll get over the border without any problems?"

"It would be wise to pray," remarked Tahireh harshly, driving the Cruiser to the front of the store where a boy filled the tank. "They will be expecting a man to be driving us, of that I am certain. They will not be able to believe that three women, all by themselves, crossed the desert by jeep. We have that advantage, but it is a slim advantage."

"I understand," said Zhara. "Should I practice my American accent?"

"Wouldn't hurt," laughed Tahireh, trying hers out.

When Jani had climbed back in, they set off. The moment the Cruiser pulled up onto the narrow highway, Zhara began talking. It was as if all the tension came pouring out of her. She kept it in English and as much of it in American slang as she could remember.

"I can't wait to see Emil again. He has Charlotte. Mom, did you know that Emil has been keeping Charlotte for me?"

"No, I didn't realize your puppy was still alive."

Zhara nodded and faced Tahireh. This was to be a story, a long story and Zhara was determined to tell it all. "You know how I got my dog, Tahireh?" Zhara didn't wait for an answer. "This was years ago, at least eight years ago. I was riding in the limousine and it slowed, it slowed enough for me to look out and someone had just hit a dog. A stray. She, a she dog and she was in heat. Oh, it was so terrible. All the male dogs were fucking her as injured as she was. Those males kept mounting her, and she was screaming. The chauffeur drove by and I begged him to stop. He just waved his hand at me as if I were nobody. Finally I pounded on the window between him and me and I demanded he do something. 'Don't worry, he said, she will die soon. Another car will hit her.'

"But she could live, I said, she could live and be pregnant and crippled and have to care for puppies and...

"'She is a bitch dog,' said the chauffeur, 'forget her, she is worth nothing.' He drove on home."

"What did you do?" asked Tahireh, amazed at what was coming from the princess. Jani sat silent and stunned at this flood of words from her normally haughty daughter.

Zhara continued, "I sent one of my personal servants out. He found the dog. He took her to a vet, and she lived. She was crippled, but she has done well. I have loved her for many years. And she, me. I truly believe she is grateful. Her name is Charlotte—after the spider?" There was a deep silence for several moments and Zhara went on, "She reminds me constantly that we human females are like bitches in heat to most men. These men, who cannot see beyond their arrogance, go blind and senseless. And take pleasure from it. They care not a bit. When my father told me I had to marry that old sheikh, I knew I would be hurt and become crippled like Charlotte and be attacked like the dogs that attacked her. I knew almost all human males were no different from those dogs. That's when I decided I had to escape. Thank you, Tahireh. Thank you. Thank you for getting my mother out too."

Jani said nothing. She leaned forward and put a hand on her daughter's shoulder and Zhara grabbed the hand and clutched it for a moment. Jani sat back. Tears rolled down her cheeks.

There was a long silence. The border crossing was coming up. The whole thing was rather ludicrous as the gate had no fence attached, only miles and miles of flat desert stretching out for kilometers. The guard on both the Saudi side and the Kuwaiti side scrutinized the women carefully giving them very sexually explicit stares. The Kuwaiti guard muttered something about American husbands letting women, their wives even! run around on their own and how they should be ashamed of themselves. The papers Tahireh presented were not really read, and they were waved all the way through. In another few kilometers, Tahireh turned north onto a large highway and the Cruiser mixed in with heavy traffic. The women relaxed a little more.

On the outskirts of the air base, Tahireh glanced at Zhara and said, "I'm glad I was able to save you, both of you. Now you must help others. Isn't that so?"

"Yes," they both answered.

The MPs guarding the American military gate were far more cautious. All three women were told to get out of the Cruiser and stand aside while contact was made with Captain Lonnie Maxwell, the agent in charge of domestic personnel issues. Fifteen minutes passed before a thin blonde woman in an air force captain's uniform drove a jeep up to the gate and screeched to a halt before jumping out. She looked tough as nails, all bone and taut, tan skin. "I was told there would be one man and two women," she declared firmly.

Tahireh stepped forward. "I'm Tahireh Ibrahim. The haji is not with us. But here are the Princess Zhara i-Shibl and her mother, Jani Felice i-Shibl. We were able to get both of them out."

"Good work, Ibrahim. I'm your contact. Captain Lonnie Maxwell. Now come along."

Captain Maxwell motioned the women back into the Cruiser and ordered, "Follow me." They drove several kilometers passing landing strips and hangers and bunkers. Finally, in front of an old barracks painted a hideous puke-brown, Captain Maxwell pulled to a stop. Tahireh parked beside her.

"You can come with me," the Captain said and the four women entered the door marked Counselor. It was a small room filled with standard-issue-ugly military office furniture. Its only redeeming feature was a well-stocked kitchen toward the back. "Thirsty? Want some tea or coffee? Sit down, you must have had a hell of a trip. Can't believe you drove all the way from the Grand Wadi."

Zhara dropped into a chair and leaned back. "I'd die for a Seven-Up."

"A strong cup of tea for me," said Tahireh and went to the kitchen to help herself. The Captain fetched a soda from the fridge. "Mrs. i-Shibl? What would you like?"

"Tea also."

"I'll fix her some," offered Tahireh.

The captain sat on the edge of a desk near Zhara. Her face had deep lines in it perhaps from years of living in the desert. Her eyes were an icy blue. "Forgive me for asking, but there was supposed to be a man with you? A haji?"

Tahireh was just setting the tea, cream, and sugar on a desk near Jani. With a thump, the tall Parisian model dropped into a chair, her face going pale. Suddenly tears flowed down her cheeks. "They gunned him down," she said in a whisper.

"Who?"

"The head of Arab military security, Commander Yusef and his men," answered Jani. "We'd reached the Cruiser that Tahireh and Habib had hidden in a bushy grove. The security men didn't see us, thank God. But we could see them. The helicopter passed over first."

"No! That's terrible!" exclaimed Captain Maxwell. "We'll file a complaint!"

"Won't do any good," said Zhara, shrugging her shoulders. "No one will talk."

"So much of this goes on and no one says a thing," Lonnie Maxwell sighed.

Jani laughed sharply, "It's done in the Arab countries all the time. You're tried, hung, and convicted before sunrise."

"But a holy man!"

"They shot down two other holy men who were with him." Jani went on, "We were awfully lucky to have been well hidden. Thanks to Tahireh."

"I should say," said the Captain. "Oh, I've been getting frantic calls from our contact, Siddhu Prakash? You should call him. Then you'll all want to get a bath and sleep for a while? We've made arrangements for Princess Zhara here to fly out this evening. Obviously, we'll tell the pilot he's taking you too, Mrs. i-Shibl."

"Are there passports for us?" asked Jani.

"We'll have to come up with something for you, Mrs. i-Shibl, but Zhara has a new name all done up for her. Zoë. How's that? Mrs. Zoë Feldenstein, a new bride who's been visiting her husband."

"I've become a Jew?" Zhara grinned. "What next?"

"American Jew at that," Maxwell laughed, "from West Hollywood, California. I think we can have something ready for you, Mrs. i-Shibl. I hate to make you Zoë's mother, but you two look so obviously related."

"Jani, please."

Captain Maxwell stood, "Until tonight. Got a preference for a new first name?"

"Might as well use Felice, that's my Irish name," said Jani.

"Nah. They'd know that. We'll come up with something. Go get a bath, get some sleep. Then we take some passport photos. The third door on the right, the room's all yours and the bathroom's at the end of the hall."

The two women, feeling their exhaustion, took their drinks and left the office. Captain Maxwell handed Tahireh the telephone.

Within moments, Siddhu was on the other end of the line, jabbering. "Are you all right? Is the princess with you?"

"Shhh," said Tahireh. "Both the princess and her mother are with me, completely safe." She went on to relate the death of Habib. Siddhu began shouting at Dr. Legesse, who came on the phone. "So he's dead?" was her dejected comment.

"Yes, I saw him fall." Tahireh took a deep breath. "What should I do next?"

"Get some rest," said Dr. Legesse. "Then come back to Israel."

"What about the Thai girl that Habib was going to help rescue here in Kuwait?" Tahireh inquired.

Siddhu spoke up, "Too dangerous. We are certain it is a trap. We have made efforts to convince Habib's friend, Shamsi Granfa to back away from it. He laughs at us."

"They will execute her," insisted Tahireh, "you know they will."

Halima Legesse said, "Yes. We want very much to save her. Our information tells us plans are underway to prevent anyone from stepping in on her behalf."

"Who told you?"

"There is a man who has just come to Haifa," Dr. Legesse explained, "a defector from the Agency named Russ Snow. The baron allowed him to find us. He thinks Snow may be valuable to us. Anyway, this man, Snow, used to be the computer expert in charge of making all the contacts between Tidewater and Yusef and Sadiq-Fath. He insists these men are all poised, waiting to strike."

"They've already struck. It was an Arab Security Force helicopter that fired on the hajis," responded Tahireh sadly. "Could I at least call Shamsi from the base? I could talk to him safely from here."

Grudgingly, Dr. Legesse agreed. "You may call him. Nothing more, understand? We have lost one of our great heroes this week, we don't want to lose another one."

"I understand." Tahireh sat back, "Now tell me about the baron. Has he found his ladylove?"

Siddhu laughed loudly, "He has. As of right now, as we speak, they are meeting."

"God, I'd love to be a fly on the wall for that," smiled the model. "One can only imagine Which I will do as I take my bath and sleep. You send the baron my sincere apologies that we could not bring Habib with us. Oui?"

"Yes, Tahireh, you go rest. Thank the lord you made it." Dr. Legesse hung up.

"You only *talk* to Shamsi Granfa," Siddhu ordered kindly, "then come to Haifa. See you soon." He too hung up.

Tahireh handed the phone back to Captain Maxwell. "I'll go see if there's any hot water left. Are there clothes in my room?"

"Just about any costume you need, Miss Ibrahim." The captain walked with her to the office door. "You're doing a great service and anything I can do to help, anything at all that's in my power, you let me know." She extended a bony hand and Tahireh shook it firmly.

"Thank you, Captain."

Halima Legesse sat slumped in her chair with her head thrown back and eyes staring at the ceiling. It was a very uncommon pose for her and Siddhu did not know what to do. She had gone totally silent, unresponsive to his queries as to whom to call first. It would not have occurred to him to touch her or comfort her. That was not his place. Finally, at last, he decided the best thing to do was to call Dr. Legesse's best and only friend, Rachel Bar-Fischer.

Russell was eating lunch in the communal dining room when Dr. Bar-Fischer entered the large room. She stopped to speak to a black, matronly woman whose daughters were digging into lunch as if starved. The woman was smiling with pleasure and grabbed Dr. Bar-Fischer's hand like someone saved from drowning. It took a bit of pressure for the Israeli woman to pull away and when she had managed to do so, she did not speak to or respond to any of the other numerous greetings from staff or clients. With direct speed, she threaded her way through the tables and delicately sat down next to the Native American. Leaning close to him, she whispered, "Habib Mansur is dead."

Russ slowly laid down his fork. After a moment, he asked, "And Tahireh Ibrahim?"

"She and the two women she rescued are alive and safe."

He looked hard at the handsome Israeli doctor. "What do you want of me? I am sure you wouldn't have told me this news if you didn't want me to do something to help."

Rachel Bar-Fischer nodded. "Siddhu thinks maybe...perhaps Commander Yusef will send an official notification to the Agency and perhaps to Darughih Sadiq-Fath by computer. He wants to know if that assumption is correct and if so..."

"...can I retrieve it?" Russ finished her question.

She nodded.

"Yes. In addition," Russ went on, "the chances are very good that Yusef will send photos of the body, maybe even of the autopsy. He likes to do that sort of thing, sort of as proof he actually accomplished what he said." Russ pushed his tomato, onion, and olive salad away. There was an herb in the dressing that was too mysterious for his palate. He turned to face the doctor. "He'd contact Agent Tidewater at the Agency first, as Siddhu guessed, and then Tidewater will notify Sadiq-Fath. Yusef never contacts Sadiq-Fath directly, or vice versa. Those two guys have never spoken or written each other directly. Ever. Not in the cards. Too risky. They use agents or better, they talk through Tidewater."

"Can you retrieve anything for us?" Bar-Fischer appealed to him. She had turned away from Russ's eyes and put both her hands palm down on the table.

He gently laid one large hand on top of one of her small ones. "Yes. Get me on a computer right now. We don't want the files to be too deep. That would take me hours to search out. I gotta get on now."

She nodded. "Come with me."

A half an hour later, Russ stood in front of a computer. He waved his hands dismissively, "I can't work with this piece of crap."

Siddhu cringed.

Devi, the receptionist-secretary chortled softly, "Told you, Siddhu. I've told you that for months. This machine is garbage."

The American Indian looked at the East Indian and said, "Right now, we go to a computer store and we get what I need."

In the palms up, hands out gesture Siddhu Prakash used to show hopelessness, he responded, "We don't have that kind of money!"

"How expensive will it be?" asked Rachel Bar-Fischer, "I might be able to get it through the drug treatment funds. We'd have to submit a purchase order."

Russ laughed sharply. "No time for that nonsense. I'll buy it. There's an account I can use that Tidewater won't have traces on."

Siddhu shuffled his feet.

"Now!" demanded Russ. "Those files will get submarined and we won't get access."

"Wait here a minute," Rachel told Siddhu and ducked out the door.

Devi lifted the phone and pushed in the numbers to summon Taqi on his pager. When it went through, she smiled and set the phone down. To Siddhu's horror and Devi's glee, Russ began clearing the table of the old computer system. Devi motioned toward a small table in the corner and Russ smiled. The two quickly pulled that table into a U-shaped configuration with the desk and long table already there and Devi was instantly on her hands and knees pulling plugs and phone wires.

"Is that the only surge protection you have?" Russ asked her as she held up a multiple set plug.

"Yep. It's a wonder we haven't fried everything in the office." Devi motioned toward the printer, "Can we get a real color printer too?"

Russ grinned, "Yes. But you will want to keep that old clunker to do files and long print jobs. The ink is much less expensive."

"Gotcha," Devi acknowledged and patted the big machine.

"You can buy us a good computer outfit?" Dr. Legesse strode into the office, Rachel beside her.

"No problem. I'll have the trust fund investment managers write it off as a donation, which it is."

"You would do this for us?" Dr. Legesse seemed nonplussed.

"Not a big deal. We have to give away a percentage of that money every year or we don't meet the trust requirements. Quit worrying about it." Russ zipped up the front of his jacket and waved at Devi to come with him. "Let's do it. No more pussy-footing around."

The front door opened at that precise moment and Taqi, hair mussed, looked in. "We go somewhere?"

"Yes," said Bar-Fischer grabbing Halima's hand to silence her. "Yes. Go buy the computer."

"I will go with you," insisted Siddhu.

"You don't know a modem from a monkey," laughed Devi.

"I want to come," insisted the little man.

"Don't argue," said Russ and led the way out the door.

Gently, firmly, Rachel pulled Halima into Halima's office and impelled her into a chair at the desk. Rachel sat down beside her, leaned toward her, and put a hand on the telephone. "My friend, it is time to call Carl-Joran." Halima looked at her with so much pain in her eyes that Rachel began to cry.

***

They were sitting down to lunch when the call came. Gustav, on his creaky old legs, hurried to Carl-Joran's side and in a whisper told him that Dr. Legesse was on the phone. Carl-Joran glanced at the assembled family, Bonnie, Trisha, Sture, and said, "Be right back."

Trish was sitting across from Sture and they glanced at each other with another of those inquiring dart-like looks that indicated their complete puzzlement over their new status. Bonnie and Carl-Joran had told them last night. Trisha had taken the news with high amusement and, with a loud braying laugh, promptly slapped Sture on the shoulder. He had turned beet-red and croaked, "*Far, hur kann det ga?*"

His father had smiled sadly and responded, "*So war det.*"

Reluctantly, Sture hugged Trisha, released her quickly saying, "*Mina nya syster.*" To his father he said, shaking his head, "I wondered that she acted so much like a Swedish woman."

"*Ja so,*" his dad agreed sagely and broke out the *konjak*, a particularly good five-star brand from Armenia. The toasts went on until they were all tipsy.

The next morning had been met with good cheer. Sture announced at breakfast that he was finished with being on a forced vacation and would return to the Karolinska Institute that evening. Trisha decreed her intention to go back to California within the week. She had already put too much of a burden on the substitute teacher and besides, there was a very important basketball game coming up the end of the month. Trisha loved all this adventure, true, but her true role in life was to coach. So she announced.

Bonnie and Carl-Joran just grinned with that look satisfied lovers have the morning after and held hands.

That the newly conjoined family had all gathered for lunch was an accident of timing. Astrid had fixed her split pea soup, the thick kind that almost had to be cut with a knife to eat, and Sture had returned from skiing with Katarina early. He told them that the Arab contingent of agents had followed him and he had felt very uncomfortable putting Katarina in harm's way.

Wanting exercise but not wanting to go skiing again, Trisha had found a basketball in the stables. After only a few minutes outside in the bitter cold, she had discovered to her consternation that the basketball froze and cracked and her eyelids and nose hairs were frosted. Krister had come out and shaken his head at her, indicating that she was crazy. He had laughed at the basketball's plight.

Bonnie and Carl-Joran spent the morning talking with Inge Person. No words could describe the look on the advokat's face when she walked into the baron's office to discover him alive. When power of speech finally returned to her, she shook Bonnie Ixey's hand with appreciation saying, "It is good to put a face to the voice." Signing the accounts into Bonnie's name, with an addendum that the will had not yet been probated, therefore such action was only temporary to release funds, took merely a little over an hour. Inge Person promised to deal with the hated Algbak herself. "It would be a pleasure," said the advokat, "to straighten out that woman. Of course I will not tell her about your being alive, my dear Baron, but I will be more than happy to install Bonnie as heir apparent...*fur narvarande*...a little while."

Now, Carl-Joran rose from the lunch table and strode ahead of Gustav leaving the retainer to make his halting way down the long hall. Sitting at his desk in his big office, he gingerly picked up the receiver. Halima told him immediately, without preamble.

Carl-Joran was only able to say, "I want to see any photos Snow is able to retrieve."

"I will tell him that," Dr. Legesse agreed, "He can e-mail them, I am sure."

"That should be no problem," said Carl-Joran softly. "And Tahireh said Yusef couldn't take the body? They say it's still with the Bedouin?"

"That's what she told us."

"Okay. Maybe we can find that tribe. Now you tell Miss Tahireh Ibrahim that I insist she come back to Haifa and not go to help Shamsi. She is not to try to rescue that Thai girl. We cannot lose another fine operative."

"I have told her and I will tell her you have ordered it," Halima Legesse sighed, "but you know as well as I how headstrong that girl is."

"Ah, yes, that is why she is one of our best people. Okay. One question more. May I come alive? Enough of this being dead. I will take Bonnie to Switzerland and we will see the bankers. We will meet Freda Englich and the women. I want to hear the mother's story for myself."

There was silence on the other end of the phone. The doctor had been struck when she was too weak to retaliate with strength against this very powerful man. Slowly she managed to say, "No."

He swore in Swedish, "*Fy fan!*"

"Don't you swear!" Halima Legesse came to, shaken awake by the words. "Listen to what I say: not yet. We are very close, Carl-Joran, but not yet. We want to have Sadiq-Fath out in the open and if you move too soon, all our work, Habib's sacrifice will have been in vain."

"That's a low blow," growled Carl-Joran.

"The truth though, it is the truth." She was regaining her determination. "Still, if you can go to Switzerland incognito, you and Bonnie, you could meet the princess and her mother. Then you could come here. Can you do that and not be caught? Or recognized?"

"Certainly." He sounded insulted by her doubt.

The sigh of resignation that came over the phone was almost palpable. "I will agree to your doing that, Baron. Nothing more. Straight to Geneva. Straight here."

"I promise," said the big man.

"Until we see each other," the doctor said and hung up.

Bonnie was standing in the doorway. The look in her eyes told Carl-Joran that she had been there some time. He motioned to her to come to him, which she did. "A very good friend of mine has been murdered," he whispered, "doing work for Emigrant Women."

Bonnie threw her arms around his neck. "It wasn't me, was it? It wasn't because I didn't arrive sooner and get money to him?"

"No, no, no." He pulled her close. "Money would have made no difference. The Arab commander simply shot him down. That is all. He shot down two other holy men who were with Habib, just like that. No compunction."

"How horrible!" said Bonnie in shock.

"We are leaving for Geneva."

"We?"

"You and I, tonight. Rather, we will take the four a.m. shuttle from Vasteras to Oslo and the SwissAir from there to Geneva. You must pack." Carl-Joran stood up. He had also decided that the time had come to clean up the local environment. His son's medical studies were important and his new daughter should not be bothered by those pesky agents following them around. He rang for Krister and started for the door. He paused to hug Bonnie. "Don't take much and don't pack anything you would miss if we cannot retrieve the baggage or if we get picked up. All right?"

"I understand," said Bonnie, hugging him in return. She laughed sharply. "Two weeks ago I would have been outraged at being told such a thing. I guess it takes only once to learn the reality of being stalked, of having someone hate you enough to kill you. An enlightenment I owe all to you, my dear…husband."

He shrugged. "It is the Iranian Darughih Sadiq-Fath who has the more murderous operatives tracking us. He does not hate us. He does not have that kind of emotion. It is business for him. Strictly business. His pride has been hurt because we in EW, especially I, have been able to elude him for so long. No, not hatred."

"I don't understand," said Bonnie as they walked down the long hallway.

Carl-Joran's face became somber, "Don't try. This kind of hell and deceit does not become you."

"Lies do not become you either," she said up to him.

A crooked smile spread across his face, "All of my life is true."

"Even the lies?"

"Especially the lies."

Darughih Quddus Sadiq-Fath gloated. "Are the agents in place?" he asked Muhit, stepping into the bulletproof Mercedes. The car still dripped steaming water from its morning wash. The driver closed the door behind the darughih.

As the car pulled away from the heavily guarded residence, Muhit, bundled in a thick bomber jacket, turned in his seat to look at his boss. "We have reached an understanding with the judges who are to try the Milind Pandharpurkar case. The verdict, and the punishment, should be swift."

"That was a given regardless of our interference," said Sadiq-Fath, wishing he had put on his warm overcoat. "Driver, turn on some heat back here." Around them, covering the higher suburbs of Tehran, a thin layer of snow frosted the lovely gardens and trees. House servants were busily sweeping steps and patios. A few maids were slipping and sliding their way to market. Here and there, the big black Mercedes had to circumvent cars and trucks that had not made it up, or down, an incline.

Almost immediately, warm air filled the back of the Mercedes and Sadiq-Fath relaxed. He hated to be cold. "We have information from the prison guards that there is a man who is trying to rescue the Pandharpurkar girl, he's been dealt with?"

"Shamsi Granfa is his name. He is under constant surveillance and his phone is tapped." Ali Muhit watched the road.

"Is this man connected to EW? That isn't clear to me," Sadiq-Fath commented.

The old soldier pushed his chin down onto his chest. "It isn't clear to us either." His hand lay, out of long habit, on the butt of the 9mm pistol in the holster on his belt. "We don't believe he is one of their regular operatives. He's new on the scene and his calls to them just began with this case. In fact, his calls went first to Lori Dubbayaway in Bangkok, whom we are certain is EW. We do believe he will be contacted by the EW administrator, Prakash, about the Pandharpurkar girl and that EW money will be put in Granfa's hands sometime this afternoon. Of course, that will be too late for Milind." Muhit leaned onto his hand on the gun butt at this waist. "There is another servant girl in prison. One EW will feel compelled to try and rescue. We're hoping this Granfa bloke will also want her."

"Why?"

"She is pregnant by a Kuwaiti dignitary who has asked that she disappear."

"This dignitary can't send the girl home?" The question was mere curiosity. Certainly Sadiq-Fath did not care one way or another.

"Too dangerous. Her father is a low-wage clerk in the Thai government, Bureau of Parks, I believe, and the mother is a teacher. He and his wife might come after the baby's father for money, not that they would be able to collect. Still, it would get to Amnesty and the other humanitarian organizations and cause unpleasantness for the dignitary." The car was pulling into the courtyard of the security agency office building. Muhit unlocked his seat belt and put on his hat.

The driver parked and jumped out to open the darughih's door. Together, Sadiq-Fath and the aged assistant walked into the tightly guarded building. It was cold in here also and Sadiq-Fath grumbled, "Why must I be chilled everywhere I go?" He shouted at a nearby secretary, "Have the heat turned up."

Eyes averted, the man replied, "The furnace is not working, sir, we have been freezing all morning."

"Has a repair man not been called?" asked Sadiq-Fath in astonishment.

"I believe so, sir, yessir," said the secretary, cringing, "I can check to see what is happening if you want?"

"Find the building manager. You aren't responsible for heat, he is. Have him report to me."

"Immediately, sir," the man responded and scurried away.

As they entered the darughih's office, two other male secretaries were plugging in space heaters. It was a couple degrees warmer in this room already. "Thank you," Sadiq-Fath acknowledged as the two men left. Turning his rear end to a heater, Quddus Sadiq-Fath looked at his assistant. "So it is all in place?"

"We will plan to pick up Granfa, and whoever else we can catch, interrogate them, and hold them until the people at EW give us the location of the women they have taken from Iran."

The darughih nodded. "And then we execute Granfa and this whomever person, perhaps after a trial of some sort?"

"That's the plan, sir," smiled Muhit. "I personally will bring Granfa and any associate here to Iran and we will execute them."

Jani's hair had been cut and bleached and dyed a charcoal salt and pepper. Tahireh had expertly applied makeup and Captain Maxwell had chosen an ostentatious pantsuit that screamed Rodeo Drive. The addition of oversized earrings and a clunky necklace finished the job. When Jani stepped in front of the full-length mirror, she gasped.

Zhara covered her mouth to keep from exploding in laughter.

"But look at you!" exclaimed Jani. The two stood side by side. Zhara's long dark hair was sun-bleached blonde with a streak of flashy silver and perfectly straight, her exposed skin a creamy tan. She looked like a teenage model right off Malibu beach. Her attire consisted of tights and an open-knit, baby doll top over a turtleneck jersey and high-heeled sandals. There was an engagement ring and a wedding ring on her finger. She hugged her mom with one arm and peered into her passport with the other hand. "Mrs. Zoë Feldenstein. Eighteen…no, just turned nineteen. Born in Hollywood, California on Christmas day. What a blast!"

Lonnie Maxwell handed Jani her passport. "You are Mrs. Myrna Feldenstein. A widow from West Hollywood, you and your daughter-in-law are going home after a visit to your son Paul, who's a pilot serving in the air force. Memorize everything. Your birthday, birthplace, all the countries you've visited. Do those rings fit?"

Jani…a.k.a. Mrs. Feldenstein Sr. twisted the diamond ring on her ring finger and then flicked through the stamped pages of her new passport. "My goodness, I have certainly traveled a lot!"

"You'll notice that most of them are takeoff points for cruises. You're husband hunting." Lonnie grinned. "Think you can manage that?"

"No more husbands, thank you," Jani laughed in return and picked up the large handbag to sort through the rest of her stuff. There were also two entire carryon backpacks for Jani and Zhara to explore.

Zhara had shaken out her small fanny pack purse and was going through her new possessions. "When do we leave?"

"In an hour. You'll be flying out on a military transport to Frankfurt, Germany. There you'll go by taxi to the civilian Frankfurt airport and get onto a Lufthansa flight to Geneva. Mrs. Englich will meet you in Geneva. She'll take you to her private school and there you'll stay."

Tahireh, who had gone to the commissary after finishing Jani's makeup, came back. She dropped a couple newspapers onto the table. "The Saudi newspaper has an article about the death of the hajis. Only two paragraphs and it says they were murdered by Bedouin discontents. Sort of a silly thing to say since two of the hajis are known to be Bedouins." She pointed down at the women's photos on the front page of the paper. Jani was in full mufti standing next to her husband and the one of Zhara showed her in school uniform. Tahireh smiled with satisfaction. "You turned out well. No one could possibly recognize you. Come on, we better get you to the plane."

"I can take them," Lonnie Maxwell said and gathered up her uniform jacket and jeep keys. "Do up those packs, put the passports in your purses, let's go!"

"God, I have butterflies in my stomach again," exclaimed Zhara-Zoë.

Jani-Myrna had no time to grieve any more. A flash of emotional pain went through her and that was all she allowed herself. Quickly, she zipped up the packs and loaded them onto the wheeled carryall. "Ready to go!"

Captain Maxwell turned to Tahireh Ibrahim. "You need sleep. You need rest. I expect to find you doing both when I get back."

Tahireh smiled and nodded. The moment the jeep engine started, Tahireh picked up the phone and dialed Granfa's cell phone number.

Shamsi Granfa sweated. In his late thirties, he looked years older. Overweight, flushed, he came away from the small grocery store that was his secret currency exchange depot. Anyone who did business in Arab countries had their source for receiving and sending foreign currency. It was a necessity. He had thought about running a money exchange from his own business location, but exchanges were often raided by the security forces. His business affairs had to be kept absolutely free of government interference, and so far, because of the clientele who sought him out, he had been left strictly to his own devices. This was good for what he called his extracurricular activity of rescuing victims of the Kuwaiti purges.

His familiarity with the word extracurricular came from a long career as a student at the University of Washington. Of all things, he had a doctor of science in nursing and pathology. Years he'd spent in Seattle attending university—years! to keep himself from being thrown out by the American HS, back to Iraq and certain death as a Kurd. When he did get his final degree, he also picked up American citizenship, which allowed him to come to Kuwait as an investor three years ago. He still felt like a foreigner in Kuwait and he probably always would.

Sometimes memories assailed him. He would watch his mother dying in the gas attack on that lonely mountain pass in north Iraq while he and his younger sister hid in a tiny hole in the cliff. Everyone in the group perished. He and his mother and his older sister, Rané, were trying to join up with his father and his two brothers in Turkey. But his two brothers never made it out of Turkey; they were shot as spies. Shamsi and Rané nearly starved on that cold pass. Only by the grace of some higher power did a herdsman find them and feed them. That amazing man managed to slip them over the Turkish border disguised as sheep. Allah be blessed, that herdsman had wrapped sheepskins over them and had them crawl, in the dark, past distant border guards and into a border village to the man's cousin's house. To this day, Shamsi retched at the smell of raw lanolin.

They had not got off free though. The cousin had raped Rané. They'd run again. A missionary family from Seattle had gathered them in and sent them to America. Sounds simple in retrospect. Simple, except for the recurring bouts of terror.

Rané, actually, was all he had left of his family after his father died last year. She had managed to get into University of California at Fresno six months ago and was supremely happy in her college studies. One of the reasons he did the work he did was to have money to send to her. Thus, in every way that counted, he was alone and he hated being alone in the world. He wanted family, he wanted to belong to something, to someone. Maybe he'd take better care of himself when that something or someone became genuine.

Shamsi hurried along the busy sidewalks. It was noon and offices and stores had closed for midday prayers. Allah u abha! came the first call from the muezzin tower and many of the people around him knelt, facing Mecca. Religion was another thing he'd cast off when he cast off Iraqi citizenship.

His cell phone vibrated. He looked at the caller ID. Not one he knew...wait, it was a prefix for the American air base. He answered, confirmed who it was and said in careful measured instructions, "Yes. The alley behind the courthouse, south side. Dress as we agreed."

This too was good. He'd long wanted to tie in with the EW's cause, and now it was doubly official. He not only had money committed to him, he had an operative.

CHAPTER 13: SNOW IN THE DESERT

Dinner at the Hanley Arms was always worth the wait. Although Tidewater had palmed some very large currency into the maitre d's pocket, it still took close on to fifteen minutes to be guided into the smaller of the private dining rooms. The waiter carried their drinks and luckily, taken the meal order as well. Marion stretched, rolled up his cuffs, put his arm around the buxom Lily, and his beeper vibrated.

"Damn!" he groused, looking at the number. It was Norm, his new assistant who had been given strict instructions not to disturb his boss unless the heavens were falling. Marion Tidewater shrugged and said to Lily, "Gotta make a phone call."

"Have the waiter bring a phone in here," she smiled.

"Ah, right. You, my dear," he nuzzled her, "know all about my work anyway. Such a good girl." Tidewater leaned out the doorway and waved at his waiter. A phone appeared almost instantly. "Norm, this better be…"

"Sir," the man's voice was deadly serious, "the agents we had covering the Hermelin castle in Sweden are in lockup."

"What?" Tidewater could feel the blood drain from his face.

Norm went on in one fast breath, "I just received a request over the Interpol connection to confirm identification of two men. They are our men. They were arrested in Norrkoping and put in jail in Vasteras."

"Interpol?" Tidewater was having trouble comprehending this.

Norm slowed his speech. "The Swedish equivalent of highway patrol officers arrested both agents outside the little community grocery store in Norrkoping late yesterday, six-thirty Swedish time. That was twelve hours ago."

Every muscle in Tidewater's body was in catatonic rigor. "I don't understand. How could they be arrested? On what charges?"

"I've got the booking charges here, Agent Tidewater, and they're for real." Norm could be heard changing positions in his chair. "DWIs."

"Say that again."

"Drunk driving, sir. It's a very serious offence in Sweden. Very serious. One step removed from attempted manslaughter."

"Our agents were driving while intoxicated?"

"From what I've pulled up on the booking sheet, which I had to have translated, it seems they were not driving. That is, the automobile they were in was not moving. The grocery store manager was going off shift and when he went to throw out the day's garbage, he discovered the agents parked by the trash bin in the lot behind the store. He tried to talk to the men to tell them to move on, but they were obviously too drunk to drive so he called the highway patrol. The responding officers found both agents passed out. The officers attempted to wake them up for a field sobriety test but neither agent could stand up. They were put into a paddy wagon and taken to a lockup where both agents were given blood tests and found to have such high levels of alcohol in their system that they were instantly incarcerated at a facility for alcoholics. Do not pass go; straight past a judge, into a dry-out facility."

"I can't believe this."

"Believe it, sir. Agent Warwick and Agent Kleinem are in the Swedish equivalent of a Betty Ford clinic with bars. For two weeks minimum stay. Their status and jobs mean nothing. By Swedish law, the failing of the alcohol level test is guilt. It'll be simpler to have them go through treatment than to go through the paperwork to get them out."

Tidewater pounded the table with his fist spilling his drink of whiskey and soda all over the tablecloth. "How could they be drunk? They were on duty. They know we'd fire their butts if they were drunk on duty. Then you say the car wasn't moving? How can they be charged with drunk driving when the car was parked?"

"The Swedes don't quibble about such details," Norm laughed harshly. "If you are behind the wheel of an automobile, whether it's moving or not, and you are legally drunk, you land in jail. Drunk, sir, is one glass of wine with dinner the night before testing."

"My God!"

"Furthermore, if you are drunk while riding in the car and you can't take over for the driver if he's caught, you go to jail also."

"Unbelievable!"

"Not only that, but you get sent direct to dry-out. Zap! No discussion, no appeals." Norm explained, "In addition, the Agency will be billed for the treatment and it'll be expensive!" He slowed his words down again and continued, "The only bright light in this tunnel, sir...?"

"You mean there is one?"

"Yessir. The Arab agents were also convicted of DWI and put in drunk tank, sir."

"No!"

"Yep."

"Muslims don't drink alcohol. Conservative Muslims, that is, and agents of the Iranian Security Force don't touch the stuff."

"Our agents will need to do a lot of explaining, sir," said Norm, "their agents will have to plead for their lives. Oh, and," he paused for the effect, "they were all put in the same room in the same lockup so it seems they were all picked up together."

Many scenarios went through Tidewater's mind, images of the agents being rolled out of their cars, trying to explain what had happened, and Tidewater was convinced EW was somehow behind this. He would have to ask the dirty tricks guys downstairs how inebriation can be achieved in unwilling agents. It was done all the time to civilians the Agency wanted compromised. Tidewater hung his head and muttered to Norm. "I suppose it's much too late to assign other agents. Our birds have flown."

"The last message we had from Kleinem was that the Hermelin son was seen driving down the highway to Stockholm and a reservation had been made on a flight out of Vasteras for two people under the name Ixey. Kleinem assumed Bonnie and Trisha Ixey were on their way home."

"Well, thanks for the update, Norm. Go to bed. Get some sleep. Nothing more we can do from here."

"No sir."

Tidewater clicked off and laid the phone on the table. "Lily, let's have a great evening. We are celebrating the demise of a powerful EW agent and that hasn't changed. Nothing worse could possibly happen."

"Oh, Marion, you are such a charming man," she cooed.

The small jet's wings were being heavily doused with anti-icing compound and would continue to be right up to engine ignition. Bonnie looked askance at the black runway barely visible through the blowing snow. Vasteras was a middling size city about halfway to Stockholm on the same Lake Malaran. As any large lake did, Lake Malaran generated its own nasty weather.

The captain of the plane seemed not the least concerned. Bonnie had seen her walk completely around the plane, patting it down like a horse and chatting with the refuelers before climbing onto the onramp. At the moment, she was chatting nonchalantly with the navigator as they walked ahead of the passengers. Both officers paused to greet their human cargo. The captain did a semisalute as Carl-Joran came up to her.

"*Hur ga det, min herre baron?*" she asked.

"*Mycket fin,*" he responded with a smile. "*Sshh, jag ar inte har. Jo?*"

"*Ja so,*" the captain agreed and waved them to their seats at the front of the plane.

"What did you tell her?" asked Bonnie as they sat.

"That I wasn't here," said the big man, grinning.

"Okay," said Bonnie, buckling up. As much as she wanted to be calm about this, there were still butterflies in her stomach. Her knuckles were a glowing white.

Carl-Joran took her hands in his. "Captain Johanneson was a fighter pilot in our military before she came to this airline. Don't worry."

"Women's equality, eh?"

"Women's superiority," He chuckled. The jet engines roared to life. "The Swedes have known for fifty years that women tend to be as good, maybe better fighter jet pilots as men. Same for Navy work. You see, the Swedes are far more practical than you Americans. If a thing works, use it."

Bonnie gulped as the little jet neatly pulled onto the runway. "I think it has to do with prejudice, my dear. Americans can be terribly small minded."

With a whoosh! the jet skimmed the icy runway and seemed to be lifted by the swirling white snow into the black sky.

"Well, I am glad you said that and not me," he smiled and curled into his seat for the short flight over the high mountains to Oslo.

Devi had managed to convince Russ that they should stop for lunch on the way back from computer shopping. He stood next to her and Taqi in front of the open café and drank in the smell of low tide, oiled pilings, the harbor, the odors of frying fish and strong coffee. It was his body that finally sent the message to his brain that the breeze he felt was warm, blessedly warm. He realized again that the water lapping at the dock nearby was of the Mediterranean. It was true. He was in Israel.

Lunch, consisting of gyros and salads, in hand, the three of them with their precious load of computers arrived back at headquarters. Taqi helped carry stuff. Russ had decided to buy several computers, one of which he would take with him to whatever place he would use as a residence. He set one up in Devi's office and ran cables to a neighboring room, unused except for storage, and in there he constructed what would be his onsite tech cubby. The lack of windows was a nuisance, but he understood the need for complete security that obviated any windows anywhere in the complex. Taqi stayed to help push tables, shove cabinets, and carry boxes. Meticulously, the installation evolved. Every so often they had to shoo an anxiously hovering Siddhu from the area. Finally, around eight o'clock in the evening, Siddhu stomped his feet and decreed that it was suppertime, that they'd skipped right over teatime in their obsession to work, and that they bloody well better stop to eat supper.

"We're ready to rock and roll anyway," Russ said.

"Really?" Siddhu clapped.

"Really."

"Wait, I will fetch Halima." Off he raced. Moments later, as Devi and Taqi were laying out the boxes of Chinese curry that Siddhu had ordered, Dr. Legesse strode into the front office. "We can have a toast " said Siddhu, holding up a champagne bottle in one hand and tonic water in the other.

Devi passed around small paper cups. She and Russ and Dr. Legesse took some champagne. Siddhu and Taqi took tonic water. The cups in the air, Russ reached over and pushed the first button. His main computer lit up and hummed. Devi stepped out and turned hers on. The beeps and whines and hums announced that all was well.

"Next, a webpage!" proclaimed Russ and Halima almost choked on her drink. Russ laughed and toasted, "To Emigrant Women!"

Devi, Taqi, and Siddhu echoed this. "To EW!"

"To EW!" exclaimed Halima, catching up. "You are exactly right, Mr. Snow. Next you make us a webpage, although God help us, we do not need more business at the moment! After that, your assignment is to convince Lama Kazi Padma-Lakshmi in India to obtain e-mail."

"Done!" Russ promised. "Do I have to go there to do it?"

"Maybe," Siddhu warned.

"Hand me a ticket to ride!" the tall dark man laughed happily. "Now, all of you except Devi, scram. It's time to get the Internet connections done. As soon as we're online, I can do some serious work."

"Those photos, please," begged Halima.

"Yes, those are first on my list," he promised and while the others dug into the Chinese curry, Russ took his plate and sat down in his own very small, but very high tech cubby. He'd been pleasantly surprised at the ease with which he could get absolutely fresh gear from Haifa stores.

In fact, the selection was from a worldwide market: Japanese, American, Russian, French, Dutch, British, even Chinese and some places he had never heard of. Kid in a candy store, he was content. Before he logged on, he pulled the beaded headband from his pocket—the infamous headband that had started his move to Israel. He put it firmly over his scalp. He was home.

A warmth suddenly hung over his shoulder. He glanced up. The gawky tallness of Dr. Legesse bent to tell him, "Captain Maxwell at the American air base in Kuwait called me just before I came in here to tell me that Tahireh Ibrahim is not there. She has put on a disguise and has left to join the man we know as Shamsi Granfa."

Russ breathed in, and out slowly. "Get me Maxwell's e-mail address. Immediately. And Granfa's."

"Captain Maxwell I can get. Granfa is a complete puzzle to us." Dr. Legesse straightened up. She turned to Devi. "Give Russell what he needs."

"Of course," Devi scurried to her desk.

With a shake of his broad shoulders, Russ said, "If Granfa has e-mail, it'll be in my file before midnight."

Dr. Legesse poured herself some more champagne. "We hope Tahireh can tell us she is safe before midnight."

"We can do more than hope," said Russ firmly and sent out the first search order. It took only seconds to show a website in Granfa's name. "I got a hit." Russ announced. The others gathered around. The screen was white with ten language choices. "This is a huge site," he explained, and grimly went on, "it's heavily encrypted."

"What does that mean?" asked Siddhu.

Devi spoke up, "It means you can't get in without a password."

"It means," Russ turned to them, "that this man runs a kind of business where only those who are given permission can enter. You want to pay this man money; he has to approve of you first."

"What could the business possibly be?" Halima sulked.

Russ clicked the keys. "All I can tell you is that the search engines find his site with the words: adoptions, transplants, hearts, livers, medical supplies, biomedical consultations...here, see for yourself."

They looked over his shoulder. Siddhu jerked upright and whispered in dismay, "Does Granfa sell babies and body parts?"

The late afternoon sun tried its best to warm them. The frigid air trapped in the alley between the large courthouse and larger jail made Tahireh's skin crawl. Frost glittered in the darkest shadows. Dressed in a white clinician's coat and pants with a long tan trench coat over both, her head and hair covered in a white and checkered *burqa* and a wide moustache tickling her nose and mouth, she looked male, Arab and professionally medical. Her hands, clutching a thin leather portfolio briefcase, were in thick camelhair lined gloves, for which she was very thankful because she'd been waiting almost twenty minutes.

Suddenly a wheezy voice behind her commanded, "Step back."

She sidled backwards into the darkest icy shadow of the alley. "Are you...?"

"Shhh. Take these," and a pudgy fellow an inch shorter than she, opened a wide metal case and from the upper section pulled out a sealed plastic baggie containing papers. He shut the case and from the baggie handed her a pocket protector, pens, a clip-on identification card with a blurry photo of her as a man minus the moustache, several files which she put in her thin briefcase, and a clipboard with a short stack of official, filled-in forms attached.

She read the ID card: Sami Aql-Hadi. "I've had so many names this month, what's one more!"

"Shhhh." Mr. Granfa was sweating, in this terribly cold air, the man was sweating. "You must memorize how this will work," he insisted, "you must follow every direction I give you without question." As the man explained, Tahireh felt herself grow numb. Her brain would not register his words. All she could think of was how much she wanted Shamsi Granfa to see Dr. Legesse. Surely the man was diabetic and didn't know it. Surely... "Can you do all I have said?" he concluded.

Tongue-tied, Tahireh, alias Sami Aql-Hadi nodded.

"I believe you can. I have heard of your bravery." Shamsi smiled, satisfied.

"How long have you been doing...this?" Tahireh managed to squeak.

"The business? About three years. It is very profitable." He smiled.

She grimaced. "I imagine it is."

"We should go in." He stepped ahead of her. Over his shoulder he said, "The rescues I only began six months ago, by accident. A fortuitous accident."

They were starting up the steps.

"Oh?"

"Shhhh."

Sami Aql-Hadi shed any hint of Tahireh Ibrahim and took up the assigned role. She had become assistant to a man whose profession gave him access to anywhere he chose to be, anywhere the to-be or freshly dead could be found. He had complete, total omnipotence over anyone whose life hung on the fate of these poor souls.

Into the courthouse they went and were immediately saluted by one of the guards that phalanxed the lobby. "The third interview room," said the man sotto voce and Shamsi nodded, motioning to Tahireh to follow as he hustled down a long flight of steps. It became more and more drear. That such morbid dampness could exist in the middle of a desert could only be due to the sheer volume of human excreta permeating everything. Centuries of human sweat and urine and shit and vomit and blood and the undeniable stench of fear. Tahireh choked and Shamsi grabbed her arm. "Not here, don't throw up here. Keep it down. It becomes much worse."

"Your new assistant having problems?" sneered the prison official that stepped out from behind the first security gate. The guard left them, hurriedly.

"Mr. Aql-Hadi will answer to me if he loses his lunch while you and I are doing business," growled Shamsi Granfa and Tahireh was stunned at the transformation of her new boss. Vampirish was the best description. A shiver cascaded along Tahireh's vertebrae.

"You have interview room three," the official said and Granfa smiled, canines showing, "You are keeping close watch on me today."

The official shrugged. "We play expensive games."

Granfa spun on his heel and shoved his face into the official's. Nose to nose. The official's breath was clouding Granfa's glasses. Granfa snarled, "You? You try to bite me more?"

"There is another player at the table."

"Which bottom sucking toad is this?"

"A very important sucker," the official did his best to snarl back, but a slight tremble in his hand gave him away.

Granfa stepped closer forcing the larger man to turn into soft putty. Granfa threw back his head and laughed, "So you will demand two payments from now on!"

"Just this time, just for the Pandharpurkar girl!"

"Why her?" Granfa snickered.

"They want her to die. We're to offer you another in her place," the official said quickly and stepped into the interview room, motioning them to follow. There was a metal table with attached straps, a metal chair with the same, and a more comfortable chair in the corner. The so-called interview room was obviously set up for torture. The official closed the door behind them. "Another Thai girl, one these people feel you cannot resist taking."

"For what reason?" Granfa shrugged, "I've already tested Milind and she matches a man, an extremely wealthy man I might add, in Australia. I have not tested this new girl and you certainly don't have the capability of doing these tests."

The official was madly shaking his head. "No, no, of course we can't. It is a…a political arrangement. Someone of high status wants you, and anyone else involved in your business, to be handed over."

"You're saying the transplant business is to be stopped?" For one second, Granfa let that hang in the air and then he roared with vicious laughter. "Never."

Suddenly it was all clear to Tahireh. All the puzzling she had done about Shamsi's business became clear. Shamsi Granfa sold the body parts of executed prisoners. With stupendous force of will, Tahireh again managed to keep lunch from spilling up and out and onto the floor.

The guard was quaking. "Never, of course, never. As I said, a high political someone has asked that we make sure Milind dies and you take the one named Dim Mahesh. As you take Mahesh out, we have been asked to hand you over to a person named Ali Muhit. An old man of military bearing. He is waiting upstairs."

"This Muhit is from where?" asked Granfa.

"I don't know," said the official, "honestly I don't. He is not Kuwaiti His accent suggests Farsi? Iranian? An Iranian Security Force hummer brought him to the execution area gate barely an hour ago."

Granfa nodded again and put his metal briefcase onto the table. "How will we do this? You cannot hand me over without stopping the services I perform and at this very instant there are three Kuwaiti personages that require my services as soon as possible."

"We have a male prisoner being condemned today. We will outfit him to look like you. We will say you were shot as you tried to run." The official shrugged helplessly again, "It won't solve the problem, but it will forestall their actions. It will give the diplomats time to set up a cost. You understand."

Shamsi nodded. "As long as the cost doesn't come down on my head because I will only shift it to those who need my services."

"That is understood, I am sure." The official held out a hand, "You must give us some identification to put on the body, and your clothes." The man sidled to the door, "I...I have a guard uniform for you. Your assistant, he will have to slip out the back way with the girls and you will have to go through the door for military guards." The official began to beg, "It is the best we could do, the best I could come up with on such short notice."

Shamsi placed several instruments on the table. "Go get me the guard's uniform." Granted reprieve, the official marched quickly from the room. "Close the door," Shamsi said to Tahireh who immediately did so. "So now you understand, Mr. Aql-Hadi?"

"Yes. Regretfully."

"You remain strong. The girl or girls must be made to appear dead. I put them in body bags but sometimes an official or a guard examines them. Luckily, only cursorily. If I am to go through this charade, it will be up to you to make sure the bags are put into my vehicle." He sighed and dug keys out of his pocket and put them in Tahireh's hand.

"Thank whatever god you pray to that you could be on the job today otherwise we would never have been able to rescue these girls." He snapped on latex gloves.

"That is the part I don't understand," said Tahireh, "you say bodies, yet you say rescue." Tahireh jammed the keys into her own pocket.

"You'll see." Shamsi took out a disposable hypodermic and picked through his collection of vials.

The official ducked back into the room. He was desperately uncomfortable. He held out a uniform and Shamsi handed the hypodermic to Tahireh.

"You guarantee me these clothes do not have lice?" muttered Shamsi. The official grimaced. Shamsi shook his head, sighed, and took the uniform. For a chubby man, he moved adroitly, changing in a few swift movements. He reached into the metal case and pulled out a spare pair of glasses and put them with the clothes. "There."

The official, relieved, turned to go.

"What about the Pandharpurkar girl? I take it they do not want her body?"

"That is correct," said the official. "I assume you will take care of that as you usually do and I will register the death certificates and mortuary receipts."

"Of course."

"Good. Then I will bring her to you as soon as the executioners are finished." He was half out the door. "You do want to check over the Mahesh girl, right?"

"What use is she to me?" Granfa had turned his back to the official and Tahireh could see from his expression that he was playing on the official's fear.

It was working because the official almost begged. "She is pregnant. By some sheikh's son, a dignitary from Yemen or Bahrain I think. Please, you must take her."

Shamsi Granfa's expression perked up. He looked around and grinned. "Oh?" He pushed his glasses higher onto his nose. "A baby? Then I am interested. Bring her immediately."

The door closed with a thud leaving Tahireh to hand the hypodermic back to Shamsi who had finished buttoning the uniform jacket. "Why such an interest in pregnant girls?" asked Tahireh.

"You can't guess? And they don't have to be young girls; it can be any of the women they bring in here, as long as the baby is healthy." Shamsi chose one vial. "I offer the woman a chance to save her baby or in rape cases, a way to take it off their hands. I find good adoptive homes for the little ones." His eyes became very sad. "It was not what I started out to do, trust me, but the first time they brought me a woman who was to be executed, she was about five months pregnant. At that time, there was no way I could save her. I hadn't developed the necessary anesthetic compounds yet or the other techniques I use. All I could think at that moment was to save the baby. So, I convinced the guards to keep her alive until she came to term and I convinced her to let me adopt out the infant." He smiled, "It was the best I could do. Then. Now it is different."

A scuffle of feet preceded the slamming open of the door and a guard dragged in a shivering, emaciated Asian girl. Behind them came the official who said, "This is Dim Mahesh." The guard threw the girl to the ground at Shamsi's feet and the official dropped a black plastic roll onto the metal chair.

"Go away," Shamsi ordered the guard and the official and they quickly backed out of the room. The pudgy man motioned to Tahireh to help the girl into the more comfortable chair. "Do you want to live and do you want your baby to live?" he spoke directly into her face.

Her tiny mouth opened, shut, tears ran down her cheeks. Her head, shaven of hair, bobbed up and down.

"Okay." Shamsi leaned closer. "Do exactly as I tell you. Do not vary your actions one millimeter. Exactly as I say!"

The tiny girl frantically bobbed her head again.

"Tell me, how far along are you? Six weeks?"

"More, sir. I don't know exactly as I have lost track of time in this dungeon. I was raped the twenty-eighth of November."

"Oh! You have been starved, yes?" asked Shamsi.

"Yes."

"We will fix that." He turned to Tahireh, "Any anesthetic we give her will compromise the baby. Watch and learn." He picked another vial from the case and filled the hypodermic, deftly cleansed the girl's arm and inserted the needle. "This is a sleep potion, my child. You will feel very sleepy in a moment. Let yourself drift off to sleep. Okay?"

Shamsi tossed the hypodermic into the case. He leaned over the girl who was quickly becoming woozy. He grabbed her chin, waved his gloved fingers in front of her face several times, and in a calm, soft voice seemed to sing her to sleep. When she was completely out, he poked her arm with a scalpel. There was no reaction, not even any bleeding. Shamsi grinned and looked at Tahireh. "She's out."

"You hypnotized her?"

"Yes. As deep as I can get her to go. The muscle relaxant is to make her body seem newly dead. There is no perceptible heartbeat and very little breath." He tossed Tahireh a pair of gloves, "Put these on. I hear the guards returning. You must be ready. This is always ugly. The executioners cannot resist hurting these girls."

Tahireh managed to pull the gloves on as the door slammed open and two men in black uniforms burst into the room carrying a lumpy body bag. The official was behind them. They tossed the bag onto the hard steel table. The official caught Shamsi's eyes and gave one firm nod. The men slammed the door shut behind them and their footfalls faded down the corridor.

"You hold Dim up, don't let her fall over," Shamsi Granfa ordered Tahireh, "I must see to this one quickly." He turned loose of Dim, Tahireh caught her. Shamsi unzipped the bag on the table. Tahireh gagged. Only a massive surge of will kept lunch down. The girl in the bag had a protruding tongue, her face was blue, and a horrible gash had ripped a swathe of skin apart around her throat. "I knew it," grunted Shamsi. "Those sadists cannot resist." He glanced at Tahireh, "She was raped before being taken to the execution area. Not to worry, I'll deal with that when we get to my building."

He pulled out a stethoscope and listened and took a relieved breath in. "She's got a good heartbeat. I hope they didn't shut down blood flow to her brain for too long." He grabbed a small oxygen mask and emergency tank from the case and after opening an airway past the tongue, put the mask over her nose and mouth and almost instantly, the color of the girl's face changed. "I daren't do too much," Shamsi instructed Tahireh. "She cannot have any movement. Thus," he demonstrated and took out another hypodermic and another vial. "A paralytic agent. Just enough to keep her still but not enough to stop her breathing." That done, he tossed everything back into the case, zipped up the body bag, grabbed the black plastic roll on the other chair and shook it open. It was another body bag. "I didn't want to scare little Dim," he explained.

Tahireh and Shamsi gently lowered Dim Mahesh into the bag. Shamsi snapped his fingers several times and the girl went stiff as rigor mortis. "She'll stay that way until I tell her to come out of it." He stood. "Ready for the gauntlet?" He stepped to the door, opened it. "Go get that pallet."

Sliding out the door, Tahireh trotted to the far end of the corridor where a long pallet on wheels had been left. It was one of the clumsy kind with an unmanageable long handle. She pulled it to the room and the two bodies were put onboard.

"The vehicle I use is an ugly brown color with lots of rust spots," Shamsi told her. "You can't miss it. It's at the other end of the alley from where I met you. In the coroner's parking spot. You can wheel the pallet right up to the back doors. Trust me, no one will look at you for more than a second. People are terrified of death. Get the girls in and leave the pallet back in the alley. Start the engine. Be careful not to flood it. Be ready to pick me up. I have no idea what these guys have planned."

"I can do that," Tahireh assured him as he wedged his metal case between the bodies.

"I know you can." Shamsi looked out along the corridor, "Go. There is a double door exit to the right, way down there. That leads directly out into the alley. Go."

She went, dragging the heavy pallet behind her. It took all her strength to raise the meter-long lever off the doors. She was amazed that the entire hallway was empty. The alley was also empty of guards, of people, of everyone. The bribes had worked, surely that could be the only explanation for the clear path. She heard a volley of gunfire from somewhere close and shuddered. Her stomach was sickly sour.

A dirt-colored ancient army medic's vehicle was parked exactly where Shamsi had said and because of her surging adrenaline levels, Tahireh jerked the bodies into the back of it with a minimum of grunting and heaving. The medical case she laid beside them. The pallet shoved back into the alley, Tahireh got the van engine going. Minutes passed. She turned on the heater. Suddenly, without warning, the pudgy form in uniform popped out of a side door along the other back street that T'd to the alley. The form waved. Tahireh jammed into first gear as she leaned over and unlocked the passenger side door and Shamsi was in.

"Drive back to my building," he ordered.

"I don't know where that is!" she retorted.

"Turn left onto the main boulevard and keep going. Just keep going." Shamsi squeezed between the seats and into the back of the van. Tahireh heard him unzipping the bags, clicking open the case. She heard him order Dim awake and mere moments later, the shaken girl was crawling into the passenger seat. Little Dim was laughing and shivering and crying at the same time, hysterical and ecstatic. Fumbling, Tahireh managed to get the heater going. Shamsi shouted directions for Tahireh to drive and after fifteen minutes they pulled up behind Shamsi's building. He was still working on Milind. "Is the driveway clear?" he asked, wheezing.

"All clear," said Tahireh.

"Help me get Milind inside. You two, come on." He pushed open the back doors.

"Will she live?" were Dim's first words.

"Yes," said Shamsi as they carried her. "She'll have a nasty scar on her neck, but that is a small price to pay. Tahireh," he smiled with satisfaction, "make sure to remind me to have her take the abortion pills before she leaves here."

"You think of everything," Tahireh remarked in awe.

"A lot of experience, a lot of planning," was his response.

"How could it happen!" Darughih Sadiq-Fath screamed into the phone at Ali Muhit. "I can't believe it's the wrong person!"

"Our doctor suspected as much when he examined him," Muhit explained in as calm a manner as was possible. "This man has been in jail for many years. His teeth are bad; he's much older than Granfa is. I don't know why the Kuwaiti officials would do such a thing when you gave a direct order."

"And paid a lot of money," Sadiq-Fath added. "I will find out. Dispose of that body. Wait there in Kuwait for further orders. I will get back to you as soon as I talk to someone in authority."

"Yessir," Muhit agreed. "We'll be at the hotel."

The night sky was filled with dust. Quddus Sadiq-Fath had decided to come home about an hour ago. It had not been a good day. He was mulling over whether or not to have the two agents in Sweden executed or to bring them back to Iran and strip them of all rank and put them in jail for the rest of their lives. Yet, obviously, it did not make sense that both agents, highly trained, skilled at their jobs, should have such high levels of alcohol at any time, not to mention at the same time. It frankly did not make sense that even one of them would drink. They were both conservative Muslims. Something was done to these men and the Swedes were taking advantage of a law meant for Swedes.

Besides, he was extremely unhappy about Ali Muhit being there and not here. Ali was too old for this kind of work, his vision was poor...yes, all in all, Sadiq-Fath decided, no more missions for him, it was time for the old warrior to retire.

Sadiq-Fath rang for the servant girl to serve him supper and for his boy of the night to prepare the bath. The darughih needed to relax.

"There is another suite of rooms at the Nof Hotel," said Siddhu. "It is not on the roof like the baron's suite. It is only on the second floor, above the kitchens. Still, it is comfortable and has an excellent view."

Russ looked up from the monitor screen. "I haven't a clue what you're talking about, Siddhu."

"You can't stay at the drug rehab center any more. Dr. Legesse told me to find you living quarters."

"Ahhh, I see." The tall man smiled. "Hotel rooms are not my style. I'd rather find a place of my own."

Siddhu shrugged. "The suite would be temporary."

"Okay, temporary." Russ turned back to the screen. 'By the way, I'm in."

"In?"

"Into Tidewater's files. His new computer jockey isn't very skilled at making firewalls."

Russ put a finger onto the screen, "Okay, okay...here we are. Photos from Commander Gurgin Yusef. Downloading as we speak. Bing! Saving them onto this computer. Take a minute to open."

Siddhu came closer. He bent down. His eyes widened. "You are sure those are the photos of Habib's body?"

"You read the writing under the photos. I don't know Arabic."

Siddhu peered into the screen and spoke, "Yusef's assistant, a guy named Faruq, describes how the hajis were shot, the wounds, the way the bodies were carted off by the Bedouins, everything. Let me see that close-up of the face they say belongs to Mansur. Oh!" the Sikh straightened up. "Oh!"

"What?"

"It is not Habib Mansur. It is not our haji."

"Seriously?" Russ demanded.

"Absolutely. It is not Habib."

"I'll be damned," said Russ. The Indians' eyes met and Russ's head leaned to one side. "If this isn't Habib Mansur, then what happened to…"

"Indeed." Siddhu shook his head, perplexed. "Does this mean our haji is alive?"

"You better tell the doctor and the baron."

Siddhu threw up his hands, "Yes. I will tell everyone here and you can e-mail the baron and his wife at the school. You have the e-mail for Professor Englich's school?"

"The Weisburg Hochschule. Yep. Even have Freda Englich's private e-mail address. No problem!" The smile of satisfaction on Russ Snow's face was matched by the smile of relief and gratitude on Siddhu's.

"Thank you," said Siddhu.

"Hey, I only found out this guy wasn't him."

"Perhaps it is a good sign." Siddhu danced out of the office and down the hall. His voice trailed back, "Dr. Legesse! Halima!"

"Go for it!" shouted Russ and began running a search to find access to Bedouin websites. He could think of no other way to obtain evidence of the continued existence of Haji Mansur.

Geneva, Switzerland was cold, but not as cold as Vasteras, Sweden. Geneva in the dark was stunningly beautiful. A city of exquisite jewels strewn around a lake and onto the sides of precipitous mountains, twinkling like stars fallen to earth. So thought Bonnie as they rode in the taxi from the airport to downtown. Dawn was breaking over the Alps and she wanted nothing more than to go to bed and sleep. Breakfast would be nice too. The big man beside her was snoring gently. As he had many,

many years ago, Carl-Joran could fall asleep anywhere, any time. It was a handy talent to have.

The taxi pulled up in front of a small hotel that faced onto the white, icy lake. The city lights were blinking off. Bonnie shook Carl-Joran awake and they climbed out as the taxi driver handed their small amount of luggage to the doorman.

"Good morning, sir, madam," said the doorman in perfect English, "your rooms are ready. Follow me, please."

"Could we order breakfast?" asked Bonnie as they crossed the lobby.

"Of course, I will take the order myself," said the man, holding open the elevator doors. "What would you like?"

Shortly after noon, Carl-Joran gently awakened Bonnie. After a pleasant cup of coffee with bowls of fruit—at Bonnie's insistence—her calorie intake had to be cut she asserted, they went out to do business. It was amusing to watch the bank manager's expression as he came to terms with Baron Hermelin's being alive, but still dead. Ms. Person had forwarded all the paperwork. It did not take much time at all to have Bonnie sign the requisite forms.

What surprised Bonnie was the ease with which the bank manager quickly accepted the situation. Since his English was good, Bonnie inquired and the manager pursed his lips while squeezing his chin against his neck. When he glanced up at her through his thick half glasses, he allowed himself a tiny smirk. He leaned close to her and whispered, "You would be shocked, madam, to know how common such arrangements are."

Having confessed this, the manager scooted them out of the bank and on their way. From the hotel room, as Bonnie packed, noting that her baron had not changed his untidy habits one bit, Carl-Joran called Siddhu and told him the EW's account was accessible again. There was a fairly long conversation in Swedish about Tahireh and two Thai girls and then the baron called Carin Smoland in Stockholm. This conversation was about the Thai girls also and heated. Bonnie heard the name Barbara Monday over and over and finally, a sigh and the big man hung up.

"Let us go to the airport and meet Professor Englich and Princess Zhara." He smiled and took Bonnie in his arms. "Ready?"

"Yes. But what was that I heard you talking about on the phone, about Monday?"

"We need an emergency place for the young girls Tahireh has rescued. One is sixteen, one fifteen. Children really. We, Carin and I, do not want to send them to Lama Padma-Lakshmi in India because they both need medical care. London is out and Carin has her hands full with Fumilao and her two daughters who arrive today in Stockholm."

"Fumilao? I've missed the history on all these people, dear."

"Fumilao Makwaia brought her two daughters to the EW shelter to keep them from being circumcised. You know what a vicious procedure that is? No? I will explain later. Judge Kandella Moabi in Uganda was their supporter. We arranged for Fumilao to settle in Uppsala near the university in a community of other African refugees. Carin should be meeting the mom and her girls at the airport very shortly."

Bonnie shook her head in amazement. "I had no idea how extensive EW's work was. Somehow I thought it was like a big women's shelter, sort of on a multicountry scale."

"More like an underground railway. We have at least one agent in every country. Some agents have more power to help than others. Barbara Monday, for example, works through a United Nations organization and oversees women escaping from the United States. Barbara helped you through Kennedy Airport. At the same time, I might add," he grinned, "that she was supervising the escape of the wife of a famous athlete out of Miami."

"How did all this come about?"

"You mean Emigrant Women? It grew. Fast. We were astonished at the rate it grew. Our biggest problem has been to vet the huge number of people who want to help. Men as well as women. For example the Lama in India and Vaughn Eames in London and the pediatrician in Berlin, Dr. Norbert Nusbaum. Health organizations and battered women's shelters and military adjuncts like Captain Lonnie Maxwell in Kuwait who got into it when she was doing counseling for military officers' spouses. The list goes on and on. Communication has been a nightmare and I sincerely hope our new agent, Mr. Snow, can fix that."

"But those men following Trisha and me at Kennedy, they weren't there to help."

"No, my dear, they were there to stop you and for some moments you were in grave danger." He stood, zipped up his duffel and her suitcase, and put a smile back on his face. "We better be on our way."

"That is one part I do not understand," said Bonnie, "why anyone would impede efforts for finding safety for these women."

"And children, like these two Thai girls. Come on," Carl-Joran urged, "we have to go."

"But why?" Bonnie followed after him.

"I cannot explain. Maybe Halima can find the words, but after all is said and done, you must reach an understanding of the great hatred of women on your own." He indicated she should punch the elevator button. "I certainly do not have any rational answers."

The concierge quickly ushered them through the lobby and into a waiting cab. When they were settled in the taxi, Carl-Joran went on with, "I have loved two women in my life, you and Heda, the mother of Sture. Perhaps it is because I am Swedish. Perhaps it is because I am of royal blood. Perhaps it is because of you. In my life it has never once occurred to me that a woman had any less status than a man."

"To an American woman that is a bizarre concept; a man who truly considers a woman his equal."

Carl-Joran thought for a while then he kissed Bonnie on top of her head. "Are you okay with my being royalty?"

Bonnie laughed. "When I knew you so long ago, you were not much of a prince, my dearest Carl. In fact, you were just a big clumsy frog and no one expected much of a change in you."

"No one?"

"Well, I was so much an optimist back in those days, I believed kissing a frog would produce a prince."

"Should I hop about?" he laughed. "My dear, have I not changed at all?"

"Not really. You have grown into the man I expected you to become—sweet, caring, concerned. It was always there. I sincerely hope I could claim some tiny bit of credit for helping you become who you are today."

"Bonnie, you were the crossroads of my life, and I took the path that led me here because of you. I saw you as my lover, my older woman, so mature, so sure of yourself. I adored you."

"In such a short time together, I gave you that much?"

"Yes, without question." He leaned forward and told the taxi driver to stop at the Lufthansa arrival area. As they gathered up their luggage, he said to Bonnie, "We have eternity now."

"As long as that lasts, yes, yes."

"Baron?" A dumpy little woman, who could best be described as square in shape, wearing a severe wool, long-skirted suit and high-top practical shoes, interrupted them. "Good to see you. Is this your new wife?"

"Freda!" Carl-Joran smiled and hugged her, making her very uncomfortable. "Bonnie, meet Professor Freda English, our Swiss representative." The two women, of the same height, shook hands, sizing each other up as they did so. Two alpha women, Carl-Joran noted and as such, the behaviors were completely predictable. He smiled. "Shall we put our luggage in your car?" he asked the professor.

"I brought the bus," said Freda and pointed out into the vast parking lot. "Why don't you take the bags," she handed the baron the keys, "and Bonnie and I will pick up the princess and her mother."

Carl-Joran recognized that this was not a suggestion, but an order and saw it as a good sign. Freda was taking Bonnie on as a comrade, not a challenger. He picked up the keys and the bags. "I'll recognize this bus?"

"It has Weisburg Hochschule written on it and an image of our mascot. Right? You will find it near the rental cars. Come," the professor linked arms with Bonnie and tugged her along. Bonnie waved as she was dragged into the terminal. Freda chattered on, "I really like that the baron has a wife again. He is such a fine man." Bonnie nodded at appropriate moments as they plowed through the crowd. "Here we are," the professor stated with a flourish that loosed Bonnie from her grasp. They had reached the immigration exits. An announcement, repeated in four languages, said that the Lufthansa flight from Frankfurt had landed. In the same wide movement, Freda slipped two photos from her handbag and held them up.

Bonnie shook her head, "How will we recognize them?"

Freda shrugged. "Maybe they will find us. Their cover names are Myrna and Zoë Feldenstein."

Passengers began exiting the immigration area. They were about half German business people and half American tourists with a few Swiss and French citizens thrown in. Freda wasn't at all ready for the Hollywood pair among the tourists.

It was Bonnie who instantly fathomed the disguises. "Those are our people," she said.

Jerking her head back in amazement, Freda struggled for words. Bonnie waved her hands in true California audacity and shouted, "Myrna! You can't be serious! How could you wear that outfit in Geneva!"

Without a blink, Jani threw her hands in the air also, waving them, and she and Bonnie kissed each other on the cheeks like best shopping buddies on a thousand-dollar spree. "What else did I have to wear?" She reached a hand to Zhara and pulled her next to them, "Remember my daughter-in-law, Zoë? Would you believe I've a son old enough to make me a grandmother?"

Bonnie grabbed Zoë's hand and pulled both women along to Freda's side. "Myrna, you gotta meet a friend, Professor Freda Englich."

Whispering, Zhara leaned over Bonnie and asked, "If she's Dr. Englich, who are you?"

"Bonnie Ixey. Well...Hermeln now," Bonnie whispered back.

"We better move along," insisted Freda. "I wouldn't be surprised if your husband doesn't have private investigators already working to find you, as well as Saudi security."

"How would they know we were in Switzerland?" asked Jani as they hustled after the little professor.

"Wealthy men have resources we can only dream of," said Freda. "You don't have bags, right?"

"No. Just these packs," replied Zoë.

"Good. I wouldn't want to hang around waiting." Freda hustled along. Immediately outside, at the curb, was a small bus, its engine running. On its side was Weisburg Hochschule in Germanic letters and a funny drawing of a Yeti snowman. The four women climbed in and the baron started along the road before they'd even gotten into their seats.

His eyes busy with traffic, he commented, "I thought I saw some Arab-looking fellows near the rental cars. Could have been tourists or businessmen, but they seemed to have some interest in me. Just as well we do some backtracking and zigzags before heading for the school."

"Good thought," agreed Freda in the passenger seat next to him. She definitely had one foot on an invisible brake and the other planted firmly on the bus floor displaying her discomfort at not being in the driver's seat.

Two hours later, they were winding down the side of a sheer valley as the sun set in the V at the far end. Glaciers all around took on an orange popsicle cast. Icy brooks tumbled from cliff sides and met up with a fast flowing river at the bottom. Bonnie was in awe. Such beauty was difficult to grasp in one glance. She shook Jani awake and pointed to the small farms, the remains of a castle, the impressive buildings of what must be the school. Jani nudged her daughter and in silence, they drank in the postcard scene.

Finally Zhara leaned forward and asked Dr. Englich, "That's the school? That's where we'll be living?"

"Yes. And working. You will be a student. It is a university prep school. Your mother has a position as a teacher's assistant. You will like the school." With a wide grin, Freda Englich said, "There is a surprise waiting for you."

"Oh, tell me!" exclaimed Zhara.

"No. Wait. You will see."

To get to the school, the bus had to go through several narrow lanes and a big gate with a guard. There was a high fence around the property.

"Why the security?" asked Bonnie.

"We have many students of famous families here," explained Freda, "and truthfully, the security is to keep the paparazzi out. Most of the families are careful not to tell their children's location, but," she sighed, "sometimes famous people are famous because they like the spotlight. So, we must take charge and make sure the spotlight does not land on their children."

"I can understand that," said the baron, parking the bus near the front entrance.

Just as they climbed from the bus, a shaggy yellow dog raced from the building followed by a gangly young man in school uniform. "Charlotte!" he shouted in French, "Come back here!"

Zhara screamed in delight and embraced the squirming, barking dog. "It has been so long. Oh, I missed you so much!"

"How about me?" laughed the youth.

Releasing the dog to romp about them joyfully in the snow, Zhara threw her arms around the youth. "Emil." A bit embarrassed, she turned around and introduced him, "Mom, Bonnie, this is my boyfriend, Emil Falleur."

The baron held out his hand and they shook. "You've taken good care of the dog."

"It was not always easy," said Emil. "Several times agents of the Saudi security almost killed her."

"And you!" said Freda. "This is one brave young man. Come along everyone. We'll get you to your quarters."

As soon as they went inside, a matronly woman not unlike Freda came bustling up and told Carl-Joran that a message awaited him in the main office. He hurried off after her while older students, appointed as helpers, took the Hermelins' suitcases and guided Bonnie down one hall, while other students took Zhara and Jani to their new residence along with Emil and the very happy, bouncing and now snow-covered Charlotte. They exited the school at the back and went along a path in the snow to a small cottage.

"This is for us?" asked Jani, astounded.

"Yes," said Emil, "for you really. Zhara will eventually be staying in the dorm most of the time. That's where I live too. You don't mind, do you, Zhara? Charlotte will be here with your mom."

"How could I not be happy?" laughed Zhara. "I am free, I am alive, my mother is alive."

Her mother said softly, "Daughter, we are home."

In the main office Carl-Joran was led to a computer. After a few moments, he pulled up the message waiting for him. It had attached files to download. His first reaction was satisfaction that Russ Snow was now sending messages and had obviously done something about the computer situation. His next reaction was on reading the message all the way through. In hesitant disbelief, he opened the downloaded files and examined the photos. It was true. This was not his beloved friend the Haji Mansur. Carl-Joran also instantly asked the question, silently, to himself, "If this is not Habib, then, is he alive?"

He quickly answered the e-mail message with encouragement for Russ to keep looking through Bedouin websites and an added instruction for Siddhu to start calling contacts in the Bedouin community. Surely, if Habib was alive, the tribe would want to get him back to them, or so the baron hoped. He read a second message from Carin Smoland about the situation with the Thai girls that Tahireh rescued. He breathed a deep sigh of relief knowing his most favorite stubborn French model was safe. But, what could be done about Dim and Milind? They couldn't stay too long in Granfa's building. Carin was correct. She had her hands full with Fumilao and her daughters. This quandary he must solve immediately. He smiled. He had Bonnie to discuss it with. That's what he would do. He would encourage Bonnie to step in and devise a solution.

He sent Carin a short note to hold tight and wait and to tell Tahireh to do the same. Just a few hours more. He'd get back to Carin as soon as possible. As the messages went off into cyberspace, he looked around to find the professor hovering near. In a few words, he told her.

"We will celebrate at dinner," she said. "Now, you go rest along with that lovely wife of yours. Go! I will have a student guide you to your rooms." She turned toward the hallway and a waiting student and hollered, "*Kommen sie heir, Dagmar.*"

At dinner, Jani heard the news. She felt the hope rise in her and forced herself to put it on hold. She had known the man a mere two days. He had seen her as a spoiled rich man's wife. Hadn't he? A nuisance to be dealt with. His kindness was a part of his personality, something he lived and practiced. A rescuer. What right did she have to hope that his survival would mean more than his continued ability to rescue more women, like her?

Morning found Tidewater standing near Norm's cubby, reading over the young man's shoulder. Slowly Tidewater turned and went back to his own office. He picked up the phone as it buzzed. He'd been waiting for this call. It was Darughih Sadiq-Fath.

For fifteen long minutes the two men talked. Upon hanging up, Marion Tidewater asked Lily to get hold of an intelligence agent from the Kuwaiti embassy here in Washington, DC, and he ordered Norm to find all the information possible on Shamsi Granfa. Next, in the quiet fury that had begun last night on receiving the news from Interpol about his agents being in a drunk lockup in Sweden, Tidewater punched the extension for the special area of the Agency which only he, in this office, had access to.

He had absolutely no qualms about ordering the disposal of Barbara Monday. In fact, his specific instructions were, "If she can't be McCarthyed, then Silkwood her."

Carin's ancient black Volvo chugged up to the imposing gate of the Hermelin castle. She didn't have to get out, for which she was very thankful as the frigid fog was sticking to everything. Krister had raced to open the gates and as soon as she'd entered, he closed them, jumped into her passenger seat and they drove to the front parking area. Krister offered to take the old Volvo to the barn and plug it into a heater but Carin told him to leave it there in front.

"It's tough," she said, patting the rusty fender.

Gustav opened the front door and, after she'd shed her boots and heavy wool coat, she followed him to the nicely warmed television room. An extraordinarily tall, red-haired woman stood and held out her hand.

"Hi, I'm Trisha Ixey. Bonnie's daughter. The baron said you spoke pretty good English. Right?"

"Yes, it is okay." Carin pulled her knitted stocking cap off her frizzy brown hair. She was one of the dark Swedes. Her mother had explained to her as a child that the women of the family were descended from Lapps. Be proud, her mother had adjured, we are of the wolves and the reindeer. Still it hadn't helped to have curly brown hair and gray-ashen eyes in classrooms of tall blonde kids. Carin had learned early about prejudice. Of course, that was before the surge of dark-skinned immigrants. Now brown, even black-haired children were not so unusual.

"I told Astrid to get us some lunch. I know it's early, but you gotta be hungry after that drive from Stockholm." Trisha motioned Carin into a comfy chair.

"Actually, I am famished. Coffee too would be wonderful."

"Yep, she'll make coffee." Trisha sat back down on the divan. "Mom says you need me to help with a rescue?"

Carin loved the directness of the Americans. Had Trisha been British, they'd have been conversing politely for a half-hour before getting to the heart of the meeting. "Yes. You see, we, here in Sweden, have accepted our limit of...how shall I say? Hidden women? Women with no legal passports? For this month. I cannot arrange for any more."

"Mom explained that," said Trisha as Marie brought in a large tray with Astrid's delicious concoction of sandwiches and hot blueberry soup. Gustav followed with another tray bearing a thermos coffeepot, cups, cream, and sugar. "Want anything else? Astrid would be happy to make it."

Carin shook her head. "I am happy with this."

Trisha nodded at the servants who quietly disappeared. "Mom, or the baron told you that I'm going back to California tomorrow?"

"Yes, and that is good. Ummm, yum," Carin dug into the sandwiches and sipped the hot blueberry brew. "Excuse me, I have been awake since very early. I was responsible to transfer the woman from Uganda, with her daughters to shelter people who take her to Uppsala. Then I drive here."

"You must be bushed," said Trisha with sympathy.

"Bushed? Tired, yes." Carin poured a cup of coffee and doctored it liberally with sugar. "Did your mother explain that we hope you can rescue two girls?"

"From Thailand? They're sitting in some building in Kuwait City and they need to get out really fast."

"Yes. We know now that this building is a medical facility, much like a mortuary, and the girls are hiding there. It is not a comfortable situation."

"I can believe that." Trisha finished off three of the small salmon sandwiches. "You want me to house them on the Posey Farm? I can't keep them in my apartment that's for sure. But Mom thought they'd be safe on the farm."

"We can make up papers for them. They are only fifteen- and sixteen-years-old." Carin sipped her coffee and groaned in pleasure. "Could they be students at your high school?"

"Could the papers say they're exchange students? Then it would be easy to register them and even get some money for their support."

"I see no problem with that. It is an excellent idea. Now, here is the tricky part. Can you wait in San Francisco and pick them up when they land? Can you make sure they get through immigration all right?" asked Carin. "It is possible to have someone from a local battered women's support group there to help you."

Trisha rubbed her forehead. "I really should be back teaching in school by Monday. When can you get the girls into San Francisco?"

Carin opened her notebook. "Depending on flight schedules, we should have them there no later than twelve hours after you arrive."

"And you let me know and I show up to get two foreign exchange students? That's all?"

"Yes. We will give you papers also. You must tell us what to say on the papers, what makes them legitimate," the Swedish woman explained.

Trisha nodded. "I can do that. I'll call Misimoto, our caretaker, right away and have her get two cabins ready. Will the girls mind living in cabins? They were built years ago for workers. One room with a bachelor kitchen, not fancy but cozy, warm, and comfortable. We haven't used them in years. Might have a mouse or two under the floor."

"They have a WC, bath, and everything?"

"Toilet and shower. Yep."

Carin laughed, "You must understand, Trisha, these girls came from very poor families. To be on your farm, to go to a real American high school? They will be so happy."

"Neither of them speaks English."

"No, they do not."

"That's okay. There's a special class at school, English as a Second Language. We can handle it." Trisha smiled. A sense of satisfaction washed over her. She had not felt such pleasure at helping in a long, long time. What her mother was doing was making much more sense to her. "Tell me exactly what will happen in San Francisco and I'll get it done."

"I will outline every step and the women who help you at the airport have done this before," said Carin. "Always remember that this work can be dangerous."

"I understand, really I do. I mean, I don't understand why, but I understand that it is," responded Trisha.

***

Barbara Monday held her suit coat closer around her neck to keep the nasty, dirt-filled breeze from her silk blouse. In the same hand, she clutched her purse and with the other hand, she pushed her cash card into the machine. Moments later, Barbara was horrified to read that her account was empty. To make matters worse, the machine refused to give back her card. Eight o'clock in the morning, the bank would not be open for another hour, what was she to do? She had only enough money for a taxi to work. She punched in the numbers for her savings account. Frozen.

A scream of rage started up her throat. How could this happen? Since the machine would not give her card back, she thought for a moment about putting in the other charge card and taking some cash on account. But, slowly, like a painfully grinding clutch, her brain registered the fact that perhaps this was not a mistake made by the bank.

Cautiously, carefully, she moved away from the ATM and made her way down the busy sidewalk and returned to her apartment building. Yes, there was someone following her. She slipped into the florist shop next door and immediately out the rear exit and into the locked back door of her building. She raced up the steps, into her apartment and picked up her phone. It was dead. She was not surprised.

Quickly she went down the back stairs, through the alley and onto the corner where she caught a cab to her office. She didn't dare use her cell phone. Too easy for someone to eavesdrop.

Her office was in a highly secure part of the UN building. She would be safe there. Perhaps. To be doubly sure, she went to the accounting department in the basement and used their phone.

In Haifa, Devi picked up. "Everyone else went home for a couple hours," she said. "It's suppertime. Hold on, I'll get Siddhu."

A moment later, Siddhu clicked onto the line. Barbara could hear an Indian movie with loud music and screaming heroes as well as the sounds of children talking and Siddhu's wife clinking dishes in the kitchen of their apartment. Siddhu listened to Barbara attentively. "We will send you money," he said quickly. "Tell us a place to send it. Not your apartment or your office."

"Okay. How soon...?"

"Immediately." Siddhu asked, "Are you safe?"

"I don't know," she answered.

"Don't take chances," the little Indian man ordered her, "you leave New York if you have to. You still have all those passports and IDs?"

"Yes, yes. But I should be safe in my office at the UN," Barbara Monday assured him.

"I will tell Baron Hermelin," said Siddhu. "Perhaps also, there is a way to help you from here. Maybe. I will ask."

"Whatever you can do," begged Monday. "I hate this."

"You will know within the hour," Siddhu assured her.

As soon as they hung up, Siddhu called the Nof Hotel and was rung through to the second floor suite. Stepping from the hot shower, Russ grabbed up the phone. As he rubbed his long black hair dry, he nodded, "I'll take care of it. Someone's zapped her financial records. I have to go back to headquarters. The hotel won't give me a secure modem line. Can you tell Taqi to pick me up?"

"Of course," said Siddhu. "Do you need me?"

"Nah. This'll only take an hour or so. Don't worry. I know how it was done and I'm darned certain who did it."

It was good Russ went back to the EW building because as he arrived, Devi was leaving. She smiled up at him, shyly, which didn't suit her tough demeanor. She caught herself actually fluffing her very short hair with her free hand and made herself put that hand in her pants pocket where it wouldn't give her away. Solemnly, with the other hand, she tossed her jacket over one shoulder and announced gravely, "Carin Smoland wants to talk to Siddhu about papers for the Thai girls. I called him just before I tried to get hold of you."

"Thanks," said Russ, passing right by her and sitting down in his cubby. "Okay. Did Carin manage to arrange something?"

Devi followed him into the office. "All done. As soon as they have ID and passports, they can go to California." She looked over her shoulder. "You know, Tahireh won't be coming back here. She'll fly straight to Paris."

"Oh?"

"She doesn't..." the Israeli girl pursed her lips and shook out her jacket before putting it on. " Is Taqi still out there? He can give me a ride home."

"Yes." Russ stood and came to the desk. "She doesn't what?"

"Nothing." With a skip, Devi slammed the front door and was gone.

It took about the hour Russ said it would to find who had erased Barbara Monday's life history. It was a thorough job, extremely well done. Nothing remained of the person known as Barbara Amy Monday. Her financial records he could redo because he tracked where the funds had been sent and retrieved them. Her birth records and Social Security he established from old bank records that had long ago been archived. At least she could have money back. Yet, the more he delved into the origins of this, the more he thought her reappearance was a bad idea. He had gone to the empty dining room for a soda when Siddhu entered. Russ shook his head at him. "Not wise, not wise at all."

"What is not wise?" asked Siddhu.

"Tell Barbara to pack what she wants to keep with her, order the moving men to put her furniture in storage, and get the hell out of New York. In fact, it would be wisest to come directly here."

"She is in danger?"

"Very much so."

"Oh, my," said Siddhu. "But you can get her money back?"

"That's the easy part and it's already done. Whoever did this," he rummaged in the fridge, "wants her gone, completely gone."

"I will tell her but she is not a lady who takes orders like that easily," Siddhu related with doubt in his voice. "Come, help me arrange passage for the Thai girls. I show you how it is done. Also, we need to buy Tahireh a ticket back to Paris."

"So she really is going back there." The disappointment was clear.

Siddhu gazed steadily at his own shoes. "Ummm, yes. That is where she always goes after an assignment is finished. That is where she works and where she lives."

"I understand," said Russ.

Siddhu shook his head. "No, you don't, really. But that is okay. One day you will."

As predicted, when Siddhu got Barbara on the phone again, she went ballistic. She shouted, "No! I won't have this done to me. No! I'll fight it. If they get away with this, they'll do it to anyone who works at EW: you, the Ixeys...no!"

Siddhu and Russ were standing by the speakerphone. Russ asked, "Can you stay in the UN? Or at a foreign government residence?"

"Sure. That's no problem. But you think I should put my stuff in storage? Get out of my apartment?"

"Yes," said Russ, simply.

"I know you, don't I?" she asked. "We met."

"Briefly, at Kennedy airport, sort of."

"Siddhu," came Barbara's voice, worried, "Baron Hermelin trusts Mr. Snow?"

"Yes, Barbara. I am coming to trust him too."

"Okay," she said with an enormous sigh. "Can I at least get my records and money back?"

"That's done," said Russ, "and I've encrypted everything this time so that only you can have access. Barbara, do you really, really want to fight what they've done to you?"

"Yes." She sounded determined. "Siddhu, I'll arrange to stay at the Ugandan consulate. Prince LaFoon isn't there right now, but his assistant will gladly put me up in the guesthouse. Snow, you find out all the names of all the people who did this to me. Find the complete trail of evidence. Send it to me. All right? Is that clear?"

"Yes, ma'am!" he responded with a surprised laugh of respect. It was like bargaining with his tough old grandmother.

"Good. Talk to you later. Bye." She hung up.

Siddhu turned to Russ. "Now we make sure the two girls get out of Kuwait safely, as well as Tahireh."

"You got it," said Russ, clicking off the speakerphone. His entire concept of women had taken a dramatic right-face turn.

Blowing sand and dust glittered in the glow of the mercury lamps and made the tarmac around the transport planes almost invisible. It was as if the jets and trucks and loading tractors and people were floating on a shimmering sea. Jet engines whined continuously. The smell of jet fuel hung low in the air. One plane was taxiing in as another pulled away from the loading area leaving thin trails through the dust sea. Two other jets waited for parking space.

In the midst of this eerie scene of ordered hustle and bustle, Shamsi Granfa dropped off three young men wearing baseball hats and dressed in American style jeans and white T-shirts bearing the insignia of the air express company. He waited outside the gate long enough to see them met by one of the supervisors, a thickly muscled German fellow; then Shamsi Granfa with a smile on his face, drove away. His job was successfully completed.

The three young men were handed clipboards with papers that looked exactly like bills of lading. They followed the supervisor to the plane they were to ride in.

"Next stop Paris," said the man in German. "Buckle up tight. These planes don't coddle passengers. We don't even serve drinks! All aboard!"

The pilot and co-pilot, in their seats and going through the preliminary checklist, smiled and shouted a warm welcome as the three took off their hats, put on their seat belts and settled back. The navigator passed by them, saying to Dim and Milind, "We'll make sure the two of you get onto the first flight to San Francisco. You may have to go via some other strange destination, but don't worry. You'll get delivered."

Tahireh translated and the girls grinned.

"Thank you so much," whispered Dim, just now coming to terms with being free. Her seatmate, Milind sighed and leaned back on a big box. "I will sleep," she said as Tahireh translated their words to the navigator who nodded and continued on toward the cockpit.

"I will be so glad to get back to Paris," Tahireh said more to herself than the girls and shook her long hair out. "Oh! I can hardly wait!"

The navigator took his seat, the engines roared, and not more than five minutes passed before the jet was airborne.

CHAPTER 14: RESURRECTION

"Monday is compromised?" Baron Hermelin remarked calmly between mouthfuls of thick oatmeal mush. He poured on more milk as he listened to Russ's answer, then said, "She has a lot of powerful friends in the UN health organizations. She'll have a way to get whoever did this."

Bonnie and Jani came into the staff dining room and sat down across from Carl-Joran. Zhara had gone to eat with Emil and the other students. Freda Englich was busy with teacher conferences. Midterms were about to begin and she had meetings back-to-back until Wednesday. A student quickly came by with bowls and spoons for Bonnie and Jani and another student served them coffee.

"I would give her all the information you find, Russ, yes. Really, she can take care of herself, you watch." Carl-Joran held up his cup for more coffee. "What else have you found out? Siddhu? Yes, good morning, Siddhu, good to hear your voice. You got a phone call? From Beirut? Okay. I cannot go to Beirut. Halima would have a cow. Can they come to the border?" He put a hand over the receiver and said in a whisper to the women, "Siddhu got a call from a Bedouin agency, very mysterious, maybe about Habib." He focused back on the voices over the phone, "We have to go to Beirut?" Shaking his head he sighed. "Tell me when you know more. Okay." He hung up.

Jani asked, "Habib has been found?"

"The message was left on one of our answering machines about five this morning. This machine is for the private phone line that can be used only by shelters that we have direct contact with, shelters we trust. Except, we have no such shelters in Lebanon. In Jordan, yes, in Saudi Arabia, yes, but anyone in Lebanon or Syria or Afghanistan must get word to a neighboring country to call. That's why it is a mysterious call. It is why I think it must be Habib himself behind the message."

"What did the message say?" Bonnie wanted to know.

"A friend of ours is ready to come home. Those were the exact words." Carl-Joran finished his mush and with a grimace pushed the bowl away. "I think it is time to go to Haifa. My dear wife, can you be ready to fly on the first plane out of Geneva?"

"And leave this beautiful valley?"

"Yes. I will call the airlines immediately."

She hung her head, "No rest at all, eh?"

"Nope," he replied and stood. "I suspect tomorrow morning will be the earliest we can leave for Tel Aviv."

"When will you have more information about Haji Mansur?" asked Jani softly and Bonnie glanced at her.

Carl-Joran shrugged. "It is not in our hands, Jani." He left the room and Freda's voice could be heard from far down the hall, "You aren't staying any longer?"

Bonnie laid a hand on Jani's arm. "You have feelings for Mr. Mansur?"

"Mister?" laughed Jani, "Habib, you mean." She sighed. "There is a lot of pain in here," she patted her left breast, "and I hear his kind words, I feel his rough hands helping me over the rocky path, through the sandstorm. I see him fall." She smiled, achingly. "Perhaps it is just that he was the first kind man, a truly kind man, whom I have ever known."

"Like Carl is?"

"Yes. Like your husband," said Jani, "only Habib spoke a language I understood. If you know what I mean."

"I think so," Bonnie answered. She squeezed Jani's hand and smiled in empathy. "Well, I guess I must go pack. Again. Another week of this and I will be homesick for my farm."

"You have a farm?"

"Yes. My husband's, or rather my first husband's," and Bonnie shook her head, "no, I mean, Ike's farm. Where I lived most my life. We grow flowers and herbs."

"How wonderful!" exclaimed Jani. "I would love to see it one day."

"Maybe you shall," said Bonnie, "one day." She finished her coffee and mush and stood. "From now on, I simply won't take anything out of the suitcases."

"Please," Jani grabbed her hand, "please tell me the moment you hear about Habib."

Bonnie patted the cold hand. "I will, I promise."

Ali Muhit rubbed his eyes as he came from his morning bath. They hurt. The strain of looking through the perpetual fog of the cataracts was becoming too much to bear. Soon he would have to take time off, perhaps even retire. He had dreamed about being released from his job, dreamed for years of being free from the tyrant Sadiq-Fath. He wanted nothing more than to sit with his grandchildren and watch them play in the sun. He gazed out the window of the hotel. The glaring winter sun did nothing to dispel his gloom. It was time to call his boss. He would not be pleased.

Walid answered the call with a salute. "Muhit, sir, I have news for you."

"You have news? Of what?" queried the old man.

"We have just received a message from our operative in Lebanon. Ahhh, the darughih has entered. Wait a moment, he wishes to speak to you."

A brief silence ensued before the gruff voice of Quddus Sadiq-Fath came on the line, "Muhit, you must go to Beirut."

"You do not want to know what I found out about Shamsi Granfa?"

"Yes, of course I do," said Quddus, "but I also want you to hear the good news. Someone is telling EW that the haji we thought was dead, the one Commander Yusef in Saudi said he killed? This man may be alive and there is a Bedouin group that has contacted EW."

"No." Ali Muhit cautiously expressed his disbelief.

"So our agent says. He has been monitoring telephone calls from the Bedouin support group office in Beirut." Sadiq-Fath assured his personal assistant. "I want you to check it out."

"If you so order," said Muhit, "although I do not see why the haji's being alive is a good thing. Did we not want him dead, as Yusef wanted him dead?"

"Yes. But, if he is alive and the Bedouin try to get him back to EW, especially through Lebanon, we can capture the agents who come to get him. If we are prepared."

Ali Muhit thought about this a moment. Did he dare speak his mind and admit he believed the entire EW pursuit was a fool's mission? As close as he was to the darughih, for as many years as he had served the man, still it was not his place and never had been his right to overtly contradict him. Reluctantly, he said, "I will go to Beirut and see what can be done. Now, about Granfa…"

"Yes, what happened with those women?"

"I have been told by the Kuwaiti prison authorities that the women are dead." Ali Muhit turned as the door to his room opened and a bellhop brought in breakfast. "As far as Tahireh Ibrahim? She has vanished again. I have asked our agent in Paris to watch for her and to tell us when the model Gillé returns to work. As for Shamsi Granfa…sir, this is a very important man. He has connections all over the world and that includes Iran. We cannot touch him." Quickly, Muhit explained to his boss why Shamsi Granfa was to be left alone and waited for the darughih to come to terms with the information.

When Muhit had finished talking, Quddus Sadiq-Fath instructed him, "Go to Beirut, track down what is happening. See what you can do. Plus," he added, "We have a short report from an agent in Geneva. He claims to have seen a man who looks exactly like Baron Hermelin. That could not be true, right?"

"Baron Hermelin is dead, sir. That is a fact."

"And Haji Mansur is dead our friend Tidewater tells us," snickered Quddus Sadiq-Fath. "Maybe we have been played for fools all the way around."

"I don't think that is possible!" insisted Ali Muhit.

"Anything is possible," said the darughih.

"Yessir," Muhit had to agree as he hung up the phone.

Overnight, New York City had been layered with three feet of snow and morning traffic had wrenched itself into a total gridlock. Barbara hated being trapped and sequestered in the Ugandan consulate. She had to admit the small garden behind the kitchen below her was magical in the snow. Resigning herself, she pulled back the thick duvet on the single bed and crawled in between the cotton sheets. She was exhausted and a couple hours sleep was what she needed more than anything at this moment. She'd told the consulate secretary to wake her around noon.

About midnight last night, Barbara had reached her friend, Kumiko Yokochi in the United Nation's central computer operations office. Kumi was responsible for investigating financial fraud reports submitted by operations personnel. Kumi preferred working when no one else was around, and she loved the little chore Barbara had implored her to do.

"I'll come up with something you can use," Kumi promised. "I'll page you when I'm ready."

Barbara had paced back and forth in the long embassy hallways and up and down the elegant stairs, from the immense kitchen that smelled of wicked peppers, sweet yams, tapioca, and other more exotic African foods to the closed front office to the bedroom she'd been given. Finally, about four in the morning, Kumi buzzed her on her pager and Barbara called her back on the consulate's secure phone line.

Kumi said simply, "You can go home tonight. Not now. You wait until I know this stuff has been read. But trust me, you and Emigrant Women will never be bothered again by Agent Marion Tidewater."

"How…?" Barbara started and Kumi hissed, "Better you never find out."

There had been two delays getting the transport plane out of Vancouver, because of the huge bank of fog filling the San Francisco basin. Trisha Ixey grouched around the San Francisco airport for hours wondering if it would have been quicker to rent a car and drive to Los Angeles and meet the girls there. A dapper young man from a local attorney's office had appeared right as she had disembarked from her own arrival last night and handed her a large manila envelope full of official-looking papers. Trisha had had more than enough time to read through them and memorize all the information.

Each girl had been given a new name and identity. They had complete high school transcripts from the Philippines and exchange student permits. Supposedly, in Vancouver, both girls were given passports that matched.

Finally, about midmorning, the sun managed to burn off enough fog to allow the airport to open and by noon the jet carrying Dim and Milind arrived. Like an express load of freight, the two girls were put out on the tarmac and Trisha found them gazing in astonishment at the rolling high fog, the buildings, and her.

"You are big!" exclaimed tiny Dim in stuttering English.

"Hey, I'm a basketball coach, I gotta be tall," responded Trisha and took both weary teenagers by the hand. The immigration officer met them at the exit gate and, although a little skeptical about their means of arrival and the fact they were dressed in the express company uniforms, seemed pleased by the excellently completed paperwork and Trisha's credentials. A woman from the local battered woman's shelter had shown up also. She translated for them.

"We appreciate having the sponsors show up to get their foreign students," said the officer, smiling, "makes it go a lot easier."

The girls ooh'd and aww'd at Trisha's van and were even more thrilled with a stop at Denny's Restaurant for a late breakfast. As hard as they tried to stay awake to see the Big Sur coastline, first Dim fell soundly asleep and then Milind. They didn't wake up until lunch at San Simeon where they sat outside on the patio of a cafe and ogled the tourists loading onto buses for the castle tours. Trisha promised them that one day soon, she'd bring them back so they too could tour Hearst Castle. The two girls smiled as if they understood every word.

The only problem encountered on arrival at the farm was Gryphon who instantly decided to be their personal slave and protector. Both girls were terrified of the massively furry dog and it took Misimoto's firm remonstrance to make him postpone his quest for doggy knighthood. Trisha left immediately for her own place to prepare for classes the next day. The school bus would pick up the girls. They'd be enrolled in ESL classes. It was all arranged.

Of course, it didn't take a lot for the two girls, with gestures and pleas to coerce the dour Japanese caretaker into helping Dim and Milind shop for clothes at the mall in San Luis Obispo that evening. Trish found out about that excursion when they came into the ESL class the next morning looking like they'd hung out on the boardwalk their entire lives.

Bonnie and Carl-Joran had been dropped off at the Nof Hotel two hours earlier by Taqi and had time for a quick shower and a quicker lunch. Taqi was soon back at the front entrance to pick them up and take them to EW. He chattered the entire way about the possibility of Habib's being alive. As with most first-timers, Bonnie was taken aback by the ugly steel warehouse, the noise and bustle of the busy harbor all around the building, and the smell of low tide. Once inside, everything changed. Two different worlds, she thought as Siddhu rushed to meet them.

The baron nodded approval to Devi at the rearrangement of the front office. Besides all the computer equipment, the room was bigger; the closet alcove was open and full of more equipment and a large, dark man in T-shirt and jeans who instantly turned to greet him. Carl-Joran had almost not recognized his newest recruit. He took Russ's hand in his and pumped it hard. Devi hung back with a silly grin on her face, and when the baron noticed, smiling, she blushed. Russ gave Bonnie an impromptu hug, and she decided to ask him later about the expression of relief on his face.

Immediately, Dr. Legesse entered. She towered over Bonnie like a giant black stork. "Come, I want to show you around," she exclaimed and motioned the small woman to follow her. "This is where your money goes! This is what you do for women!" To the men she declared, "I convene a meeting in ten minutes. Siddhu, have everyone there."

"Very good, yes, doctor," he acknowledged.

Russ, Siddhu, and Hermelin pulled up chairs near the new equipment. Devi hovered over Russ's shoulder as he and Siddhu reviewed all the information they'd put together about the haji. Russ also showed the baron an interesting e-mail from Barbara Monday who was back in her own apartment and gloating.

"Got any idea what she's up to?" asked Russ.

The baron shook his head. "Something really sneaky if I know her." He looked at the wall clock. "We better head for the meeting room. Time to induct Russ and Bonnie formally and," he chuckled, "let them know who is really boss."

"Dr. Legesse," sighed Siddhu.

At that second, the private line rang. Devi grabbed it, listened, and handed it directly to Siddhu. "The Bedouin contact," she said and carefully switched on the speakerphone.

"I have a message for the baron," said the young male voice in Arabic. "The message is for him to come to the Good Gate above Kiriat Shimona tonight at eight o'clock. Tonight. The baron must come. Be ready to collect an important package."

Devi translated and Siddhu looked frantically at Carl-Joran, who nodded and whispered, "It is a sign from Habib. It is he who is sending the message. Tell him we will be there."

Into the phone, Siddhu replied in English, "The Good Gate, eight p.m."

"Okay." The caller replied in English and hung up.

"It's a three-hour trip to the Gate," said Devi.

The baron turned to Russ, "Bring what you have there and let's get to the meeting."

Dr. Legesse had seated Bonnie to her right at the long black table. The others took their places. She listened, pursed her lips, looked down at the tabletop, and tapping it, signaled she had come to a decision. "I believe it is a true message. Only Habib would send the message directly to Baron Hermelin, only he knows the baron is still alive. The boy giving the message probably does not even understand the words."

"But Halima," Siddhu argued, "how do you know they will bring the haji through the Gate? How do you know this is the truth? That Habib is alive, that it isn't a trap?"

"We don't," said the doctor, "so we prepare. Devi, tell Taqi to get the Mercedes ready, then I want you to contact the Defense Force commander at the Good Gate. Make him understand the danger that is possible tonight."

"Yes, ma'am, and I will bring my weapons." She quickly left the room.

Ann Fillmore

Russ leaned toward Carl-Joran and whispered, "Her weapons? She seems like such a mild-mannered kid."

Carl-Joran roared with laughter. "You don't know about Israeli girls, do you? They serve in the military just like the men. Devi Hamberg spent two years as a tank commander and four years as a UBX officer."

"She disarmed bombs!" Russ exclaimed. "I thought I was coming here to help rescue women. Jeez, I really do gotta develop a whole new attitude about women!"

Pounding the table for silence, Halima Legesse was trying hard also not to laugh, "There are women, and there are women, Mr. Snow. Soon you will know the difference."

"Damned right," he muttered.

"Baron," Dr. Legesse went on, "here is how tonight will go. Are you ready?"

"Of course," replied the big Swede.

The snow had reached Washington, DC and was continuing south with no letup. Whereas New York City took snow mostly in stride, DC did not. Roads quickly became impassable and impossible. Most office managers early on decided to send home as many workers as could be spared from their jobs. Tidewater let his staff go early and he decided to start the long commute to Virginia and his house. Little did he know that a courier had arrived at his front door minutes after he'd left for work to hand a large cardboard envelope full of papers to Arletta Tidewater in return for her personal signature. Arletta had never received such an important looking document with the big words: FOR YOUR EYES ONLY stamped on the front.

She had been seriously considering going to her mother's for the weekend. The news of closed roads and delayed trains had convinced her to reconsider. Instead, she had made herself a cup of Earl Grey tea and opened the envelope. The return address meant nothing to her. Some obscure department at the United Nations. Despite all her husband's warnings about strange packages, Arletta decided that something from the United Nations was a safe enough bet not to contain a bomb.

Thus it was that when Marion Tidewater arrived at his front door about four in the afternoon, he found it not only locked but his keys no longer worked. A note attached to a stack of printouts, all in a plastic bag to protect them against the snow was tacked on the door. He ripped open the plastic. The note stated simply that he should let her know where he would be living from now on so she could send him some clothes. Also so her attorney could send him the divorce papers, and if the thought crossed his mind to try and do her harm, she would forward on the copies of all his charge receipts and expenses to the Agency's Department of Internal Affairs.

Jerking the stack of printouts from the plastic, he flipped through them and went cold. Marion Tidewater had no doubts as to the origin of this material.

A frigid wind hurled sand and dry leaves through the black night of narrow wadis and valleys that cut the terrain above Kiriat Shimona, the northern-most kibbutz in Israel. On the border, several miles further on, was the Good Gate. Here is where Habib Mansur had crossed into Lebanon, here is where he was to be delivered. Harsh mercury lights illuminated the entire three-meter-high border fence, the complicated zigzag wire fence structure which contained the actual Gate and went down into the staging area for tanks, missiles, rockets, antiaircraft guns, and other military machinery. The twenty-four-hour cafe at the taxi turnaround was busy as usual and Taqi parked close.

Devi, in her army uniform of khaki pants and dark green sweater with leather elbow patches, her rifle slung over her shoulder, and her pistol on her hip, went to talk to the local defense force commander who was expecting her. She saluted, he saluted. Carl-Joran remained sitting in the Mercedes, slumped down, hidden. Bonnie, dressed in one of Devi's army outfits and Russ, in a thick bomber jacket and heavy boots, took seats in the light at the cafe. They ordered tea and coffee respectively.

The baron was not happy about this arrangement. Halima was still not ready to let him show himself outright, so he sat with the back door unlatched, ready to jump out. The boss had spoken, he would follow her orders.

They waited, and waited.

Around midnight, Bonnie, her stomach finally loosening the tight clench it had been in since leaving Haifa, considered for the umpteenth time talking her husband into giving up for the night and going down to the hotel in the kibbutz. Not a single person had gone through the Gate either way for hours.

At that instant, a thin young man hesitantly, cautiously, began walking from the Lebanese side of the zigzag toward the Gate. The Israeli defense force commander and Devi, rifles resting on their arms, went to meet him as he stepped through. They took all his weapons off him: rifle, pistol, knives, and his papers were scrutinized before Devi led him to Bonnie.

"I am to talk to women?" the young man squawked toward the commander and Devi translated.

"Prove to me you are Bedouin and that you bring Haji Mansur," Bonnie insisted, hoping her voice didn't crack and give her tremendous fear away. She felt Russ's big presence behind her, but still, she knew she was face on with a dangerous man.

Devi translated.

"Who are you?" the young man spit at Bonnie and Russ took a step forward, as did Devi.

"The baron's wife."

"Your gray hair will not protect you if you lie," said the young man with certainty. "Follow me to that side of the Gate. If the haji agrees, he will come forth." The young man did not look directly at anyone anymore. He kept the hood of his burnoose tight around his head and face and brushing Devi aside, started back to the Lebanese entrance of the zigzag fence.

"Can we assume the enemy accompanies our haji?" Russ said after him and when Devi had translated, the young man nodded.

The Israeli commander stopped at the borderline. Devi continued alongside the small group. "I go in front. Russ, walk next to Bonnie."

Pushing the Mercedes door open a bit further despite Taqi's admonition, the baron stuck a long leg out, wanting very badly to be at his wife's side.

Going only as far as the first checkpoint in the zigzag Gate, the young man stopped and spun on his heels. "I am sure the baron himself must come," he insisted.

"No! It is enough your comrades and the haji see me," declared Bonnie. Devi shouldered her rifle, finger brushing the trigger as she translated. Russ Snow towered over all of them and felt like the primary target.

"Perhaps my chief cannot allow the haji to come through," warned the young man.

"Your chief is not a cruel man," Bonnie continued. "He will not keep a dying man from safety. The enemy will not influence a chief such as yours, will they?"

At that, the young man's eyes sought out Russ's eyes, the only other man in the group.

"There is danger in the Gate. You would let women lead the way?"

"Two women in fact," shrugged Russ with a nasty grin.

"So be it," said the young man, resigned, and led the way into the final leg of the zigzag enclosure. Russ with Devi behind him and Bonnie behind her followed quietly, committing themselves to the penned-in area.

From the other side, a group of men in Bedouin burnoose robes embarked on their walk into the zigzag, carrying a larger man in an arm sling. That man was obviously weak, his head lolled and he seemed barely able to hold himself upright. At the exact center of the enclosure, the men carrying the man gently let him onto his feet. He instantly fell forward and Russ jumped quickly to catch him.

At that very moment, four of the men threw off their robes and grabbed for the big Indian. The remaining men—the real Bedouin, including the young messenger, still wrapped in their burnoose, quickly traversed the Lebanese side of the zigzag back the way they came and disappeared into the black night.

In a flash, as the four aggressors, each with a hand on Russ, pulled guns from under their shirts, Devi jammed her rifle under the first man's chin. Stalemate. She shouted at the fallen man, "Habib! Is that you?"

"Yes," came his faint voice.

Devi glanced at Bonnie. "Get him out of here."

"I will do my best," she responded and reached down and lifted the haji putting one of his arms over her shoulder. It was slow going. Bonnie staggered with the load because Mansur had almost no strength at all.

Devi Hamberg pushed the first man's head back with her gun and snarled, "Notice that the commander of the Gate guards is ready to fire several rockets across the border. I know you are not Lebanese and if you return over there, after the rockets land, they'll kill you."

Slowly, the four men's weapons lowered. Devi and Russ disarmed them and Devi motioned for all but their leader, the small guy with Devi's rifle bore under his chin, to leave. Russ grabbed him and dragged him forward. They made their way back through the Gate and through the zigzag, catching up to Bonnie. Devi held the rifle behind their captive while Russ lifted Habib Then they moved faster.

The commander and the baron, who finally could not stand it any longer and had jumped from the car, were waiting as they came out and they helped Russ put Habib in the Mercedes. Russ climbed in the front, the Carl-Joran and Bonnie in the back.

"We will meet you at the hospital in the village," shouted Devi as the Mercedes sped away, but by the time she arrived there, Bonnie and Habib and the baron had been airlifted by helicopter to Haifa. It was up to her now to take care of the prisoner. The commander had released him to her. She phoned Dr. Rachel Bar-Fischer who agreeably responded yes, of course Ali Muhit, the personal assistant to the Darughih Quddus Sadiq-Fath, could be incarcerated at her facility. With pleasure.

Emergency medical staff were waiting on the roof as the Medivac landed. The two paramedics on board the chopper had already stripped off the dirty robes and awful bandages that had held Habib together for the last few days. Bonnie heard the woman paramedic comment that they'd be lucky if he didn't have gangrene.

"GWS through the right shoulder downward, lower back, thigh, and left calf," shouted the paramedic handing Habib down to the ground crew. A stream of shouted statistics followed the crew into the hospital. Bonnie, Carl-Joran, and Russ found themselves left behind in a lounge near the operating theatre. Waiting again.

"You go to your rooms," the baron ordered Russ, "and take Bonnie to our suite. You don't need to stay here."

"I'll go," said Russ and as Bonnie started to refuse, a doctor came from the operating room. Tired, he did smile though as he pulled off his mask.

"Mansur has one strong constitution. How he made it through, I really can't explain." The doctor pulled off his gloves. "We got two of the bullets out; the one in his shoulder that went straight down into an arm muscle and the one that went into his hip. We've put him on a regimen of antibiotics and antifungal medications. Hopefully that will kill the bugs he picked up along the way. You folks might as well go home. He'll be asleep until morning."

"Thank you, doctor," said Carl-Joran standing.

"Just tell Legesse she owes me on this. She's been onto me already, on my cell phone in the operating theater for God's sake, and I want to make sure that woman knows her precious haji will live." With a sigh, the doctor wearily pulled off his apron and tossed everything into a nearby bin.

The bright winter morning peeked over the Haifa cliffs and the golden dome of the Bab as the three took a taxi to the Nof. Before

Bonnie joined her gently snoring spouse, she called the Weisburg Hochschule and left a message for Jani that included the phone number of the Haifa hospital. As sleep caught up with her, she wondered how Trisha was doing and she felt a pang of homesickness. No matter how wonderful the company, how great the adventure, there is nothing like your own bed in your own home, she thought.

Ali Muhit was numb with exhaustion and contrition. An Israeli woman doctor had ordered him into a locked room in a building surrounded by razor wire. This woman was in charge. She gave the orders and workers dressed like nurses followed these orders. Although food was offered, Muhit didn't feel like eating. He couldn't sleep. For the first time in his life, he was helpless in front of women.

He couldn't tell if it was day or night when they came for him, the woman in charge called doctor and a tall black woman who dominated the entire small room where they took him. To his total and complete mortification, she was also called doctor. The women tried several languages: English, French, Arabic, and he pretended ignorance. A quick whispered conference and in came a well-dressed man with the clean, sharp features that obviously identified him as descended from the ancient Persians. He spoke eloquent Farsi.

Muhit was about to answer when he noticed the ring on the man's finger containing a large flat ruby with the inscription Allah u abha Baha'u'llah. Muhit's lips scrinched shut in a tight line. First women in power, then the only speaker of Farsi was a Baha'i. Naturally, the Baha'i man would take orders from a woman. Baha'is believed women were equal with men. Heresy. Ali Muhit could not respond to any of this. It was not in his remit. It did not fit the order of his life. He hung his head in absolute shame.

"That's all right," said the Baha'i man, "we're negotiating with your commander, Darughih Sadiq-Fath. The terms will be easy for even him to swallow. Hear what I say even if you cannot find it in yourself to respond."

Ali Muhit swung his chair away to face the wall.

The Baha'i man went on, "In return for absolving the fatwa on Baron Hermelin and his entire family, you will be kept here and kept alive. As long as the fatwa remains gone, you will live. Is that not a good deal?"

To the wall, in a very muted voice, Ali asked, "And my family? Will they be safe? Will I ever see my grandchildren again?"

"That is not in our hands," said the black giantess in Arabic, "it is in the decision of your superior."

"Then I am doomed," murmured Ali, "to loneliness, for the rest of my life. He will never let my family out of Iran."

"We can discuss that down the road a way," said Dr. Legesse and the Baha'i man translated it into Farsi as she and Dr. Bar-Fischer stood up. Ali Muhit peered around, wondering what they meant.

As Rachel closed the door to the interview room, she said to Halima, "Think we could get those cataracts of his taken care of? It's such an elementary procedure."

"When can you schedule it?"

"Early next week?"

Halima nodded. "Anything to make life easier for the old man. Go ahead. Bill it to us and the contact lenses too, if he needs them."

Siddhu reluctantly held out a sticky note with the code on it. Russ had almost had to pry the code from Siddhu's brain with a can opener, or so it had seemed. First had come Singh Siddhu's long lecture in florid British English about keeping secrets and how important it was not to interfere in Tahireh Ibrahim's life once she had returned to Paris and became the famous model Gillé.

"We cannot have her as an agent if she cannot become this other personality when she is home. She is famous, a bloody famous model, who stands in great spotlights!" Siddhu, with waving arms and fluttering hands, insisted as Russ tried valiantly to nod in agreement at all the correct junctures. Siddhu ended with, "You do not disturb her. You understand?"

Russ nodded again. "I do not disturb her, ever." He gently plucked the note from Siddhu's finger. "I promise on my mother's ancient name, Snow-from-Night-Sky, which is an honorable name, I promise!"

"Bloody right," sighed Siddhu and backed out of Russ's alcove. He conferred briefly with Devi and then took off for a briefing with Dr. Bar-Fischer and Halima over the cataract operation for their prisoner.

As Russ plugged in the code for transmission to the Hospital de la Croix St. Simons where the Torture Treatment Centre was housed, Devi came up behind him.

"My mom sent me some fresh lamb from the kibbutz. Want to come to dinner tonight? My apartment? I know the kitchen in your little house really sucks."

"Well, a stove that doesn't work and a sink that's all plugged up doesn't help." Russ had found a small, abandoned dwelling on the outskirts of Haifa and had great plans to rebuild it. At the moment, it was more like camping out with the biggest problem being the neighbor's goats who had considered it shelter for years and were cranky at being evicted. They'd twice eaten their way through the scrap wood he'd put over the holes in the walls. Russ carefully composed the message to the model Gillé, who so graciously volunteered her time at St. Simons, saying Habib Mansur was doing well and would be back on his feet in about a week. As the message was sent, Devi leaned against the doorway.

"She doesn't date," said Devi.

"I'm not sure I follow you," Russ looked up the Israeli girl who sported a new hairstyle and a pretty blouse. She seemed slightly uncomfortable in both.

"Tahireh doesn't…" Devi blushed and suddenly Russ caught on and helped her with the explanation. "You mean she keeps her life simple."

Devi said, "Yes. I mean, she's not gay. She's famous. It's difficult for her."

"I understand," Russ insisted, "I really do."

"So, do you like lamb? I make a super curry, hot enough to clear all your sinuses in one go."

"Sure," Russ grinned. "What time?"

Jet lag didn't seem to affect Bonnie at all. She was up with the birds and out with Misimoto surveying the ginger crop and a new pond for catfish that had been dug in the upper pasture. Groundwater was slowly seeping in and would reach the correct level in a couple days. Misimoto was worried that the catfish would arrive before the water had clarified, but Bonnie pointed out that catfish were not too particular about water clarity and, in fact, liked mud. Gryphon enjoyed the muddy pond immensely. For a brief while, he forgot his constant surveillance of ground squirrel activity.

Carl-Joran slept late and spent his waking time practicing his martial arts or hiking. Bonnie went back to work with her library research. Trisha taught health classes and her basketball team won two and lost one. The Thai girls flourished, their English improving by leaps each day. Misimoto's stock of catfish adjusted to their pond without any problems, just as Bonnie had predicted.

Fourteen days passed before the phone call came. It was Barbara Monday and she talked with the baron. There was a woman in Montana. That wasn't far from California, right? The wife of a wealthy cult leader, she'd managed to escape to a shelter in Helena, but the entire shelter could be in danger if she stayed much longer. These cultists were end of the world freaks and carried big, ugly guns.

And where would this poor woman go if they could get her out of Montana, Bonnie had inquired of Barbara and the baron.

Barbara explained that Halima Legesse had already arranged for Crystal, the woman's new name, to go to India. Before her cult entrapment, she'd been a third grade teacher. Lama Kazi Padma-Lakshi could use a teacher in his village. How soon could Carl-Joran and Bonnie have her safely on a flight out of San Francisco?

Carl-Joran looked at Bonnie who promptly said, "Within the week."

END

www.ingramcontent.com/pod-product-compliance
Lightning Source LLC
Chambersburg PA
CBHW031112030726
47496CB00002BA/509